STELLA GIBBONS

Stella Gibbons was born in London in 1902. She went to North London Collegiate School and studied journalism at University College, London. She then spent ten years working for various newspapers, including the *Evening Standard*. Stella Gibbons is the author of twenty-seven novels, three volumes of short stories and four volumes of poetry. Her first publication was a book of poems *The Mountain Beast* (1930) and her first novel *Cold Comfort Farm* (1932) won the Femina Vie Heureuse Prize for 1933. Amongst her works are *Christmas at Cold Comfort Farm* (1940), *Westwood* (1946), *Conference at Cold Comfort Farm* (1959) and *Starlight* (1967). She was elected a Fellow of the Royal Society of Literature in 1950. In 1933 she married the actor and singer Allan Webb. They had one daughter. Stella Gibbons died in 1989.

ALSO BY STELLA GIBBONS

Cold Comfort Farm
Bassett
Enbury Heath
Nightingale Wood
My American
Christmas at Cold Comfort Farm
The Rich House
Ticky
The Bachelor
Westwood
The Matchmaker
Conference at Cold Comfort Farm
Here Be Dragons
White Sand and Grey Sand
The Charmers
Starlight
Pure Juliet

STELLA GIBBONS

The Yellow Houses

VINTAGE

1 3 5 7 9 10 8 6 4 2

Vintage
20 Vauxhall Bridge Road,
London SW1V 2SA

Vintage Classics is part of the Penguin Random House group of
companies whose addresses can be found at
global.penguinrandomhouse.com

Penguin
Random House
UK

First published in Great Britain by Vintage Classics in 2016

www.vintage-books.co.uk

A CIP catalogue record for this book is available
from the British Library

ISBN 9781784870287

Typeset in India by Thomson Digital Pvt Ltd, Noida, Delhi

Printed and bound by Clays Ltd, St Ives plc

Penguin Random House is committed to a sustainable future for our
business, our readers and our planet. This book is made from Forest
Stewardship Council® certified paper.

For dear Laura

'Guardian Spirits are ex-human souls, reconditioned for reissue by the Lower Hierarchy.'

'Uncovenanted Mercies' from
Limits and Renewals, Rudyard Kipling

'Resolute imagination is the beginning
of all magical operations.'
Paracelsus

BOOK ONE

BOOK ONE

1

The handkerchief

It was a beautiful afternoon, warm and still, with clouds more cream-coloured than white lingering in the hazy blue of the September sky. In Lorrimer Park a robin whistled in the shrubs; the children's pool rippled in the sun, and the children splashed in the water and sailed pieces of wood and the first fallen leaves. The orange berries on a rowan tree glowed in the scene of gently-moving, ordinary life.

The town, Torford, was smallish, lying some seventy miles from London on the side that goes east towards marshes, and the villages where the sailing people gather.

In the final months of the war its ancient heart, where the old houses and a few mossed pitted crosses and troughs of stone were cherished, had been badly hurt by the rockets. But this ancient heart was alive some thirty years later, with shops looking as near as they could get to the shops in London: boutiques and steak-houses and Chinese restaurants. Estates of bungalows, white and clean as daisies, curved over low surrounding hills; and there was talk of a new motorway.

The man sitting on the seat below the rowan tree seemed to express in himself some of the town's prosperity. His overcoat was newish and of good quality; his collar as white as the distant bungalows. *Respectable* was the word that had come into the minds of the one or two strollers who had glanced at him: a fair-skinned, ordinary type of man, who had probably looked sturdy up to three or so years ago, but had now turned into his middle sixties and was, oh yes, decidedly elderly – and a little too thin to carry off that coat. And what could be interesting about the purplish composition of the path where his well-polished shoes rested? Or was he dozing – with his head forward on his chest like that?

It was about half past four; the shadows were lengthening. The children and elderly strollers turned homewards.

Three little girls lingered, puttering with leaves and rowan-berries in a game of nursing; and it was while the man on the seat was allowing his eyes to move desolately over them that he began to cry.

He sobbed aloud. The children neither looked towards him nor stopped their play. His tears blurred his sight, and the children disappeared into a rainbow caused by the late sunlight glittering on the pond. He was shamefully aware of sitting there crying in public, and shamefully aware that he could not stop.

But he did hear slow, lounging steps approaching; heard them distinctly because, from the moment his crying began, he had dreaded that someone should come past and see.

The footsteps stopped. He did not look up, but waited, with a sudden anger. Staring. Someone was staring. *You would think anyone would have the decency to pretend they hadn't noticed.* He kept his head down while the tears ran on.

The figure which had stopped was a long whitish blur to him: someone wearing a light raincoat, perhaps, with the sun on it.

He kept still, with his head lowered.

The scene slowly cleared, and he heard the robin's song, making him want to cry again. All the time he was struggling to drive off the lingering intruder; flinging anger towards it – man or woman. *Go away, go on, go, go*, shouted the weeping spirit inside his motionless body and averted head.

A little time passed. Nothing moved. How soft fell the robin's notes. Like the robin in the garden at home. The evening sun was warm. But suddenly he felt cold, and shivered. Had the figure moved away?

Something touched the hand clenched on his knee, the one furthest from his obstinately turned head. Startled, he glanced down. A handkerchief, large and white, rested against his glove.

'Mop up,' said a voice, low-pitched and cheerful. Someone was sitting beside him.

But this was the last straw. This was treating him like a tearful child. He snatched away his hand and thrust it into his pocket, while muttering something – he hardly knew what – some sort of rejection, some sort of assertion of his 'all-rightness'.

But he had come out of the house without a handkerchief.

Six months ago, in the other life whose last solidities had been whirled away from him that morning, such a thing wouldn't have been possible.

Pat had always said that his position at the Town Hall deserved, and needed, such small marks of respectable achievement as a daily, spotless linen handkerchief, and a dozen of these, initialled and prettily wrapped, had always been her Christmas present to him. None of your slovenly paper things for Pat. '*Dad's wipers!*' This had been one of Mary's jokes.

But there was nothing in either pocket of his coat; he was feeling in the right one now and here was Mary's letter. *Christ!* he swore to himself. But nothing else.

He had been shrinking from the figure in the white coat, leaning as far as possible towards the end of the seat. But at the contact of his hand with the letter he forgot everything but searing pain. The tears gushed again.

The man's handkerchief moved slightly towards his hand. He could just discern its white blur.

Blinded by tears, he accepted it and put it to his eyes. It kept the faintest of scents that reminded him of something. Ferns?

'Thanks,' he said hoarsely in a moment. 'Be all right now – had some bad – a bit of a shock. Sorry.' He held out the handkerchief as if to return it, at the same time slowly lifting his head.

A nice face, kind. Long, pale brown, clean-shaven. Wearing a hat, but not old. In his forties, Wilfred Davis judged. And – he searched confusedly for a word – middle-class. A doctor? Perhaps. Or a clergyman?

'Hang on to it, won't you? I'm often here in the late afternoons. We'll see each other again, I expect. My name's Lafcadio Taverner. Goodbye for now.'

He got up – how quickly he moved! – and was walking away, turning to give a last smile before he was lost to sight behind some rhododendrons.

Lafcadio. That was an unusual name. Yet Wilfred was certain of what he had heard.

The three little girls straggled past, looking chilled and pale, the smallest with a spray from the rowan tree drooping in her hand. Their long hair hung limp in the cooling air. Mary! Wilfred's heart went out to them. He wanted to call to them, gently take the youngest's small cold fingers in his own. But he did not move. Perhaps they would shout at him and refuse his gesture. Girls were not gentle nowadays.

He looked down at the handkerchief, then pushed it into his pocket. His crying was over; now he must think – about *so much* – and the washing and ironing and the returning of the handkerchief presented its own small addition to the vast, the over-toppling total sum of his difficulties.

The grass, the paths, Lorrimer House seated small and white and serene on its gentle slope amid dark shrubberies, the cold pond – all had an air of desertion. It must be near closing time.

Lafcadio Taverner. The only kind look, untouched by curiosity or duty, that had been given to Wilfred that day. He sat on for a moment, looking absently, wretchedly, about him while making ready to go home.

The little girls' chatter was fading in the distance; his eyes followed them while he was deciding cautiously that he did feel a little better; sort of numb; that was it, numb, as if an injection had been given to a throbbing tooth.

If the numbness could only last . . .

'Well, Mr Davis. And what brings *you* out so late in the afternoon?'

Round the rhododendrons, accompanied by the sound of panting, came Mrs Wheeby, who lodged in Wilfred's house, and suffered with her chest. She was bundled in layers of elderly wool, and wore a hat of felt; hard in outline and fawn in colour, cocked above an unmemorable face.

'Very cold, isn't it,' Mrs Wheeby began. 'Well, seeing you're here I may as well sit down. I should have never done if I was alone. I heard an elderly lady was struck down just about here only last week. I'm just on my way home.' She lowered herself carefully onto the seat, and now put a laden shopping bag down at her feet.

'I always *have* said you save five minutes coming this way, though Mrs Davis never would have it . . . said it was quicker by way of Cartwright Road. I've been to the supermarket, the one that used to be Reynolds's. It's no use, I shall never like it. Nasty noisy place and so inconvenient, through you do get things a bit cheaper, I suppose. That decimalizing, Mr Davis, I shall never get used to it, never. It stands to reason – people of our age can't. Why they wanted to change everything round I can't imagine. Nobody likes it. Nobody can make head nor tail of it. I passed three little girls a few minutes ago. The eldest can't have been more than eight. What their mothers can be thinking of, *I do not know*. Not a soul about. Anything might happen to them . . .'

She paused to pant.

'The times are terribly dangerous, Mrs Wheeby,' Wilfred said faintly. 'Even for boys . . . in the paper . . .' The thought of Mary to whom *anything might happen* struck his heart.

'Dangerous! I should think they are. Oh boys. I don't care about *them*. They can look after themselves. – By the way, I didn't hear Mary go off shopping this morning. She got a cold?'

An eye, like a chip of grey granite under the fawn felt, fixed him.

He had read of the blood draining from a heart. Now it
drained from *his* heart. That was exactly what it seemed to
do. But instantly – and surprisingly – a picture of Lafcadio
Taverner's face came before his inward eye.

'She's gone to stay with her auntie in London,' he answered,
at once and steadily.

'Oh that's funny. I never heard her go. Yesterday, was it?
And I hear most of what goes on. When did she go, then?'

'Early this morning. Before you were up, I expect,
Mrs Wheeby,' and he even smiled. Mr Taverner's face was
still clear in his mind.

'What part of London? I used to live there, you know. I
lived there for a year when we were first married, but we never
liked it. How long has she gone for? Just for the weekend, I
expect . . .'

'I don't know for how long, really. Her auntie's found her
a job in London.'

'A job! And Mrs Davis working all those years to pay for
her schooling. I thought it was all arranged she should go to
university. She isn't seventeen yet, is she . . .'

Not seventeen. Oh God. Oh God.

'It was *hoped* for, Mrs Wheeby,' Wilfred answered slowly
and as if repeating something he had learnt by heart. 'But
her – Aunt Beatty, my sister, you know –'

'Never knew you had a sister, Mr Davis,' panted Mrs Wheeby,
not removing the eye.

It passed through Wilfred's mind that there was no reason
why Mrs Wheeby, who had been their lodger for only eighteen
months, should know it. But that was not the sort of thing one
said to people – at least, he didn't.

'Oh yes. My sister is three years younger than I am,' he said,
while his imagination stayed with Mr Taverner's face. 'She . . .
runs a little dress shop in . . .Watford . . .'

'Watford isn't in London. Twenty miles outside London,
Watford is. *That* I *do* know.'

Dusk was growing rapidly. The lights in the houses shining through the park's bare trees looked homely and cheerful. A few yellow leaves rattled dryly along the path.

'Wanstead, I should have said Wanstead. She wanted . . . my sister . . . a girl to help her in the shop, so she wrote . . .'

'Not much of a job working in a shop, I'd say.'

'Well, you know Mary likes clothes . . .'

His voice was almost a whisper. The kind face in his mind's eye had vanished. He looked wildly into the dim face of Mrs Wheeby, dim and pallid in the dusk. What had happened, where had it all gone, his life, that he should be sitting in Lorrimer Park with his lodger, tear stains on his cheeks, telling fibs about Mary? Where was the order, the pattern of everyday, that had gone on for nearly seventeen years?

'Yes, we all know that, Mr Davis.'

She meant the row about that . . . what was it . . . micro-mini skirt? Pat had shouted at Mary. The house had . . . resounded. He could not bear to remember it . . . and Pat had been defied . . . and two months later she was dead.

There was silence. Then Mrs Wheeby turned to look at Lorrimer House on its hillock, palely reflecting the last of the light. How clear the air – and not a cloud in the darkening sky.

'Do you remember the Japanese Room?' she asked in a different tone.

'Japanese – oh, in the house. In Lorrimer House, yes. Mrs Wheeby, oughtn't we to be getting along? It must be nearly closing time.'

'I was taken to see that when I was six. Six, I was. I recall it perfectly; sixty-four years ago, that was. They had a lot of pretty things, all Japanese: little cabinets, and a red rope to keep the public off – though no one would have dreamt of touching anything in those days – and a statue, life-size it was, over life-size—'

'Kichijoten,' said Wilfred suddenly, sounding surprised.

'Yes, yes, that was the name. Fancy you remembering. She was meant to be the Goddess of Fortune. All in palest pink, holding an apple. And there were little boxes, I remember. Carved ivory. Every week I used to be taken to see the Japanese Room, if I'd been a good girl; and when I came to my schooldays I would often go by myself. I loved that room, Mr Davis, and all through the war, the first one I mean, the 1914 one, it was there, and they were our allies then, of course, and no danger from bombs. And then I went to live in London. But I always meant to come back to Torford – and the Japanese Room was one of the first things I went to see when I did. But in the second war of course there were the air raids, and the things had to be stored away. For safety.'

'Mrs Wheeby, they will be shutting the gates . . .'

'I'm *telling* you, Mr Davis. I did so look forward to seeing those things again after the war. And when it was opened again, at last, I went. And there they all were, as pretty as ever, and it was such a *pleasure.*' Mrs Wheeby laid a wool-gloved hand on his arm. 'The ladies on the screen, and the white silk storks. Every week I used to go and study them. But then, as time went on, you know, lads didn't take any notice of the rope, and they got to touching the things, and later on they damaged them; there was no one to look after them; the council could only afford to pay an elderly man . . .'

'Yes, Mrs Wheeby, the council was . . . I remember it all, perfectly, we couldn't get a grant . . .'

'. . . gangs they were, lads in gangs, and they took to breaking the things. *Vandals,* Mr Davis. So at last the room had to be closed, and I don't know where all the things went to. I often think of that pink goddess. I should like to send those lads to a reformatory. Breaking up pretty things like that. It's my belief they hate anything pretty.'

Wilfred felt a faint surprise at the vehemence of her tone. He looked at her hat, from the hard line of which a pallid shapeless section of profile stood out. *Mrs Wheezy,* Pat had called her.

'We really must go, Mrs Wheeby.' He got up, then stooped to lift her shopping bag from the ground, and together they began walking slowly towards the gate.

Lorrimer Park covered no more than the forty acres, which had been the park of the family house two hundred years ago, and at no point were its trees, now half denuded of their leaves, thick enough to hide the glow from lights on the roads that ringed and hemmed it in.

He could hear the roar of the home-going traffic.

It was the same road he had always known (though its gentle curves had been hacked away and straightened) but its flawless surface and its merciless stream of cars had nothing in common with the tarry-scented, warm wood-blocks over which he had tottered, pulling a wooden horse on a string, and just ahead of his smiling young mother, sixty-three years ago.

2

The canary

The next day was Sunday.

At six o'clock, Wilfred awoke with the start that had brought him up through the blest worlds of sleep on so many mornings since Pat's death; but on this morning his first thought was not *Pat's dead*, but *Mary's run away*, and the pain was worse because with it came fear.

He reached for the clock on the table between the twin beds, (the one with its burden of wide-awake, wretched man, and the other bed smooth and empty), and, seeing the time, sighed and lay back and put his arms behind his head. The house and the road outside were silent; a fragment of bright sky looked in between the curtains; it was sunlit, out there, and the brilliant faces of Pat's dahlias, with cobwebs glittering between them, would be staring across the lawn.

He turned to look at Mary's letter on the table beside the clock. The square, modern-style writing of the word 'Dad' hurt him; it seemed to set Mary away from him in a young, secret, hard world of her own.

Dear Dad,

I'm off to London to get a job. Not to worry I am nearly seventeen and not silly like some of them. I shall be alright and as soon as I've got the job I shall write but

not any address because then you'll be after me, I know
you. In London, so huge and glamorous, I shall have a
better chance.

Love

from

Mary

Love from Mary. What a letter, what a frightening mixture
of a child's inexperience and the decision of a woman! What
a thing for a father, still dazed and stunned from the death of
the child's mother, to find beside the tea cosy, on the neatly
set breakfast table, propped against that cosy's gay, psychedelic
patterning.

'London so huge and glamorous.' *Wicked, dirty place, loveless
and –* his thoughts turned in sudden affection towards the
streets and shops of Torford – *heartless and rotten too* . . .

This time last week, Mary had come slowly in with the tray
of tea for the two of them, one cheek still creased from the
pillow and her dark eyes slitty with sleep.

They had drunk their tea together, she sitting on Pat's bed,
in her navy dressing-gown, and they had had one or two of
their little jokes.

Not pretty, perhaps. A bit on the plump side. But her hair
was really something, her mother used to tell her. Pat had
meant as well as any woman could, and done everything for
the best. *Keep your mind on your studies*, she would say. *Pass your
exams, and get into university and get your degree. Plenty of time
for boyfriends afterwards.*

But Wilfred remembered an afternoon, nearly two years
ago, when he had idly picked up from the lounge table a
book bound in pink plastic and lettered *True Confessions* and
belonging, if the inscription on the flyleaf were true, to
Sandra Bailey.

Under the heading *Ambition*, on the page signed by Mary
Patricia Davis, were the neatly written words: *To get married
and have three children. Max, Hugh and Cilla, in that order.*

Whew! Putting down the *True Confessions* quickly, with one glance round the bright, silent lounge, Wilfred had wondered about Mary's hours of evening study, up in her room. Nearly six years of them. French and Latin Grammars, and the New Maths book, lay on the table. But what ruled in Mary's head? New Maths and Grammars or daydreams about Max, Hugh and Cilla and their possible father? In what order?

Secretive Mary. When had either he or Pat ever heard her say the names of those children, the bearing of which was her ambition?

He had never told Pat about that page in the confession book. He had been warned by Pat's reaction on the occasion when Mary had suddenly said, at the tea table, that she would like to work in a shop.

'What kind of shop? A bookshop? Of course, that's —'

Pat had pounced, but Mary had gone on, undisturbed, buttering a half-slice of bun: 'Not a bookshop — a shop where they sell clothes.'

'Well really, Mary, I must say . . .'

For seven minutes (Wilfred had looked stealthily at the clock) Mary's expression had remained placid under the spate of sensible, kind, unanswerable words, and her answer to the final, 'Now don't you?' had been an un-sulky 'M-mm' which might have meant anything.

But when Mary did say something, it was something that could haunt a father; revealing, as those three names in the *True Confessions* book had done, depths beneath the sunlit surface of family life.

'You think exactly what you want to think.' Mary's flatly spoken sentence had cut across the flow of her mother's irritable words during the scene about the micro-mini skirt, and although Pat apparently had not heard them, Wilfred had, and he had never forgotten them.

The micro-mini skirt, fully twelve inches of it, had been worn once by Mary. She had come home from school wearing it, gone straight up to her room, and come down wearing the school's grey pinafore dress and white blouse.

'Thought better of it? That's right; I thought you would,' Pat had smiled, pouring tea. 'Sensible girl.'

'It wasn't *me*.'

Again, no inflexion, no expression.

The skirt had never again been seen on Mary's womanly thighs. But, now that she had gone, Wilfred painfully felt sure that this moment, and none other, had been the moment when Mary had made up her mind to run away.

Yesterday – only yesterday! – he had awoken at six, and waited for her to come in, sleepy and smiling, with their tea. Five minutes – ten minutes – she must have overslept. (Not Mary.) He had got up and put on his dressing-gown and gone along to her room and tapped on the door. Again – louder. Again. Then opened it.

Her bed was neatly made. The air of a fine morning stirred the curtains at the open window. Staring, his heart starting to beat hard, he had seen the note, and from that moment, anguish and fear, unceasing anguish and fear.

Now he struck the bedclothes, suddenly, with the back of his hand. Where to *begin*? Where should he *start*? Even that chap's handkerchief, lying crumpled on the dressing-table, had to be dealt with.

Steady strokes from the tower of St Peter's church sounded from the heart of the town, touching him with the comfort of familiarity. Seven. In half an hour Mrs Wheeby would begin to bump about in her room as she prepared herself to attend the church's eight o'clock service.

At that moment, there was a ring at the front door bell. It could not be the paper boy who did not deliver the *Sunday Express* until half past eight. Mary?

He hurried out of bed, hurried across the room, dragged the curtains apart, pushed up a window and stared down, breathing fast.

No. A face, of a bluish-purple colour, stared back at him, topping a collection of clothes which caused the word *rags* to touch the beholder's mind.

'Good morning to you and a fine day it is,' said a voice. 'Here he is, and I brought him along early because I'm off to see me sister in London and the train leaving the station on the stroke of half past eight, and me living the other end of the town, and never a bite of breakfast in me yet. So you'll excuse me, I know,' and here a largish object muffled in a piece of dirty blanket was held up. 'He's sleeping sweetly, but off with the cloth and he'll start away like he was one of the Beatles.'

There was a pause. Then Wilfred, feeling that the top of his head would fly open, demanded in a hoarse weak voice:

'What is it?'

'Why, a canary, of course.'

The muffled object was gently swayed to and fro as if in demonstration. 'Bought off me for two hundred new pence (and a black day *that* was for us all, it coming in, God help us) by the old lady. There was I, sitting on the seat, and she sitting by me, and us getting into a chat, as people do, and her saying she wanted a canary, and hadn't I the very thing by me, looking after it for me sister who's gone to live in London, and writes me a postcard this last Saturday saying she don't want no more of him? Wasn't it only yesterday the postcard come, and me meeting the old lady the very same afternoon as if it were the hand of Providence? Name of Wheeby,' concluded the voice, relapsing into a less lyrical style, while its owner nodded in emphasis.

'I'll – I'll come down. Wait . . .' Wilfred muttered.

'Me train goes on the tick. Not a moment will they wait.'

Passing Mrs Wheeby's door, Wilfred gave it a thump. It instantly opened, and his descent was arrested by the appearance of his lodger, white silk hair neatly gathered into the smallest conceivable knot at the back of her head, and looking at him severely over a steaming cup.

'What is it, Mr Davis?'

Mrs Wheeby, like Wilfred, wore a dressing-gown; a Marks and Spencer one, of red flannel bordered round the collar with red satin; and the fact that Wilfred's own sturdy garment had come from the Men's Department of the same Universal Provider seemed to unite him with Mrs Wheeby in a common bond of humanity which he did not want at all.

'It's your canary, Mrs Wheeby,' he said shortly. 'The man has brought it early – because . . .' his voice died away. Really, he could not go into all that about sisters and trains.

'Ah, my Dicky,' Mrs Wheeby exclaimed. 'I will come down. But no. Better not. My tea will get cold. Perhaps you could bring him up, Mr Davis?'

'Bring –? The man?' Wilfred was poised at the head of the stairs.

'No, that isn't necessary, I meant Dicky, a little thing like that with tiny bones can't be heavy. Have you ever held a bird in your hand, Mr Davis? And felt its heart beating? It is *nothing* but tiny bones and feathers.'

'No I haven't, Mrs Wheeby, and Mrs Davis always said *No Pets*. She made that quite plain the day you came to us. I remember it perfectly.'

'Mrs Davis is dead,' Mrs Wheeby said – right out, not lowering her voice, as if she were saying it was a nice morning. He stood and stared at her silently. She took a sip or two and stared back.

'Not a minute will they wait. I'm warning you,' came the voice from below, apparently through the letter-box.

'I'm COMING,' Wilfred shouted, and ran down into the hall and opened the front door.

'His seed box is filled up and his water's there, all fresh an hour ago, God bless him. And now I'm off and good morning to you. It's a bit of groundsel does his heart good twice a week. Ye'll have some in the garden. It grows whether ye want it or not. I'll be off, for me stomach's calling to be filled,' and thrusting the cage at Wilfred the Irishman went quickly down the path and away, leaving the garden gate open.

Wilfred went to shut it against visiting dogs, leaving the cage just inside the hall by the open door. But quick as he was, next door's cat had slipped out of the bushes and was sniffing at the cage, while Mrs Wheeby was descending the stairs, panting.

'No, pussy, no. Mr Davis, can you drive Bella away? No, pussy, no.'

'Get OUT,' shouted Wilfred, making a pouncing movement at Bella which caused her to rush off, with tail erect, turning back to present a malevolent mask.

He turned to Mrs Wheeby, who had set the cage on Pat's immaculately shining hall table and was fumbling with its mufflings.

'Poor little man, I expect he's frightened. I hope the water hasn't spilt. Mr Davis, can you just undo this string? My fingers are all thumbs, first thing.'

'Mrs Wheeby –' Wilfred was struggling with the stout piece of cord which kept the blanket about the cage. 'Really . . . wasn't it rather . . . rash . . . Oh *bother* this thing . . . to pay a man you'd never seen before two hundred new pence for a canary that . . . *damn* . . . mightn't have existed? He might just have cleared off with the money. And there's another thing . . . you know Mrs Davis told you . . . she said quite plainly, when you first came, No Pets . . .'

He did not finish the sentence because he did not want to hear again Mrs Wheeby's voice telling him Pat was dead.

But he conquered the knot, and Mrs Wheeby eagerly pulled off the cover.

Sunlight was streaming into the hall through the glass panels in the front door, where white storks and white lotus flowers paddled and floated in a yellow river. And immediately the occupant of the cage came out, a trill of piercingly sweet noise soared up to greet this light.

Wilfred instantly felt that this joyous spun-glass sound was going to be unbearable.

'Little beauty,' Mrs Wheeby was gloating. 'Like drops of silver, isn't it, Mr Davis? It reminds me of Yehudi Menuhin,

but if you were to ask me – I should say it's *better*, because
Dicky has never been taught to sing, and Yehudi Menuhin had
lessons. Oh yes, I like Dicky's singing much better. I shan't go
to the Eight O'Clock this morning,' she ended, and sat down
abruptly beside the hall table.

Wilfred again felt that impulse to clutch at his head. 'But
you always go to the Eight O'Clock, Mrs Wheeby! You've
been every Sunday without fail ever since you came to us. In
all weathers, too; Mrs Davis used to be quite worried about
you, some mornings.'

'Very good of Mrs Davis, I'm sure, but I can take care of
myself, thank you. I never did *like* going, but Duty is Duty,
Mr Davis. I like Dicky better than Duty, so I shall stay at
home, and perhaps I'll go next Sunday and perhaps I shan't,
we'll see,' and she nodded, allowing a pant to come out, as she
sat looking up at him.

'Just as you please, of course, Mrs Wheeby,' he said after a
pause, and while Mrs Wheeby was nodding, as if to imply that
she should hope so, he made an attempt to assert himself by
adding, 'I'm . . . I'm not sure . . . I don't think . . . the fact is
I can't stand that noise all day, you know. It's downright . . .
piercing. People may complain.'

He lowered his voice at the end of the sentence, because he
was struggling with an impulse to cry aloud *and it's so awful
about Mary. I can't bear any beautiful thing because of Mary.*'

'Alternate hours,' Mrs Wheeby said instantly.

'What? . . . I beg your pardon?'

'Alternate hours, Mr Davis. Eight to nine he sings; nine to
ten he's covered up; at eleven I uncover him, and at twelve
under he goes again. Oh we shall soon get accustomed to it,
Mr Davis. So long as people know where they are. It's like
when my sister Minnie was learning the piano. Ten to twelve,
practice every morning. She was so fond of the loud pedal,
nothing could cure her. But after twelve everybody could settle down. Well, I suppose my tea must be stone cold by now.
Come along Dicky. Goodbye for the present, Mr Davis.'

Slowly, allowing the pants to emerge freely now, setting two small feet in bright slippers on every tread, up the stairs went Mrs Wheeby, carrying the cage, and Dicky's song seemed to be wafting them upwards as they went.

I won't have it, I simply won't have it, Wilfred was thinking as he went into the kitchen to make his own tea. *If Pat were here – if Pat were alive – she would never have dared.*

First Mary, now Mrs Wheeby. Taking advantage of Pat's death. Well, hadn't they? Both of them.

He put cereal and milk, absently, into a bowl.

He was sitting at the table, staring unseeingly past the curtains at some large, yellow objects on stalks eight feet tall: the giant sunflowers that grew at the garden's end, towering over the fence.

Oh Mary. Where are you?

The long day shone ahead, empty, yet brimming with the sensation that so many things were waiting to be done.

Two months ago, Sundays had seemed too short, what with gardening, and perhaps an hour or two at the decorating that had been going on in one of their eight rooms ever since he had retired five years ago; watching their favourite television programmes; sometimes (though not often because on Sundays the roads were too crowded with cars making for the sea) – sometimes a drive. And always the feeling of comfort and safety because Pat was there and Mary was upstairs in her room studying, or calling from the front door that she was just going round to Sandra's for half an hour and would be back to tea.

He got up, unable to endure his memories and wandered over to the window and stood there, looking out, chewing on the sodden flakes.

Across the railway, there glimmered a line of dim grey; the old houses of Hardy Crescent that had been badly bombed in the war, when the Germans had been aiming at the railway line. They had grown more ruinous every year since, and were (as Wilfred knew, and he knew all the details too) a recurring subject of argument and suggestion at meetings of the council. Should the money be allocated to recondition the houses, or should they be pulled down and the land sold? It was always pointed out by someone, as the discussion continued and the councillors began to think of a waiting pint or television programme, that on one side they overlooked the town's cemetery and on the other the railway. Not points to attract purchasers of land, even today.

As if everywhere weren't noisy.

Wilfred swallowed the last of his sapless meal.

That bird was still at it. He would, he supposed, have to let Mrs Wheeby keep it. It seemed disloyal to old Pat.

Pat had been so . . . certain . . . about everything. So practical; so sensible. So kind. This, and the smooth rosiness of her face, had attracted him as he met her, every day, going about her work in the Town Hall. Her modishly dressed hair had gleamed, her clothes were always bright-coloured and fitted close to her sturdy body, her shoes and her fingernails shone. She was ten years younger than him; and Mary had not come until they had been married longer than either of them had liked to be without a child.

While Pat was still working at the Town Hall to pay for Mary's fees at Redpaths House, the cancer which she had suspected but never spoken of to anyone had become obvious.

There had been some weeks in hospital; daily visits from Wilfred (now retired and on a good pension); the 'gallant fight' expected by relatives and friends and neighbours; a bright expression, attention to hair and dressing-jackets and make-up. The approach of death had been ignored. But it had come: unconsciousness, incontinence, an unrecognizable face and body – then quietly, death.

We were so *happy*, Wilfred thought, and pushed aside the empty bowl. He tried not to remember the acrid, tigerish smell of the dying: a live smell, although the body exhaling it would soon be alive no longer.

So happy. We had our ups and downs, of course. She didn't always understand how I felt. She liked to wear the trousers (bless her), but we were happy. And now I've got nothing. Nothing.

But Pat's cure for what she called the blues had been action. She had proved that it worked, she used to say, over and over again.

After a moment or so of sprawling, weak in body and despairing in heart, Wilfred got up, and, having forced himself to rinse the bowl and spoon and inspect them, he put them away and went upstairs to fetch Mr Taverner's handkerchief. He might as well fill up some time by washing and ironing the thing.

He had mooned over his breakfast longer than he had realized, for nine o'clock was sounding on the autumn wind from St Peter's as he passed Mrs Wheeby's door, and, even as he did so, Dicky's silvery torrents of sound stopped as if cut off by a switch. Mrs Wheeby had been as good as her word. But even as the thought occurred to him, he was brought to a stop by an outbreak from her room of another noise.

At first he thought that she must be having some unprecedented and alarming form of what is loosely called an attack, and his selfish reaction was one of angry despair: how much *more* was he going to have to put up with?

But, the sounds swelling and growing more peculiar, he decided that Mrs Wheeby had, so to speak, burst out in another direction (Hindi, perhaps, this time, or Urdu as she seemed attracted to the East) and had purchased, and was practising on, some exotic musical instrument.

He wondered if she were going mental . . . And he was as nervous as he was angry when he sharply tapped on the door, which he himself had deftly, eighteen months ago, painted with glossy white Crown, and waited.

During the brief pause that followed, the giant mewings, and the swooping and cooing sounds convinced him that they could not come from any imaginable sort of human throat. The door opened.

Mrs Wheeby's right hand was upon the doorknob and her left held a bowl of milk-sopped cereal. It added to Wilfred's annoyance to see, on the table behind her, a packet of the same brand which he himself had recently been swallowing. Fate seemed bent upon linking him with Mrs Wheeby.

'Mrs Wheeby!' he exclaimed, his irritation increased by her unfuffled air, 'what *on earth* is that *extraordinary* noise?'

'Whales, Mr Davis.'

'Wails! I should think it is wails – I never heard such a row in my life – I really can't have this, you know. First that bird, and then—'

'*Whales*, Mr Davis, hump-backed whales. Fish, if you can call them that. It's on my gramophone. There was a wireless programme about them, most interesting, I never enjoyed anything on that Third before, it's usually philosophy and that sort of thing, or those plays, meant to be clever, where the people talk like you and me only it means something different. This was taken on a tape recorder by some man who went after them (the whales, I mean). It's them calling to each other, a kind of warning, and singing too. Fancy that! It said you could buy the record if you sent the money to some place in California, so I sent it, and back came the record – so neatly packed, all that way, quite surprising really. Listen!' She held up the bowl of cereal, looking at him with bright eyes. 'That's them calling to each other across a hundred miles of sea. I love this part. Listen!'

The sound was hurrying along in waves: a mooing, wavering rush of notes that brought suddenly into Wilfred's mind the clear gloom of the ocean where it is deepest and furthest from man. Lonely beyond any loneliness the human imagination can conceive, yet inhabited. Oh yes, inhabited – by vast sombre indigo bodies gliding under the ever-darkening and deepening weight of three miles of salt water, and singing and calling one to another as they glide.

He came back to the white door, and the narrow passage and Mrs Wheeby, feeling oddly cooled in mind, even faintly chilled in body, and as if he had been, for a moment, a very long way away under. The unhuman sounds were swooping on.

'Whales, is that it?' he murmured, staring over her head and out through the open window. 'What a . . . I've never heard anything like *that* before.' The sounds were dying away; they ended. He heard the faint noise of the disc revolving.

'Nor me, Mr Davis. I'll *have* that record, Edith my girl, I thought. You've listened long enough to the electric kettle boiling, and Mrs Davis's Hoover, and those jumbo jets – not half as nice, not one quarter, as a *real* jumbo – give me elephants every time. And layabouts on the wireless singing about how they'll overcome. *What*, I should like to know? What will they overcome? Soap and water, or a visit to the barber or those drugs? A pity they don't make a start by overcoming *them*. But the whales, they're free, Mr Davis, and don't have to sing about overcoming anything. You and I, Mr Davis, aren't free to walk across the road in safety, in the town we were both born in, so that's why it does me good to hear those whales and so it will you. You come up here any time you like, well, say in the evenings, when we all feel a bit solitary – I know I do – and you'll be welcome as sure as my name is Edith Wheeby. We'll listen together. Goodbye for now, Mr Davis.'

3

Old Mr Davis

The days, with their dull little duties, soon began to have one hope only: a letter from Mary.

None came. And her father did nothing, told no one about her flight. But four days after she had gone, there came a telephone enquiry from the school. The secretary would like to know, please, why Mary had been absent since last Friday. Was she ill? If so, why hadn't the school been informed? Wilfred muttered something about writing.

While putting down the receiver, however, he decided that he would go to see Mrs Anstruther, the headmistress.

Absent since Friday. She must have taken the day off to make arrangements . . . frightening, sensible Mary.

With shoes shining, and collar turned up against the stiff breeze that rakes the streets of east coast towns, Wilfred walked across Torford. He left behind the tree-lined roads of small, red-brick houses for wider roads of larger ones, whose frontages had been replaced by shop windows full of goods that wearied his eye by excess of choice.

There seemed to be more cars about than people; the moving air bit the cheek and rang with noise; all was busy, prosperous, and ugly. Only the sky, the East Anglian sky of Cotman and Constable, offered consolation. Its noble autumnal colour was occasionally stained by the roar and stench of a passing air-liner, but the blue remained. *The blue remains* thought

Wilfred, briskly carrying his load of pain across Torford, and remembering Pat saying, *everybody has their troubles* and *there's always someone worse off than you*, and thinking that, true though these sentences were, they did him no good this morning, while *the blue remains* did.

The new Town Hall loured at him across the square, too large for its setting; heavy, menacing, adorned by a frieze of concrete bars divided into bundles, each bar set askew. He actually shut his eyes as he walked past its purple brickery. He had agreed with Pat that its design was 'fully contemporary', and therefore must be admirable, but he had never liked it.

We mustn't live in the past: it's morbid.

Why mustn't we? Wilfred found himself thinking, *Why mustn't we?*

As for the Town Hall . . . fit for witch doctors, it was, and enough to frighten the primary school children.

He remembered the decorously festive week in which it was opened, and how tired he had grown of the words *civic pride.*

On this side of the town the roads were wide and some big trees, once growing in meadows, had been left standing when Torford's largest houses had been built here a hundred years ago, by Torford's richest men. Each house stood in an acre of garden, where hothouses had once glittered in the sun; at the back of one or two, there were stables. Dark green conifers spread their shadows on the neglected grass. Redpaths: School for Girls had once had its yard and stables, and the stables had had a weatherboarded tower with a clock that chimed the hours.

Gone, now, the creamy wood slats covering the pepperpot tower; gone the softly insistent note of the bell. The paved yard contained a compressed-looking, concrete building with too many windows: the new Science Wing. Murderous powers seemed imprisoned in it and bursting to get out.

Wilfred went through a low wooden gate, and along a drive past a mighty cedar, and up six steps raying out in a satisfying half-circle, and rang a brass bell-push.

The door was opened by 'Slutty' Singer, now aged (if the town's collective memory was reliable) forty-three, and the despair of Torford's social workers.

Five illegitimate children, whose fathers were not even putative, were flourishing like dwarf green bay trees on the Torford ratepayers' money. Slutty was generally assumed to be mentally deficient, the ratepayers preferring to take this attitude rather than face the fact that there was, alive and well and living in Torford, someone who had more than once said, to trained psychiatrists, 'Mind your own effing business.'

Wilfred had never accepted the mentally deficient theory, believing, for his part, that Slutty was what Pat had called *careless*, and the twelfth century would have called *fruitful*.

But he was decidedly not pleased to see her at Redpaths. The school, with its wide, lofty hall paved in black and white marble, and certain esoteric and threatening contemporary pictures on its apricot walls, had for him an aura of half-comprehended values that had nothing to do with getting on or with money. *A nice class of girl* went to Redpaths. But if Redpaths was employing Slutty Singer, it must be hard pressed indeed for staff, and could it be going downhill?

Mary had been at the school for nearly seven years, and Pat had worked hard and fiercely to earn the fees: Redpaths was a part of the Davis family history and he did not want it to go downhill.

'Hullo, Mr Davis,' beamed Slutty, all crumpled white working coat and dusty red hair; she knew him, of course, because of living in the same street as his father, a fact which Pat had not liked.

'Good morning,' he answered unsmilingly, being in no state of mind to smile at unmarried mothers – and was going to say 'I want to see Mrs Anstruther' when there came from Slutty a kind of warning howl.

'Oh she don't see nobody not without a 'pointment, never does, can't be done – but I'll see what I can do for *you*, Mr Davis,' she ended with a conspiratorial smile. Then out from an office (formerly the morning room) swept Miss Turner; mini-skirted, mermaid-haired, cool and tidy as a plastic flowerpot, and hopelessly entangled with a married man twenty-two years older than herself.

'I'm Mary Davis's father,' Wilfred said, looking her full in her wide hazel eye. 'I want to see Mrs Anstruther.'

Miss Turner gave Slutty, who was lingering, precisely the right smile, and Slutty wandered off.

'Mrs Anstruther doesn't usually see parents without an appointment. But – do sit down, Mr Davis,' said Miss Turner, and went away.

Wilfred sat. On a black William Morris kind of chair which might have been part of the house's furniture at the time of the sale, thirty-six years ago. The notices on the green-baize-covered board stared at him whitely.

Miss Turner reappeared.

'Mrs Anstruther will see you, Mr Davis' – and he followed her across the hall and down a passage to a door, at which she knocked.

Mrs J. Anstruther was sitting at a desk in a pale blue and dark blue room; not luxurious – the curtains were hessian, the carpets felt – and making no attempt to be impressive.

Nevertheless, her plain pale face, fair hair drawn upwards into a knot, neutral wool dress, and bracelet and brooch of carved cornelian, impressed Wilfred. He had only seen her, previously, at a distance on the school's Open Days; had never spoken to her, although Pat had always made it a duty (which he was certain she had feared) to *have a word* with the Headmistress.

He had never before been face to face with a woman who seemed to him both gentle and hard. It must, he supposed vaguely, be something to do with education.

'Good morning, Mr Davis. Do sit down. Now what is the matter with Mary? Is she ill?'

'No. She isn't ill – so far as I know.' He sat leaning slightly forward, with anxious eyes fixed on Mrs Anstruther's. 'She's run away.'

'*Has* she!'

He was astounded; there was no disapproval or surprise in her voice. What was there? It couldn't be – enthusiasm? He stumbled on.

'She – she left a note. She wants to work in a dress shop.'

Mrs Anstruther nodded. She put up a hand (roughened by housework, Wilfred noticed, and the fact, curiously, comforted him) – and pushed back a hairpin.

'This is a small school, Mr Davis,' she began, 'and because there are only a hundred and twenty girls here, I know them all, and something about each one. Would you like me to tell you what I know about your Mary?'

Your Mary: a delicious warmth of feeling flooded him. Just to think *I love her* lessened his pain. He looked gratefully at Mary's headmistress.

'She isn't an intellectual girl,' Mrs Anstruther continued. 'She works hard, and her results are quite good, but no more than average, in spite of her application. The taste, the – passion – for learning, simply isn't there—'

'I've always thought so,' he interrupted, 'always. And I didn't care. Mary's . . . enough for me as she is. It was her mother. My wife never . . . had the benefit of a university education, and she felt the want of it, always did. She was the one who was ambitious for Mary.'

'Yes, that's a common mistake parents make, especially mothers . . . Mary, Mr Davis, is the type of girl who marries young and has three or four children rather quickly, makes a thoroughly good wife and mother, and is perfectly content to be what she is.'

He was leaning forward listening to what she said as if he were drinking it in.

'But seventeen, Mrs Anstruther – not yet seventeen! And in London, alone. I'm so afraid some bad type of boy will get hold of her . . .'

'Well,' Mrs Anstruther paused, considered, and plunged. '*That* might not be such a tragedy as it sounds. Experience deepens and enriches character. The richer the temperament, the more likely a woman is to satisfy—' She broke off. 'I don't think you need be afraid. Mary won't let a bad type of boy get near her.'

'Really? You honestly think so? You . . . aren't just saying that to . . . relieve my anxiety?'

'Indeed I'm not. Mary's strongest characteristic is common sense. I've always thought so. That was why – I'm talking to you quite frankly – I was, well, rather pleased just now to hear she'd run away. It isn't good for the young to be too sensible. If they don't get adventure out of their systems while they *are* young, they try to do it when they're middle-aged, and then the results are seldom satisfactory. Not that one wants it *all* got out of the system, of course, especially for women—'

'So you wouldn't go to the police?' he interrupted.

'The police? Oh no, not unless you want to make things much worse. I . . . my husband says that my prophecies, which often come true, are just . . . lucky. But they aren't, Mr Davis, they're based on *really* knowing about girls: what they're truly like, their potentialities, and what they want from life – things they sometimes don't know about themselves. I am quite certain about your Mary. She is going to be . . . what you, as her father, would think of as perfectly "all right". Has she any money, do you know?'

'Well! I never thought of that. (Her mother would have, of course.) She's got forty pounds in the Post Office. To tell you the truth, I haven't had the gu— I just haven't really looked round her room. But I will do. Soon as I get home. I'd feel better if I knew she had that Post Office book with her.'

Mrs Anstruther glanced down at some papers on her desk, and instantly he got up and made a movement towards the door.

'Goodbye, Mrs Anstruther, and thank you.'

She smiled, and managed to convey 'goodbye' with her head. She spoke again as he reached the door.

'Mr Davis.'

He turned and looked at her.

'I've talked to you absolutely candidly, of course, because I'm so sorry you've had this new worry, following on your loss, but also because I know you're someone one can talk to candidly . . . Will you keep this conversation private, just between ourselves, as two parents?'

The school, with its small Board of not-too-obtuse Governors, was flourishing as only a school offering something better than the state or grammar schools offered, could flourish, in a town where the level of prosperity was rising steadily every year. Mrs Anstruther did not want her views on the enriching of the female nature by running away from home to reach the ears of parents who had daughters aged eight or nine to be educated.

'Of course, Mrs Anstruther. I . . . I . . . took that for granted.'

As Wilfred followed the helplessly captive Miss Turner across the hall he suddenly decided that to go home at eleven in the morning would be unbearable. Thirteen hours before bedtime and the world of sleep. No. He would go and see his father.

Old Mr Davis, now aged eighty-five, lived on the east side of the town; in the low part across the railway.

So back across Torford walked Wilfred, his thinning hair blowing in the cold wind. Occasionally he nodded and smiled at an acquaintance.

Soon people would begin asking where Mary was. That must be expected because Sandra Bailey and the rest of the schoolfellows would talk. Not that Mary was what you might call popular. Sandra lived in the Davises' road, and her father was their dentist; Wilfred had always suspected that the friendship was one of propinquity rather than mutual attraction. Well, one friend, or perhaps two, was enough; girls who had what Pat had called a *full social life and nice friends* weren't necessarily happy.

That – happiness – was all that he wanted for Mary.

Blinking against the wind, he crossed the road and went down Lesley Street, where the shops still looked bright and clean; tottering on the edge of insolvency, possibly, but *putting up a gallant fight*, as Pat had always said about anyone or anything struggling against odds.

She had always made *an allowance* of majestic proportions for Wilfred's father. Old Mr Davis lived half in the street, with the front door permanently open, and three or four of the street's children, for whom there were not enough pre-primary schools in Torford, sitting on the floor watching the television (also permanently on).

This morning, there were two little girls in the dusky, crowded little room, dressed alike in scarlet maxi-coats to their ankles. They were sitting on the mat in front of the fire smouldering in the basket grate; and Mr Davis, a large, stout, rosy old man with remnants of curly dark hair, was stirring a saucepan balanced on the fire, and addressing them.

'. . . then, when yer caught 'im, know what yer does? Yer ketches hold of his skin and yer *pulls it over his head. Right* over his 'ead, see? and he's all ready for the sarsepan. In he goes – see? with a shake of pepper and a bit of salt, and a bit o' parsley and an ongyon or two wot you as by you, and then what does yer do? You tell me, young Kelly,' pointing at one of them with the spoon.

A silent shake of her head, with its fall of long fair hair.

'Hullo, Dad,' said Wilfred, appearing at the door.

''Ullo. Don' know? I never see such gels fer don't knowing. Yer *stews* 'im, that's what, stews 'im very slow, so he comes out as tender as a babby and his flesh fair falls off his bones.' Four eyes were fixed on him, entranced.

'Morning, young ladies,' said Wilfred, coming into the room and, having lifted off a pile of *Daily Mirrors* and *TV Times*, he sat down in an ancient springless armchair (an old enemy of Pat's, and still in use, while all her energy and cheerfulness had gone).

The children's eyes turned to him, but they said nothing.

'I'm just a-showing these two 'ow to stoo a rabbit,' his father said, standing upright with a hand on his back. 'Two o' young Ginger's, they are,' he added in a lowered tone. 'She's got a job up your Mary's school – re-abiliting 'er or summick. Funny ideas people 'ave nowadays, I will say – carn't leave anyone alone. But funny ideas – I don't know.'

He opened a drawer in the old wooden dresser and took out two cleanish pieces of rag, and supervised the tucking of them into the necks of the scarlet coats.

'Regular little images they look, don't they?' he murmured. 'Out of the Ark.'

The little girls were standing by the fire peering down into the saucepan. 'That's right. Now 'ere's yer mugs.' He took down from the dresser one made of blue plastic, and an earthenware one decorated with those pale magenta flowers seen only on cups made when Victoria was Queen. 'And 'ere's yer broth,' ladling out the rich creamy liquid. 'Samantha, you put that bit o' mat on the doorstep. Don't want yer ketching cold in yer little bums, do we? And eat up. And don't let's 'ear a word out of neether of yer.'

When they were seated side by side in the doorway and supping the broth, and their attention was fixed on the people passing in the street, he settled an old tin kettle on the hob.

'I wonder you could –' his son was beginning, beguiled by the familiarity of his surroundings into making a comment that was also familiar, but Mr Davis caught up the sentence and carried it on.

'– Wonder I could use a sixpenny kettle, what I got from Woolworths when it *was* Woolworths? Well, *I* like what I'm used to and no thenks I *don't* want you wasting your money buying me a 'lectric one. Boil over before you can turn round, fuse up, and cost the earth having it repaired. Going up again, too. I 'eard it this morning.' He moved his head towards the television, glaring and flickering soundlessly away in its corner. 'And if it wasn't for the football I wouldn't 'ave *that*. I don't trust 'lectricity.'

Wilfred felt no impulse to retort or argue. The dust and clutter in the little room, and the reek of ancient Old and Sweet tobacco (which had celebrated its centenary last year), and the narrowness and obstinacy of his father's opinions, no longer irritated him. He himself – though Pat disliked him recalling the fact – had been born in one of the two rooms upstairs, and had been carried to the window in a shawl to have his first view of the world outside.

As for Old and Sweet – his hand strayed absently towards the pocket where he had kept his pouch. He had given it up at Pat's repeated entreaties. She had brought out the word *cancer* with such difficulty and fear that he had been touched to his heart. She had been frightened. Giving up had been a sacrifice, but worth it, because he had been able to comfort her, and that was something he was hardly ever asked to do.

Nevertheless, he still missed the peppery-sweet taste of Old and Sweet.

'Yerss. Yer ought to start again.'

He stared at his father. 'What?'

'Yer pipe. I saw yer feeling for it. You don't want to notice what they say. Where's the 'arm? Be afraid to go outside yer own front door if yer took any notice of some of 'em . . . I was listenin' the other night,' and he nodded towards the television, 'round about twelve midnight it must a bin . . . nice thing to send yer to bed on, I don't think . . . some bloke goin' on about eatin' fat. Eyes fair coming out of 'is 'ead, and that solemn – might a been preaching a sermin. And another bloke up there with 'im, to be the example. '*Ad* a stroke, seemingly. All along of eating fat. Don't tell me. Why, a nice bit o' crispy brown an' white inside – that's *good* fer yer . . . Same as yer pipe. – 'Ere.' He handed Wilfred a cup of tea.

'Me and Kelly don't like fat,' came a piping voice from the doorway.

'You and Kelly don't know what's good for yer. 'Ave yer soup and shut up.'

Mr Davis put his upper lip and moustache into his cup, sucked, and sucked again, shutting his eyes.

'Nex' thing,' he announced, emerging, 'you'll 'ave ter think about getting rid o' that great 'ouse.'

Wilfred felt too wretched to put forward sensible remarks.

'And you're in with the council, aren't yer? They'll 'elp yer . . . ought to go off quick, too, a great place like that wi' a bit o' garden, get a good price, I shouldn't wonder. Set yerself up in a *little* place. Comf'able.'

Wilfred did not answer. What would Pat have said to the imputation that Lamorna, with oil-fired central heating, double-glazing in the bedrooms, fitted carpets and a fridge, and electric blankets, was not comfortable?

'Might get married again,' his father added casually, packing his pipe with Old and Sweet, and giving full attention to the task.

'Dad! That's unfeeling! Pat hasn't been dead three months . . . besides, at my age . . .'

'Sixty-five's no age nowadays, besides . . .' But here Mr Davis recollected the presence of the virgins on the door-step, and checked himself. He suddenly shouted, loudly but unalarmingly: 'Samantha! Young Kelly! You be off. And say thenk-you-Mr-Davis-for-the-soup.'

'Thank-you-Mr-Davis-for-the-soup . . . Mum said can we come in after dinner 'cos she's goin' out?' they said, in chorus.

'Yer can knock on the door . . . I may be asleep . . . enough's enough. Be off, now.'

They contrived to delay their going by rinsing their cups and putting away their rag bibs, and the mat on which they had been sitting, but ran off at last.

'Be in trouble, the pair of them, before they're fifteen, unless someone frightens the vests off of 'em,' Mr Davis said grimly. 'Young Ginger's no use to 'em – not in that way, tho' she do spend a bit o' money on their backs . . . no – it's me as will 'ave to.'

Mr Davis never called Slutty anything but Young Ginger, having known her, so to speak, before she was born. Her baptismal name of Gloria he ignored.

'Soon as they're turned eight, I'm giving 'em a talk,' he went on.

'Haven't they . . . isn't there . . .?'

'No there ain't. Gawd only knows 'oo their dad is – a rozzer, I *'ave* 'eard, but I don't believe it – rozzers ain't that 'uman . . . Young Ginger's mum and dad snuffed it, couple o' years ago . . . their aunties and uncles is all bad lots . . . well, layabouts, I don't say outside the law . . . so it's up to me. Merrige or nothink, I'll tell 'em. 'Bout the clap, too. No use in 'ushing anythink up,' Mr Davis ended severely, and poured out more dark red tea.

'Oh well . . . I must be getting along, Dad.'

'Wot's the 'urry all of a sudden? Stay and 'ave a bit o' rabbit along o' me.'

'All right – thanks.'

What was there to do, anyway? The room was warm, it smelt of Old and Sweet. The news, pre-digested to a kind of curried pap by a young man with a Liverpool accent, babbled on in its corner, ignored by them both, and Wilfred remembered the plain green hills that used to smile through the cottage's windows in his childhood.

'Besides – about the house, Dad. There's Mrs Wheeby.'

'Mrs Wheezy? She's had a good run for her money – it won't hurt her to go into a 'ome.'

During the trying hours of last Christmas Day, while his father was paying his obligatory yearly visit to Lamorna, it had become plain that he disliked Mrs Wheeby. Not because he wanted to live with Wilfred and Pat, occupying the room that she now filled; indeed, he would 'sooner go on the road' than do so. No, it was because in Mrs Wheeby old Mr Davis had instantly detected one who liked her own way, and, in so doing, was a rival of anyone else who liked theirs.

'It's not her, Dad, it's me. I shouldn't like to turn her out, not after Pat going to all that trouble.'

'Yer can't let some old basket stop yer selling yer own house. Don't be so soft.'

Wilfred drank more tea and decided not to answer. Other sentences sounded in his memory. *You old softie. How do you ever expect to get anywhere if you're soft? You let anyone put on you.*

'Yer a good lad, Wilf,' his father said suddenly, stooping over the saucepan with his back to the room. 'Too good for some, if you arst me.'

Wilfred knew that his reply to this should have been sharp, because *some* was Pat. But the truth was that his father's words were so comforting that he could do nothing but drink them in, settle them into his bruised heart, and thank god in a shame-faced muddled way that the 'low', obstinate old man was still in the land of the living.

As Wilfred was an Englishman, the immediate result of these thoughts was that he got up, saying that he thought he must be going, accompanied by coat-buttoning.

'Sit down – sit down – 'ere's yer dinner,' said his father soothingly, and poured half the saucepan's contents into an ancient soup-plate, 'dumplings and all. Out of a pecket, but 'oo cares so they tastes all right?'

It was like eating beside a campfire; like being a Scout again. The savoury taste, the warmth, the company familiar as his own right hand – which asked nothing and gave approval and affection. Wilfred at last felt enabled to say what he had come to say. 'Mary has run away from me. She has left me. She's gone to London.' And when their plates had been wiped clean with bread, Mr Davis had ended the visit by saying exactly the right thing to round off the half-hour of peace.

'Mary! She'll be married before yer can turn round . . . that stout quiet sort always is. Let 'er get on with it.'

Here was the second person that morning to tell him that Mary was the marrying kind. Who could be more different from his father than Mrs Anstruther? . . . yet, from both came the same comforting verdict.

4

Mary

When Mary got out of the train and walked down the platform at Liverpool Street station, she was not awed or confused by its noise and crowds, because she had been there before. Once with the school, and twice with her parents, to see some of the sights of London.

And she knew exactly where she was going.

On her last visit, eighteen months ago, she had noticed, immediately outside the station and situated on a corner where it would catch the attention of passers-by, a shop window full of pink-and-green, purple-and-orange patterned dresses. Some of them had overflowed the window and were hanging in the doorway, fluttering in the wind among strings of coloured beads, glittering chains set with pearls, and large broad-brimmed hats of bright felt.

Mary, having given up her ticket, went straight towards this shop.

A little woman wearing black, nearly bald beneath a frizz of hair dyed bright brown, with a flat face and shrewd eyes, was sitting behind the tiny counter, surrounded by more dresses, beads and hats, and working at some figures. She looked up as Mary's solid shape appeared in the doorway between the blowing shifts.

'Hullo, dear – vant a frock?' Her eyes travelled over Mary. 'Size eighteen, it'll be . . . what colour?'

The pink-and-purple patterned dresses drifted against the dim blue autumn sky and the people – *Londoners* – hurried by with their heads up, not looking at anything. Mary could feel their stir and haste going past her back as she stood there.

'Good morning . . . thank you. I don't want a frock yet, though I shall later on. I want a job. I remembered your shop from the last time I was in London, and this is the kind of shop I want to be in, so I thought I'd ask you.'

Mary was what is called well-spoken. Her words came out slowly, for so young a girl, and her voice sounded placid. Her dark green coat, her gleaming knee-high black boots, and her thick well-brushed hair suggested that behind her was a respectable home. It was all these things, as well as some surprise, that caused Mrs Sadie Levy to moderate the righteous indignation, which she felt on hearing Mary's statement, into a mere tartness, rather than give the shriek in which she had at first meant to indulge herself.

'I daresay you do,' she snapped, flinging down her pencil. 'I-dare-say-you-do. And how many girls in London vant the same, you think?'

'Thousands, of course,' Mary answered calmly. 'But I'm me, not them. And I'm good at arithmetic and I can spell and—'

'Where you from?' demanded Mrs Levy.

'Torford. That's—'

'And you vant twenty pounds a week and commission, I suppose –'

'I'd start at twelve, but I'd certainly want commission . . .'

'Vell you can't come here,' Mrs Levy interrupted, 'because there isn't room for two. You see that, I think. Besides, I don't need you or anyone. I've had some. You all want the same. In Hamburg where I grow up, I start at age thirteen. Up at six, vork all day and just fifteen minutes for lunch until nine at night. And for how much I do this?' demanded Mrs Levy, at last permitting herself the shriek. 'For ten of your shillings – gone now – a veek. Und then the war come, und ven ve lose it, of course—'

'Did you lose it when the Russians came?' Mary interrupted, wishing to prolong a conversation which seemed, to her, to have taken a not discouraging turn (at least she hadn't been dismissed in a sentence) and remembering her mother's remarks about old folks liking to reminisce.

'Russians?' Mrs Levy stared. 'Vot Russians? Is before the war I'm talking about. Is 1920.'

'Oh.' To Mary, 1920 and 1220 were equally remote.

'Yes, *Oh.* So we all starf, my mutter (she yet alive, thank Gott), my sisters, me, until things better. Gott in His Heffen, how we work! You girls, you don't know you're born. Layabout. Vot you all are nowadays, layabout – vere you off to?'

'Oxford Street,' breathed Mary, half out of the door, and all her common sense could not keep a note of excitement from her voice.

'Und vot chance you haf *there*, you tell me?'

Mary halted in the doorway, unhurriedly pushed aside a purple shift that had blown across her face, and stood looking steadily at Mrs Levy.

'Listen . . .' Mrs Levy struggled up from behind the counter. 'I just got new grandchild; fourth one; the first boy – a lofly boy. I can't see him all I vant because I must be in the shop . . . You a loose girl? You go vith boys?' She leant across the counter, resting her hands on it, and studied Mary.

Mary shook her head.

'Vell . . . I take a chance. You haf boys in my shop, and *out you go* . . . Mr Foster across the road selling cigarettes alvays keep an eye on you . . . just like you *alvays* feel you can go back home if you don't like to live in London, hein?'

Mary looked down. The thought was like an anchor at the back of her mind.

She looked up. 'Oh yes,' and her eyes became long, smiling slits. 'But not till I've got a job.'

'You haf one,' Mrs Levy said crossly. 'Every afternoon you come here und look after the shop while I go see my grandson. I pay you vun pound per day.'

'Good!' Mary exclaimed, and a pink shift from the other side of the door blew out and hid her face for the second time. 'But where am I to sleep tonight? I must –' she brushed it aside and caught the strap of her wristwatch in it. 'You see –'

'Not here. Certainly not here,' interrupted Mrs Levy. 'Be careful, for Gott's sake don't tear it. That's right. It is forbidden by the law and nothing upstairs but my stock und holes in the floor.'

She glanced upwards, as though her eyes could penetrate the blackish ceiling of the two-storey ancient little house perched on a corner near Broad Street and Liverpool Street stations.

'I tell you vot,' Mrs Levy went on, sitting down again. 'You go across the road to Broad Street station and take a train to Gospel Oak. Is nice, respectable neighbourhood, Parliament Hill. You find a room there. Und you come here tomorrow, one o'clock. Sharp.' She looked down at her sheet of figures, shaking her head. 'I don't suppose I see you again . . . vot's your name?'

'Mary Davis.'

'Ha! Vy not Jones?' demanded Mrs Levy, obviously suspecting an alias, but Mary said, 'Good morning, then. Tomorrow at one, and thank you,' and went out between the floating dresses and across the road and up some steps leading (so she was informed, on enquiring, by her prospective mentor in the tobacco shop) to Broad Street.

Mary possessed a sense of smell too acute for her comfort. She did not like the smell of London. But she kept her head turned towards the open window of the train, and, after they had passed a more than usually broken, ruinous and confused stretch of wasteland, there was a change.

Her nose reported a new freshness and coolness, almost a sweetness, though it was unlike the biting sweetness of the air at Torford. And suddenly – a high green hill, with green meadows sloping up to it, was gliding past.

The train stopped, and the name of the station was Gospel Oak.

Mary did not like the look of it.

It had an old-fashioned, Torfordish air; and she was convinced that Oxford Street, and the even more glamorous King's Road, Chelsea, were a long way away. She had had quite enough, during the last seventeen years, of peaceful roads with trees, and, across the fields, she could see the same kind of place.

She went down some steps and turned to the left, under a railway bridge that spanned the road then past some old, whitish houses. There was a good deal of traffic. *Oh bother*, thought Mary, rather confused, and she turned off impatiently down a side track leading onto the meadows she had seen from the train. Her case felt heavier, her spirits were definitely falling. *Nearly twelve. Of course! I'm hungry.*

Seeing some shops in the distance near a bus stop, she marched towards them, following a path under trees. Passing the playground of a boys' school, and finding a café near a sub-post office, she went in, and ate an eggy, sausagy lunch.

Full, she sauntered out again. The fading trees shone gold in the golden sunlight. *This Parliament Hill must be quite a big park. I may as well have a bit of a breather*, thought Mary. *I suppose I don't want to start looking. Let's face it.* She weighed her case, thoughtfully, then turned into the sub-post office.

'We're just closing,' warned the sub-postmistress, observing Mary taking out her purse.

'If I gave you five new pence, would you kindly mind my case while I go for a walk?'

'I don't want your five new pence . . . I'll mind your case for you,' said the sub-postmistress, taking the case and settling it, in reassuring privacy, under the counter. 'Half past two, we open again. Now you mind how you go, there's vandals about.'

Mary sauntered on.

The green fields climbed undramatically until they reached a summit where there were seats, and boys were flying a big white and scarlet kite shaped like a butterfly.

Far below, all old London; spreading away, away, filling the vast valley from east to west; a flittering, smoking, golden-grey mass from which towered up stark white cubes. Mary's eyes smiled with pleasure, as she thought: *Oh I'm glad I came! I've got a job, and forty-three pounds in the Post Office, and I'm glad I came.*

She turned, and looked north. All green there, and the horizon hidden by a long rolling line of golden woods. After glancing at her watch, she set out towards them; across more meadows and down through a wet valley full of beech saplings and patches of boggy turf.

Once in the trees' shade, she paced more slowly; along paths darkened by rhododendrons and smelling of autumn. It was not solitary. She passed young families strolling, tourists consulting maps; elderly women, well-dressed and ceaselessly taking. If the setting of golden stillness was too pensive for her taste, at least there was plenty of company.

She sat down on a seat under a beech tree laden with yellow leaves. A squirrel ran out onto the path and she watched it, a little bored.

A youth of about twenty came tramping round the rhododendrons; he had a white face pinched into a shape suggesting a snout, a thin moustache and flowing hair.

She had hardly time even to think how unattractive she found his appearance, before he was coming down upon her – nearer – nearer. She stared, unable to believe what was happening – and then he flung himself onto the seat, almost on top of her, with a force that jarred the wood. He pressed his body close against her side; she caught a faint, bad smell.

'Come on . . .' he said, out of the side of his mouth without looking at her, 'over the fence and into the bushes.'

Mary was too astounded to feel frightened. Indeed, his voice was so low and thick that she was not certain what he had said. She got up instantly, and moved without hurry towards two people who came at that moment round the bushes at the other end of the path.

'Excuse me –' she said, stopping in front of the pair, 'but may I walk on with you? That boy on the seat is annoying me.'

'I'll do the lot of you,' shouted the boy, not moving, his head thrust forward on his breast.

'Oh dear,' sighed the woman. 'Is there no peace anywhere? You had better walk between us.'

The man muttered some words that appeared to confirm both his complaint and her permission, and the three went on together.

'Oh dear!' exclaimed the little woman again, as a distant shout from the boy reached them. 'It makes you feel quite bad.'

'After this morning,' said the man.

'Yes . . . we've come out for a breather,' the woman said to Mary. 'We had a *most* unpleasant experience this morning with a tenant who was leaving. Our windows broken – and such language as I never hope to hear again!'

'I'm sorry,' said Mary, now wishing to be rid of these apparent saviours who had too rapidly turned out to be themselves in need of comfort. 'I shall be all right now, thanks very much.'

They had followed a path leading out of the rhododendrons and were walking beside a lake covered in lily pads and bordered by beds of brown reeds.

Mary was turning aside, intent on leaving them, when the man said: 'I don't think we ought to let her go alone, Florrie. We should never forgive ourselves.'

'No . . . I suppose we shouldn't. – What's your name, dear? I'm Mrs Cadman and this is my friend Mr Grant.'

'Hi,' said Mr Grant, and made a vague gesture intended to bridge the generation gap.

'Hi,' said Mary, smiling. 'I'm Mary Davis.'

'I could just do with a cup of tea, Harry . . . Is that café place open? In the Old Stables? . . . That's shaken me up all over again, that boy's shocking language has,' Mrs Cadman said, appropriating to herself the tremors that should have been Mary's. 'Such a dreadful-looking creature! The homes they must come from!'

'He smelt horrible, too,' said Mary.

'Soap's cheap,' said Mr Grant deeply.

Mrs Cadman's little face was, Mary now observed, carefully
tinted with make-up. Her lipstick was pinkish-orange, and
thirty years ago she must have been deliciously pretty. Her
expression, in spite of her doleful words, was cheerful. *I made
the best of it*, one could hear her saying.

Mary's thoughts had been straying back to the scene on the
seat. Had Mrs Anstruther ever confided to this pupil her theories
about the enriching of the female temperament by untrammelled
experience, it is just possible that Mary might have regretted
an opportunity for enrichment, lost for ever between the beech
tree and the rhododendron clump. As it was, her good sense had
not been dented, and while they all walked up yet another hill
to a gate that led out of this big park onto Hampstead Heath
(that was the name of these rolling meadows and coppices and
big old trees, Mr Grant said,) she told her rescuers a carefully
prepared recital, omitting her flight from home.

'And now I've *got* to find a room,' she concluded.

There was silence. Mary was again preparing to take off,
but something in the two friends' manner, an expression on
both elderly faces, kept her lingering.

'What do you think, Harry?' asked Mrs Cadman, turning
to him.

'Suppose we say a week's trial, Florrie?' was Mr Grant's
reply.

'Mr Grant and I were thinking,' announced Mrs Cadman,
'that you seem a respectable girl, and, as it happens, we do
have an empty room at the moment. An attic. I suppose you
require furnished?'

'Oh yes,' said Mary, with inward amusement at a picture of
herself roaming Gospel Oak followed by a van full of furniture.
'And what were you thinking of asking, Mrs Cadman?'

She knew instinctively that the coarse words 'How much?'
must not be uttered.

'Two pounds a week, seeing you're so young,' smiled
Mrs Cadman, and Mr Grant smiled too. 'And that includes
the use of gas ring and light.'

Then Mary realized just how sensible she had been to find out from Sandra's friend Linda all those facts about the cost of renting a bed-sitter in London, for she could murmur, with strong feelings of satisfaction as well as honesty: 'But that's *wonderfully* reasonable!'

'Ah well,' Mrs Cadman sighed. 'All Mr Grant and me ask is a little peace, on the downward slope of the hill.'

'Here, here,' Mr Grant protested, 'steady on. We've got a good many years before us yet.'

'. . . And after our recent experience we're prepared to let it go a little more reasonably than we would normally. But I will be frank with you,' concluded Mrs Cadman with emphasis, looking full at Mary, 'it would have been three guineas to anyone else, and whether it *remains* at two pounds will depend on whether you *suit*.'

"Then that's settled,' Mr Grant said. 'She'd better come back with us now, hadn't she, Florrie, and see the room.' They were drawing near to the bus stop and the sub-post office.

'I must just pick up my case . . . The lady in the post office is taking care of it for me,' said Mary.

'Oh . . . Miss Drewer . . . Yes,' and Mrs Cadman gave a slight shake of her head, and this dismayed Mary, reminding her of Torford, where people often made a face or shook their heads when other people's names were mentioned. She had taken it for granted that in glamorous London there was none of this.

'You do that, dear. Mr Grant and I will go on home and make us all a cup of tea, and you can see the attic. It's *nice*, isn't it, Harry?'

'Best attic in Parliament Hill Fields – and we have a high standard in attics in this neck of the woods,' said Mr Grant.

'It's Twenty Rowena Road. You have to cross over,' called Mrs Cadman, as Mary hurried away.

Two hours later, Mary was on her way to Oxford Street.

En route to the bus stop she had pushed a postcard into the letter-box: 'Have got a job and a room. In a nice neighbourhood so don't worry. Will write once a week. Love, M.'

She got back at eleven, and was in time to see Mr Grant marching up the stairs behind Mrs Cadman, who was carrying two hot-water bottles. She wore a fluffy blue shortie dressing-gown.

'Goodnight,' called Mrs Cadman, looking round at the head of the stairs and smiling down at Mary. Then she and Mr Grant went into a room and shut the door.

Well, thought Mary. *Suits me.*

5

Egg-putters

Mary's postcard gave Wilfred a comfort out of proportion to its scanty message. If she wrote that a neighbourhood was respectable, then respectable it was. If she wrote that she had a job, then she had one. His first impulse was to bound upstairs and show the card to Mrs Wheeby, but then he remembered having told her that Mary had gone to a job with her aunt. So he put the postcard in his pocket and stood staring, with a lift to the corners of his mouth that was not quite a smile, around the white and cherry-coloured (no, it was not a true crimson) hall.

Who was it who had loved crimson and white as the height of beauty in furnishings and dress? Ah – poor Charlotte Brontë, in the person of tiny, fiery, fascinating Jane Eyre. Wilfred went absently along to the kitchen, where he had just switched on the heating for the winter and the air was pleasantly warm, thinking about Mr Rochester, and hoping that when Mary found a husband, he would not resemble that gentleman. *Nor Heathcliff either*, thought Wilfred, opening the refrigerator to get himself a can of beer, *nor Heathcliff either . . . Too much of a good thing, both of them, if you ask me.*

On this earth there are egg-putters, people who, because of their nature, are obliged to fit their allowance of eggs snugly into just the one basket. No one had ever warned Wilfred, a born egg-putter, against this habit. And it had not occurred

to Pat that egg-putters existed, much less that her dozy old
Wilf was one.

He felt so thankful and so much happier that he decided to
walk that afternoon through Lorrimer Park, past the seat where
he had encountered Mr Taverner, taking with him the washed
and ironed handkerchief nicely folded in its clean envelope.
He would doze for an hour in the big armchair in the lounge,
then set out.

But he couldn't doze, because this was one of Dicky's singing
hours, and the trilling, shaking, silvery sounds were dropping
down through the silent house. He went over to the window,
pulled back the curtain, and peered aimlessly out.

It was a grey afternoon, threatening rain, and every colour glowed soft and clear: the bluish slates of the old roofs,
the sooty grass on the far side of the railway cutting. Even the
ashy material between the railway lines was rich steely-black,
and the great sunflowers were a sulky gold. *In this sort of light,*
Wilfred thought vaguely, *you don't want bright colours.*

His eye moved to a painting, which was of the view from
this very window. It hung on the opposite wall, and was one
of Pat's. She had had enough energy left, when housework, her
job, and the refuelling and supervising of Wilfred and Mary
were achieved, to attend evening classes in painting. *Dear old
Pat, how she had loved bright colours.* His widower's eye turned
from the picture, with the guilty thought that he would rather
look at the real scene.

In the gentle crescent of the houses across the railway, a
colour suddenly caught his eye: one line of bright white gold. *A
really nice colour,* thought Wilfred. *The sun shows it up. Now that
is a colour – delicate but strong too. Funny, because –* he glanced
up at the leaden sky – *there isn't any sun.* He stared, interested
and fascinated.

What was that yellow line?

No, it wasn't sunlight from some distant break in the clouds.
Just a thin golden line, in the curve of the grey crescent.

I'll get my glasses.

His field glasses had been a present from Pat, bought from a war stores surplus shop after she had decided that he must have bird-watching as a hobby to match her painting. In his retirement, he had dutifully used them, summoned many a time from a book or mooning fit by the robust shout – 'Wilf! Quick! There's a jay on the fence!'

He secretly resented birds (with the exception of his garden robin, which he looked on as a member of his family) because they ate the buds of his primulas in May, pecking out the unfolding cups of blue or crimson before he had had time to perform his usual laborious protective operation with black cotton and sticks.

But looking at distant roofs, or windows giving on mysterious dim rooms, going with his eyes into toppling ziggurats of red evening cloud – that was enjoyment. He had never told Pat of his private studying of old brick walls and grimily curtained windows, because she would have said that it was a kinky thing to do, and people would be surprised if they caught him 'at it'.

The glasses were good ones. They brought roofs and trees and windows so near and so large that a simple and unsuspected beauty was revealed; Wilfred had sometimes thought that it wasn't possible to realize how beautiful an ordinary sight, such as an expanse of wet slate, could be until he had seen it through his field-glasses.

His sight was bad; a wound sustained during the Second World War had affected it. Now he took off his spectacles and settled the glasses against his eyes.

Ah, the familiar curve of the beech hedge below the sunflowers. Something – he knew nothing about the laws of optics and cared less – in the structure of these two thick rounds of glass made any nearby tree or bush studied through them take on a convex curve . . . After a satisfying stare at the yellowing leaves growing along the graceful bending line that he knew was, in reality, straight as a hedge can be, he tilted the glasses and focused on the line of white-gold gleaming among the old houses.

Somebody had painted a house. The rest of the houses were all the same colour, neither white nor grey nor cream. That had been their last coat of paint – in 1939, before the bombs came. But one house shone out in the colour that had lifted Wilfred's heart.

Dicky's song stopped, as if turned off by a tap. It must be three o'clock.

Best be off, Wilfred thought, putting on coat and muffler in the hall; *it's nearly dark by four, and I don't want to hang about. Of course, he may not be there.*

But when he turned the corner by the rhododendrons, there was Mr Taverner, sitting on the seat where they had first met, and again wearing his white raincoat. He glanced up as Wilfred approached, and smiled.

'Good afternoon,' Wilfred said.

He had expected to feel embarrassment; the last time this man had seen him he had been crying. But he felt only pleasure at the sight of Mr Taverner's lanky figure draped along the seat, as if he had recognized a friend. He seated himself alongside him.

'Not too bad, now, is it?' he ventured.

Pat had disliked the dim, white *something* that frequently rolled into Torford late on winter afternoons. The sea was only fifteen miles away, and old Torford hands called this something 'the sea mist'. Wilfred, while liking the mystery it gave to streets and houses, had never until today said anything to anyone that implied an affection for it. The setting sun was now looking redly through it, and already the trees were ghostly.

'I like this kind of afternoon,' said Mr Taverner, but said no more.

In the pause, Wilfred brought out the clean envelope from his pocket-book. 'Here's . . .' he began, and for the first time he felt embarrassment. 'You may not remember . . . but . . . you lent me a handkerchief that afternoon . . . when we first met, I mean.'

'So I did.' And Mr Taverner, a little to Wilfred's surprise (surely it would have been more tactful to put the envelope at once and unopened into his pocket?) tore it open, flourished the contents about his long pointed nose, and shied the envelope unerringly into a nearby litter bin.

'I . . . I expect you thought I'd made off with it,' and Wilfred gave a nervous little laugh. 'I . . . did mean to bring it back the next day, but . . . that day, you know, I was a bit upset about something . . . it all mounted up . . .'

'I didn't think you'd pinched it. I knew it would be back. Handkerchiefs and umbrellas — other people lose 'em. I never do.'

'You're lucky, then,' said Wilfred. The wet scent of the mist, his companion's indolent voice, and the very pose of his angular body along the seat, were all soothing. *It's a long time*, he thought vaguely, *since I felt soothed.*

'Yes, I'm lucky,' Mr Taverner answered, turning his large, light-haunted eyes on Wilfred. 'And so today you're feeling better?'

'Yes . . . my daughter wrote to me. Only a postcard, but . . .' and then and there he began to *tell.*

He told it all without thinking. At the back of his mind there was a slight feeling of surprise at thus pouring out to a stranger more freely than he could have done to his own father. But the feeling was not strong enough to restrain him. Though when, at the end of the recital, Mr Taverner only said: 'Won't you come home and have a cup of tea with us?' Wilfred's common sense took over.

Was it *natural* to feel this intimacy? He recalled Pat's earnest reading of certain Sunday papers. There were odd types about nowadays — loonies, psychopaths, schizophrenics. One didn't, of course, *condemn* them. They were sick. But only a b.f. would go home to tea with one.

Mr Taverner continued to look at him mildly, with the suggestion of a smile.

'Thanks very much,' Wilfred said. 'I'd like to.'

They set off through the thickening mist, walking in easy silence along several roads of elderly houses where grew plane trees whose annual leaf-dropping threatened the shopping expeditions of the retired people living there. The roads ended in mist tinted to coral by the setting sun.

The footsteps of the few people who were about sounded without echo in the muffling dimness. It did not occur to Wilfred, among his barely formulated fears, that Mr Taverner might be a murderer. There are fashions in bogeys, as there used to be in hats, and murderers were not real; they belonged to thrillers and television.

They turned a corner, and there was Hardy Crescent curving away before them; hushed, deserted, graceful, with its miniature pillars and bay windows veiled in mist. It ended in a rosy blankness, beyond which lay the railway cutting.

'Empty, aren't they?' observed Wilfred, glancing up at boarded doors and down at broken stone steps.

'Not all. Two or three are let out in bed-sitters.'

Wilfred was going on to say something about the council deciding to bulldoze the place any day now, but did not. The houses were beautiful, and their beauty laid a restraining finger upon his lips. Instead, he said:

'There's a nice . . . I was noticing, earlier this afternoon . . . our house overlooks the railway and I can see the Crescent from our kitchen windows . . . someone's painted one of them yellow – a really wonderful yellow . . . it is most unusual.' Mr Taverner turned to him attentively. 'Kind of a pale gold; got a lot of white in it. If I hadn't almost decided to sell my house – as I was telling you – I'd do up my daughter's room that colour – *if* I could buy it anywhere. I know she'd like it. We always have liked the same colours.'

'I'm glad you like it.' Mr Taverner laid a hand on a low gate of scrolled iron. 'Here we are.'

The mist had crept up on them while they chatted, so thickly that now it was not possible to see more than a few yards ahead, but Wilfred glanced up at the house behind the gate and exclaimed –

'Why, this *is* the yellow house!'

'Yes. That's why I'm glad you like it.'

Mr Taverner stood aside to let Wilfred pass along a little walk, paved with black and blue tiles, running between beds of yellow chrysanthemums drooping heavily in the motionless air and giving out that aromatic scent of which some people never tire.

The front steps of number 7 were so white that they appeared to send out a glow into the dusk, and with a feeling of pleasure Wilfred recognized the humble yet stout presence of *hearthstone*, which he remembered his mother using on the doorstep of their cottage sixty years ago. He could see her tumbling knot of fair hair and the curve of her young back and the sweeping movement of her strong red arm.

'You don't often see steps hearthstoned, nowadays,' he observed, as they stood in the portico.

'Whizzo, Promesseing (with an e), and Sensuelle,' said Mr Taverner, producing a latchkey. 'But Miss Dollette and I *like* hearthstone.'

'You're lucky to get a woman to do it,' said Wilfred, remembering various failures to secure such services (Pat never could 'get on' with daily women). Mr Taverner was making fun, of course, of the telly adverts with their fancy names.

'Mind you, those electric things save a lot of work,' Wilfred added, feeling a vague disloyalty to Pat, devout user of the time-saving household devices.

'I-do-it-myself,' Mr Taverner sang, as he fitted the key into the lock. 'Work. Work. It keeps me off the streets and out of the pubs.'

Wilfred was feeling a little uneasiness. *This certainly was a queer kind of chap; seemed to make fun of everything. Odd way of talking, too.*

'And *not* early in the morning when everybody is asleep. About twelve, when they're just about waking up. That's when I do it.' Mr Taverner swung open the front door.

That's nice, I like that, was Wilfred's first thought at the sight of the octagonal hall, and the staircase curving sweetly upwards, and the ceiling with its medallions lustrous in that same glowing colour. But then astonishment banished every other feeling.

'Why, it's Kichijoten!' he cried.

He spoke the exotic syllables of the name without shyness, having sometimes repeated them over to himself in his times of what Pat had called mooning.

Taller than a real woman, the figure smiled down at him in her pink draperies. In one long hand she held some rosy fruit.

'How on earth did you get hold of *her*?'

'Oh, I . . . spent a lot of time and took some trouble.'

Mr Taverner lowered himself onto some six of the stairs and reposed there comfortably, watching his guest with a gentle half-smile while Wilfred continued to stare up into the placid smiling face of the goddess.

She wore large pins of tortoiseshell and mother-of-pearl in the black coils of her hair. The pose of her body was benevolent, inclining slightly towards the beholder. The only angularities about her were her hands, thin and delicate, cherishing the apples that were only a little smaller than one of her white-stockinged feet.

'Is it really the same one that used to be in the Japanese Room in Lorrimer House?'

'I'm – not quite sure.' Mr Taverner sounded drowsy. The hall was in deep twilight now, yet its walls seemed to give off enough light to see Kichijoten.

In a moment, however, Wilfred began to feel that he was behaving like a half-wit, and turned towards his host; at which Mr Taverner came up off the stairs and stooped over a table. There came the scritch of a match being struck, and a wide blue flame slowly expanded in the middle of a brass lamp.

'Haven't you electricity?' asked Wilfred. 'No – I remember now, it was never put on again after the bombing, was it?'

'We like oil here.' Mr Taverner was settling the pearly shade onto the lamp.

If you can see, of course ... But Pat's impatient voice in Wilfred's head was silenced by the quality of the light beginning to waver up. Up, up soared the lamplight with an effect of gaiety and triumph. *Someone ought to be dancing*, he thought confusedly.

Mr Taverner was opening a door. 'Felicity? A friend: Mr Davis,' he said, and stood aside to let Wilfred enter.

Here it was: a kitchen. Wilfred thought at once: *the* kitchen.

The old wooden floor was painted a pale, shining yellow, and a large old table was scrubbed to a warm white suggesting the bleaching work of the sea. It was half spread with a white cloth, on which stood brilliantly red and peacock-blue china, and a breadboard incised with a decoration of wheat sheaves, on which sat a flat, golden-brown loaf. The walls were painted a deeper yellow, and another pearly-shaded lamp filled the room with amber light. There was a built-in dresser having cupboards underneath, laden with more bright china of all colours and kinds and disposed with homely lack of arrangement.

A woman was standing by the large range where the fire was in precisely the right state for making toast; that is, on the very point of declining from a long fierceness, as if its tide of heat were on the turn. She held the bread at the end of a long wire fork, and it was browning gently.

For years, Wilfred's picture of a woman had been bright-coloured and a little stout, with immaculately arranged hair. This was the outer picture. Behind it, overshadowed and softer, was another. The other had tendrils of hair that blew across her eyes, and her clothes were softly tinted and rather shapeless. She had no voice to set against the loud, kind, sensible voice of the other picture. Only God, and the subconscious memories of a silent, rather observant little boy, knew where and when this second picture had been born. She was not his mother.

Miss Dollette wore a soft greenish dress and her hair was pale wheat colour, streaked with a silvery grey. The tendrils strayed about her small face and large eyes. She was a small woman, shorter than his five foot six.

'Good afternoon,' she said, smiling up from the range. 'Do you like dripping toast?'

'I won't say no,' Wilfred said, smiling too.

He would have liked to sit down. The change from the bitingly cold air in the streets and the momentary forgetfulness of his anxiety and grief were making him feel drowsy. The light of these lamps: that had something to do with his state. It was so steady and splendid – but it was tiring, too.

'No, I won't say no. Thank you,' he repeated.

'That's right – say "no" as little as possible,' exclaimed Mr Taverner, pulling chairs up to the table. 'Try saying "yes" a hundred times before breakfast – "yes yes yes yes yes yes yes yes." Makes you feel like a snake.'

Hissing was the kind of joke that Wilfred enjoyed with Mary (if anything so silly could be called a joke) and which Pat had always heard with an impatient smile.

'Then I'll say "yes", Yes and thank you . . . Just the right afternoon for dripping toast, isn't it?'

'It's always the right afternoon for dripping toast,' said Mr Taverner. 'Mind you, I admit that on August the Eighth – (sounds stifling, doesn't it?) – one might falter before a plateful. But on every other afternoon – yes.'

This was the point at which Pat would have begun to look irritated. Miss Dollette neither spoke nor looked anything. She added a sixth slice of toast soaked in dripping to the pile on the plate standing at the cool end of the range.

'Assam tea, we're having. Oh-what-an-ass-I-am tea,' Mr Taverner ran on. 'Sit down, sit down, Mr Davis,' and he waved at three stout old wooden chairs. Wilfred settled himself thankfully between the hard, comforting old arms, and felt the support of the curved back, and observed: 'Now this is what I *call* a chair, this is . . . feel you really are sitting down in this.'

'I'm glad you like it. I made it.'

Wilfred was about to exclaim in admiration, when Miss Dollette turned her head just a little in Mr Taverner's direction.

'Well . . . that is . . . I took some trouble and spent some time,' Mr Taverner said quickly.

'I see. Like you did over the statue of Kichijoten.'

'Oh, that was more dif— Do help yourself. The salt's in front of you.'

Wilfred took a slice, soggy with rich gravy-impregnated fat, and put it on his plate. He took the linen napkin from under the plate and wiped his fingers.

'Eat it up,' Mr Taverner urged. 'Devour and consume and absorb it while its savoury vapours exhale and fume upwards.' The toast drooped and dripped from his long fingers. 'Because when it's even the *least* bit cold, it's hellish — I mean in the sense of Shakespeare's "thrilling regions of thick-ribbed ice".' He bit into the toast and mopped unashamedly at the dripping running down his chin. 'I say,' he went on, with his mouth full, 'we're like the Three Little Ghostesses —'

'"Sitting on posstesses,"' Miss Dollette went on for him, looking dreamily out of the window into the mist.

'"Eating buttered toastesses,"' Wilfred capped eagerly. 'Only it ought to be "dripping toastesses". My father used to say that to me — goodness only knows where he got it from, for he — isn't a reading man.' (Wilfred recalled copies of two papers called respectively *Ally Sloper's Half Holiday* and *The Police Gazette* lying about the cottage sixty years ago. The cover of the latter often showed a murdered girl — lying across a kitchen table with hair streaming down to the floor. *Usually showed her knickers, too. Well I s'pose Z Cars is better than that*, he mused. *Of course, in those days, knickers . . .*

'"See how the gracetises

Roll down their facetises –

Dirty little basteses!"' Mr Taverner capped. 'Irish ghosts, wouldn't you think? I've always imagined those postesses in the middle of an Irish bog.'

'I never went into it,' Wilfred answered, suddenly prim and self-conscious.

'And a good thing too – very prudent!' Mr Taverner's laughter was a musical shout, and Miss Dollette's chiming with it, a bubbling gush, seemed to escape of its own will. Wilfred laughed too, enjoying the silliness as he used with Mary.

Miss Dollette handed him a cup of red tea, and he sipped.

'"Swoon to the timeless taste of Tiddlers Twoshy Tips",' said Mr Taverner. 'Actually, it's quite good.'

'I always did think there's a lot of rubbish talked on those TV adverts.' Wilfred said this aloud for the first time in his life. Pat had studied the commercials as a Shakesperian critic might scrutinize a manuscript for clues.

'And now, about selling your house,' said Mr Taverner, setting down his cup.

Wilfred was instantly alarmed. He too put down his cup, fixing his gaze on Mr Taverner's face, and did not immediately answer.

'You see, it's Mary,' he said at last. 'I must have a home for her to come home *to*, when she *does* come. She's only seventeen – well, seventeen next month. And besides, there's Mrs Wheeby, the old lady I was telling you about. What would I do with her? She – she *relies* on me. She said so. Or as good as.' He broke off. Mr Taverner continued to munch and keep his eyes on Wilfred's face. 'It would be a big upheaval, you see,' Wilfred continued. 'We've been there nearly twenty years – bought it just after the war. It went for a song – being on the east coast, you see. People hadn't started to come back. But I got out of the Army early (first in, first out), and if you were on the spot you were lucky . . . But there's all the trouble of selling it . . . moving . . . finding somewhere else . . . The fact is, I don't feel I can face it. And I must keep a home for Mary.'

In the silence following his speech, a cat came wandering in and rubbed itself against his legs, and he put down a hand and absently caressed it. Miss Dollette murmured: 'Antony, aren't you a nuisance?' and the cat went across to her and rolled over on the floor at her feet, looking lovingly up at her. It was shining black, with brilliant eyes.

Wilfred was hearing voices: sensible voices, warning him that Mary might take up with some young layabout, down in the City of Dreadful Night; that something terrible might happen to her there; that she might never come home again.

'I'll have to think about it, you see,' he said at last. 'It isn't a thing you can make up your mind about in five minutes, selling a house.'

A door slammed somewhere, and Miss Dollette sat upright, while her face seemed to come alight with a gentle glow of pleasure. 'There's Katherine,' she said.

'It isn't a crime, of course, *never* to shut a door quietly,' Mr Taverner said, as if to himself, and Miss Dollette laughed.

The kitchen door opened, and in swirled a scarlet cloak. Inside it was a tall woman. Her lipstick and headscarf matched its glow, and her mouth was large and smiling.

'Hullo, dears,' she said in a loud, rich voice. 'Hullo,' with a friendly nod to Wilfred.

'Mr Davis — Mrs Cornforth,' said Mr Taverner, and Wilfred felt as if the temperature of the room had gone up.

'We've eaten all the dripping toast,' announced Mr Taverner, 'and if you want any, Katherine, you must make it yourself.'

Off came long gloves (real suede, Wilfred noticed, and she wore a big red stone set in a gold ring). 'Where do you think I've been?' she swept on, slicing bread carelessly, while her large bright eyes danced over the three faces.

'In a pub, I should think,' Mr Taverner said. 'There was a little boy outside, waiting for his brother who had popped in for a quick one, and you simply had to go in and buy him a packet of ham-flavoured crisps—'

'Absolutely right!' cried Mrs Cornforth. 'He was a poppet –
tiny, and looked frozen. But you're wrong about the crisps;
they were cheese and onion. A sailor wanted to buy me a
drink.'

'Look out, you're burning the toast. How did you know he
was a sailor?'

'He smelt of the sea, of course . . . but I said no, thank you,
and flew outside again . . . and what do you think the poppet
said?'

She sat down at the table and bit into her toast, while
Miss Dollette refilled the teapot.

'"That's about the best thing you ever done, *Miss*." Miss! Do
I look like a "miss"?' turning suddenly to Wilfred.

It was as if a warm searchlight had focused on him, and
his impulse was to shrink and mutter. But she called to his
manhood; and he compelled himself to overcome the shyness
and slowly utter a sentence which was at least what he wanted
to say, though he could not prevent it from sounding clumsy.

'No one could think *you* had been allowed to remain unmarried, Mrs . . .' here the sentence died off into an embarrassed
mutter, because he had the English habit of never attending to
people's names. 'But he probably meant it as if he were speaking to his teacher at school – respect, you know.'

'I love to be respected,' she said instantly, looking at him
over her cup. 'I suppose it's because hardly anyone ever has.'

'Katherine dear. You will give Mr Davis the right impression!'

Mr Taverner had lifted up the cat, and was looking at her
over its gleaming black head, and his demure tone was almost
a purr. All three broke into affectionate laughter, and Wilfred,
laughing too, thought: *Oh, if only Mary were here.*

'Mr Davis was talking about selling his house,' said
Miss Dollette, taking up some embroidery.

'Well . . . hardly that, really,' Wilfred said. 'Selling a house, it
isn't a thing you can make up your mind about in five minutes.'

'Oh but that's just what it is!' Mrs Cornforth exclaimed. 'If
you've ever even thought about wanting to leave it, if you can

bear the thought at all, five minutes is just the right time. *I've* moved twenty-five times in my time.'

'Yes, for some no doubt –' Wilfred was rather carried away by the recklessness of these remarks, but moved to argument. 'But I mean, selling a house – it isn't like getting rid of an old lawnmower. There's how much you paid for it in the first place, and the time of the year – people like to buy a house in early summer, when the garden's looking nice – and local prices at the moment, not to speak of the state the place is in . . . decorations, I mean . . .'

Mrs Cornforth smiled at him; brilliantly, but she did not attempt to continue the argument, and this disconcerted him.

Though his appearance suggested a certain meekness, in fact Wilfred had his opinions about most subjects, and was prepared to proclaim and defend them when necessary. This ability had been strengthened, rather than weakened, by years of living with a woman of strongly held views, in a circle of equally opinionated acquaintances.

But the apparent passivity, the smiling silences, of *these* people, 'threw' him. They also listened when he spoke, giving him time to prepare his thoughts, and he was not used to that, either. After one glance at Mrs Cornforth's face, he was silent. Then he glanced at the clock, and exclaimed:

'I must be getting along. I'd no idea it was so late.'

'I'll run you home,' Mr Taverner said, getting up, and in reply to Wilfred's polite protest added, '*Of course* it's a trouble. Going out into the cold, starting the car, steering it through that lemming-flight of unfortunate souls, and then getting it home again and putting the blasted thing away. Trouble! When aren't cars a trouble . . .? But my enjoyment of your company will make up for it.'

They can talk when they want to, mused Wilfred, picking up muffler and coat from a chair. 'I've heard other people say cars are more trouble than they're worth,' he ventured, and was startled by a rich chuckle from Mrs Cornforth.

'There are easier ways of getting there,' she said, but the words were masked by the scrape of Miss Dollette's chair as she quickly pushed it back, and stood up and smiled at Wilfred.

'You will come again, won't you?' she said. 'Please promise.'

'Of course I will. I've enjoyed myself no end,' he muttered, using in his embarrassment slang from his young manhood. 'Thank you all very much.'

Mrs Cornforth gave him a hand noticeably white and pretty. He felt the faintest breath touch his face; once, then again. *Like a pat, patting a child's cheek*, he thought confusedly, following Mr Taverner out of the kitchen. *Warm in there, very warm. But not too warm. I feel perfectly all right.*

'Katherine,' said Miss Dollette, looking at her across the table when they heard the front door shut.

'I know, darling. I am sorry. I truly am. But I couldn't resist it.'

She got up and wandered round the room, the light playing on her red-brown hair. 'I love them so. I could –' she lifted her arms in a wide movement – 'eat them,' she ended.

'Frightened,' said Miss Dollette in a low voice, shaking her head and looking down. 'Even now.'

'Poor love. Look . . . let's wash up, shall we . . . I wish Laf would get down to doing my room. That bed of yours, darling! I'm sure William Morris is approving it. I'd like something puffy and stuffy. Couldn't I have a round one? That's the newest thing . . . and for God's sake, some *pink*. Your blues and greens give me the shivers.'

Miss Dollette's laughter came out. A sound different from Katherine's, but equally pretty.

'I am sorry, I just can't . . . you'd have liked my first attempt even less, all dingy browns and greys. And just at the moment I'm busy on the dining room, and you know how it takes it out of you . . . . no, you don't, of course, I did try hard with your room . . .'

'"Hard" is the word . . . do you think we'll get our little man?'

'He's attracted, I feel, and he does need us. But Katherine, we *must not* frighten him. You and your kisses. – And Laf with his "taking time and trouble". I'll warn him again. Vanity,' she ended more softly – though her voice had not been loud – 'Pride's little sister. When will that pair *truly* not trouble us again, for ever?'

'Too soon for me.' Katherine shrugged. 'Now – washing-up'.

6

Sylvie

Autumn passed into winter, and Mary did not notice.

One morning she glanced out of the window while dressing and saw bronze leaves flying across the grey roofs and felt a certain current of air, which haunted her attic, blowing colder. She put on the warm underclothing that she had asked her father to send (*c/o 6 Hadham Street, N5 but that's not where I'm living*); her mother had drilled her into assuming it at this time of the year, and it was thick and creamy and unfashionable, like Mary's own body.

There came another morning when her boots went along sturdily through snow.

Everything was of such interest to her in London that she thought of her father as little as she did about the change in the season; though the postcard, always with its brief piece of good news or sensible comment, went off regularly every Friday afternoon – *Dad's weekend treat*, as she thought of it.

Mr Grant and Mrs Cadman continued the unvarying path of their existence, and never asked her any questions beyond an occasional 'Well, how's business going, eh?' should they happen to encounter her in the hall or on the stairs.

She had made no friends. London was endlessly interesting, and the people exciting to look at and to wonder about; but it cost money, most of fifty pence, to get to Oxford Street; and if she walked, which she did before the weather broke, she became inconveniently hungry. Also, walking wore out one's boots.

She took to staying at home on Sundays. There were clothes to wash, and hair. A burst of correspondence with Sandra had been short-lived. Sandra had suddenly decided on passing her A levels, as a result of what she described as a 'truly grisly' talk with her parents, and could spare time to write only an occasional groaning and envious postcard. For who would want to work for A levels, or even pass them, when it was possible to live in a bed-sitter in London and work in a tourists' souvenir shop?

Number 20 Rowena Road housed, in addition to Mary and Mr Grant and Mrs Cadman, Mr Bailey who had been there for seventeen years and was aged seventy-three; Miss Wayne, who recently had retired from forty years at Benson & Broadbent's Ladies Outfitters (which had turned almost overnight into one of those boutiques, thereby supplying Miss Wayne with conversational material for the rest of her life); and, in the basement, Sylvie Carano.

'You mustn't take notice of what Sylvie says. She's a liar,' was what Mrs Cadman had said, with uncharacteristic strength of statement, when Mary had said, on the landing one morning: 'I saw a girl go downstairs.'

Mary was lonely for a girlfriend without knowing it; the loneliness for a boyfriend was something different, to be approached, even in thought, with deep and conscious care.

'She'll be on to you before you can turn round,' Mrs Cadman went on, 'suggesting you go on the town. (*Up West*, it was, in my day.) *You'll* pay for everything and she won't pay you back. Now I've told you – you're on your own, as they say. And she's no more Carano than I am. She comes from Queen's Crescent, I'll be bound – there's an Italian café up there called Carano's. Higgins. I saw it on a label on her case, half-torn off. Sylvia Higgins, that's who she is. *Sylvie Carano!* Yes I don't think, to put it vulgarly. Unless I get her rent on the dot next Friday, out she goes.'

'I'll remember,' nodded Mary, thinking: *Keep your cool, she can't have had time to be all that bad, she doesn't look more than thirteen.*

But she also thought that Sylvie might be worth encountering.

Hair was what the beholder was first, and most, conscious of, on encountering Sylvie. Hers was cut in the newest mode: thinned away into elf-locks at the base of the neck, clubbed over her forehead into a ferocious fringe, and given body by some kind of goo. It was then dyed a whitish green. Under the fringe, a pair of frightened greenish eyes looked out, and a long nose. Her skirt suggested two purple wool handkerchiefs sewn together, and the top of her was covered by a purple sweater and a long sleeveless black crochet jacket. She wore white lace stockings with holes in.

'Hi,' said Sylvie to Mary, when they met a few evenings later on number 20's doorstep.

'Hi,' Mary responded.

'Quite a change to see a face under ninety round here,' Sylvie gabbled on, while both girls felt for their latchkeys. 'You living here?'

Her voice was as thin as her legs. Mary looked ten years older, in her dark green coat (but it needed cleaning now) and the nylon-fur Esquimau hood bought from Mrs Levy at 10 per cent discount, and the boots (but they needed mending).

Mary nodded.

'Like one of these here horror films, isn't it?' Sylvie confided. 'I bin here a month, but it feels like it was six.'

'I don't think it's too bad.' They were in the hall now, with its fitted carpet and gay contrasting wallpapers. Mary carefully shut the front door.

'And quiet! If there's anythink I cannot stand, it's quiet. Gets me down. You working?'

'Yes. In a dress and souvenir shop.'

Mary wanted to get up to her attic and cook a chop and eat a third of a lettuce and some grated carrot and two potatoes and a third of a bar of milk fruit and nut chocolate, but she

made no move. The attraction of a young face, even one half
concealed in pale green fringe, was stronger than that of supper.

'Thought you might a still been at some posh school. Your
gear isn't half square. Haven't been in London long, have yer?'

'No. How did you know?'

'Oh, yer can tell. Least, I always can. Kind of a look,' Sylvie
said airily, while her eyes roved restlessly about. 'I got a smashing record-player. One of me boyfriends knocked it off.'

She paused, looking mysterious; at least, Mary decided that
this was the impression intended by lowering the head and
glancing around under the fringe and dilating the nostrils.

'I reckon my record-player'd set me back thirty pounds if
I'd bought it. But one of me boyfriends whipped it for me,'
Sylvie said again.

Mary did not quite believe this. She already suspected Sylvie
of a wish to make herself interesting. *Sticking it on*, thought
Mary.

'Wasn't he afraid of being caught?' she asked, unable to think
of anything else to say.

'He didn't exactly walk out of the shop with it under his
arm, love,' snapped Sylvie with a shrill giggle. 'You trying to
be funny?'

'I got to get my supper – I'm starving. See you –' and Mary
moved decidedly towards the stairs.

'Well *I* shan't stay here,' Sylvie suddenly called after her,
standing still and staring at her from under the fringe. 'Getting
me down, it is.'

Mary made a vague gesture and disappeared.

However, about ten o'clock, when she was sitting by the gas
fire in her dressing-gown, alternately struggling with *Sinister
Street* (which she had found with some other books on top of
the chest of drawers) and wishing that she were at a dance,
there came a scrabbling on the door.

'Who is it?'

Mary stood up, and in her thick dressing-gown (which
needed cleaning) with her thick hair (which had been washed

on Sunday) tied back, she looked capable of dealing with anyone. But she did not unlock the door.

'It's me. Sylvie. You know. Downstairs.'

Oh Lord, thought Mary, recalling the warnings of Mrs Cadman, and then dismissing the notion that Sylvie might have called to suggest their going 'on the town'. Not that Mary would have minded. It wasn't *that* late – but she had no spare money.

'Well, what is it?' she demanded.

There was a pause, and something about 'a bit of a natter', and 'enough to give you the willies'. Annoyed yet welcoming the visit, Mary unlocked the door.

'Locked in, were yer? Well, I don't blame yer. That old Grant – he's awful.'

Sylvie's whining voice began at once, as she came in, wearing a pink nylon housecoat burgeoning with black frills. Mary's eyes fixed instantly upon it. But, since the incident of the micro-mini skirt, she had told herself, implacably, that such clothes were not for her.

'Thought I'd just see'f you was in,' half-whispered Sylvie, who had gone up to the gas fire and was now crouched over it.

'Well, you can see I am.' Mary's tone had something of Torford's east wind about it. But Sylvie was not the kind that notices tones.

'You got a telly?' she asked, peering up from under the fringe.

'No.' Mary did not smile. She supposed tea must be offered; even biscuits.

'*She's* got one. Won't let you get near it, though, not even for *Top o' the Pops.*'

'How about some tea?'

'I don't mind.' Sylvie wriggled like a shy five-year-old.

Mary, who was accustomed to hearing 'I'd love it' or 'Thanks, that would be fine,' when tea was offered, marched across to the cupboard and carefully measured out a single scoop of tea. She was not following the *one for each person and one for the pot* rule for Sylvie Carano-Higgins.

The room was quiet, except for the roaring of the gas fire, converted some three weeks ago to North Sea Gas, and suggesting, to an imaginative hearer, the sound of the waves from beneath which its power was drawn. The floor was warmly covered with a shabby brown carpet matching the thick, faded brown curtains. The walls were a dingy cream. In a glass vase with a gilt rim glowed one large, amber chrysanthemum.

'Mr Grant gave me that,' Mary remarked, seeing Sylvie's eyes wandering (so far as their activities behind the fringe were ascertainable) in its direction.

'Kind of him, I'm sure, seeing he's got a congservatory full. He arter yer? He looks at me legs,' and Sylvie giggled.

It occurred to Mary that, if Mr Grant did, he must be hard up indeed for legs to look at.

'Of course he isn't. He was showing me the greenhouse and I said he had some lovely flowers and he gave me that. It's lasted a week already.'

'I bet he is after yer. I bet yer. Old men, they always are,' Sylvie said drearily. 'Pinching yer bum, peeking at yer legs. All they think of, once they're old.'

'You must have met some funny ones, that's all I can say – here, have a biscuit.' Mary held out, on a plate, the remains of a twopenny packet.

'Sooner 'ave a slice o' bread – or a bacon sandwich – if you got it.'

Mary felt that the last words were a distinct concession. There was the faintest hint in them of consideration for someone else – no more than a grudging shade, but it was there.

'I've got two slices of bread. They were for my breakfast. But you can have one if you want it.' She got up resignedly and began getting things out of the cupboard. Mrs Cadman's warning had lost no time in coming true: Sylvie was on to her. But Mrs Cadman had not warned her that the skeletal, green-haired Sylvie would inspire pity. *She must come from an Awful Home*, thought Mary, remembering various verdicts of her mother's.

She silently handed a sandwich to Sylvie on the plate which had held the biscuits. She expected the girl to attack it like a wolf, as people did when half starved in the thrillers Mary occasionally read; but Sylvie dinted the soft crust with her chalk-white, pointed teeth and then, after a few minutes' silent nibbling, put the spoiled food back on the plate.

'Don't you want it?'

Sylvie shook her head. She had brought out a packet of cigarettes, and was lighting one.

'Never do eat anything up. Mum's the same – tea and fags all day. How about you?' She held out the packet.

'No thanks.'

'You don't want to take no notice of what they say. My grandad, he's gone sixty and he's smoked, oo, 'undreds a day, fer years.'

'It isn't that. I can't smoke *and* buy food, and I like food best.'

'I bet yer do.' Sylvie's giggle suggested the merriment of a spiteful elf. 'You want to take a bit off, you do.'

Mary's patient expression began slowly to alter, until she was looking sulky. She turned her head and stared at the old wood and brass clock on the mantelshelf. Even Sylvie could not fail to notice a movement so deliberate, and she at once began to cough.

'Same all day –' she gasped, 'first thing in the morning it starts, cough, cough, cough.'

'You're sticking that on,' pronounced Mary, unimpressed.

'Sticking it on, am I? I'll bloody well show you if I'm sticking it on – 'ere –' She fumbled in a pocket and brought out a stained paper handkerchief. 'See? Blood.'

'Lipstick, you mean. Blood isn't salmon-pink.'

'Calling me a liar now.' Sylvie was scrambling to her feet. 'I *done* someone, once, for calling me that.' She glared through the fringe.

'I'm not calling you anything. I just said that blood isn't that colour. Do get weaving – I'm sleepy and I want to get to bed. I've got to be up at seven.'

'Shoving me out, now . . . you aren't half mean . . . I come up 'ere trying to be matey, and you call me a liar and shove me out. Bloody stuck-up, that's what you are. You don't know nothing about anything, yer clothes is awful and yer scared to smoke—'

'Oh shut *up*,' snapped Mary loudly. 'And go away.'

There was a silence. Sylvie stood, drawing on the cigarette, staring at the floor. The gas fire hissed, the clock ticked, and across the roof outside the window floated the notes of St Anne's church clock striking eleven.

Mary made a movement towards the door, and Sylvie looked up.

'I been done,' she whispered.

Mary stared.

'Taken in – deceived, do you mean?' she asked at last.

'Taken in! 'Course not. No – you know. *Done*. Two years this autumn it was. I started something and I had it took away.'

'You mean . . . you had an abortion?' said Mary, after a pause, and Sylvie violently nodded.

'Just sixteen, I was.'

'I'm sorry,' Mary said at last. She did not know what else to say.

'Well yer bloody well needn't be, thanks. I didn't want no kid. It wasn't my day, that was all. Might have happened to anyone.'

She was silent, drawing smoke down into her narrow chest, then slowly expelling it. She crouched in front of the fire suddenly, and at the same time Mary sat down in the armchair. There was something she wanted to know.

'I suppose . . . did you love him?' she said at last.

Sylvie did not answer at once. Her head was bent.

''E done 'is best,' she muttered presently. 'I will say that. Wasn't above seventeen.' And that was all.

Mary's thought was: *a kid of seventeen, how could she?* Then she reflected that she did not know what kind of a seventeen-year-old this father of Sylvie's destroyed child had been. Some seventeen-year-olds were more like twenty. (*Like Mrs Levy's cousin's boy – great lump.*)

Her pity for Sylvie was detached, like that felt for a repulsively shaped insect, and her curiosity was strong. Although she had always sulkily refused to listen to Sandra's giggling confidences, she felt that she could both listen and talk to Sylvie. Sylvie had been on the far side of the fence that separated Mary from another country. She had been through what Mary thought of as *terrible things.*

'I'd have wanted to keep the baby and get married to him. That's what I'd have wanted. A baby! I'd . . . love to have a baby,' she said, feeling so strongly that the words came out with no difficulty at all.

'It's easy done,' giggled Sylvie. 'I s'pose you think I'm awful . . . like a bit of shit or sunnick?'

'I don't think having sex with him was awful. It's the not loving him that I can't understand and . . . doing that to a baby.'

But as she spoke, while she talked as she had never done to anyone, she realized that talking to Sylvie was like talking to a dog or a budgerigar: hopeless. *She doesn't even know what the words mean.*

Sylvie said nothing; and in a moment Mary said decidedly that she was going to bed.

'Tell you what!' gabbled Sylvie, seizing her arm. 'Let's go on the town Saturday afternoon – what say? Up Oxford Street – there's men selling beads there – smashing – you meet me outside the Dominion –'

'I haven't any money – not to spare. Besides, I've got to work. I'm sorry, I'd have liked to come.' Mary was implacably moving towards the door. 'P'raps one day next month.'

'We might knock something off and sell it.' Sylvie's pale bluish-green eyes were shining lights.

'Don't be silly . . . I'm thinking about writing to my dad for some money.' Mary had just come to this decision, and was rather surprised to hear it expressed in words, as she hadn't realized she was intending anything of the kind.

'My dad's in prison,' said Sylvie.

*

After his visit to the Yellow House, Wilfred's mind often turned to Mrs Wheeby and what he should do about her. The feeling that Lamorna was empty, dead – a mere show place since Pat and Mary had gone – was growing on him. Dead was the word for all these enamelled and Formica and Perspex surfaces. Only Pat's interest in them and her energy had maintained any feeling of life. What a housewife she had been! She had washed, and rubbed, and polished, and kept a sergeant-major's eye on it all. No new device for getting through the work more efficiently; no little rubber-suck-in-gadget for attaching tea towels to the side of the refrigerator, no new wax designed to keep a near-eternal shine upon wood, had escaped her keen eye and testing hand.

Wilfred had more than once had one of his 'kinky notions' about the furniture. Continually criticized with a view to its improvement – and the upholstered stuff every three years subjected to Pat's skilled needle – it was gasping for breath. In vain, for it was polished with some stuff that 'sealed' its surfaces. *And if you can't breathe, you* are *dead*, Wilfred thought now.

Its breath had stopped with Pat's.

What was the use of staying on here, in a house full of dead things? How he detested hoovering the carpets! Polishing he damned well drew the line at and, only that morning, dusting had crossed the rubicon. And cooking! How often, lately, had he nearly hurled the sausages or the baked beans into that bucket with a lid you lifted up with your foot . . . *Only where'd I go?*

He was so accustomed to passing the days in solitude that when a smart tap came on the kitchen door, he jumped. He looked unbelievingly at the clock – nearly midnight.

'Come in.'

Mrs Wheeby was fully dressed, but her hair was concealed by a net and ribbon cap.

'Is anything . . . up . . . Mrs Wheeby?' Wilfred was pouring milk from the saucepan into a brightly decorated mug.

She came in and sat down at the table, where preparations for imbibing Mil-ko were immediately beneath her gaze. *Hell*, thought Wilfred, and asked her if she would like some.

'Oh, no thank you, Mr Davis. I could never drink that heavy Mil-ko. Eggeen is my nightcap, very light, you hardly know you've had anything. Made out of the *whites only*. I often wondered it they use up the white left over from those egg shampoos. Rather a disadvantage' (pause, wheeze) 'in some ways being so light. But better than tossing and turning all night is what I've always said. I've had such a strong feeling all day, Mr Davis. It's been growing on me, and I felt I could *not* close my eyes until, as you might say, I had spoken out. I feel you may be going to *make changes here*, and we must prepare our plans.'

Wants to leave – what luck! he thought – *just when I was wondering what to do about her.* Then he paused, the saucepan tilting in his hand, staring at her. *Prepare our plans?*

Before he could get a word out, she was going on, with the pace and weight of a small steamroller.

'Of course, Mr Davis, let me say here and now that wherever you went, I should go too. You can be sure of that. Because if you were there, it couldn't feel strange, could it? – in spite of the furniture being different.'

Wilfred's silent response to this Ruth-like avowal was strong dismay. What! Laden with Mrs Wheeby and Dicky and the whales for the remainder of his life?

'So don't be afraid that I shall ever desert you, Mr Davis,' Mrs Wheeby said, with alarming earnestness, and a nodding of the net and ribbon cap.

A silence followed.

His lips were parting, when the steamroller moved on.

'A man needs a woman's company, Mr Davis, especially as he gets older; it's then he feels the need of it most. And you having been used to being married – you feel it, of course you do. I know I do myself, and my cousin James' (pause, wheeze) 'Jim we used to call him – he was quite desolate when Maddie

went. Not that I ever saw all that much in her, but of course
with him it must have been different, and finally, I suppose in
desperation, he married Lilian Brewer, and of course it turned
out exactly as we all expected.'

Mrs Wheeby paused again to gasp, and Wilfred had time
to hope that some offer of a home for her might emerge from
among those who had expected things from the marriage with
Lilian Brewer. Evidently Mrs Wheeby *had* had a family. Where
was it now, when it might make itself useful? Dead, no doubt:
Jim, Lilian Brewer, the lot. Still faintly hoping to be reprieved,
he allowed her to continue.

'Of course, Mr Davis, cooking is what I could not undertake,
having been married to a vegetarian and believer in health foods
for forty years. No, if I was to undertake cooking for you and
Mary' (pause, wheeze), 'should she ever want a break, as they
call it, from that job in Walthamstow or wherever you said it
was, Mr Davis, we should come to grief, as sure as my name
is Edith Wheeby . . .'

Wilfred was lifting the Mil-ko to his lips when the simple
thought came to him: *to hell with Mil-ko. How about iced beer?*
and, opening the refrigerator, he began to hunt amongst his
store of tins.

He and Pat had rarely, yet sometimes, had a beer together
on their return from the last house at the Majestic Cinema.
He took out a tin now and hesitated.

'. . . and so I decided to put your mind at rest, Mr Davis,
and lay my cards on the table— iced beer! How delicious! If
there's anything I do enjoy, especially late at night, it's a glass
of beer, and iced – delicious! Now, I'll get the glasses while you
open the tins, Mr Davis.'

Wilfred, too surprised to speak, took out another tin, and
turned to the gadget, screwed to the wall, used for opening
them. He was actually smiling, seeing Mrs Wheeby now as an
old sport rather than an old nuisance.

Mrs Wheeby neither hesitated nor sipped, but took a good
pull of her beer.

'It's nice to have a friend,' he said suddenly, as he set down his glass.

He had had no intention of saying any such thing.

'Well, you have, Mr Davis. You have. Believe me.'

Wilfred had a second's fear that she would stretch a pudgy hand across the table to seal the new bond. That would have been too much. Pat would have thought they were both drunk – and perhaps *he* was, a little? Certainly, he felt odd. *There's no . . . stability . . . nowadays*, he thought muzzily. *Nowhere*. He drained his glass.

'Well, I must be off to Bedfordshire,' Mrs Wheeby said. 'I'll just rinse these . . .' *Really, she was the right sort of old woman; rinsing glasses, going off to Bedfordshire – he and Pat had misjudged her.*

'I just wanted to have things quite clear, Mr Davis,' she said at the door. 'About our sticking together, I mean.'

'Yes. Yes, thank you, Mrs Wheeby. Goodnight.'

'Goodnight, Mr Davis.'

'Goodnight.'

7

The bargain

The next morning, Wilfred was in Dill's, the butcher's, buying the two slices of liver which Pat had persuaded him to eat once a week for the anaemia which she suspected, after reading an article in the *Sunday Times*, that he might be suffering from. He was not anaemic, and he disliked liver, but he continued, under her posthumous influence, to buy, cook and chew the stuff every week.

He was surprised when Mr Dill, having handed him the slices of liver in a plastic bag, leant across the counter and said in a mutter:

'Thinking of selling your house then, Mr Davis.'

It was a statement, not a question.

'Well I am, as a matter of fact. But how on earth did you know?'

Wilfred tried to think who had told him. Only those people in the Yellow House ... and, instantly, he was certain that none of them would have talked to Mr Dill.

None? Mrs Cornforth?

Mr Dill was going on:

'The fact is, I'd like a word with you. How about The Black Swan? Do you know it?'

'Carmichael Street, on the corner,' Wilfred said automatically.

'That's right ... half past six suit you? In the saloon bar?'

'Yes. Oh yes . . .' Wilfred held out some metal – you couldn't call it silver and coppers nowadays – and wandered out of the shop thinking *Damn*.

He disliked events to move quickly. Pat had often told him he needed more time than was necessary to think things over – *a year wouldn't seem too long for you*, she used to say.

Dill . . . Dill . . . lived over the shop, and had two little children, who occasionally put a face round the door – an old-fashioned place.

Suppose I ought to go into Ratchet's, thought Wilfred, *and ask what houses in our road are fetching . . . I suppose he wants to buy it himself. He probably wants to get out of that place; it must be a hundred years old, at least.*

Damn and blast, all the same. I wonder if she did tell him?

He didn't want to go home; he didn't want to drop in on his father; he was restless, and mildly worried, and the prospect of returning to the house was unbearable. He saw in his mind's eye the white faces of gadgets glaring at him round the kitchen and he hated them.

I'll go to the sea.

The thought came like a flash of sunlight, *I'll take the car.* It was a day when the clouds were racing. *There ought to be white horses.*

It was the first time that he had driven since Pat's death; he was a nervous driver, who had taken the test five times before passing, and he never enjoyed driving. Pat had always done it.

The trees were bare but for a few shrivelled leaves fluttering like golden rags, and where there was a wide prospect the fields were cinnamon-colour to darkest purple; the willows bordering stream and pond had a pale and ghostly look. Gradually the beauty of the landscape crept upon him, and he drove almost in a dream. He knew that this was both dangerous and the act of a bad citizen, but he felt rebellious. If he were the kind of driver who became slightly drunk on fields and willow trees, was that his fault? But who would believe such a defence if he put it forward in court? *How extraordinary it would sound . . . as if I were some barmy poet.*

He drove through small, Indian-red brick Benton, perched on its cliffs; past the handsome houses in large gardens on its outskirts; and there was the sea, the colour of a black pearl under the racing pewter sky, running in at the land with its thousands upon thousands of white-toothed waves, as if it were grinning in rage.

He stopped the car above the narrow 'promenade', whose concrete was already cracking, and stared out over the stupendous dark expanse, breathing in cold salt air. There were no other cars about; it was lunchtime, and everybody sensible was indoors eating.

He stepped out onto the wiry turf, and walked down some steps leading to the path immediately above the sea. An expanse of gleaming sand suggested that the tide was going out; and, attracted by the band of pebbles with here and there the whiteness of a shell, he descended some old wooden steps and stood there, with the hissing loud in his ears and spray drifting into his face.

The prospect was forbidding: dark sky, darker sea, shrilling wind. It must, he supposed, be the movement everywhere – skies racing, waves rushing, dry sand flying along in pale clouds – that made it exciting. He felt his spirit lift to meet it. As if he were ready to set out on an adventurous journey.

And I wish to God I were, he thought, turning away and trudging up the damp, shingly slope. *The world's big enough. There's Brazil. Places where no one's ever been. And I will have had some money from the house . . . And when I got there, I'd be as lonely as hell, and there'd be all those insects, and cutting your way through all that jungle . . . anybody'd think I was fourteen . . .*

But I could get a bit drunk, he thought as he went up the old wooden steps. *I'll go to The Woodman and have a whole bottle of wine. That's what I'll do.*

The Woodman was small, ancient, and dying. Its position in a longish, remote lane leading to nowhere in particular was disadvantage enough, without a landlord who could not be bothered to be jovial.

Wilfred knew that there had once been a stock of wine there, because he and Pat, on one of the rare occasions when he could persuade her to use the car for idle exploring, had come upon The Woodman one afternoon in summer and eaten a lunch of dry biscuits which had so outraged Pat that Wilfred had ordered wine in a spirit of reparation.

A bottle of red stuff with a foreign name had been produced.

'Last two bottles. Been down there three years; didn't see the use of ordering more than the 'alf dozen,' explained the representative of Bacchus whose task it was to keep the atmosphere in The Woodman genial and its fortunes prosperous. 'All *they* ever drink's wallop.'

Wilfred could remember nothing about the wine, except that it had tasted unexpectedly strong, and had made him a little drunk. The Woodman might have been pulled down by now, he thought. That lunch must have been all of three years ago.

But there it was, apparently unchanged, halfway down the lane, looking small and sulky in its dingy weatherboarding, with its faded sign showing a man with a bundle of faggots on his shoulder. A bog chestnut tree standing beside it had just loosed a shower of golden leaves as Wilfred drove up, and they rattled on the roof of a small, old-fashioned car parked outside. *Customers*, thought Wilfred. *Well I never.*

He pushed open the door and went into the low-ceilinged, dark little bar, and there, sitting by the window with a glass of beer, was Mr Taverner.

'Hullo. Nice blowy day,' he said, looking up and smiling. 'Are you one of the regulars?'

'God forbid,' Wilfred answered, lowering his voice because the landlord was brooding over a newspaper behind the bar. 'I just came over to have a look at the sea. Felt like it, somehow. You often come here?'

'Oh no – no. I was just tootling around. Miss Dollette wanted some beech leaves to pickle in glycerine. Have one with me?' He flourished his glass.

'Well, that's very kind of you but the fact is I won't mix them – I'm driving back – and what I fancy is a glass of wine.' The landlord had allowed his paper to drift onto the counter and was looking at him remotely. 'Perhaps you'll join *me*?' Wilfred added.

'And what can I get *you*?' the landlord asked at length, with the slightest emphasis on the last word, unsmiling. A gust of wind hit The Woodman so hard that it shook.

'A better day for riding a horse than driving a car,' observed Mr Taverner, glancing out at the rioting leaves.

'I was here about three years ago with my wife, and I had a bottle of red wine. I'd like another of the same, please,' Wilfred answered.

'There *may* be a bottle left. I'll have to see.' The landlord got himself off his stool, moving as if he were rheumatic. 'There isn't much call for wine, not round here there isn't.'

'Well, I'm calling for it now,' Wilfred retorted pleasantly.

The landlord, without looking at him again, stood at the far end of the bar and shouted: 'Freda! Go down the cellar and see'f there's a bottle in that rack we bought off of Wilson . . . left side. Careful now.' He returned to the bar. 'Always falling about, the wife,' he explained to the room generally. 'Got a weak leg.'

Mr Taverner shook his head 'A disadvantage in the circumstances,' he said, and was over the bar in a leap, and at the back door before the landlord had opened his mouth again. 'I'll get it, madam, I'm an expert in cellarage . . .'

They heard his voice, in gentle argument with a tired female one in the passage outside, and then steps rattling down a wooden staircase.

The woman's face appeared at the door in the dimness, fat and rather frightened. 'It's very kind of him, George – I was just going to ask you if you wouldn't mind going. I'm so nervous of those stairs and my leg isn't too good today . . .' The landlord said nothing and, after a quick glance at Wilfred, she withdrew.

Mr Taverner reappeared, smiling, and waving a bottle.

'This must be it,' he announced. 'Do you agree?' to the landlord.

'I don't reckon to have the customers fetching up the drinks,' said the landlord. 'Those stairs are murder.'

'We will leave you to ponder that word –' said Mr Taverner, 'and if we might have the wine . . .' He went back to their table and sat down.

The landlord occupied himself with uncorking the bottle, half filling a glass, putting it on a tray, and bringing it and the bottle across for Wilfred's inspection.

'Very nice,' said Wilfred, sipping, and the landlord retired to the bar and his newspaper.

If they kept their voices down he could not hear what they said, Wilfred assumed, and he began at once: 'I'd have liked to stand you lunch, but there's nothing but stale biscuits. My wife and I tried last time we were here.'

'Thanks, but I've brought my own sandwiches. There are three left –' he felt in the pocket of the white raincoat '– if you're hungry.'

'Well, that's very kind of you –'

'I couldn't eat a bite, my dear man. I'm full of cold partridge – here.' He handed across the packet, and, muttering thanks, Wilfred bit into the dampish fresh bread.

'Grand . . .' with his mouth full.

'Miss Dollette's baking – twice a week . . . Well, how are things?' Mr Taverner asked.

'Much the same, except that I'm meeting a man this evening who wants to buy my house, I think. I don't know what to do about it, and that's a fact . . . there's Mary, you see, as I said . . . I keep on see-sawing about it . . . Pat . . . that's my wife, would have made up my mind for me.'

Mr Taverner said nothing, keeping his fingers on the stem of his glass and his eyes on Wilfred's. The wintry wind dashed leaves against the low, small windows.

'I wish I could see Mary and talk it over with her. If only I didn't think she'd cut me off altogether, I'd risk going down to this fake address she's given me and trying to trace her. But the truth is, Mr Taverner – I'm afraid to.'

'Yes. Loving someone, one is afraid,' said Mr Taverner, and Wilfred glanced at him in a grateful little surprise. Even his father would not have understood that. Remarks about smacked bottoms sounded for an instant in his inward ear.

'I'll have to think it out, that's all – but it doesn't give you much time. I'm seeing the chap this evening, at half past six.'

'Let's have a race,' Mr Taverner said.

'A race?'

'Yes – your car and mine. You'll be heavily handicapped, because mine's more than thirty years old. We won't race side by side, of course, just to some place you can choose, each going different ways. Here ' Mr Taverner pulled out a large-scale map of the district and deftly unfolded it. 'How about Eccersley? Twenty miles.'

'That's where the beautiful church is, isn't it?'

'Yes – we might go in and look at it . . . all right then, that's on . . . but let's finish the bottle first.'

Wilfred obediently refilled their glasses. He knew that he ought, at this moment when he was sitting half-drunk with a rather odd acquaintance in a run-down pub in a back lane fifteen miles from home, to be sitting in Racket's – Ratchet's – office, finding out what houses in his road were fetching on the property market. And certainly, as a driver, not drinking.

But the wine stole over his senses in a delicious dreaminess. He looked glassily into Mr Taverner's smiling, shining eyes. How they shone! He never remembered seeing eyes so – luminous – was that the word? They seemed to glow, and he could not put a name to their colour. They had more light than colour. They were unlike any eyes Wilfred had ever seen in a human head.

A dejected-looking elderly man, with an air of retirement from the working world, had been hesitating with his half-pint, as if deciding whether to come over to their table, but now retreated slowly to a seat in the darkest corner of the bar.

'Praise God from Whom all blessings flow,' whispered Mr Taverner.

'Yes, I was afraid he might, too. I don't feel up to strangers today.'

'I *never* feel up to them . . . or almost never.'

'I – was a stranger. When you saw me on that seat, Mr Taverner. You're one of those – those who have a kinder heart than you'd admit, I'd say.'

'"I was a stranger and ye lent me a hanky,"' said Mr Taverner. 'Ah, but that was different. (Part of my reward, you are.) But that old bundle of grumble in the corner is all right; lives with a married daughter who's a good girl to him. He just enjoys a whine. We needn't be sorry about him.'

'Pat – my wife – you remember, I told you' – Mr Taverner nodded – 'used to say that it was the whiners, and the murderers and the baby-bashers too, that you *should* be sorry for. She said people like us – her and me – were all right because we could pull ourselves together, and – and be unselfish. But some people simply *couldn't*. So if you were one of the lucky ones, she said, you had to *Make Allowances*.'

'She was right – unhappily. Dead right.'

Mr Taverner's face, which could sometimes appear empty of expression, merely courteously attentive, as if a pleasingly coloured mask had been assumed, showed no consciousness of having used an unfortunate phrase.

'"Virtue is its own reward". The sergeant-major of the proverbial sayings: upright, stern, incorruptible. He said so Himself, in other words.'

'He . . .?'

'Jesus. "I come to bring, not the righteous, but sinners to repentance." Tough luck on the righteous – especially in the twentieth century. If you and people like you had been born, say, about 1853, you would have been with the saved sheep, and comfortable. Nowadays, I don't know quite where to say you are. Somewhere smug, certainly, and there's a decided inclination to blame you for being there. "You're all right. You like the right things," as someone said to me once.'

For the first time in their acquaintance, Wilfred heard bitterness in Mr Taverner's light voice and saw its shadow on his long, charming face.

'That sounds to me like downright envy,' he said sturdily, wanting to see the shadow lift.

'Oh, it may have been. In fact, almost certainly it was. But if you love someone with all your heart, *you* don't want to have something that *they* haven't got and that they envy you for having.'

Wilfred was a little embarrassed by 'love someone with all your heart'. Was Mr Taverner going to turn out religious? He could think of nothing to say. He was certain of only two facts concerning this odd Mr Taverner: first, he was kind; and secondly, not the faintest shade of meaning in another person's gesture or tone escaped his observation and – though he might say nothing – his judgement.

'But let's thank God,' said Mr Taverner, beginning to smile, 'that we still have the Goddess of Common Sense. (I knew an old German doctor once, who used to say, "I don't know why they gall it *Gommon* sense, for it is *most Un-Gommon*".) The altars of Common Sense are almost bare nowadays; little incense, few flowers. But she exists, and to her and to her Higher Incarnation and to their divine sister Reason we *can* still appeal, both for ourselves and for others, often with results.' The shadow had lifted.

Wilfred was not certain what this meant, but he heard himself saying, with an effect of notable feebleness: 'Of course it's wonderful work, looking after drug addicts and that kind of thing . . .'

'More exciting, too, than reading to deaf Aunt Betty or ironing shirts,' Mr Taverner drawled.

'Pat used to iron my shirt.' Wilfred turned to look out of the window. 'She was a good wife to me.'

'I know she was.' Mr Taverner rose slowly, tall in his white raincoat. 'You look so lost.'

Wilfred stared up at him. The coat glimmered in the dimness of the room, for the day had darkened over. It was the brightest thing there. It seemed to glow.

'Our race,' added Mr Taverner gently. 'Come along.'

The two smallish cars drove quickly away in opposite directions to find their way to Eccersley.

Wilfred knew that he was not completely drunk. He could keep an eye on the road; his touch on the wheel was firm and light; he knew precisely what was going on. He even knew exactly where he was – bouncing up a lane full of smallish potholes, running along the east side of Dunbury Wood.

Flying leaves slapped against the windscreen, hung there for an instant, were gone. Branches in untrimmed hedges whipped the roof. The car bounced and banged and Wilfred bounced and banged with it. Everything looked miraculously clear, gold and brown and herb-green in the rainy light. He had no burdens, no longings. He wished that he could drive on for ever.

The lane ended. He was out on a passable road again, and could safely go up to sixty. The wine was singing its soft, warm, crimson chant in his blood as he drove between brown fields looking as if they were asleep under the darkening sky.

He passed through a long village street, where already there was a shop with one dress in its window and 'Boutique' painted above its once-modest face; and there at the end, tall against the hurrying clouds, was the church.

Its tower was livid in the last light. He drove round the green, stopped, and sat looking up at the rooks flying slowly about the elms. The trees were naked now; their highest branches rocking slowly in the whistling air.

No one was about. Lights shone further down the street. He got out of the car and sat down on a seat under the wall of the churchyard. Perhaps it was the quiet, unbroken except for the ancient sound of the rooks, that gave him peace. The birds floated like big black leaves, turned sideways by the wind in the thin golden light from the falling sun. *Hasn't changed since they built the church, not the light, nor the cold,* he thought. *Makes you feel better somehow. But God, it's lonely.*

Down the street came another car. The hooter sounded a cheerful signal, and his spirits went up.

'Beat me to it,' Mr Taverner said, bringing his car to a halt and putting his smiling face out of the window.

'Well, yes. But I did know a short cut. Wasn't fair perhaps. I ought to have told you, really.'

'Oh nonsense. All's fair in love and war. (Quite nonsense, incidentally.) Want to have a look at the church?'

'Yes, I'd like to.' Wilfred got up.

But the oak door, studded with nails made by hand six hundred years ago, was locked.

'That's a nice state of affairs,' Mr Taverner exclaimed, having vigorously twisted the massive handle once or twice. 'Suppose a demon had been after us, and we'd wanted to take sanctuary?'

Wilfred glanced at him sideways in the dimness. He was not smiling. High up in the golden, hurrying sky, a bell struck one note: clear, soft and very ancient was the sound.

'I suppose you're joking. But . . . *not* joking, Mr Taverner, I'm interested to know what you think. You . . . do you believe in all that sort of thing?'

'Demons?' He turned away before he answered. 'Oh yes. I believe in them. Not that I've ever . . . really . . . *seen* one.' Then some kind of change, to which Wilfred could not put a name, came over his face as he looked round. 'But it's vandals, of course, not demons that make the Reverend Peter Pinkright, MA,' nodding in the direction of a noticeboard beside the gate, 'keep his door locked.'

'And ghosts?' Wilfred persisted, while carefully fastening the gate behind them. 'Do you believe in ghosts?'

'Oh lord, yes. Yes to both questions. Now, about getting back. It's half past four. I gather you're seeing this chap at half past six. Come back to us for tea first, won't you?'

＊

When Wilfred let himself into the hall at Lamorna, somewhere around ten, he was much drunker than he had been at three.

Three double whiskies paid for by Mr Dill had been necessary to bring him up to agreeing to sell his house to the latter for eleven thousand pounds; for although Mr Dill's juicy lips had never parted in his steak-like face to utter any plea of parenthood or poverty, Wilfred had had continually before his mind's eye the figures of Mr Dill's children, and also that of Mrs Dill, recently encountered at the side door of the shop, in what the newspapers used once to call 'a certain condition'.

He had bargained with Mr Dill. He had *Held Out*. He had pooh-poohed Mr Dill's contention that a house backing onto the railway meant noisy days and disturbed nights. He had even quoted the rumour about one Biggs, living in the same road as himself, whose house had 'gone' for thirteen thousand.

'Ah, but there was a big converted attic,' Mr Dill had thrust in. 'Made two bedrooms.'

'Say pokeholes. Nearer the mark.'

'Pokeholes or not, Mr Davis, they were rooms. Brought it up to a six-bedroom house in the twelve-to-fifteen-thousand bracket.'

'I never said anything about fifteen thousand.'

Mr Dill had ordered a third whisky, and Wilfred, who looked noticeably exhausted and white, broke into a pause by saying quickly: 'All right, Mr Dill. We'll say eleven thousand. The fact is, I haven't . . . had time . . . gone into the matter . . . as I should. Rather caught me on the hop, as you might say.'

'Done, Mr Davis,' said Mr Dill smoothly. 'That's settled, then. Now I s'pose you'll want everything above board and legal –'

'There's Anstruther and Coburn in the high street. Mr Anstruther's married to the headmistress of my daughter's school.'

'They're a reliable firm, I'm told,' said Mr Dill. 'Been there fifty years. I remember old Mr Anstruther. Used to come in for his veal cutlets and a bird now and then, in season, when

I was a boy . . . You'll go along there first thing tomorrow morning, then?'

Wilfred nodded.

'Chance 'ud be a fine thing . . . fifteen thousand,' said Mr Dill, as he thundered (it seemed to Wilfred that he thundered) after him on their way to the door. 'No, eleven's about right, Mr Davis – you can take it from me. No phoning up some old pal when you get home tonight and fixing up a deal for fifteen thousand?' he shouted playfully.

Outside the air was raw and icy with the Torford sea-mist. The street was empty and almost silent. Wilfred turned up his coat collar. The pale bushy willows and buffeting winds of the afternoon seemed in another world.

Money and business are dreadful. Some chap in the '20s had said that, or something like it. Wilfred had come across it in a book. *Poor bastard – took his own life. I don't know why I never really thought of doing that, not even when I was feeling worst.* He got out to unlock the garage doors. *Dad, perhaps. And Mary, of course. And Mary.*

When he got into the house, the colours and shapes in the hall struck him as entirely, completely, and undeniably dislikeable. *And it's that Yellow House that's done it,* he thought, standing in the hall and staring around. *If I hadn't been there, and seen what a home's like, I'd never have turned against . . . all this and sold it.*

He stood, looking stupidly about him. Something – an impression, a feeling, the ghost of a thought – was teasing at the boundaries of his memory.

His gaze wandered around the hall, absently, while he struggled to catch and examine the impression, and reached the mat immediately before the front door. A square white object lay there, and he darted forward.

The writing on the envelope was Mary's.

8

The break-out

Julia Anstruther did not enjoy being a mother and a housewife. As for Jeremy Anstruther, she loved him and she did not get on with him.

It was impossible, for her, to imagine herself living with any other man. She knew this, because she had tried, conscientiously, detachedly, and many times to imagine it; and found every known part of herself shrinking from the hypothetical situation. She had even, occasionally, tested herself by being forthcoming to men who seemed to admire her. She had not enjoyed her glacial flirtations.

Jeremy on the other hand, could have lived more or less contentedly with any woman who was pretty and kind. This, in his wife's opinion, gave him an unfair advantage.

My marriage isn't an easy one, she would think, when her mind should have been on lists of marks, and notes about behaviour in the Upper Third. She was 'intense', as the Edwardians would have said; 'tense' is the contemporary equivalent; Jeremy was easy-going or 'relaxed'. Continually, they clashed.

Their house was large, old, and beautiful. It was one of the first to have been built in Torford, a few years after the Lorrimers had built Lorrimer Park; on the outskirts of the town to the east where that sea-mist first made its chill appearance on the evenings of late autumn. Inside it was shabby. The furniture was good, mostly inherited, but it was worn and ill-kept.

The garden at the back was neglected; it was an acre wide and nearly an acre long, and had a small copse of aspens in one corner, and there were old swings and various mouldering huts and forts built by the children; rows of smelly cabbages put in by Jeremy Anstruther when he had believed that they could grow their own vegetables and save money; and straggling climber roses with fierce purple-red thorns an inch long that no one had the time to prune; and a lawn which had never recovered from years of football.

It had, however, a front view straight across Torford's roofs (for it stood on a slight rise) to the one part of the surrounding hills which did not display bungalows. Its back windows gazed over the garden at a distant wood where primroses could still be found in spring.

A week or so nearer the battered festival of Christmas, the Anstruthers were undergoing the daily exacerbation of family breakfast in the large, warm kitchen where a cooking fire had burned for more than a hundred years. Today, it was a smokeless fuel boiler.

'Babette, it's ten to eight.' (Ridiculous, insultingly too-feminine name, insisted upon by Babette's father.)

'Everything's under *control*, Mummy – where's my muffler? *Christ*, where's my MUFFLER? It really is simply extraordinary how people shove my THINGS away . . . Giles, have you been assing about with it?'

'So likely. The colours are enough to make one vomit.'

'Shut up, you two, I want to read. And I dislike hearing females say "Christ",' droned their father, behind the pages of the *Guardian*.

'Did you put it out ready for this morning?'

'I did mean to but I was reading.'

'Oh well, in that case . . .' Her mother's look and tone were mollified, for Babette was one of those whose natural indifference to reading is proved by their always referring to the number of pages so far conquered. 'What were you reading, darling?'

Ash-blonde hair, flowing in the mermaid fashion (Julia was tired of seeing mermaids in the school), grey eyes, large, with curving thick lashes darker than the hair . . . Yes, she was going to be a beauty in three years, even to the pale pug-face, which was contemporarily favoured together with the brown, plump, sensual face.

Unfortunately, if she did not learn at the crucial age of thirteen to apply herself to her books, she was also going to be a dunce, and Julia did not want a dunce for a daughter.

Engaged in what can best be described by the cliché *crumbling a piece of toast*, Mrs Anstruther sat staring out of the window across the awful garden and letting two streams of thought run confusedly through her mind – one on the apparently insuperable difficulty of dealing justly with the claims of everyone, including the animals, in a family of four; while the other lingered nostalgically on mornings in her flat in Kensington, when she had been Second Mistress at Warbeck House School for Girls. Jeremy had made jokes about Second Mistresses.

'Juley, you aren't eating a Proper Breakfast,' came his voice from behind the *Guardian*. 'Get on with it now. Nice eggy-bacon.'

He was right: he too often was. 'Giles, get my plate out of the oven, dear, will you?' she said.

Giles was nearly fifteen. An awful detachment, a god-suggesting calm, ruled his views and his spoken judgements.

'He *weighs his words*,' his mother used sometimes to wail to her own mother. 'And he's so dreadfully, *dreadfully* clean. It isn't natural.'

He now got up with an air managing to suggest that, although he had been interrupted in a train of philosophic thought, he was prepared to be dutiful. He carefully fetched the plate from the oven with a clean tea towel, which he first took from the dresser drawer, and set it before his mother.

'Thank you, dear.' Julia was not proud of Giles's being clever; she wanted Babette to be.

She glanced at the clock. Eight minutes before she left the house; in twenty, she would be in her room at the school, dealing with matters and people that she felt herself trained and able to deal with; not . . . floundering at home.

How sick I am of girls, Julia thought suddenly, and checked the thought in dismay. (She was in the draughty hall now, putting on her five-year-old tweed coat.)

'Oh God oh God, back to the treadmill again.' Her husband came lounging out, folding the *Guardian,* and, seeing her in front of the tarnished Regency looking-glass seriously arranging her sealskin cap, took her in his arms and began to kiss her.

'*Don't,* Jeremy, you'll make my hair come down,' she whispered irritably.

'All the better – that's what I like.'

'Well I don't – what's the matter with you?'

'Nothing – right as a trivet – just like kissing you.'

'Well don't do it *now* – so do I – I'll be late –'

'No time like the present.'

Jeremy kept an arm about his wife's shoulders while he took his overcoat from the peg with his other hand.

'Didn't you tell me that a girl called Davis had bolted from your Select Academy?' he asked.

'Mary Davis. Yes. What about her?'

'I had her father in yesterday morning. Wants to sell his house and isn't asking its current value. I couldn't convince him.'

After he had read Mary's letter, Wilfred almost decided to telephone Mr Anstruther and tell him that he had decided to take his advice and add two thousand to the price he was asking for the house.

Dear Dad,

Sorry to bother you but could you possibly let me have one pound fifty every week? It would make all the difference. I have made friends kind-of with a girl living

in this house. She is off her trolley but not too bad. Sorry
to be a nuisance.

Love

Mary

Wilfred thought resignedly that his Mary did not tell you
much. Didn't she realize that the smallest detail connected with
her was interesting to him? *If her mother had been alive, we'd
have had the girl's name, and whether she's respectable or not, and
where she comes from . . . but of course, if Pat had been alive, Mary
would never have dared to run away.*

She isn't afraid of me. The thought was both a stab and
comforting. The money would have to be sent to the accom-
modation address.

I can't face Dill about putting on another two thousand, Wilfred
thought, at last. He was sitting in the kitchen, where he liked
to be because he could look across at the Yellow House. *The
whole thing might fall through if he were to turn nasty . . . but I
know what I will do* – and in his excitement he went over to the
window and stared out at the Yellow House, which was glowing in a burst of late December sunlight – *I'll ask Anstruther
to put on something more for the furniture and fittings . . . that'll
help. And I'll sell the car.*

*I'll keep enough stuff to furnish two rooms, one for Mary, and one
for me . . .* His thoughts met a sudden jar. *Mrs Wheeby. What'll
I do about her? Oh damn everything. If only it was over – the house
sold, me in some quiet bed-sitter with another in the same house for
Mary, and the old woman settled somewhere else.*

It was not much to want. But he was learning that the less
you asked, the less likely you were to get it.

He sent Mary the money by the next post, with a letter
promising its future arrival every Friday morning and ending 'I am glad you have made a friend. Take care of yourself,
Bunny. Your loving Dad.'

They had called her Bunny until she was eleven, when Pat
had announced that it was rather a kid's sort of nickname for

a sensible stoutish child looking older than her years, and they had dropped it.

Mr Anstruther sounded pleased when commenting on Wilfred's decision.

'Always provided your furniture is up-to-date—'

'It's that, all right,' said Wilfred sourly.

'You can ask three hundred and probably get it. Carpets and curtains and beds nowadays . . . let's try, anyway,' carolled Mr Anstruther.

'It's all the bother,' Wilfred snapped, affronted by this legal joyousness.

'Ratchet's are responsible for that,' cried Jeremy, with all the energy of forty-two pushing responsibility onto someone else. 'Don't you worry. We'll tell them to ask three, and if we have to come down to two, no harm's done – or practically none, ha! ha!'

When letter and postal order arrived, Mary felt a sedate exultation. But it was a Saturday, so she would be at the shop all day while Mrs Levy pursued the religious rituals of her race, so there would be no opportunity for that excursion to Oxford Street which Sylvie had suggested.

Mary knew that she must go to work. But when, on her way to the bus, she encountered Sylvie loitering in the hall, she remarked that it seemed a shame they both had to work on Saturdays.

'Well, I'm not,' Sylvie snapped, 'so let's go Up West like I said.'

'But why aren't you?'

''Cos one of the bloody supervisors didn't like being called a rotten old cow, that's why.'

'Then you're . . . did she . . .?' Mary still felt some of the consideration for other people's feelings instilled by home, and the word 'sacked' would not come out.

'Shoved out on me arse. I was wondering when you'd notice.'

'Well, if you don't tell me . . .'

'I been ill. Had the Chinese flu, the doctor said it was.'

A pause. Mary felt that she just could not speed away. It was not feeling sorry for Sylvie; it was not even that the thought of the daily bus was suddenly unbearably dreary. The front door was still shut, and it was a solid, well-hung piece of wood nearly a hundred years old, yet through it beckoned the lure of a brilliant, stingingly cold, sunny morning. *Shopping!* Mary burned to spend some money.

'I – I suppose you're pretty skint?' she suggested, but Sylvie snorted.

'Well I'm just not, see, 'cause I got me relief. And I paid me rent, so old Orange-Face can't push me out.' She paused, and her eyes, which had grown dull, began to glitter again. 'What say we go? Oh come on.'

Mary hesitated. 'I'll lose my job,' she said calmly. 'But we'll go.'

She often thought, afterwards, of the instant in which she made that decision. The whole of her future life had unrolled from it, like a Japanese *kakemono*.

She went quickly upstairs and threw her dressing-gown into a corner of her room. Three months of common sense and frugality and prudence went with it.

In twenty minutes, she and Sylvie were giggling over a second breakfast in a Wimpy Bar in Kentish Town Road.

The luckless ones who worked on Saturday mornings were jerking past in buses. The early shoppers were on the prowl; the wind bit, the cold yellow sun shone, and a jet lumbered thundering through the thin, low, winter clouds. But in the Wimpy Bar it was warm and quiet.

'We'll see the decorations. 'Ere, I'm having another coffee. What about you?' Sylvie spoke over her shoulder as she undulated towards the counter, her hipless body moving under a black cotton skirt printed with lilac and yellow circles and reaching to her ankles.

'What decorations?' Mary asked through her beefburger.

'Xmas. Up West.' Sylvie held up her cup questioningly, and Mary nodded. It was not *coffee* — her mother had ground the whole beans in a little machine. But it was hot, and the sugar was free.

'Now where'll we go?' Mary demanded as, full and warm, they came out into Kentish Town Road.

'Oxford Street. There's blokes there sells them medals, on chains they are, and beads . . . We could have a look at them and p'raps see'f there was anything what we fancied up Selfridges.'

It was Sylvie, too, who decided that they should travel by Underground because it was warmer and, she added, 'There's more boys there.'

Side by side they sat in the Underground, and Northern Ireland, Bangladesh, Mr Nixon and the Middle East droned past their understanding like the muffled thundering of the train. Pat had worked from nine in the morning, until half past four in the afternoon, five days a week, for nearly ten years, to keep Mary at Redpaths. The rate-payers of Camden had seen a high percentage of their heavy taxes go to keep Sylvie at the Beatrice Webb Secondary Modern. Mary had listened and tried; Sylvie had sat at the back painting her nails. The result was the same in both cases: their chief, their deepest, interests were clothes, beads and boys.

Mary preferred the kind of boy who did not wear beads; but Sylvie, with a mind suggesting those Edwardian dresses whose trains swept up miscellaneous rubbish from the streets, gathered fashionable trends in much the same way and, to her, beads on a boy were all right. Groovy.

No one looked at them as they sat there. Sylvie's greenish hair and pseudo-Victorian skirt and dirty leather coat bordered with dirty sheepskin were conventional wear; while Mary's clothes were equally conventional in another and older style. Too many girls looked like Sylvie to attract the stares which she would have welcomed from the long-haired, long-legged youths; and no one but her elders ever looked at Mary.

They came out of the Underground at Tottenham Court Road, and set off at once on a slow, prowling stroll along Oxford Street.

They paused before a young man selling earrings set with pearls, and chains at the end of which swung a silvery medallion, stamped with a crude pattern that glittered in the wintery sunlight.

BOOK TWO

9

Two invitations

How Wilfred longed to ask Mary to come home on Christmas Eve and stay for the three nights of the holiday! But what kind of a Christmas would they have in the dusty house full of staring gadgets, with Pat's absence haunting every room?

'I never 'eard of such a thing – are you 'er father or some kind of a housefly?' demanded his father, when he dropped in to see him some days before the twenty-fifth. 'You make 'er come. Tell 'er she's ruddy well got to. I shan't; I meant to tell yer, young Ginger's arst me along. 'Er latest'll be there, and 'e always 'as a drop too much Christmas (Easter *and* all the year round, come to that) and 'e might get knockin' the kids about. 'Course, the three eldest'll be 'ome for the day 'cept for Marlene wots in reform but I better be there. In case,' Mr Davis swelled up a muscle under his tattered jersey and studied it with approval.

'Oh well . . . please yourself, Dad.'

'Now don't take it like that, Wilf. There's a pound for Mary,' he nodded at the mantelpiece, 'not that she'll think anything of it, but she *is* me granddaughter.'

Wilfred wished the old man a Merry Christmas, pushed a small parcel tied with red ribbon at him, and said that he must be going.

'It'll be merry, all right – thanks,' Mr Davis said grimly, and Wilfred, having pocketed the pound note and left a fifty pence piece apiece for Samantha and Kelly, took his departure.

'Thanks for the bacca,' followed him in a shout to the corner of the little street; he turned, and saw his father on the door-step, his old jersey and trousers looking more than usually disreputable in the clear winter light, waving the opened parcel at him.

Never could wait till Christmas morning, bless him, Wilfred thought, smiling and waving back.

A man of the nineteenth century, tempered by hardship and courage into what, for Wilfred, was an utterly satisfactory human being. His love took the form of the cliché *They don't make 'em like that nowadays,* and as this thought passed, his next thought was that he would write and invite Mary.

'Where was you on Saturday?' snapped Mrs Levy, her eyes narrowed and her face swollen with anger as Mary came into the shop on Monday morning. 'I phone Mrs Cadman three times. She said she don't know. I have to phone my daughter; I phone Mr Foster across the way making him trouble. My daughter vas going with a friend to see *Canterbury Tales.* She can't go because I have to come down here because you weren't *available.* Now she missed it. All your fault.'

'I went Up West,' Mary said, looking steadily at Mrs Levy. Round her neck hung a long chain on which glittered a silvery medallion.

'Oh. So you went Up Vest.' Mrs Levy nodded. 'Ver-ry good. Up Vest. I see.' She pointed, with drama, at the medallion. 'Vaste your money, vaste your time, let me down. I know. Sooner or later, I think, Mary do this to me. And vy? Because you *all the same.* 1970s girls lazy, liars, unreliable.' She paused, glaring.

Mary glanced out of the door where the gold light of a perfect winter's day beckoned.

'I felt like a bit of a holiday, so I went with a girlfriend. I've always done my work properly, Mrs Levy.' She hesitated. 'I like it here – as a matter of fact.'

'Tank *you,* tank you very much!' Mrs Levy cried.

'I just . . . felt like a bit of a holiday,' Mary ended. Her serious dark eyes stayed unmovingly on Mrs Levy's. She thought, dreamily, that this old thing had once been seventeen years old.

'Und me? Und me und the shop?' Mrs Levy banged her black woolly bosom. 'Vot become of us? Suppose I never phone Mr Foster to check if you arrive –'

'But you always do.'

'Of course I do. But suppose this time I haf a stroke or my muder, God forbid. Suppose bugglars, suppose a fire, vandals? No, you don't care. All the same, 1970s girls. Mrs Cadman already toldt me you respectable. So I should hope. But your friend' – Mrs Levy sucked in her lips – 'she's *bad*. Mrs Cadman said so.'

'She's all right.' Mary glanced out again at the morning. She would walk to St Paul's and sit there. 'Shall I go now, or do you want me to work this afternoon? I may as well, now I've spent the fare.'

Mrs Levy stared. 'Go vere?'

'Well . . . off. I mean, if I'm sacked . . .'

'Who spoke about sacking? You know well, Mary' – Mrs Levy's voice took on a note as if it were undulating like a tearful snake – 'you have advantages. Vy you did not *ask* me to give you a holiday for Saturday? – Isn't it enough you have the morninks? No – idle, idle. Und I could have stop the money.'

'Because I needed the money.'

Mary hung up her coat and unhooked the fun-fur hood. 'I'm sorry Mrs Bearstein missed *The Canterbury Tales*. If I'd known she was going, perhaps I'd have come in.'

'Perhaps . . .' Mrs Levy muttered, unlocking the drawer where she kept her ledger. 'Yes, you have advantages, Mary. Good education, good home. Perhaps your father a rich man and you do this for a joke, like in film?'

Mary could not decide if this was asked in sarcasm, or whether Mrs Levy really was wondering if her father were a millionaire.

He's better than ten millionaires, she thought warmly, as she bent over the counter and the medallion swung forward gleaming in a ray of sunlight, *and I love him.*

When she reached home that night, through the thick, rich, exciting atmosphere of preparations for Christmas, she found her father's letter.

She stood by the alarmingly hissing gas fire, slowly waving the letter about, and considering. She had not thought about what she would do at Christmas; at the back of her mind had been a vague idea that 'they might ask me down', 'they' being Mrs Cadman and Mr Grant. It would be a bore, anyway, three days with the shops shut and nothing to do and nowhere to go.

But to go back to Torford, home, without Mum (Mary's eyes surprisingly filled) and see the sad, loving look on Dad's face, and have everyone asking how she liked London, and how she was getting on – oh, she could not face it.

"Ullo? Anyone at 'ome? Knock, knock 'oo's there?'

It was Sylvie's thin voice outside the door.

'I'm just back. What is it?' Mary strode to the door and jerked it open. 'I've got enough supper for myself tonight, and that's all.'

'Don't be so mingy. I got liver sausage and cider – *bought* the cider. It's an invite.' Sylvie's eyes were glittering, as always, at the smallest hint of gaiety.

'Oh.'

Mary felt slightly embarrassed. This was proferred hospitality, this was a return for her own. Had she been unkind to Sylvie? She felt penitent (it did not occur to her that she had been unkind to Mrs Levy; Mrs Levy was old).

'All right – thanks. Sounds good . . . how did you get on today?'

Sylvie was helping with the Christmas rush at a local post office, Mrs Cadman having unwillingly recommended her for the job.

'S'like a mental 'ome down there. (Well, it's the same everywhere, I s'pose.) Come *on.*'

Soon they were crouching beside the gas fire in Sylvie's large, dim, damp basement, to which every piece of furniture in the twelve rooms of the house that was cracked, broken or near-useless had drifted. So solid were Mrs Cadman's tastes, however, and so settled her habits of cosiness, that the room was not without an air of comfort.

'Come on, let's boil the cider. Make us drunk quicker,' suggested Sylvie, unwrapping a long, greasy parcel at a table that must have been all of a hundred and fifty years old; kidney-shaped, with traces of crimson and gilt and black lingering on its battered surfaces.

'Cripes! What an enormous sausage.'

'Whipped it.'

Sylvie opened a drawer that slid forward smoothly as a dancer, and took out an old, sharp knife. 'Down on the floor it was, near the door. Some fool never put no address on it. There was a feller arter it but I got it first.' She began vigorously slicing.

'It would only have gone bad and been wasted,' said Mary, wishing to give a shade of respectability to the eating of stolen food. Sylvie grinned behind her fringe and said nothing.

'We'll *mull* the cider. Mum used to,' Mary went on.

'What in hell's that?'

'Heat it with spice. Have you got any? You know – cinnamon or that kind of thing?'

'Catch me. I got something else to do with me money – when I got any. Run and ask old Orange-Face.'

Mary did so, and returned with a minute pinch of powdered clove carefully put up in a screw of paper. As she ran down the stairs to the basement she again congratulated herself, with the whipped sausage in mind, on having a landlady who seldom asked questions. It did not occur to her that Mrs Cadman, with the aid of Mr Grant, might know all she wanted to about what went on in the house.

'She cough up? Miracles'll never cease . . . 'Ere, bung it in.'
Mary put a little of the spice into a saucepanful of cider.

'What you doin' fer Christmas?' Sylvie asked, when they had
pulled the table close to the fire.

'Oh going home, I guess. Dad's asked me.' Mary spoke
with her mouth full. She had at that moment decided that she
would go.

'You ain't half lucky.' Sylvie's voice took on a whine. 'S'pose
I could go 'ome but . . . there was some boys asked me, said
we might go some 'ouse what's empty back of the 'ospital where
there's all that building goin' on. They had this groupie, see,
and she went off somewhere, so they arst me . . . eight of 'em.
Nice Christmas I'd have . . . You like it?' she ended, sliding
her eyes round at Mary.

'Yes, it's very good,' Mary answered, lifting a piece of sausage
on her fork and misunderstanding deliberately.

Sylvie let out a screeching laugh.

'Go on! "It's very good" – when I know you ain't done it yet.
Only asked you for a giggle. There ain't much to it, 'cept—'
she broke off, stared broodingly at the floor for a second, then
added: "Course, there'll be plenty of nosh at 'ome. Mum'll see
to that. But they'll only be on at me.'

Mary dipped a spoon into the steaming cider, blew on it, and
tasted. She intended to avoid the subject of Sylvie's Christmas.

'Here.' She handed over a handleless cup, and they sipped.

'Tastes a bit funny,' pronounced Sylvie, 'but it ain't bad.
S'pose I'll have to stay 'ere and get drunk' (she did not say
drunk) 'by meself, then.'

'Oh for heaven's sake. Of course you won't have to get drunk
by yourself. Mrs Cadman'll ask you or . . . or . . . something.
I know she's having some friends in.'

'All about fifty. Thanks. *And* the mistletoe. He'll be onto that,
Christmas time, 'stead of bum-pinching.'

'Now look here.' Mary set down her mug and raised her
voice. 'I like Mr Grant, and I don't believe he's the kind that
pinches girls' bums – *I* was brought up to think that's a vulgar

word – and what's more I don't believe he's ever pinched yours. So there.'

She stared steadily at Sylvie, and Sylvie stared angrily back. 'Calling me a liar, now. You aren't half mingy,' she said at last. 'All right then, he never. But I bet he'd like to. They're all the same . . . calling me vulgar, too. Lady Toffee-nose, that's what you are!'

'Oh for heaven's sake! Have some more cider and shut your cake-hole.'

Mary's voice was a controlled shout, and suddenly, the mulled cider rollicking through their young veins, they both began to giggle.

'I'll tell you what –' Mary leant across and poked Sylvie in the chest – 'don't you stay here and get drunk on your own with Mrs C's old trouts. You come and have Christmas with me.'

'Mrs Wheeby!'

Wilfred stood at the foot of the stairs, with the telegram in his hand. 'Mary's coming home for Christmas!'

He knew that he should have knocked discreetly at Mrs Wheeby's door, but he had to shout the news to someone. And a telegram! At the sight of it, his heart had felt as if it stopped, for he belonged in the generation to which telegrams meant disaster.

The silence that followed quietened Wilfred's excitement. Perhaps she had not heard. But suddenly her door opened, and there she stood in the Marks and Spencer dressing-gown, looking at him over the top of a cup of something.

'Well Mr Davis, so I should trust and hope,' she said severely.

'I know, Mrs Wheeby, of course. But I haven't seen her for three months, you know. I'm – I'm so . . . excited.'

'Very natural, I'm sure,' said Mrs Wheeby, unmoved. 'But do I see a telegram? I'm sure I'm glad for you, Mr Davis, and that Mary knows her duty to her father, but do I see a telegram? I must put in a word of warning. I feel it my duty, though not a pleasant or welcome one. A man of your age, Mr Davis (and I take you to be in your middle sixties) should be careful and not get over-excited. There are such things as strokes, and a telegram, too . . . Shall I ever forget my husband's third younger brother? . . . On the Thursday morning at breakfast, and by tea-time – *Gone.*'

Mrs Wheeby lifted and dropped a hand.

'I expect Mary sent a telegram because the posts are so behindhand, Mrs Wheeby.' He could only wave the telegram to and fro and smile. 'Look here, you'll come to us for Christmas, won't you?' he went on eagerly. 'We'll have a turkey, and a tree. Pat – Mrs Davis – always liked a tree, you know . . . and mince pies, and all the trimmings.' Kindness shone from him.

'Well as to that, Mr Davis, I won't say that it isn't neighbourly of you, but there is one small point I must make clear and when I tell you that all my enjoyment of the invitation depends upon your answer' (pause, gasp) 'perhaps you will understand me asking a question no other circumstances – nor wild horses – would induce me to ask. Is the old gentleman to be present with us?'

'The old – oh, my father. No. No, Mrs Wheeby, I'm sorry to say he isn't. He's going to – some friends. He feels they . . . might need his company.'

Mrs Wheeby nodded, managing by the nod to imply that she had difficulty in imagining anyone needing it.

'I shall be pleased to come Mr Davis, and I suppose you will want help with the shopping. It isn't a job for a man, though I must say that Mr Wheeby could buy a pound of icing sugar with the best, though always careful to point out it was not really his duty. Such a lot to do at Christmas' (pause, wheeze). 'I suppose you will get everything from Marks? Really excellent, they are. Except the turkey. I suppose you will go to Dill's for that. I warn you, there is one thing I cannot and will not do, and that is hurry. You have left it very late. Only two days. But we shall manage somehow. How about setting forth this afternoon?'

The shopping! Wilfred had completely forgotten that any would be necessary. Turkey and tree and all the trimmings existed in his mind, shining in the glow of Mary's coming. And shopping with Mrs Wheeby . . .

'Well . . . that's very kind of you, Mrs Wheeby . . . and . . . and *considerate* . . . but – er – will you enjoy it? The shops are crowded just now and . . .'

'Oh no. I shan't enjoy it, Mr Davis. I quite dread the idea, especially with a man. And these new self-service places are so confusing. I'm sure the hunt I had for shrimp paste in Mallock's last Tuesday would have worn out one of those commandos they had in the war. Oh no, I shan't enjoy it, Mr Davis' (pause, long wheeze). 'But I must earn my Christmas dinner, mustn't I?'

While he was wondering what on earth to say next, the telephone bell rang in the hall. He muttered 'Oh bother – excuse me,' and ran down to it. It might just be Mary. *Oh, don't let it be that she can't come.*

'Torford 666.'

'Laf Taverner here, Mr Davis. Come and spend Christmas with us, won't you? All the three days. Do.'

Over the telephone, the light voice was almost indistinguishable from a woman's.

Wilfred felt strong relief – no shopping, no setting forth with Mrs Wheeby – then gratitude.

'That's very kind of you, and . . . and of Miss Dollette and Mrs Cornforth too. But I'm in a bit of difficulty, you see. It's my daughter, Mary. She'll be coming home for the three days. I've just heard. And then, I'm afraid, there's old Mrs Wheeby (my lodger, you know). She'll be alone. It's rather an army, three of us.'

'There are plenty of rooms in the house,' said the voice at the other end of the line – and something in the words touched off an echo – a memory – what was it? – in Wilfred's mind. 'So, the more the merrier. And you'll be able to have Mary to yourself for a talk whenever you feel like it, you know. Do come, all of you.'

'Well, Mr Taverner, I won't say no. I must just ask Mrs Wheeby. It is so kind of you – of all of you. I was dreading the shops, to tell you the truth. At this time of year they really are hell . . .'

'Not quite,' Mr Taverner said dryly.

'Goodbye, then, and thank you all again, Mr Taverner.'

Wilfred replaced the receiver. The thought of describing the Yellow House and its occupants to Mrs Wheeby made him shrink, and then and there he decided to write a note and put it under her door.

On his way out to buy the ritual slices of disliked liver, it occurred to him that Mrs Wheeby would want to take Dicky to the Yellow House.

Home again, he put the liver in to bake with a knob of butter, and sat down to write his note.

Dear Mrs Wheeby,

Some friends living in Hardy Crescent have asked us all – you and me and Mary – to stay with them over the Christmas holiday. This will save us all a lot of work and bother so I hope you will come. By the way, I have sold the house to Mr Dill the butcher.

                            Yours sincerely,
                                W. Davis

In the pre-lunch quietude prevailing at Lamorna, he stole upstairs and slid the note under Mrs Wheeby's door.

But the ides of March, so to speak, were not yet gone, and just before tea-time, when he was making himself tea in the kitchen, there came a tap at the door.

Mrs Wheeby entered, neat and portentous.

'Thank you for your note, Mr Davis. I must say I think the news might have been conveyed by word of mouth, and not pushed under the door, like a greengrocer's bill. But then, it hardly *was* news to me, as Mrs Dill and I are old friends, as was proved to me many times in the war with offal when she was having her first' (pause, gasp).'I will not trouble you now by asking whether you have found us somewhere else to lay our heads permanently. "Sufficient unto the day" is what I always say, and always have. As for the invitation, it is very kind of perfect strangers. Who are they? I didn't know that you and Mrs Davis had any friends in Hardy Crescent – one of the oldest and nicest parts of the town, I think . . .' She suddenly ran out of words, and sat down on a chair that faced Wilfred's teapot, into which he now poured boiling water.

He silently handed her a box of biscuits.

'No biscuits for me, thank you, Mr Davis. I prefer bread and butter with my tea, and always have.'

10

The desolate place

The houses that were 'empty, back of the 'ospital where there's all that building', mentioned by Sylvie, were more than empty.

Some of them were roofless, and some had had their sides ripped out, with streamers of wallpaper hanging down in their shattered rooms, and all were now shut in by barriers of corrugated iron. They stood in a wasteland between the busy prosperity of Archway Road and, on the other side, the quiet avenues of a private estate.

The pavements of the old streets – Cavell, Manson, Veeley, Arcott and others – still ran between the pallid metal walls, without a name or a shop or a public house left to guide the few pedestrians who made their way through the wilderness.

At night, with the low red glare thrown up from the Archway Road lights staining the sky, and the surrounding half-darkness through which the barriers glimmered, and the fearful muted roar from the distant traffic, the place was frightening.

It was also, to some temperaments, exciting.

But it was not the loneliness and its desolation that had lured into it the boy who was walking slowly along what had been Veeley Street, a few nights after Mary and Sylvie had had supper together.

No one else was there. Heavy rain had fallen. The barriers shut off acres of churned mud where, during the day, huge machines toiled and lumbered. A small cold rain had replaced the earlier downpour; he picked his way round wide pools, not quite water, not quite mud. The dim air was full of the low, threatening roar of hidden traffic. It was about seven o'clock.

He walked slowly, with bent head and hands pushed into his pockets. The zip of his jacket was fastened, but his long hair blew in the rainy wind; only softies put on anything to protect the head. It was the most terrible thing in the world – the small, savage, tight world of their gang of eight – to be a softie. He was muttering as he walked, a stream of self-pitying sentences.

Why was he always the one? Why wouldn't anyone even listen to him? He paid his share, didn't he? He did what the others suggested. There wasn't any reason for his being chucked out, but here he was: alone, hungry, jobless, nowhere to kip down tonight unless he went home, and bloody miserable. He used the word miserable – muttering it over and over again, the word that was never used by the gang.

His heart felt that it would burst with his misery. *I'm not all that soft*, he repeated under his breath. *I'm not all that soft*. It was the vilest word the gang knew: soft. *There's no one. There's just no one.*

His banishment from the gang – the seven with whom he had grown up and played in these streets – pressed upon him in an unbearable load. He could have fallen to the broken pavement with the weight of it.

Veeley Street, Cavell Street, Manson Street, Arkell Street, Arley Street – all of them gone. And his mum and stepfather moved off to the council flat, and not wanting him there unless he would go back to the factory and bring in some money.

Shitting place, he muttered. *Putting bits of metal on jars moving along a bloody conveyor belt. Let them try it, eight hours a day, five days a week. Let them try.*

Wish I could die, he whispered. *Wish I could die.*

He heard the wheels of a car crumching on the road behind him, and turned quickly. *They beat you up for nothing, sometimes.*

He'd have no chance. They might have nicked a car and followed him. *They just might . . .*

But it was a bloke in a white raincoat, leaning out of the window and smiling.

'Derek Skuse?'

'What's it got to do with you?'

Derek spoke truculently, as they always did in the gang, but, in his unbearable loneliness, he was not sorry to speak to someone.

'You'll see,' the man said.

Derek had hardly been spoken to, since his father's death three years ago, in a tone that was not impersonal, hectoring, facetious or whining. But there was a note in this voice that he remembered from Archway Secondary Modern. The young master had stayed only a term, but Derek still remembered his voice, without knowing that what it carried was loving authority.

'What's all this about?' the boy asked, alarmed, standing in the drifting rain with his long wet hair blowing back from his narrow face. 'I ain't done nothing. You the fuzz?'

'No. Please get in, Derek.'

'I'm not queer, neither. We had a groupie in our . . . mob, see, and I had her. So nothing doing.'

'I'm a friend. Get in.'

'S'pose you think I'm mental, on me own in a place like this.' Derek did not move.

'No I don't. You're wretched, and so you came to a place that seems wretched too.'

'Well yer just wrong, see, 'cos I used to live here. When my dad was alive.' He had moved nearer to the car without knowing that he had. 'That's an old bus,' he added, moved, even in his misery, by the passionate obsession with cars felt by all his gang. ''Bout 1937, I'd say.'

'Thirty-eight. Get in, won't you?'

'Where we goin', then? You can give me a lift, if you like. I . . . I got a home.'

'I'm glad to hear it, son.' The voice was quiet, yet seemed to be drawing him towards it.

'I ain't . . . I meant, I ain't like some . . . that lot that always lives reely rough. In them places.' He jerked his head towards the louring black shape of a ruined house behind the barrier. 'I ain't soft, neither. I been living in one of them places . . . only yesterday they come and put up the barriers, and turned us out.'

'I know,' the man said. 'And I want you to come and spend Christmas with us.'

'Spend *Christmas* with yer . . . Christ!'

'Exactly,' said the man amiably. 'Christ. I live with some friends in a small town not far from the east coast. Do come, Derek. Just for Christmas.'

Derek was tired. He had been living rough for three days. This bloke might be a pusher, but . . .

'And I don't push drugs. Get in,' said the irresistible voice.

'But yer *are* a bleeding mind-reader!' Derek was inside the car, in some way, before he knew it, and it was moving away.

He leant back with a feeling of comfort, and noticed a slight, fresh scent. *Must have been a bird in here recent,* he thought, and was reassured. *Bloke wasn't queer, then.* That was what he would do, if he had a car – pick up birds.

'Hungry?' the man asked, as the car moved away from the last of the barriers into a sober road with houses and trees.

'Christ, I am.'

'True . . . Christ you are. I haven't any wine or bread, but Christ will now, with my help, give you some coffee and sausage rolls. On the seat at the back.'

Moving at the unalarming pace of a 1938 model, the car had now left behind the frightening wilderness and was climbing a steep hill between walls over which looked big, leafless trees. The long hill was well lit, and there were other cars going homeward, climbing with them. *Talks funny,* Derek thought tiredly.

The sausage rolls were hot, so was the coffee. He ate and drank in silence.

'Yer not 'aving nothing?' he asked presently; he had almost forgotten the driver. It was a long time since he had tried not to drop crumbs on a carpeted floor because his mother hit him if he did, and made him get out the Hoover and take them up, but the almost-forgotten habit lingered.

'No thanks. I've eaten.'

'I asked 'cos –' he held up the Thermos with the first faint beginning of a smile. 'There ain't much left.'

'It's all right. I got it especially for you.'

Oxfam or sunnick, thought Derek. *Goes round looking for delinquents. Start on me presently – oh well, make the most of it. Warm, anyway. . . .* the thought faded.

'Can't she go any faster?' he asked presently, because the dimness in the car and the changing, passing, flashing white and red lights on the main road over which they were travelling, and the smooth movement, were making him sleepy, and if he fell asleep this bloke might dump him somewhere. Then it occurred to him, suddenly, that he might be a murderer.

'No . . . that is, no I'm not,' said the man. 'A murderer.'

Derek sat up, wide awake and frightened.

'But you *are* a bleeding mind-reader, like I said . . . 'ere . . . let me out.'

He struggled away from the white raincoat, staring in fear at the profile under the soft, old-fashioned hat. The man turned his head and smiled.

'It was a perfectly natural thought. We're getting out towards the lonelier roads. I would have thought so, too, in your place . . . Yes, she can go faster, but if I let her out as fast as she can go, you . . . might be frightened.'

'Me frightened! I done ninety, once, in a mate's bus.'

'That must remain your limit while you're with me, I'm afraid . . . do you play football?'

'Used to, a bit, when my . . . my dad took me to see Arsenal, once. Arsenal was our . . . Arsenal's tops.'

He stared aside, at the awfulness of the M1, along which they were now travelling; then said slowly: 'It's . . . like them streets . . . what they pulled down. You know, where you picked me up. This road gives you the same kind of feeling.'

'Hallelujah!' exclaimed the man loudly, turning on him a broad smile.

'You know what –' Derek said timidly. 'I don't mean it nasty-like, but are you a bit . . . you know . . . mental? A lot of blokes are, there's no disgrace. I don't mean you'd do a kid or anything, 'course. Harmless. Just not quite all there? I don't mean . . .'

'All of me is all here – unfortunately. It's all right. I only seem mental because I don't pretend. When I'm glad, I say "hallelujahs" . . . Now we're going to leave this horrifying road and go somewhere real.'

The car turned aside, down a secondary road, where a few houses stood behind shadowy fences and large trees. Overhead there was starlight. London was thirty miles behind, and the headlights shone on emerald grass beside bare hedges, while ahead lay a harmless, mysterious darkness. Sometimes ivy gleamed green and dark amid silvery thorn trees.

'Lonely,' Derek half whispered, looking aside into the briefly lit beauty fleeting past.

'But not lonely like the place I found you in,' said the man, and Derek choked. 'No . . .' and he began to weep – pouring out misery-laden words, stammering, protesting, writhing, turning on his companion in fury.

The man heard him in silence. Not once did he attempt interruption. The car was deep in the country now: not a house, not a light appeared on the dim fields. The headlights shone on withered, white grasses, ghostly and asleep.

Once the driver leant across the sobbing child to open a window, and the smell of damp earth floated in. There was no sound but the throb of the old engine, and Derek's crying. When the man slowed down a second time, it was to feel in his pocket and bring out a folded white square, with the same ferny scent that was floating in the car. He put it into Derek's hand, and presently Derek slowly wiped his eyes.

*

When Wilfred opened the door for the fifth time on Christmas Eve to inspect the weather, he murmured 'Right – for once,' meaning the BBC. It was snowing.

Crystals drifted through the dark air and there was a thin white carpet covering the path. He looked along the road, whose leafless laburnums and maples were already whitened. A white Christmas. She had said she would be home about seven; he had decided not to meet the train in case they missed each other.

He had hardly sat down before the television again when the front door bell rang.

Oh, it was a moment. He opened the door to see her longed-for, smiling face; it was framed in a hood of dark fur. She was thinner . . .

'Hullo, Dad . . .'

He could not speak, and she drew him towards her and gave him a calm hug and a kiss.

But who was that, standing behind her in the shadows? Someone else . . . a fuzz of pale hair, a coat to the ankles . . . boy or girl? Oh, had she got herself a boy, *looking like that*? But she was turning to the bizarre figure, keeping a hand on his arm.

'This is my friend, Sylvie Carano. You know. She was going to stay at Mrs Cadman's alone over Christmas and get drunk, so I brought her along. Sylvie, this is my dad.'

Mary's laugh was a little nervous.

'Hullo,' came out in a mumble from behind the green hair, and the head moved. How her eyes shone! *Was she mental?* Wilfred wondered.

'Hullo, Sylvie. Glad to see you. Any friend of Mary's . . .' he said, wondering what Mr Taverner and his ladies would think of this? 'Come in . . . come in, both of you. Here, let me have that,' and he picked up an airliner bag, through whose broken zipper some grubby pink frills showed.

In the warm, bright living room there was silence while Mary took off her hood and shook back her hair; its glossy ends were wet with melting snow. She looked round the room, then at her father and he just moved his head. The word *mother* flew silently between them.

'Well . . .' Mary said quickly, 'Sylvie and I'll go up and get her room ready and then I'll cook us some supper – we're starving . . . come on, Syl.'

'Just a minute, love – we aren't staying here over Christmas,' her father broke in. 'We're going to some friends of . . . of mine . . . nice people. You'll like them,' he added, firmly.

'Who are they, then?' Mary asked, with a little curiosity. The Davises had few friends outside the small circle made up of stout, talkative, sensible, salt-of-the-earth-and-down-to-it women whom Pat had known for years. 'Now, what have you been up to while I've been away?' She smiled at him and his heart glowed with love.

'Bet you wish I'd never come,' Sylvie said suddenly, 'goin' to friends.' Her voice was so low and hoarse that he could hardly make out the words.

'Now, Syl, don't start,' said Mary authoritatively. 'Dad wouldn't know people who weren't nice and friendly, and we're going to enjoy ourselves. Cheer up, or I'll ruffle your wig.' She made a gesture at the damp mass, and Sylvie dodged, while a grin showed on her face.

'Let's all have a sherry,' Wilfred suggested. 'I bought a couple of bottles to take along with us as our contribution . . . to . . . to the feast, as you might say.' He turned to the sideboard.

'Syl, sit down,' commanded Mary, and Sylvie slowly subsided into one of the armchairs and began to undo her coat, revealing as odd a collection of garments as Wilfred had ever seen thrown upon a human body.

'I shan't get drunk,' she said suddenly, not looking at anyone. 'Might of, if I'd stayed at that old b— cat's, but not 'ere.'

'We'll all get a bit drunk,' said Wilfred playfully, pouring out.

'That was a joke, what Mary said,' said Sylvie.

'I know – I've had some of Mary's jokes.' (*Missed them, too. God, how I've missed them.*) 'But I hope we'll all be a bit cheerful by the time Mr Taverner calls for us.'

He held out a glass, the correct kind of glass to drink sherry from and part of Pat's pride in her home. 'Merry Christmas, Sylvie.'

'Here's . . . mud in y'eye,' she muttered.

They drank. Wilfred was just wondering if he could get a word with Mary about doing something to modify Sylvie's appearance before they arrived at the Yellow House, when slow steps were heard descending the stairs, and Mrs Wheeby appeared, muffled in six or seven wool scarves and cardigans, and carrying the equally muffled cage of Dicky.

'I *cannot* think how it came to escape my memory,' she began. 'It may have been the shock, a pleasant one, Mr Davis, of being invited away for Christmas; but quite suddenly, only an hour ago it was, when I thought – Why, there's Mary! Just the same, only thinner. How are you? and how is business? – Who's this?'

Mrs Wheeby's eye, suddenly pebble-like, became fixed upon Sylvie.

'This is my friend, Sylvie Carano,' Mary put in smoothly. 'Mrs Wheeby lives in our house, Sylvie.'

''Ullo.' Sylvie waved her glass.

'Won't you join us, Mrs Wheeby? Just a small one for the road?' asked Wilfred.

'Thank you, in a moment. But first about Dicky. I can't of course leave him here alone for three days, nor make my way across town to feed him' (pause, gasp). 'And it is said snow is coming, and sure enough here it is. They were right. (*I* think they often are, and people don't do them justice. I'm sure I shouldn't like the job of saying what the weather will be tomorrow afternoon.) Nor could I trouble anyone to get out their car just to feed and water a canary. No, it wouldn't be *right*' (gasp). 'So I got him ready, and here he is, and I only hope our friends won't mind. You know he's well trained. Now *you*,' turning to Sylvie, 'remind me very much, Sylvia, of my cousin Alice's eldest girl, Georgina. She had your type of features and wore her hair all over her face to hide them. I'm sure I don't know why, because she looked much nicer when you could see her face. If you like,' concluded Mrs Wheeby, accepting a glass from Wilfred's now slightly trembling hand, 'I'll show you a prettier way to do yours.'

Sylvie opened her mouth, but at that moment Wilfred thankfully heard the front door bell.

'She's here!' he said conspiratorially as he opened the door to Mr Taverner, tall and white against the drifting snow. 'Mary.'

Mr Taverner smiled, and Wilfred called: 'Ladies! Your escort has arrived.'

Out they came in a procession, led by Mrs Wheeby bearing the silent Dicky, Mary looking curiously at her father's new friend, and Sylvie. Swaggering was the word for Sylvie's gait.

Wilfred hastily made introductions, remembering through his agitation to present the man to the ladies and not the other way round. (Pat would have been pleased with him. She had known what was correct on such occasions, though shyness had usually made her sing out, laughing: 'So-and-so, meet such-and-such!')

Mrs Wheeby's steamroller advanced immediately. 'Well, what a night, isn't it, Mr Taverner? Quite like the song. Here is Dicky, my canary,' waggling the cage slightly. 'I hope you won't mind my bringing him along . . .' The account of her hesitations, fears and assumptions continued as she moved out onto the snowy path with Mr Taverner's hand under her elbow.

Wilfred lingered, to put out lights and lock up.

Lamorna's gadgets were left in darkness, motionless and therefore even more uninteresting than usual. Icy crystals floated against his face as he hurried down the path, and in the air was the unmistakable, secret hush that whispers *snow*. He felt extraordinarily happy and, as always when he was happy, was silent.

Mrs Wheeby had wedged herself next to Mr Taverner, remarking that she had heard it said one was less inclined to be so dreadfully sick if one sat next the driver, having first handed Dicky over to Sylvie. ('There you are, Sylvia. Now mind he doesn't shake about.') Mary and Sylvie were squashed next to Wilfred in the back seat, giggling.

'All right behind there?' Mr Taverner asked.

'Dicky must be a blinking eagle, I sh'd think,' snapped Sylvie, on whose knees the cage rested. 'Weighs about a ton,' and Mr Taverner laughed.

'I'm glad someone thinks it's funny,' Sylvie said. 'Me knees is nearly in half.'

'We'll soon be there, I expect, Sylvia. A little thing like that, all feathers and tiny bones, can't be all that heavy. Let's hope we don't have a skid. But I expect Mr Taverner is an experienced driver, aren't you?'

'You might say that, Mrs Wheeby. Yes.'

11

Thinking

Wilfred was oddly relieved to see that a wreath of holly decked with red ribbon hung from the Yellow House's knocker; and in one window a Christmas tree gleamed with globes of pink, blue and silver. Candles burned motionless along its branches. *Just like everybody else's house, really.*

'Well, what a pleasure! Candles instead of electric lights!' (wheeze, pause). 'I know some people say it's dangerous, but not if people have their wits about them.'

Mrs Wheeby was slowly preparing to emerge.

'No danger,' smiled Mr Taverner, holding open the car door. 'Our wits are all about us.'

'Dead quiet,' muttered Sylvie, to no one in particular, and Mary silently agreed: she would have welcomed more sound and light.

Suddenly, she had both. The door opened, and a glow shone out from the hall, and there stood a tall woman with an apron over her dress. She seemed to float, rather than run, down the snowy steps.

'Merry Christmas!' Her deep, warm voice came out boldly into the hush.

'This is Mrs Cornforth,' said Mr Taverner.

'But please all call me Katherine,' cried Mrs Cornforth, smiling round on them and taking Mrs Wheeby's woolly hand in her own. 'Hi, Sylvie! Mary! Come in, come in, supper's nearly ready . . . And this is Dicky,' to Mrs Wheeby, who had taken the cage from the more-than-willing Sylvia. 'Oh *can* we have him out to sing for us while we eat? Let me take him.'

Mrs Wheeby had painstakingly mustered her hostesses' names, making Wilfred give her instruction in how to pronounce, even to spell, them, with much comment upon the queerness of 'Dollette'. Now she came out unhurriedly with:

'Thank you, Mrs Cornforth. But as for having him out at supper – Oh and a Merry Christmas to *you*, and so kind of you to ask us all, especially when *one* is uninvited – I'm afraid it won't be Dicky's time until ten o'clock. You see, I have trained him very carefully and dare not break his routine' (pause, gasp). 'It's like a child – begin as you mean to go on.'

Slowly they all climbed the steps, Katherine going ahead.

'I *quite* understand. We'll all look forward to ten o'clock.'

'Merry Christmas – welcome,' said a low voice. Another woman stood in the doorway. The light fell on her shining hair and blue-green dress, against which she nursed a black cat. 'Mary – Sylvie dear – come in, come in. You must be cold . . .'

Mrs Wheeby's eyes became fixed on the cat even as she successfully brought out: 'Good evening, Miss Dollette,' on a gasp.

Mr Taverner said quickly: 'It's all right, Mrs Wheeby. Antony doesn't go for birds.'

'Well, I'll take your word for it, Mr Taverner, though I never met a cat yet who wouldn't, if it got the chance.'

They moved into the hall. The cat's green eyes were fixed steadily on the cage. In the background, Mr Taverner moved a finger, and the eyes blinked and glanced aside.

'Oil lamps! Well I never.' Mrs Wheeby's voice had a note that Wilfred had never heard in it – could it be delight?

Out of the corner of his eye he could see that Sylvie was looking sulky. *Doesn't like it*, he thought. *Instant TV and chips is more her mark. Hope she won't spoil things.*

He had introduced her to Mr Taverner as 'a friend of Mary's', and Mr Taverner had accepted her without comment as an extra guest.

'You'd like to see your rooms,' announced Mrs Cornforth. 'Dears –' to Mary and Sylvie, 'go straight upstairs. You'll see your names on your doors.'

'Mrs Wheeby, I thought you might be more comfortable without stairs to manage, so you're here –' turning to her. She led the way to a door opening off the hall, but almost immediately Mrs Wheeby stopped dead.

'Well I *never* did, I never *did*,' Mrs Wheeby said. 'Kichijoten, as sure as *my* name is Edith Wheeby. Now where in the world, Mr Taverner, did you get hold of *her*?'

'I bought her,' Mr Taverner answered at once; rather loudly, Wilfred thought. 'The – some – the authorities let me have her.'

The statue stood in a niche, instead of in her previous place by the front door; she was on a wooden pedestal enamelled in black and gold, and the additional height gave majesty to her sweet, calm, unsmiling expression. She looked down at them, benevolent yet apart.

'Well, you were lucky, very lucky, Mr Taverner. This house is full of things I never thought to see again.'

Mrs Wheeby moved on, and Katherine opened a door on a room that appeared to be furnished entirely with pillows, cushions and a puffy white bed.

Mr Taverner turned to Wilfred. 'I say, will you mind sharing? With a boy I asked along?'

'Of course not.' Wilfred was dismayed. *What sort of a boy?* But he reinforced his acceptance with a nod.

'He's up in one of the attics now, watching a football match. Come along. It's all right, you'll like him,' and he went up some stairs.

Wilfred followed, not at all sure that he would. Mr Taverner pulled aside a curtain of yellow brocade, shredded and faded at the edges, and a scent of fern came out, growing stronger as they went down a passage. He opened a low, yellow-painted door.

'If . . . we aren't comfortable in here, Mr Taverner, well, we ought to be,' said Wilfred, after a pause. 'Of course, I can't speak for *him*. But it's just my cup of tea. *And* a fire! But the work! I hope your ladies haven't been wearing themselves out?'

'No. Oh no. And we do have some help. A couple come in,' Mr Taverner assured him.

Wilfred was staring absently at one of the two wickerwork bedsteads, with their white quilts and eiderdowns covered in softly coloured patchwork. An extraordinary phrase had shot through his head. It had left a faint uneasiness, strengthening the oddity, the inexplicability, which had been teasing him. The phrase had been *a couple*. He turned to his host, and could not be certain whether or not the ghost of a smile was just passing from his face. *A couple of what?*

'Bathroom and loo in there.' Mr Taverner pointed to a curtained alcove. 'Now I'll leave you. Supper in the kitchen – you know your way, don't you? Take your time – nice to have you here.'

He nodded, smiled, and was gone.

Wilfred stood by the fire, looking down into the million-year-old enchantment of the flames. How quiet it was, and how odd he felt. But the oddness was familiar. He had experienced it before in the Yellow House.

At that moment, as if to remind him that he was in the real world, a diesel train thundered along the railway at the end of the Crescent.

Dismissing the sentence *a couple of what* as the memory of some silly joke, he crossed the carpet (just the colour of a yellow plum) and, going to the window, parted the curtains and looked out.

The light from the window shone downwards on withered ferns laden with snow, growing in a wall above water, rippling over bright brown and grey pebbles. The back of the Yellow House must overlook the Tor, he thought; yes, he could remember playing on its banks in the railway meadows, sixty years ago – nearly. Trains and tiddlers. He and his chums could have asked for no more. Those meadows had been perfect.

How clear the water was! Not a scrap of litter anywhere. He
dropped the curtains, and turned back to the wickerwork furniture, the white-rose walls, the soft, shabby comfort of his
bedroom. A pair of pyjamas on one of the beds caught his eye.
They had an air of good quality. But probably Mr Taverner
had lent them to this boy. Oh well . . . it might be all right . . .
How had Mrs Cornforth known Sylvie's name? He had introduced
Sylvie to Mr Taverner in his own hall as 'a friend of Mary's'.
There had been no telephone call by Mr Taverner to the Yellow
House between that and their leaving. Mr Taverner had not
shouted out, 'Katherine, here's Sylvie, a friend of Mary's', on
their arrival.

Mrs Cornforth's greeting – 'But please all call me Katherine –
Hi, Sylvie, Mary' – had been instantaneous with Sylvie's first
appearance.

And Miss Dollette. Miss Dollette, too, had said 'Mary
Sylvie dear – come in, come in.' She had known, as well.

He remembered so clearly – could in fact see the scene as if
it were a picture. The glowing house, the street lamps veiled
in drifting snow, the party getting out of the car.

'But please all call me Katherine . . . Hi, Sylvie, Mary.'

How – how on earth had she known?

'Well,' said Katherine eagerly to Mr Taverner in the hall, 'does
he like it?'

'I think so. Unfortunately, I made a gaffe.'

'Well thank goodness for once it was you, and not me . . .'

'You made one too, my sweet . . . a much worse one. Who
carolled out "Hi, Sylvie"?'

Mrs Cornforth's eyes widened and one ruby-ringed hand
flew to her mouth.

'Gosh I didn't!' she almost whispered.

'Gosh you undeniably did, dear Katherine . . . How does
Mrs Wheeby like hers? . . . Yes, yes, I'll tell you what *I* did
in a minute.'

'Oh, she loves it. But she can't call me Katherine.' Mrs Cornforth began to giggle. 'Most unfortunately, an aunt of her husband's had a really unpleasant daughter who was called Katherine and it's given her – Mrs Wheeby – a *dislike* of the name ever since. Nor could she *possibly* invite me to call her Edith (no reason given). But she hopes we may come to it. Now tell me what you did – quick.'

Mr Taverner told.

'I don't call that so bad, Laf. It sounds quite ordinary.'

'Unfortunately, I was also thinking.'

'Oh. Well.'

'And I'm pretty sure our dear man has started to think too in his way, of course. But he's started.'

'You be careful, then . . . oh . . .' she linked her arm in his. 'I love them all. I love them so much. *Aren't* we lucky?'

'We are. And you be careful too, Katherine, my sweetie-pie.'

Most of the time they were at supper, Mary was thinking about her bedroom.

She saw her bed, covered with a quilt of amber cotton and a dark red eiderdown, and the picture on the wall opposite: darkest blue irises, and their flat, greenish-blue leaves, and above them the kingfisher, so throbbing with the life and energy of spring that it seemed dancing in the air. It looked, to Mary, like a Japanese picture. She liked it very much.

She glanced across the table at Sylvie, who was sitting next to Mrs Wheeby (and no doubt Mary would hear plenty about that, after supper). Sylvie looked slightly dazed. Mrs Wheeby was placidly disposing of a mound of mashed potato.

Mary wondered if Sylvie liked her bedroom? Mary herself had only glanced in through the door, and had received an impression of pale mauve, a large record-player, a pile of records on the floor, and a gas fire roaring away as if preparing to blast off.

Sylvie had turned away from a last passionate inspection of herself in a long glass, and came undulating towards the door in red velvet trousers and a grubby white lace blouse.

'What say we 'ave a play of them records arter supper,' she began at once. 'We don't want to be with Grandma and that . . . lot.'

'I think they're nice,' Mary said in a low tone as they went downstairs. 'Mrs Cornforth's gorgeous.'

Sylvie gave a warning sniff. 'They'll be on at us. I bet yer.'

'No they won't, if you don't do anything to make them.'

'I never done nothing! What 'ave I done?' It was the usual whine.

'Oh Syl. I only said *don't* do anything.'

"Ere – like me blouse?' Sylvie twirled herself round, eyes glittering, as they paused outside the kitchen door.

'Smashing,' Mary said loyally.

'Tell yer sunnick.' Sylvie put her face closer, but, for the first time since she had known her, it did not seem ugly to Mary. "E give me that.'

A pause. 'That . . . boy? So you mean . . .'

''Oo d'ya think I meant?' A snap, and the face was drawn back.

'Well, *I* don't know, Syl, you—'

Mary checked herself; she had been going to say that she never knew how Sylvie felt about 'that boy', but what was the point in saying that? *She isn't so mingy since we got here*, decided Mary as they went into the kitchen.

The starched white cloth covering the long table touched the floor on all sides, and the china was blue and red. *Not posh*, thought Mary. I thought there'd be wine – Mr Taverner's a wine sort of man – but goody, we're having tea.

'What a nice kitchen,' she said sedately to Miss Dollette.

'I'm so glad you like it, dear. Will you ask Mrs Wheeby how she likes her tea? I'm afraid she won't hear me.' Mary thought so too; she could hardly hear Miss Dollette.

It was noisy, though agreeably so. Mr Taverner was saying something that made everybody laugh; Mrs Wheeby was announcing that she had never hoped to see an open range again in this world, and Mrs Cornforth, gesticulating with a spoon, was asking people how many sausages they could manage?

'You make it sound as if they were . . . horses,' said Wilfred daringly, at which everybody laughed, and Sylvie came out unexpectedly with 'Hope not,' and everybody laughed again.

Where's the boy? Wilfred wondered. *Cut supper to watch his football, I suppose. One of these young louts or soccer maniacs. Nice lookout for me.* But then he decided that even if his unseen stable-mate was a football maniac, Mr Taverner would know how to manage him.

Mrs Cornforth dominated the conversation . . . 'There I was on the pier with the lobster hanging onto my skirt . . . the fishermen were absolute lambs . . . so I treated us all to ice creams . . .' the stories floated on.

Miss Dollette, at the head of the table, occasionally murmured to Wilfred. Did he think the sausages were too highly flavoured? They came from a farm in Lincolnshire belonging to a friend of Mr Taverner's. What beautiful hair Mary had . . . Yes, she herself had arranged the mistletoe, Christmas roses and miniature gnomes in the middle of the table.

'I am *so* fond of gnomes,' said Miss Dollette.

Funny people. Nice people. Wilfred was tired by the unaccustomed voices and laughter – the company – after months of living alone.

He leant back for a moment, while Mr Taverner was assisting Mrs Cornforth in removing plates (the older guests had been forbidden to help), and looked dreamily down the long, brightly lit table and the smiling faces. He saw it, for a tiny flash of time, as a picture: a clear and happy picture. He liked them all, and the darling of his heart was beside him.

Outside the Yellow House, there was the snowy darkness over the sooty, littered fields; the crammed and snarling traffic; the millions of people who were vaguely unhappy. *Not much real happiness in this world,* he thought, *except here and there. In flashes, as you might say. In flashes.*

The pudding was treacle.

'I'm slimmin',' said Sylvie instantly.

'Right you are, apple or orange jelly?' Mrs Cornforth's question was carolled out almost before Sylvie's sentence was finished.

That's the style, thought Wilfred.

'Oh come on, Syl,' from Mary.

'All right – seein' it's Christmas.' Sylvie grinned suddenly, and Wilfred thought uneasily of the lecture Pat would have given her.

But how would the people in the Yellow House deal with someone who wanted to do something really bad? His thoughts, uncomfortable for a moment, turned again to the unknown boy.

'No washing-up for guests. Rule of the house,' proclaimed Mr Taverner, when the pudding had been eaten, deftly sliding himself between Mrs Wheeby and the door of the scullery (and that's a word I haven't used for a good many years, thought Wilfred). 'Won't you all come along?'

Sylvie paused in the hall, while the others were following Mrs Cornforth towards a door opened by Mr Taverner, revealing a room furnished in yellow and once bright, now faded, pink brocade. Sylvie caught at Mary's arm.

'Comin' upstairs? Play them records? We don't want to go sittin' round . . . be on at us about something, you see.'

'I want to be with Dad,' Mary answered in the same low tone. 'You go, if you want to . . . they won't mind.'

'They better not!' Sylvie flashed. 'See yer.'

She glided up the stairs, and Mary just caught the delighted, amused smile that Mrs Cornforth sent after her. *Liberty Hall. Suits me,* thought Mary, and settled herself on a tuffet, in front of a splendid fire, at her father's knee.

Sylvie went quickly up the stairs. The silence, and the golden glow from the walls, excited her, and she was full of good food. She found the door with 'Sylvie' so surprisingly running across it in silver writing – then paused.

Someone was using the record-player; she heard the familiar voices of the Seekers. *Cheek! Bloody cheek, and who could it be?* She flung open the door.

She stopped dead. A thin boy with limp dark hair to his shoulders was hunched before the fire, rocking in time to the sounds. As the door opened he looked up, and ceased to move. His expression changed. A mask seemed to come down, and he stared at her steadily. He did not speak.

'Well I'm buggered,' Sylvie said at last. 'Look 'oo's 'ere.'

There was silence. The voices howled on and the gas heater hissed. There was a sweet woody scent in the room.

'Wouldn't never a come if I'd known *you* was goin' to be 'ere,' Sylvie muttered at last, not moving from the door.

'Nor me neither,' he said hoarsely. 'Don't you worry. Never wanted to see you again, I didn't.'

She stared downwards, moving a foot to and fro.

'How'd you get 'ere, anyway?' she demanded at last.

'*He* picked me up. The long guy. In Veeley Road. Says he wants me to spend Christmas with him.'

'You seen 'im before?' she said sharply.

''Course I never seen 'im before. Come up in a car – bleedin' perfect stranger.'

'Veeley Road – that's all knocked down now,' she said, and the boy stared at her stonily.

'Tell me sunnick I don't know,' he said.

Sylvie moved slowly forward, drawn by the warmth from the fire.

'I come with a friend. *'E's* a friend of 'er dad's. The long one is, mean t'say,' she said slowly, watching him.

'S'pose it's a bloody coincidence, then. But it's funny. It's very funny. That's all I got to say. Last person in the world I expected to see,' Derek said.

'Last one yer wanted to, too. Go on, say it.'

'I never said that, Syl. I said . . . never expected to see you again. That's all.'

'Then I must be the last one you wanted to see – mustn't I?'

'Oh belt up.' He dropped his head onto his hunched knees and was quiet.

'Well, it's not me wot's going 'ome. Don't see why I should.' Her voice was a whine.

'And nor 'm I.' He raised his head. 'I been here since last night. I was here first.'

'An' sittin' in *my* room!' she suddenly almost shouted. 'Cheek!'

'I never knew it was yer room. *He* said, just make yerself at home, and I didn't want to see nobody, so I was having a bit of a look round, had me tea early, upstairs, took it up meself, and – and I come in 'ere.'

'You could see me name on the door, I s'pose.'

'Wasn't on the door.'

''Course it's on the door.' She whirled round and flung the door wide open. 'You blind or sunnick?'

'I never see it, Syl. The bleedin' door was 'alf open. And if I had I'd – I wouldn't have thought it meant *you* – I'd have thought it was just a – a sort of coincidence, like. 'Sides, it says "Sylvie". You used to be Sylvia.' His voice died off into a mutter.

Sylvie suddenly dropped onto the hearthrug; beside him, but at the other end.

'Funny kind of place,' she announced. 'Quiet. Tea wasn't too bad, I s'pose – did you 'ave any?'

'I told yer. Early.'

While they had been exchanging these sentences which suggested in pitch and intonation the noises made by two animals rather than the voices of human creatures, the Seekers had also been making their contribution to subhuman sounds.

''Erc –' said Sylvie in a minute after they had sat for some moments in silence staring at the floor. 'Let's 'ave another, shall we?' She began to turn over the pile of records. 'Wot you been up to since . . . two years, innit? I dunno . . . you was goin' in with Blakers, wasn't you?'

'He went bust,' said the boy sullenly.

'Then wot you do?' Sylvie put on a record and more sounds began.

'None o' your business . . . oh well, nothing much. Went around with Brian Holey and that mob.'

'In them 'ouses back of the 'ospital.'

'That's right.'

'They 'ad that groupie.'

'That's right. Doreen. Went off.'

'They arst me, but I wasn't 'aving any, thanks. Over Christmas, they said.'

He looked at her now, without lifting his head; then he said: 'Funny if you'd of gone with them and I been there.'

'Comes to the same thing, don't it . . . know wot? I ain't all that sorry to see a face I know.'

'Nor me, Syl,' he said, after a pause.

They said no more, but sat in the stifling heat, letting the waves of sound roll over them and stun them into a waking dream.

12

Christmas Day

On the evening of the third day, Wilfred acknowledged to himself certain feelings about the Yellow House. Certain *strangenesses*, that was the word, would not leave his mind. And they joined each other, as if making a chain. Or could it be an arrow – an arrow that pointed? And did it point in any direction? He didn't know. It only seemed to point to – strangeness. In the middle of the cheerfulness, and the little jokes, and the eating, and the helping, and the kindness, it would roll into the front of his mind. Not frightening; not threatening; not even demanding to be thought about. Just – strange.

Everyone got up late on Christmas morning. Wilfred breakfasted in the kitchen with Mary and Miss Dollette, and Mary made them both laugh with stories of Mrs Levy and her great-nephew, Artie.

No one went to church, although behind Mrs Wheeby's door about ten o'clock the sounds of a service being relayed from St Ethelburga's, Little Hudnut, could be heard: boys' voices soaring in 'O Come All Ye Faithful', and piercing through the thumping and wailing coming from Sylvie's room.

That boy did not seem so bad, to Wilfred, who had been aroused on the first night, just as he was dropping off, by slight sounds, and, turning a drowsy head, had seen a thin young silhouette with flowing hair peeling off its clothes in the moonlight.

The boy had apparently been still asleep when Wilfred got up on Christmas morning, but had lifted his head to mutter "Ullo – Merry Christmas', as Wilfred went out of the door. *Looks rather crushed*, the latter thought, hurrying downstairs towards a smell of bacon.

He had Mary to himself for the whole of Christmas morning in the room he had heard Miss Dollette call the drawing room. A coal fire burned in the gleaming grate; the flames ate voraciously yet lightly into the glittering jetty masses of coal that suggested precipices and crags to the dreaming eye; blue, green and orange flames, unchanged in the sixty-odd years that had passed since the six-year-old Wilfred had watched them in the little basket-grate in the cottage in Derby Row.

'Your Mr Taverner doesn't mind breaking the law, seemingly,' observed Mary, from her deep armchair opposite his own.

'What? Oh – the coal fire. Yes . . . funny.'

The strange wave, the pointing arrow, came singing softly forward in his mind. 'That law's been going for at least five years. I remember it being passed by the council . . . perhaps he doesn't know. I don't know how long he's been living here.'

'Doesn't care, more like. Oh well. Suits me,' said his daughter lazily. 'I should think he's like that.'

'Like what? Don't you like him, Mary?'

'Oh yes, I like him.' Mary paused, wearing her no-expression. 'He makes me laugh. – Dad . . .'

Her tone changed, and she sat up and leant forward. Her hair streamed smoothly down onto a dark green jersey. As usual she wore her medallion on its silvery chain, and her skirt was dark red, slit at the side to show a striped red and green petticoat, made from one of those rolls of material, salvaged from fire or flood, and bought occasionally at cost price by Mary's employer.

'It is good for trade that few girls know how to make petticoat nowadays,' Mrs Levy had observed sombrely, on parting with two yards of the striped stuff for fifty of Mary's pence. 'But I also think it good you sew, Mary. Is womanly.'

What a ghastly word, thought Mary, bestowing on Mrs Levy a grateful smile. *Who the hell wants to be womanly?*

Her father was thinking how charming she looked, and wondering uneasily if Mr Taverner, as well as living in a strange house, was – lawless. Lawless?

What secrets were singing under Mary's well-brushed hair? She looked as reliable as Her Majesty herself; but what was he about to hear?

'Not one single, solitary boy have I met in London that I'd give you *half a penny for*,' announced his child. 'Mind you, I haven't met many. Only a couple of Sylvie's (awful, *they* were, plain awful), and tourists coming into the shop. All sorts. Try it on if they get the chance, too. (Not all of them, 'course.) Mrs Levy's usually there, and she's very down on sex . . .'

'I don't see how you can say that, love.' Her father was a little embarrassed, but also flattered by the calm, woman-to-man tone. 'You can't have goings-on in the shop, you know.'

'Well, she is. Seems to think everybody wants to be at it all the time. Always on at me. *And* she's made me learn "Good morning, can I help you?" in five languages.'

'Well, that's good for business, you know, if you get a lot of tourists in. What languages? Say some, love.'

'Oh – some French I knew, of course – and some German, or half knew it. But Italian and Spanish and – just fancy – Japanese. *Japanese!* That really was the last straw. Thought I'd finished with school. I had to go to the Public Library.'

'Let's hear it – come on.' Wilfred leant forward eagerly. 'Say the Japanese one.'

Strange sounds came out onto the quiet air, where the silence was only deepened by the fluttering of the flames. They sounded odd indeed in the beloved, familiar voice. There was a pause.

Wilfred, strangely moved, turned away to look out of the long window curtained in faded pink brocade. Sparse flakes of snow, brilliant in the dark air, were falling singly. How quiet the house was! The snow was like a shower of white bells. And the peace! He wished the moment could last for ever.

'It's a queer sound. I've never heard Japanese spoken before,' he said at last.

'Nor me. I got a Japanese girl who came into the shop to correct my pronunciation. It's right now . . . I wonder if Sylvie's going to stay in bed all day? I'd like a walk.' She turned to glance out of the window.

It was only natural that she should want to be with those of her own age, yet how he wished that she would stay!

'Dad,' Mary leant forward again. 'You needn't worry about me. The house is all right where I'm living, and Mrs Levy's all right (a bit too all right, if you ask me) and . . . I'm all right. Really I am.' She looked at him affectionately.

'Then . . . you don't think of coming home, love?' he said timidly, after a pause, and she shook her head.

'I thought so.' He did not know what to say. He loved her so, his darling child. But what would her mother, with those plans for higher education and a really good job, have said?

'You know, love,' he blurted out at last . . . 'I'd feel just that much better if you'd let me have your real address.'

There. It was out. And surely it wasn't much to ask – most fathers . . .

Mary considered, and the snow bells drifted down, and Wilfred waited.

'All right,' she said at last. 'It's only fair, really. That one pound fifty has just made all the difference. Dad, you are an old dear.' And she got up and came over to him and put her arms round his neck and gave him a great kiss. 'Thanks a lot,' she ended.

Her father said: 'That's all right, love,' in a rather muffled tone. And then Mary said, 'I'll write it down now, while I remember,' and was feeling in her shoulder bag when the door opened and Sylvie's head, freshly goblined and gooed, came round the door.

''Ullo.'

'Hullo.' Mary had begun to write, and continued without looking up. 'Merry Christmas.'

"'Ere's Derek,' announced Sylvie, half turning to an impression of reluctance, shuffle, height and flowing hair behind her. 'Come on in – don't be shy,' with a shrieking giggle.

Then Mary did look up, saw a dark thin sulky boy and turned down a mental thumb at one glance, though she remembered her mother's training, and smiled and said: 'Hullo – Merry Christmas.'

The boy nodded.

Mary glanced at the window.

'Feel like a walk, Syl?'

'In the *snow?* You nuts? We come down see'f you'd come up and play some records. Comin'?'

'All right.' Mary smiled at her father and dropped an old envelope on the table beside him. 'See you, Dad.' She was off.

He leant back and watched the falling snow, now ordinary again; no longer brilliant in dark air, no longer like white bells; then glanced at the address she had scribbled. It made him feel a little nearer to her.

He ventured to break up a small piece of coal with a long brass poker. In the midst of which action, necessary to relieve his feelings, Mrs Cornforth came in, smiling to see him thus engaged.

Katherine's reddish hair flowed about her face; her housecoat of thin red cloth moulded her statuesque shape. The room was pleasantly warm, yet surely it was warmer since she had come in? (The wave, the arrow, moved stealthily forward again in his mind.)

'Have you seen Mrs Wheeby this morning?' he asked, forcing the feelings away from him.

'Oh yes, I looked in on her after breakfast. She's enjoying herself.' Katherine nodded, her large dark eyes dwelling on his – affectionately?

'Oh – I'm – I'm glad to hear that. You see, the fact is, I was certain Mary would enjoy it here because she and I like the same kind of people and places . . . I wasn't quite sure about Mrs Wheeby.'

'She's pure gold and steel.' Katherine came forward and sat down in the chair Mary had occupied. 'A marvellous mixture.'

'And . . . I was just a bit afraid . . . she doesn't get on your nerves?'

'I have no nerves,' said Mrs Cornforth. 'I ride on Life, and the bigger the waves the more I enjoy them.'

'That's wonderful,' he said softly, watching a face that seemed to him as beautiful in its way as Mary's.

'Is it?' She smiled mischievously. 'Don't let Laf hear you.'

'Why? . . . Doesn't he – approve?'

Katherine shrugged, and her smile faded.

Wilfred was not unaccustomed to being alone with women, and talking to them. There were Pat's friends: bright-natured women, slightly overweight by modern standards, who joked about diets, and tried to diet and failed, and tried again; loyal friends; good citizens; kind, firm mothers who managed their husbands and the family income with success. He listened, rather than talked, when he chanced to meet one out shopping or give one a lift in the car. Sometimes they had *a bone to pick with him*, and said so, and Wilfred disliked bones. It had sometimes seemed to him that these bones were too small to be of importance, and had been disinterred because Pat's friends enjoyed lecturing a man and telling him what he ought to do.

He was not accustomed to sitting alone, in silence, with women like Mrs Cornforth . . .

If there were any other women like Mrs Cornforth.

The thought came with the wave–arrow sensation before he could check it. *She was not like any woman he had ever met or ever seen – except in certain pictures. That was it – in certain pictures.* The Belle Dame who leans sideways on the knight's charger in that forgotten Edwardian painting; the red-haired girl, drowsy with love, caught up in the shepherd's arms in *An Idyll*; the women in other drawings by Maurice Greiffenhagen, who illustrated the books by Rider Haggard that Wilfred had taken out from the Public Library when he was fifteen. *A picture-woman; that was it; a romantic, beautiful, unreal picture-woman.*

He must say something; the silence was becoming embarrassing.

'I hope you'll let Mary and her friend help with all these fires, Mrs Cornforth,' he said, clearing his throat and summoning all his social sense. 'What a terrible lot of work fires make!'

Katherine roused herself, smiling.

'That's sweet of you. I'll certainly ask them, if we get desperate. But I think we can manage – we have a couple who – who live quite near and come in at the crack of dawn – as *if* dawn cracked, you know; it ought to creep! They get us started for the day. You see, I thought Mary and that little goblin friend of hers might like a real *laze*. I know girls are strong; one forgets *how* strong; but they haven't got their full strength in their late teens, and Sylvie looks half starved.'

'More than I can say for Mary,' and he laughed. 'Though she's lost weight. That's London, I expect, and being on her own.'

'But I expect she looks after herself sensibly, doesn't she? I feel she *is* very sensible – and so beautifully calm. One hardly ever sees a *calm* girl nowadays; it isn't a fashionable quality, of course. You're her father, Mr Davis –' Katherine leant forward, with bright, dwelling eyes. 'Is she really calm? Inside, I mean? Or is it a mask?'

At that moment Miss Dollette came in, and Wilfred turned to meet her smile with a feeling of relief.

If Mrs Cornforth made him think of a picture-woman, turning the air warmer with her colours, Miss Dollette was like a – a snowdrop.

13

Enter the hero

The room was the best in the house: the largest and the quietest. Forty acres of garden and cultivated land absorbed the ceaseless roar of traffic.

It was also the only room into which no hint or suggestion of the West had been allowed to intrude.

Its shutters, open to let in the radiance of full summer, filtered the light to a golden glow, reflected from the pale matting. Bright reds and violets glowed in the picture above the shrine, and the air was very warm because, in spite of the morning's heat, a charcoal fire glowed in its pot.

Great-grandfather, once a sailor who had fought at Port Arthur against the Russians and who had risen to the rank of Admiral, was now ninety-three, and head of the family of Tasu, and he felt the cold.

Yasuhiro knelt with hands laid flat on his thighs and his eyes lowered. He could see the pallor of the matting, the dark greens and shining greys of the garden, glowing beyond the open shutters.

As always in this silent room with its sacred memories, he felt that he was two people: Yasuhiro Tasu who had grown up in an exquisitely ordered world ruled by Great-grandfather's thin, remote yet loving voice; but also a graduate of Tokyo University who rushed about on a motorcycle, and sat chattering with girls in coffee bars. The student Yasuhiro felt slightly self-conscious in the dark blue robe embroidered with storks which had been Honourable Great-grandfather's parting gift. He would be relieved to get back into shirt and jeans.

He was just beginning to feel slightly cramped (or bored, if he told himself the undutiful truth) when Great-grandfather spoke.

'I could say many things for your instruction, but time is short. (It has been short, to me, since The Ending – yet too long.) All I have to say to you is this: do not return to the home of your ancestors with a demon-woman as your chosen wife.'

Yasuhiro bowed his head in surprised silence.

He too felt the disgrace of The Ending, the defeat of Japan in 1945, and the descent of the Divine Emperor to the status of an ordinary man. He felt it proudly and keenly, but not of course with the perpetual shame and despair with which it afflicted the ancient spirit of Honourable Great-grandfather. Yasuhiro had not been born when the bomb fell on Hiroshima. It was the reference to his possible wife, not to what Great-grandfather called The Ending, that had surprised him.

He moved his young body stealthily inside the stiff, archaic robe. Great-grandfather's idea of honour was an older one than his great-grandson's, though a branch of the same tree.

'May I speak, Honourable Great-grandfather?'

'Speak, dear one.'

The head, suggesting that of a tortoise, inclined slightly forward above the silvery-grey robe, in an effort to concentrate the hearing, while the heavy lids lifted slightly to focus the failing sight.

'This dutiful one,' said Yasuhiro, keeping his voice on its deepest note when it attempted to slide up into a boyish squeak, 'seeks only to improve his English.'

No answer.

'Not to . . . find a wife.'

No answer.

'On his journey to Britain, Honourable Great-grandfather. I mean . . . this dutiful one means . . .'

'I know that,' said the old man at last. 'But young men's eyes are young. And their hearts.'

'This one . . . this dutiful one knows well . . . in the small time that he has given to the matter between his studies . . . what kind of woman he will choose. When the time comes . . . This dutiful one is not yet twenty years old, Honourable Great-grandfather,' Yasuhiro ended, almost pleadingly.

'And his body is virgin.' It was a statement, in the thin, authoritative voice.

Yasuhiro bowed his head. 'And his body is virgin.'

He had had his own strong, secret reasons for keeping it so.

'Therefore –' Honourable Great-grandfather was saying, in a voice in which austerity battled with sleepiness, 'keep heart and eyes to heel, as a good dog keeps.'

'Sure, Honourable Great-grandfather.'

'"Yes" will do,' snapped Great-grandfather, suddenly wide awake at the Americanism. 'And now go. The plane – the Sky Dragon –' he laughed sarcastically, 'awaits you. The United States' (he always gave them the full name) 'likes to think that these picturesque names linger in our simple Japanese hearts. They are mistaken. Go. And mind that you write to me – *not* postcards. Letters.'

'Of course, Honourable Great-grandfather.'

Yasuhiro lifted his head, and for a moment the clear dark young eyes looked into the old filmed ones. Then Yasuhiro bowed once, rose, and deftly went out of the room, still bowing, and backwards.

Fifteen minutes later, in white shirt, jeans and jacket, he was edging his way through the fierce traffic on his Honda, rucksack on back, with the memory of his sisters' laughing faces and his mother's plump, rueful one, fading from his mind's eye. Europe, the West, lay before him.

But always he was thinking: *I am Mishima.*

14

The explanation

The night before the house party broke up, everybody except Wilfred went to see a pantomime called *Pull in Hot Pants*, put on by the local repertory company. He had said that he felt like a quiet evening and an early night.

The truth was that he wanted what he thought of as 'a long think' – an exercise (unless it was concerned with strictly practical affairs) with which he was not familiar.

But he did not begin it at once, as he sat before the fire in the drawing room, enjoying the first moment of quiet that followed the shutting of the front door. He . . . didn't want to begin.

So he leant back in the deep chair, conscious of the silence. The lamp on the table beside him was turned low, the faded pink of the walls glowed softly, he had his pipe going, and a packet of Old and Sweet given to him by Mrs Wheeby for Christmas.

It's no use, I've got to think it out, he decided, settling his head into the cushion. *Here goes.*

There's Mr Taverner's way of talking; he's said some funny things, very funny, since I've known him. 'I spent a lot of time and some trouble,' about that statue of Kichijoten, and 'I'm glad you like it. I made it,' about that kitchen chair. (And *I've* seen no sign of carpentry about, though of course he might have made it some time ago. That's possible.) . . . The breath of warm air – almost like a kiss – that had touched his cheek, wafted by Mrs Cornforth's hand on that first evening as she had said goodnight to him. And the clearness of the Tor, unfrozen, running below his bedroom window – seen with his *own* eyes, through his *own* glasses. But the . . . the . . . *real* Tor, inspected by himself during a walk over the railway meadows taken yesterday for his health's sake, had been fouled by ancient rags, old tyres, rusty tins and plastic containers.

And above every other odd circumstance, there was the . . . the *atmosphere* surrounding these three people living in the Yellow House. *Not ordinary people, not ordinary types at all,* mused Wilfred, frowning at the sleepy fire. *They don't argue; they don't snap; everything seems to glide along with little jokes, as if . . . as if . . . I suppose if Paradise was real and I got there, it would be like it is here . . . in a way . . .* And then there was what had happened last night . . .

Mrs Wheeby had gone to bed early. The others had been playing a cheerful game of poker in the drawing room (Mary showing a surprising capacity for bluffing) when Wilfred had had occasion to go out to the lavatory opening off the hall; and on his way back, he had paused for a moment to listen to the sounds made by Mrs Wheeby's whales. Evidently she had decided to enjoy their voices before going to sleep, and the particular ululation now cascading down the staircase was that part of their singing which always seemed to call to Wilfred most strongly.

He was standing, listening, looking absently at the expanse of yellow wall directly above the staircase. The watery inhuman sounds were swooping on their way. Suddenly, he saw a great shadow come gliding out onto the wall: dark, humped, unmistakable in shape – it could be nothing else in the world. And its blue-blackness dimmed the light of the hall into a mysterious soft gloom. *It was more than a shadow.* It moved onwards. It seemed that it would never end. The blunt snout went over the edge of the wall and disappeared (where?) and the great body glided on – on – until, while he watched in a trance of wonder and awe, there appeared what he had known, from the shadow's first appearance, that he would see – the fins. They gave a quick upward jerk that implied enormous strength, then followed the bulk of the body – away, simply away, out into nowhere.

Wilfred sat down on the stairs, trembling.

The benevolent, detached gaze of Kichijoten met the stare of his own: no help there. Had he had too much alcohol during the last three days? (Certainly, he had drunk more than he usually did.) Was it indigestion? Was he developing an uncontrolled imagination in this Yellow House, under the influence of his unusual new friends?

There might be everyday explanations for all the other small oddities that had struck his notice. There might. But this – this was utterly different. This was very, very strange indeed.

Now he sat, puffing at his pipe. The peace in the dim room, with the scent of fern that haunted the whole house, was strong and comforting . . . oh, the place was peace itself, and yet –

What was going on in this Yellow House where everyone was happy and kind?

His long thinking had answered nothing.

He sat up, knocking out his pipe. *It's no use*, he decided. *I'll have to ask him. Get him alone somehow, and ask him.*

The next morning they were all going home. For the last few hours everyone did what they pleased. Derek had shown a wish to spend every minute, when not eating or sleeping, under Mr Taverner's car out in the garden. But Sylvie had continually importuned him – to come and play records, to scuffle on the sofa in the drawing room, to watch television in the attic, even to admire her in the ankle-length, Kate-Greenaway-type dress given to her for Christmas by Mrs Cornforth.

'Smashing,' Sylvie had breathed, for once betrayed into admiration by the cream-coloured folds and the soft greens and blues of the pattern, and the low neck. ''Ow'd yer know me size?' as she eagerly pulled it over her head. 'S'just right.'

'Oh . . . my great-grandmother was your size,' Mrs Cornforth had laughed.

'I bet,' retorted Sylvie, twisting about in front of the long
glass. 'I bet it cost yer a packet, too.'

Mrs Cornforth had smiled. Miss Dollette, who was assisting
at the display as admirer, looked tired this morning, but Sylvie
did not notice when people looked tired. 'Thanks,' she added,
as an afterthought.

Now, in the middle of the morning, she and Mary were in
the latter's bedroom looking through a wardrobe full of old
dresses, richly embroidered ribbons and ancient hats. Sylvie was
wearing the dress. They were trying on the clothes, though
Mary frequently had to recall Sylvie from the window where
she could see Derek's legs emerging from under the car.

'Do leave him alone, Syl, if he's happy.' Mary felt strong
sympathy for Derek.

"'Appy! Muckin' about with that old crock in the snow!'

'Well, if he likes it . . .'

'And the other one – makin' a snowman like some great kid.
Off their trolleys, if you arst me, both of 'em.'

'No more than trying on hats.'

Mary solemnly balanced a mighty creation of 1902 on her
head. Deprived of the padded, back-combed hair that had once
balanced it, it fell over her eyebrows, and there were shrieks
of laughter.

Then, in her turn, Mary wandered across to the window.

She was a little fascinated by Mr Taverner: his lankiness, his
kindness, his odd way of talking. Mrs Cornforth came easily
under the heading *gorgeous* – clothes, face, manner, ruby, hair-
do and all – while Miss Dollette was merely nice (the precise
word for her, though not as Mary used it). Mr Taverner was
both *nice* and interesting. Old, of course, but undoubtedly
interesting.

Mary pushed up the window and leant out into the pale,
sparkling light.

'Who's that, Mr Taverner?' She was yielding to the first
impulse of coquetry felt in her life – and she also felt vaguely
that Mr Taverner was *safe*.

'Snubbia. Goddess of Common Sense. Come down and see,' he called, looking up and smiling.

Neither Derek nor Mr Taverner looked up from their tasks as the girls picked their way across the frozen snow. Mr Taverner, wearing an old battledress and balaclava helmet, was vigorously shaping a snowman; while Derek, lying on a space cleared of snow by himself that morning, was only half visible under Mr Taverner's car. He was surrounded by a number of large and small pieces of metal, the mere sight of which caused a sensation of boredom in both girls so strong as to be almost pain. Tools and metal fragments were arranged, with care, on an old piece of dirty, greasy rag.

Well, I shouldn't look up if I were sewing the corner on a square neck, like the one Sylvie's dress has, thought Mary, excusing the males' absorption by reference to her own experience.

She admired Sylvie's dress, but she thought Sylvie looked downright dotty in it. She did not want it for herself.

Small, continuous and very bitter, like chips of aspirin chewed every hour for four years or so, had been Mary's struggles to give up the wish to dress like other girls – so bitter that now the sight of crochet jackets, shapeless, pseudo-Victorian skirts, Afghan coats and cloaks still gave her a sharp little inward pain.

But the robes of the Japanese ladies, in the pictures on the walls of her room at the Yellow House, gave her a pleased interest. Dark blue as the evening sea, flowing like its waves. What woman could look anything but romantic in those folds?

She paused beside Mr Taverner, while Sylvie strolled on towards Derek.

'Called Snubbia because she snubs the operatic types, don't you know,' confided Mr Taverner, looking up with a smile. 'Do you like her?'

The figure was naked to her sturdy waist. Mr Taverner had put a necklace of wooden beads, of a warm pinkish brown, about her round neck. Her hair was pulled back into a knot

exactly on the lower part of her skull, that most difficult place
to fasten a woman's hair.

'The Goddess of Common Sense!' Mr Taverner was laughing. 'I think she ought to be called Mary . . . How about a
snow-fight? I want some exercise.'

He turned towards Derek. 'Derek – want a snow fight?'

Sylvie was looking down at Derek's legs, all her features
seeming to pout forward in a mask of sulky resentment. She
stood as motionless as Snubbia herself, staring downwards.
Her hair glinted green in the sunlight.

'Sylvie? How about it?' Mr Taverner called.

Derek wriggled backwards far enough to get his head out.
'Nope,' he said, with decision, and wriggled back again.

Sylvie moved forward. She extended a thin leg, veiled in
the muslin of her new dress, and slowly dragged the hem
across the array of metal objects and gleaming tools, so that
they swirled away after it into confusion, falling into the snow.

"Ere!' Derek came out quickly from under the car again, his
face white with rage. 'What the hell are you doing? I just got
all that straight.'

'Too bad.' Sylvie gave her malicious giggle, and sauntered
away.

In three steps Mary had caught up with her, whispering
angrily: 'Syl! You fool! Just when you were getting on with
him. 'Sides, what a rotten dirty trick.'

'Oh, —' It was the strongest expression Sylvie had ever
launched at Mary, and she jerked herself violently away. You
'ave 'im – since you're so mad about 'im.'

Then she was off. She glided away, with her stealthy cat's
gait that always suggested suspicion and concealment, and
disappeared into the house.

Mary stood looking foolishly about her. Mr Taverner came
across, leisurely brushing snow from his hands.

'So that's that,' he observed. 'Pity.'

'You don't mean – she hasn't *gone*, has she?' demanded
Mary, startled.

'Oh yes. In a minute or two you'll hear the front door slam.'

'But that – that's *crazy*,' Mary stammered.

She looked about her as if for help; the sun had come out fully, and the snow sparkled and the trees glittered under the deeper blue of the sky. Snubbia's round, calm face, with the hint of a smile on her full lips, seemed to be saying: 'Really! How unkind and silly. But that's how some people are.'

'She can't just go off—'

'Oh yes she can. (You mean that *you* couldn't't, because of manners, and feeling sorry, and all kinds of reasons.) Yes, she's gone, and you won't see her again for a – you won't see her again.'

'Not – even in London? Where we live?' Mary asked like a child, staring up at his long lean figure silhouetted against the sky.

'She may drop in there to pick up her things. But she won't be there when you get back.'

'It's *sickening*,' Mary said, anger and disappointment, as always, making her sullen. 'And I sort-of-feel-it's-my-fault –'

'Well, you will, of course,' lightly.

'They seemed to be getting on so nicely. I thought everything was going to be all right.' She hesitated. 'He was the one, you know . . . they . . .'

'I know.' Mr Taverner nodded.

'I wanted them to get married!' she burst out, but keeping her voice low as she glanced at the long legs protruding from under the car, and was not soothed when Mr Taverner laughed and said:

'*You* want to get married, you mean. But not Derek and Sylvia – to each other. He'll be all right, dear. You must think of him as . . . *all right* . . . Let's go and comfort ourselves with another look at Snubbia, shall we?'

Snubbia's breasts were those of a young mother, heavy yet firm. Her necklace and her nipples were the same warm colour. Mary's feelings calmed as she looked at her.

'Wish I had a photo of her,' she said suddenly. 'It'd cheer me up when – this sort of thing happens.'

'We'll try,' Mr Taverner said, and was halfway to the kitchen door before she could speak again.

He came back with an Instamatic, and took two photographs. Mary thought that Derek was watching the happenings from beneath the car, but he did not come out.

'There.' Mr Taverner put the camera away. 'Your father can send it on to you . . . By the way, do you think he'd like to come and live with us?'

'Here, do you mean? At . . . the Yellow House, as he calls it?' Mary's mouth stayed open, in her surprise.

'Well, it is yellow. Yes. Do you think he would? He's got to find somewhere, you know . . . would *you* like him to live here?

He had begun to stroll back to the house and she had fallen into step beside him.

'I don't know,' she said at last. 'I don't much mind our old house going. It . . . isn't the same without Mum.' She paused. 'What I'd like best is for Dad to have a flat here, and then I could come and stay sometimes – in Torford – I mean. It's grand here – in this house, I mean, Mr Taverner. I do like it. It's been a super Christmas, really it has. But I'd like . . . our own home . . . if you understand.'

She glanced at him.

'I do understand. But if I ask him to come, and he wants to, but won't because of keeping a home for you somewhere, will you say you don't mind?'

She was silent.

'Well!' exclaimed Mr Taverner, 'if I tell you that in six months you'll be married to someone you love, and who loves you, "with a serious and unchanging love", as a friend of mine once beautifully said – *then* will you say you don't mind?'

'It's like fortune-telling,' said Mary, with a shake of her head. 'How can you possibly tell, Mr Taverner?'

'Well . . . you think I can't, of course. You think I was only trying it on . . . But will you? He'll be painfully lonely, all by himself.'

'He'll have Mrs Wheeby and Dicky and the whales.'

Mary felt that the conversation had got rather beyond her, and she wanted to get into the house and to make certain that Sylvie really had gone.

'I'll tell him that you think he'll be very happy here, then,' Mr Taverner said calmly, and he shut the kitchen door behind them, to which Mary answered, feeling defeated and wanting to change the subject: 'Have you studied sculpting, Mr Taverner?'

'No, Mary, I haven't . . . I say, I could do with some tea and hot buttered toast, couldn't you?' He was laughing as he turned away.

Mary went upstairs to Sylvie's room, regretting that she had not run after her at once.

No goblin head was lifted from the pillow of the unmade bed, though the gas fire was roaring as usual. The drawers were pulled out and empty, the wardrobe doors gaped wide; there was no sight of the airliner bag with the broken zip. Not a shred of anything remained to prove that Sylvie Carano had ever been in the Yellow House, except the presence of a scent, cheap and pungent, named 'B.B.'

Derek, summoned to tea and toast from beneath the car, stood by the kitchen table gulping and chewing and staring absently at the wall.

'Well, and haven't you anything to say about it, young man?' demanded Mrs Wheeby. 'She was your "girlfriend", wasn't she? Going off like that, ungrateful little monkey.'

Derek shrugged. He had one thought in his head: how would he get back to London? He had no money. Not just a few new pence; *no money*. Not one new halfpenny. And if he did manage to hitch-hike, where would he go?

They wouldn't have him back: he couldn't go back to the rooms darkened by rags at the windows and the wildly danger-ous fires blazing in the grates too small for them, and the icy wind pouring down through the holes the mob had knocked in the roof for a giggle . . . until the navvies and the guard dogs had come. He wanted to think about that bit of bother in the

1938 Renault's engine; that was interesting, that was; but you always had some bloody thing on your mind . . .

'I spoke to you,' Mrs Wheeby said, 'and you heard me, I'm sure. You remind me of my cousin's—'

'She's always goin' off,' he muttered. 'Run off from home, run off from our mob. She's off her trolley.'

Mary, who was sitting at the table looking sulky, said: 'I'll be seeing her when I get back, I expect,' for she did not believe her host's airy prophecy. 'Any message?'

'Nope.'

Mary slowly went deep pink. 'She's on her own. She didn't mean . . .'

'Well,' announced Mrs Wheeby, setting down her cup, 'that was very welcome, thank you Miss Dollette. All good things must come to an end, and we should be making a move, and Dicky's all ready in the hall. I was careful to dust your record-player, Mr Taverner, and I put the duster back on the bookshelf in its place. Thank you for the loan of both. A great pleasure; I'm sure my whales appreciate the use of such a fine machine. Well, Mr Davis, Mary, I'm sure you're all packed and ready, aren't you?'

There was general bustle, and everyone moved into the hall.

'Oh – my toothbrush!' exclaimed Wilfred, pausing.

'Dad, you are the limit! I'll get it.'

'No, love.' He lowered his voice. 'You give Mrs W. a hand. I'll go – really –'

He was whistling under his breath as he reached the landing; really, it had been a . . . a lovely little holiday . . . and Mary was coming on so nicely . . . a good thing that other little piece had taken herself off . . .

He went quickly along the passage. Some of the bedroom doors stood open, and as he passed them he glanced in, partly instinctively, and partly because – he admitted the impulse – here were rooms he hadn't seen in the Yellow House.

One room, furnished in a style that instantly suggested Katherine Cornforth, was full of sunlight, blazing up from

the dazzling snow. He noticed the low, wide bed covered in
crimson, the dressing-table crowded with glittering bottles,
the dark shining furniture – vaguely, because his eyes were
drawn to the fireplace.

Something was moving there. The grate had been cleared of
last night's ashes and was ready for the laying of today's fire.
And in front of it . . . the sunlight was so glaring . . . he
could hardly see . . . in front there crouched *two things* . . . were
they dwarfs? Brown children? . . . *What* were they?

The light hurt his eyes. He peered, suddenly very cold, and
the things turned their faces . . . were they faces or masks,
brown masks? . . . toward him, mischievously smiling.

They were naked, male and female; and there was a rudimentary quality, that was yet not repulsive, about testicle and breast.

Then they had gone. The sun poured into the low, wide,
rich room scented with fern. There lay the coal in its metal
bucket, and the bundles of freshly chopped wood; and that
was all.

He turned and went back along the corridor, cold and
shaking.

They aren't evil, he thought, over and over again; *not evil.*
That's all I'm sure of. Not evil – so long as someone can control them.
But what, in God's name, is going on here?

He descended the stairs slowly, to give himself time to
recover. Just halfway, he found himself looking down into the
lifted face of Mr Taverner. No expression beyond the mild
concern of a host for a departing guest's welfare. None.

'All clear?' Mr Taverner drawled, and Wilfred nodded. He
remembered the toothbrush above the basin in his bedroom. It
would have to stay; he was not going upstairs again.

They went out into the snowy light under the azure arch
of the sky, and Mrs Wheeby exclaimed to see an unusually
large car, mint-new and precisely the colour of crème caramel,
drawn up beside the gate.

'*Cor!*' breathed Derek, who had loitered in the wake of the
party. 'Where'd you whip that, Laf?' His face was transformed.

'Hired it – since the innards of mine are all over the garden. In you get, loves –' addressing them collectively as he opened the back door of the car. 'You'll give Miss Dollette a hand with the potatoes, won't you?'

Derek went straight to the kitchen, still thinking about getting back to London. Whip something and sell it? Miss Dollette was alone in the house now . . . Something stopped the idea before it took shape.

'Oh . . . Derek – would you very kindly peel the potatoes for me?'

Miss Dollette's voice was almost inaudible; so faint that he noticed it even in his preoccupation. He glanced at her.

'You all right, Miss?' he demanded. 'You aren't half white – your face, like.'

'Oh yes . . . yes, thank you . . . perfectly all right, it's just . . .'

''Ere,' said Derek, as a thought struck him that he did not like at all. 'You aren't – well, a bit scared like of me, are you, Miss? I mean, us being alone, and that?'

It was odd to see Miss Dollette's amused smile on her pallid face, and he was not sure that he liked the implication either. She shook her head, so that its wheat-coloured, silver-streaked hair slipped about.

'Oh *no*, dear boy, of course not. You couldn't hurt anyone,' she said, low and rapidly.

'I'm not soft, you know,' he tried to growl. It would never do to tell her about the groupie, and sleeping in ruined rooms, and hunger, and small thefts, and being dropped by your mob.

'You aren't soft at all; you're rather brave, as people go,' she went on, still very quickly. 'No – it's just that I have something to ask you, and it's enjoyable – that is, I think you'll be pleased – and it's so *very* difficult . . . for me to talk to people unless I – I know them very well, you see.' She stopped.

'Here, I'd best get on with those potatoes,' Derek said, pushing up his sleeves and turning to the sink. He began to peel the skin off in chunks.

'Mr Taverner – thought it would be good for me to tell you, you see. *Ask* you (oh dear, I *am* so bad with words and people. Now if you were a *bulb* or a *shrub* –)'

Derek suddenly gave a loud, boy's guffaw without turning round, a completely different sound from the sneers and sniggers and mindless roars uttered by the mob; a childish pleasure in sheer silliness sounded in it.

'If I was, I couldn't peel these here potatoes, could I? Look funny, that would, a bulb peeling –' he laughed again.

'You *aren't* peeling them, you're – my dear boy! Thinly, *thinly* – here –' Miss Dollette came over to him, distractedly sweeping aside hair from her brow. 'Let me show you.'

'No, I'll manage – thanks. What is this bit o' good news, then?'

'Well,' she was back at the kitchen table now, with her hands in the pastry bowl. 'How would you like to go and work with a friend of Laf's? He lives in a little seaside town in Wales. He's nice. He's married, with a baby boy. Would you like it?'

He turned, letting the knife sink into the mess of skins and potatoes in the basin. He looked full at her, and his eyes were suspicious, and behind the suspicion was the child's longing and instinct to believe.

'Is that on the straight?' he asked, surlily at last.

She nodded.

'I ain't – I've got no money, Miss.'

'That's all right. Laf will drive you down. And Tim Stanton – that's his friend – will pay you a week in advance.'

'And I'm not trained, not proper. But there was a chap I was going in with, to help in his garage. He went broke, but he always said I had a gift for cars, like. Come natural, he used to say.'

'Then do go!' she exclaimed. 'I – I like so much to think of you working with cars and enjoying it.'

'I thought you didn't like cars, Miss.' He smiled, teasingly, as the excitement rose in him. 'And I've no overalls.' He spoke solemnly, as if confessing some secret crime.

'We'll buy you some, Derek. Really we will. Oh *do* say you'll
go. It's just the right thing for you – I'm certain of it. I – I
see you there.'

So did Derek. The child's imagination in him, blessedly sur-
viving five years of artificial manhood, ran towards a vision of
screws, little bolts, nuts, jacks, brick Volkswagens and ageing
beauties made by Rolls-Royce, oil, and bright mornings, and
himself smart as a new spanner in his overalls. The air smelt
of the sea.

'All right,' he said, turning back to the murdered potatoes.
'I'll buy it. You tell Laf when he comes in.' His voice was flat
and rather bored.

Then he turned quickly, staring. Something warm, like a
kiss, had touched his cheek; and Miss Dollette was standing there laughing, minute floury hands palm to palm in a
soundless clap.

Outside Lamorna the car was being slowly emptied of
Mrs Wheeby, Dicky, Mary and Wilfred.

Wilfred glanced at Mr Taverner, who was arming
Mrs Wheeby up the slippery path to the front door.

'Give her a hand upstairs, love,' he said in an undertone to
Mary. 'I want a word with Mr Taverner.'

Having run up the stairs with cases and Dicky, and paused
at the door to say something that left Mary giggling and
Mrs Wheeby wheezing in a way that suggested laughter,
Mr Taverner came lightly down the path. He was smiling.

Pale and disturbed, Wilfred stood by the car, waiting. And
how, in the name of heaven and earth, and he hoped no further,
was he going to begin?

He swallowed, and said quickly: 'Can I have a word with
you?'

'Of course. Get in, won't you – it's nippy.'

They settled themselves side by side; the great car smelt
faintly of the man-made substances covering the seats, but
Wilfred was at once aware of another smell – oh, he knew, he

knew – fern. It stole over his senses like music. Mr Taverner turned attentively towards him.

A prolonged pause.

'It's so *difficult* –' Wilfred broke out at last.

'Well, perhaps I can give a hand . . . would it clear things up at all if I told you that our Yellow House is supposed to be haunted – always has been?'

Wilfred stared at him. Yes, it would clear 'things' up; of course it would; *but was it true?* The smile that had just hovered on the mouth and luminous eyes had vanished. *Grave as a judge*, thought Wilfred resentfully.

'Not by the usual miserable "ghost",' Mr Taverner went on, oh so lightly. 'But by odd happenings; slipping back into the past; memories?'

'Yes.' Wilfred nodded.

Yes, that could account for . . . yes, he supposed so.

'*I* never heard anything about its being haunted,' he said at last, with a touch of sulkiness. 'And I've lived in Torford all my life.'

'*I* don't know . . . everything . . . about it,' and Mr Taverner's tone was unmistakably final, and one hand moved towards the dashboard, 'but people who've lived there have had peculiar experiences. Nothing unpleasant. Just . . . peculiar.'

'Have – any of you?'

'Lord, yes!' Mr Taverner said heartily. 'Very rum indeed.'

Another pause. Wilfred knew that the natural thing would be for him to ask what experiences, and in what way were they rum?

I don't *want* to know what's going on there, he thought suddenly. Let it *be* haunted. He felt helpless, and bewildered, and longed to get quickly into Lamorna with Mary, and Mrs Wheeby and Dicky, and the dusty unused gadgets, and the whales safely *imprisoned in their gramophone record.*

'Well, thanks for putting that straight,' he said at last, managing to smile. 'I – don't think I'll bother telling you what I did see – or thought I saw.'

Mr Taverner nodded, all soothing attention.

'So – well – thank you all again for a very happy Christmas. It . . . I mean I was dreading being alone . . . you know . . . for Mary, I mean. The first time after her mother passed on.'

'We've all loved having you.' Mr Taverner's smile had come back. 'I'll ring you soon, and a happier New Year.'

Wilfred was outside again; the door was shut. Mr Taverner lifted a hand and smiled, and the great crème caramel glided away under his expert control.

'What was all that about?' Mary asked indifferently, standing at the entrance to Lamorna. 'It's OK, you're safe for a bit, she's making some muck for herself.' The house was already ringing with the song of Dicky.

'Just thanking him . . . did you enjoy it, love?' He picked his way carefully along the path towards her.

'Of course. It was smashing. I like *them*, too. But,' she slipped her arm through her father's as he stepped into the hall, 'I'm ever so glad to be home again, with you, all to ourselves.'

He lifted his arm and put it round her shoulders and they went into the house.

'What did you say, Laf?' Katherine asked eagerly. 'How did you get out of it?'

Mr Taverner looked at her for a moment in silence, with judging eyes, then said gently: 'I know it excites you, Katherine. But do try to remember, all the time, that he needs us, and what our work is, and that we aren't sitting on the edge of our stalls at some bloody thriller.'

'I know – I know –' she said at once, biting her lip, but also half-laughing. 'I do try to remember . . . What *you* can never remember is that *you* aren't *me*.'

'No, indeed.' Mr Taverner was leisurely hanging up the white raincoat as they stood in the hall. 'You can – as they say – say that again.'

'Children,' Miss Dollette said under her breath as she passed them on her way to the kitchen.

'All right – I'm *sorry*. I'll try to remember – I *will* remember. Now tell me what you said.'

'I went into the "haunted" routine,' he said over his shoulder as he opened the kitchen door.

'Do you think he believed it?' Miss Dollette breathed anxiously.

'Oh no.' Mr Taverner's tone was cheerful. 'Not by a long chalk. You see, he saw our – helpers.'

'Oh my goodness!' from Katherine.

'Yes. This time, I'll have to give them a *real* ticking off. I suppose the temptation was simply irresistible – I don't imagine he saw them for longer than a second or so, if that, and of course he couldn't believe, he isn't sure – if he really did see anything. But it was *very* naughty. They could feel he was the most responsive one of the five.'

'And they *must* have felt him coming *and* smelt him, too,' Miss Dollette put in. 'They've no excuse there.'

'Of course they did. I'll bet they were grinning all over their unbelievable little faces . . . The trouble is, when I'm ticking them off I always want to laugh,' Mr Taverner said.

'But they don't know that, Laf,' said Katherine. 'I *do* laugh, that's why I'm not much use. Now Felicity is useful, aren't you, love?' turning to her.

'I suppose I am, yes . . . it's like babies. Sometimes you want to laugh at the baby because it's so funny – beautiful –'

'Your favourite "funny-beautiful",' Katherine said, teasingly yet gently.

'. . . Yes. But behind this laughter there's always the solemn feeling: it's so important . . . I try to remember that feeling when I'm giving them a little talking-to,' Miss Dollette ended.

'Only *they* aren't human souls.' Mr Taverner was extended in the big armchair, arms linked behind his head, staring into the fire. 'Solemnity . . .'

'But they will be,' Miss Dollette said distinctly though softly, as always.

A long pause.

'And what do you think *I* did!' she said in a moment, beginning to laugh. 'When that boy said he would go to Wales I – I kissed him! And I was then feet away. He did turn round, but I don't think he knew anything.'

'Oh, he's going, then?' cried Katherine.

Miss Dollette nodded. 'I persuaded him,' she said cautiously. 'I really believe I did.'

'Jolly d and congrats,' Mr Taverner said, brightening. 'Where is he, by the way? – And when we've got visitors, also by the way, we really must censor our conversations. I suppose we could always say we were MI5, but that won't convince some people . . .'

'He's under the car, of course – Just *look* at these potatoes! What am I going to do with them?' Miss Dollette almost wailed.

'Make us some more, love,' Katherine half-whispered, and all three burst into stifled laughter in the firelit quiet kitchen.

15

Mrs Wheeby's cousin Fred

Mrs Cadman was not the kind of landlady who rushes at lodgers returning from holiday, ravenous to hear and impart news. For three days after she got back to Rowena Road, Mary saw her only from a distance, cleaning the lower stairs, or setting out to shop with a large wicker basket.

However, on the third morning she met her in the hall. Mary had been down to see if there was a letter from Sylvie. There was not.

'Have *you* any idea where that silly friend of yours has got to?' Mrs Cadman asked, questions and answers about a nice Christmas having been exchanged.

'Haven't the foggiest. *I* was going to ask *you*,' Mary answered rather pertly.

'Oh well.' Mrs Cadman sighed. 'Her rent was paid up, I will say that, though I reckon it wouldn't have been if I hadn't asked for it before she went off with you. But rushing in here, wouldn't say a word (not that I asked her much, *I* didn't care what was the matter with her), banging about in her room. We were watching TV and Mr Grant was asleep. She woke him up, trust her. And the state of her room! Bed not made, lipstick all over the pillow, bits of fluff on the floor, dirty cups . . . oh, it was a picnic.'

What else did you expect? was Mary's unspoken thought.

'And now I suppose I'll have to set about letting that room. Oh well. I shan't hurry myself. It'll need a good turn-out before I show it to anyone.' Mrs Cadman paused. 'It isn't one of the best rooms, of course.'

Mary made some kind of an acceptable noise and escaped up to her own room. It looked cold and shabby in the winter light. She stared round, rather stonily. She had pains, and disliked telling Mrs Levy, who was apt to transfer any situation to Hamburg in the 1920s. Girls in Hamburg before the war had had pains, *and* starvation, *and* only ten marks a week. Gretl Tuber, the forewoman, had write, yes *write*. Well did Mrs Levy remember. But what had Gretl Tuber done? She had *vorked*.

Mary decided that she would bring back a bunch of anemones that evening to brighten the place.

(It was not until the next occasion that she realized that Mrs Levy had meant *writhe*.)

But life in London, she decided, lying comfortably under the eiderdown, wasn't as exciting as it had been. She had no friends now that the tiresome Sylvie had Run Off; and not enough money to go to a disco. . . *I might find some club, though,* she mused. *I can't be the only girl in London with no friends and I have nearly forty pounds in the Post Office. Only I don't want to blow my savings and join a club – I don't know why. As for getting another job – though it's nice not having to work mornings – yes, now that, I might . . .*

No, commanded a voice within her, clear as a telephone bell, STAY WHERE YOU ARE.

Oh well, s'pose it isn't so bad, she thought, her half-intention deflected so firmly that she hardly realized it had existed. *At least I do know old Levy, and she isn't too bad.*

The truth was that Mary was a corner-maker, as irrevocably as her father was an egg-putter.

Her flight from Torford had been caused by the strongest desire in her nature: to find a husband. Torford had only been boring because she felt that it held no boy for her; London had only been thrilling because it had more chances of finding one.

Oh well, she thought, *p'raps something will turn up, and at least I'm not tramping round in this wind with green hair and a broken airliner bag and torn clothes and no job.*

At that precise moment, the object of her thoughts was sitting in a stifling hot kitchen/living room, half a mile away, eating fish and chips out of a newspaper and swallowing with them the sharpest ticking-off of her life.

Mum, the perpetual consumer of tea and fags, the eternally reliable – had *Turned Nasty.*

'Now you listen to me, Sylvia Higgins. I haven't said all that much, so far. Let her learn, I've thought. Well, seemingly you haven't. I'm telling you straight, next time you've *had* it. I got enough on me plate.' (Down went the smoke, into the lungs coated with tannin.) 'This time, *you go off and you don't come back.* You stay 'ome, and you get yerself a job, and you pay me 'alf what you earn, and you take up again with Chris Pollitt –'

'Mum! He's wet!'

'And what are you, I'd like to know? Bone-dry, I s'pose. Look at yer hair, look at yer cloes – enough to frighten King Kong . . . His dad *owns* that shop and come a year or two, Chris'll be managing it. He's always asking about yer –'

Sylvie hooked a finger through a strand of green hair and twiddled it.

'Now you get out o' that chair and you put on *that* –' throwing a plastic apron at her – 'and you get weaving on that washing-up. I'm off to work. We don't want me bloody well on the Assistance as well as your dad.'

A time both dull and exhausting now began for Wilfred.

Long before the final settlements were signed, Mr Dill took to *marching into the place* (this was how Wilfred put it to himself) 'to see what wanted doing'.

'What's got to be done in such a hurry?' Wilfred asked surlily. 'The place looks all right to me.'

'Oh it isn't a bad little shack as places go, but it badly needs modernizing . . . *that's* coming down for a start.'

Mr Dill jabbed a finger, suggesting one of his own beef sausages, at the wall dividing the dining room from Pat's dearly loved lounge. 'Mrs D.'s set on having one large room. Better for entertaining. *And* a picture window in the best bedroom. That she *must* have.'

Wilfred said nothing. He didn't want anything, except to be settled and have a bit of peace with Mary.

'A new bath,' announced Mr Dill.

'That bath was new three years ago!' cried Wilfred, aroused. 'A brand new pink bath –'

'The wife doesn't go for pink. And we may have to run up another room in that loft. I been having a recce.'

Wilfred knew this. The lumping and swearing had been audible in the kitchen. He took down his raincoat. It was sleeting, and when it sleets in Torford, it sleets.

He spent one of the most depressing afternoons of his life, walking at a determinedly brisk pace from street to street, looking for rooms.

There were simply no small, cheapish, cosy rooms to be had. At about four o'clock, he turned homewards as determinedly as he had set out. It had just occurred to him that he could have kept at least warm and dry by using the car. But the car had never played a large part in his life, and he had simply forgotten it in the press of his worries.

I'm sick to death of this, he thought. *But I won't give up until I've done every part of the town – except where Dad is. I couldn't stand that now. Funny, when I like going there. But there's him, of course – oh well—*

'Hullo, stranger! Where've you been hiding?'

He turned, just as he was entering his own road. It was one of Pat's sensible, sharp-eyed, cheerful friends. As 'hiding', in the sense of deliberately avoiding these women, was precisely what he had been doing for months, guilt was added to his irritation and dismay.

'Oh . . . hullo, Shirley . . . nice to see you . . . yes, it is a long time . . . Oh, I don't know. Haven't been out much, I suppose.'

'Now that's naughty, Wilf. I guessed you hadn't. I was only saying to Maurice the other Thursday – no, it must have been the Wednesday, because I'd just come in from my Flower Arranging class . . . *I haven't seen Wilf for months*, I said. *I bet he's just lying down under it.* What *you* want to do is to get out, see people, distract your mind, join a club – the Liberals are always clamouring for members, I can give you the address – but I suppose you couldn't, of course, being Labour. Or even come round and see little us! You're always welcome, you know that.'

'Yes . . . I do . . . thank you. It's very kind of you.'

'Oh, kind – rubbish . . . *Who are these new people you're running around with?*' Shirley's eyes had become suddenly sharper; they were fixed on his own. 'Big woman, always wears a pinkish coat, and a long chap in a greyish raincoat? Don't they live in Hardy Crescent?' It was a pounce. 'I've seen you in his car.'

'Oh . . .' Wilfred's words died away. Presumably she meant Mrs Cornforth – but *big* and *pinkish*? Katherine, who made him think of *An Idyll* and 'La Belle Dame'? And her favourite scarlets and crimsons . . . Katherine? And *greyish*? The familiar raincoat that seemed to glow?

'New friends,' he found himself saying, as lightly as Mr Taverner himself.

'Oh? Interesting? I adore meeting interesting people; you know me. Come and have a coffee and tell me all about them – on me, of course!'

In another minute, he thought, she'll have got me.

'It's very nice of you, Shirley, but I can't – I'm – I've got someone coming to see me and I'm late now – I was just –' he looked at his wrist.

'Oh? Anyone exciting?'

'A medium . . . I'm trying to get in touch with Jack the Ripper.'

He realized the implications of what he had said when he saw Shirley's astounded stare.

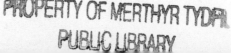

'Well, really, Wilf,' she said, crimsoning but managing a laugh. 'Look us up soon, won't you? I did call once or twice but you always seemed to be out.'

'I'm sorry . . . The fact is I've been a bit under the weather.'

He knew that she had called; he had twice seen her sturdy silhouette through the glass panels of the front door as he lurked in the kitchen.

'You must cheer us up . . . the Big Man didn't let Pat linger on for years, you know, like some do . . . bye-bye.'

'Bye-bye,' said Wilfred savagely.

Why must great fat women talk like toddlers? And why must they call God Almighty the Ancient of Days, the Big Man?

And what's wrong with Shirley and Sheila and Joan and the rest of them? he demanded guiltily of himself as he shut the front door. *They're kind, they're sensible, they're good wives and mothers, and not so thick as you'd think. She knew I meant I wished the Ripper would get her, when I said that . . . not really, not really, of course . . . It's awful, the feelings one has buried inside oneself . . . but I can't stand it. Give me Mrs Wheeby any day.*

His search the next morning in the region of large old houses, with spacious gardens, was no more successful. Twice, an au pair girl heard his enquiry for rooms with an uncomprehending stare ending in giggles; several houses were let out in separate rooms, but could not accommodate three; some, on closer inspection, were falling into ruin; and some had the staring word DEVELOPMENT on boards in their gardens.

At last, about the time the cold January sun was going down the yellow sky, he turned homewards. He felt ashamed at having thoughts about hot tea as early as half past three in the afternoon, but they were there, so why not admit their existence?

Doesn't mean I shall give way to them, he thought, walking quickly past the glaring, blazing shops through the delicate winter light. *Mustn't start pampering myself.*

Another thought which had quietly taken possession of him was that he would leave the finding of rooms to Providence.

Perhaps Providence could manage it. Certainly Wilfred Davis couldn't.

It's daft, said part of his mind. *Well, we're told to trust in Providence, aren't we?* said another part tartly, which could not face any more tramping about in fruitless search. *So you shut up! And I'll take myself home a doughnut. Have it hot. (Pat was always afraid I'd put on weight.)*

Mrs Wheeby was planted in his kitchen. As he opened the front door he saw her bulky shape, standing by the table.

'Oh there you are, Mr Davis. I was just beginning to wonder where you had got to. It's nearly dark. I hope you'll forgive my having unlocked the kitchen door. I noted you keep the key hanging on that drawer-knob in the hall – not wise, if I may venture to say so. They could see it through the letter-box. – Now you' (pause, gasp) 'will never believe what has happened. Quite providential.'

He saw that she was holding an opened letter, and her downy cheeks were slightly flushed and her eyes behind the thick lenses were shining.

'I'm sure you must have heard me speak of Fred, Fred Garston, my husband's second cousin. Such a coincidence. He and I were chums when we were all teenagers. But I haven't heard from him – not to say *heard* –' (pause, gasp) 'for sixteen years, though we always exchange cards at Christmas *and* Easter. I attach importance to that, Mr Davis. It shows someone *really* has you in mind, if they send at *Easter* as well. – Now you just read *that*,' and she handed him a letter.

In clear, old-fashioned handwriting Cousin Fred proposed that Cousin Edith should come to share his house in Chelmsford. It was getting too big for him. They could each have their own half, because he knew she liked a bit of peace and quiet as much as he did, and they would manage nicely. Would she excuse him not giving her longer notice, but the idea had come over him rather suddenly, and would she please let him know soon. And he was hers, affectionately, C. F. Garston (Fred).

Wilfred put the letter down on the kitchen table. Providence *had* stepped in, right smartly. But would Mrs Wheeby bow to Providence's arrangements?

He fixed his eyes on her anxiously as she began her steam-roller tactics.

'Well, Mr Davis, what do you think? I'm most *eager* to have your opinion, and of course I haven't forgotten my promise to stand by you through thick and thin. But the truth is, financial matters do *not* improve' (pause, gasp) 'as the years go by, and Fred has always been well-to-do. He comes from a well-to-do family, and I have no doubt at all he intends me to go as his guest. The fact is, Mr Davis, he was sweet on me when we were both eighteen; and I think if Mr W. hadn't come back from India at that time he would have Proposed. My dear mother always believed so, to her dying day. Now what's your opinion, Mr Davis? I'm really anxious to hear it.'

'Do sit down Mrs Wheeby, won't you? I was just going to make some tea – perhaps you'll share it with me?'

Providence had done him so handsomely – and so quick off the mark, too! Old suitor, comfortably off, second cousin of late husband, own house in Chelmsford, sufficiently far off for Wilfred not to feel obliged to go rushing round there at a minute's notice if the scheme went awry! His only fear was that the splendid gift might, so to speak, flutter off before he had caged it.

Now don't overdo it, he warned himself, as he took down the teacups.

Mrs Wheeby had seated herself, and was studying him with a touch of anxiety. He began to speak slowly, as he plugged in the kettle.

'Well, Mrs Wheeby, my first thought is that I shall be sorry to have you so far away as twenty miles. But we must . . . we must use our heads, not our hearts, mustn't we? And there is no doubt at all, that I can see, that you would be much more *comfortable*. I don't mind admitting to you, now that this offer has come up, that I've been out room-hunting most of this week, and had no luck at all.'

'Well, I never thought you would, Mr Davis.'

'. . . And of course, it's been all the more worrying, Mrs Wheeby, because of finding somewhere suitable for yourself and Mary . . .'

'I think you'll find Mary won't be on your hands for long. Much improved in looks and thinner too. More attractive nowadays.'

'. . . and so, on the whole, I must say it seems quite providential . . . though perhaps you would have liked a bit longer to think it over . . . Cousin Fred seems in a bit of a hurry, doesn't he?'

'Only because of my promise to you, I do assure you, Mr Davis. Only because of that. I feel every confidence in Fred, and I don't mind him being in a hurry – affections formed in youth, you know, have a way of lasting – yes, every confidence.'

'Well, I shall miss you, of course.' Wilfred paused. But the situation seemed to be moving so surely towards the position designed for it by Providence that he felt he might safely indulge in a little kindness. 'I had quite looked forward to . . . to . . . our all setting up housekeeping together.'

'Oh, I was positively dreading it.'

Wilfred retained enough control not to turn and stare at her.

'Yes, really dreading it, Mr Davis. I've lived in your house for nearly two years, and it's been ever so much better since Mrs Davis died.' (*Well! Plain-speaking indeed. Astounding Wheeby.*) 'But we don't really *know* each other, not the way I know Fred; and I'm sure I never could resist putting in a word about Mary now and then, if we all lived together. I can tell you now' (pause, gasp) 'I was really shocked by her unkindness – going off and leaving her father with her mother not six months dead – job with auntie or no job with auntie!' (Wilfred quivered inwardly.) 'Downright heartless, I thought, though I did send her a birthday card. But we'll say no more about that, and I hope you'll find somewhere *really your style.*

You know, Mr Davis, there are the whales and Dicky – and my ways are not yours and Mary's ways.'

Wilfred smilingly set before her a cup of tea.

'So I shall write to Fred this very night. Let me see, the last post goes at seven. I will just drink this up quickly, and get down to the pleasant task.'

'But you mustn't go out in the cold, Mrs Wheeby. It's bitter this evening. You'll let me take it for you, won't you? I can be there and back in no time.'

'Well that's very kind of you, Mr Davis, but you *are* kind. You always have been.'

They sat sipping their tea in silence.

Hallelujah, thought Wilfred. *Hallelujah*.

16

The golden offer

Wilfred took to Cousin Fred. It would not have mattered if he hadn't, he supposed, yet he would not have liked to see his old brick of a Wheeby handed over, for the last years of her life, to a bully or a sponger.

Cousin Fred was tall and bald – he might have been any age between fifty and seventy – and silent, with an infrequent smile which was pleasant on a usually solemn face.

'It's a relief to me, knowing Mrs Wheeby's going to be settled with a relation,' Wilfred confided to him while they were waiting in the hall for Mrs Wheeby to come downstairs. 'We've become friendly in the last six months – me being on my own, you see – and her in the same boat.'

Cousin Fred nodded.

'Edith has always been Rather Original,' he said in a lowered tone, with a glance up the stairs. 'Now I like that, Mr Davis. At nineteen, Edith was quite unlike the other young ladies in our little circle. *Outstanding*. I shall enjoy her company. I always have enjoyed it.'

So long as you're prepared for just how Original Edith is, thought Wilfred, but said no more.

Clearly Cousin Fred was taking to live with him, not a stout old woman of well over seventy, but an Outstanding Girl of nineteen, with large grey eyes and a lot of – but it wasn't possible to guess what colour that hair had been before it turned to white silk.

Mrs Wheeby reported, in quiet approval, on her new home.

'It is really *commodious*, Mr Davis, *and* a conservatory. I am fond of a conservatory. Fred specializes in fuchsias, and I am to have my own sitting room, and Fred is having a second bath and toilet put in on my floor' (pause, gasp) 'and a regular man comes in to help with the garden once a fortnight, and a regular woman comes in every day to clean thoroughly – at least, she is *supposed* to clean thoroughly . . . "I cannot imagine, Fred," I said to him, "where you find these people . . ." When I remember the difficulty Mrs Davis had . . . I am certain, Mr Davis, that Fred's having been a regular eater of health foods for forty years has much to do with it . . .'

Wilfred was silent, sitting with her before the television; he had invited her down to see a programme about dolphins. He waited, knowing that some Wheebyism would follow.

'You see, Mr Davis, Fred is not *inwardly poisoned*, and people can *feel* it, and therefore they know that he will be a good employer.'

'Yes. Yes, I see, Mrs Wheeby.'

Mrs Wheeby paused. Her eyes, fixed upon the faces of the celebrities on the screen, slowly became pebbly, but whether because of the kind of faces they were, or because of her next sentence, was not clear.

'I hope, I very much hope' (wheeze, gasp) 'that I shall not have any trouble with Mrs Bedford. That is Fred's cleaner, Mr Davis. Mrs Bedford.'

Wilfred neither hoped nor feared. If she did, he knew who would win.

The desolate month drew on, in the icy spring light, with the earliest shivering flowers. Doggedly, Wilfred continued to search for two bed-sitters, and to find nothing. Mrs Wheeby's preparations for her departure rolled on, and Mr Dill bullied him into letting the workmen start on knocking down the thin partition separating Mary's room from the room over the porch.

'Dressing-room for me; very "with it" the wife is,' Mr Dill said.

Since's Pat's death, it had never been cheerful to return to Lamorna; now, with the dust, and the trampled garden, and the ceaseless whine from the men's transistor, Wilfred almost preferred his fruitless tramps through the bitter streets. He put off turning homewards as long as possible, pushing open one more gate, lingering to inspect a last house that promised cosiness and cheapness, before turning slowly away and moving through the lengthening January evening, towards the Commedia dell'Arte.

It was not his idea of a place you dropped into for a cup of tea, having a black and gold front and 'all this Italian nonsense all over the place'. But it was warm, and he could get a hot doughnut there, and he had taken to dropping in after his afternoon search.

On this particular evening, he pushed open the massive glass and chromium door with fretful thoughts, and worked his way in between table and banquette.

A small elderly lady came up to the glass door and began to push at it; a waitress loitered up to Wilfred's table; and finally, behind the small elderly lady there loomed the familiar tall figure in the white raincoat.

Wilfred's spirits lifted. He sat up, smiling, while Mr Taverner pushed open the door easily, with a long arm over the elderly lady's head, and held it for her.

'Yes?' asked the waitress, shifting her chewing gum.

'Two, no, four doughnuts, please, and may we have them hot.' Mr Taverner slid into the seat opposite to Wilfred, looked round him, and began to laugh. 'What an absurd place . . . and TEA,' he hallooed after the waitress '– hot, hot and very hot, and bad for our poor nerves.' The waitress disappeared smiling – sourly, but it was a smile.

Wilfred felt, comfortably, that although he might not see Mr Taverner for a week or so, they always resumed their friendship as if there had been no break.

'Well, how have things been going? Katherine tells me that she has telephoned you "again and again", but always without any luck.'

'I've been out every afternoon,' Wilfred said shortly. He didn't want to start relating his experiences; it would sound like grumbling – and Pat had been so down on grumbling.

'Oh . . . well, no doubt, being Katherine, she telephoned *once* . . . however . . .' Mr Taverner paused.

'I've been looking for rooms,' Wilfred blurted out. 'For Mary and me and I can't find a thing. Not a thing.'

Mr Taverner looked sympathetic but the tea and doughnuts now arrived.

'You see,' Wilfred went on, 'Mrs Wheeby – you remember Mrs Wheeby?'

'Of course. What do you take me for?' Mr Taverner nodded, sucking a finger burnt by hot jam. 'Nothing more bracing than boiling jam on a January afternoon,' he confided. 'Greed was ever my besetting sin.'

'I suppose I could have taken some makeshift place for myself, and then when Mary came up – but they were all so depressing, Mr Taverner! I just couldn't think what to do. You see, Mrs Wheeby being . . . but what do you think has happened?'

'She's off your hands, I hope?' smiling.

'Yes, that's just it.'

Wilfred began to tell about Cousin Fred, going into details with enjoyment. That tongue, on whose taciturnity Sheila and Shirley and the rest had rallied him (when they remembered to, for they were accustomed to apparently dumb, or at least monosyllabic, men) now rattled along. Mr Taverner listened, sometimes throwing back his head in laughter. It was a happy story; Wilfred realized this while he was telling it.

'And just at first, you know, I thought at last *she's* out of the way, and things'll be all right . . . but I haven't seen a single place, not one, under ten guineas a week; and when they were clean they . . . they . . . sort of glared at you – if you know what I mean?'

'I know very well.' Mr Taverner nodded.

'I just don't know what I'm going to do, and that's a fact,' Wilfred ended. 'It seems hopeless.' The word came out before he could prevent it.

'Come and live with us in the Yellow House,' Mr Taverner said. Wilfred stared at him.

The warm, dim place was quiet; there were only two other people drinking coffee in the further shadows, and outside the windows, Torford's rush hour was going past, its roar muffled by the plate glass. Mr Taverner's expression was easy, his faint friendly smile comforted; it might almost have been that he was joking. Yet Wilfred felt that he wasn't; in fact the offer had not really surprised him.

Hadn't he thought *I'll leave it to Providence,* and hadn't Providence provided Cousin Fred? Now Providence had come up with this.

The pause lengthened. He was seeing in memory his bedroom at the Yellow House, with the white-rose walls and cane furniture.

'Look here,' he broke out, 'there's Mary, you know. She's got to have somewhere. With me, I mean.'

'Mary too, of course. The more, as they say, the merrier. You know there's plenty of room.'

Wilfred nodded. That faint sensation swept him again like cold air: stars, vast space, immense vistas. It passed.

'You'll let us pay something, of course, won't you?'

'Four quid a week for you, two for Mary when she's there – I take it she won't always be.'

'But, Mr Taverner, that's . . . ridiculous. You know it is. I never heard such . . . (As you say, she won't always be there.) But four!'

'An aunt left me a goodish fortune a couple of years ago,' Mr Taverner gabbled. Every line in his face was smoothed

out, his eyes were clear as the Cornish sea. 'And Katherine and
Felicity have enough to canter along on – (not jog, I wouldn't
say jog), and . . . we would so like to have you.'

But Wilfred felt that it was his duty to make Mr Taverner
fully aware of what the plan would mean.

'Another thing . . .' he began slowly. 'Could your ladies manage? It means extra work, and it's a big house. You did say
you have some help?'

His voice trailed off, as there sprang into his memory, with
an astonishing clarity, the faces of the two creatures he had
seen, or imagined he had seen, kneeling before the grate in the
room he had assumed to belong to Mrs Cornforth.

Had those – those – *things* . . . been, unbelievably, clearing
away the ashes and re-laying the fire?

Mr Taverner was pouring himself a second cup of tea. His
heavy eyelids were lowered. Now he swept them up, and looked
limpidly at Wilfred.

'More tea? No? Yes, a couple do come in to help' (exactly
the same words!) '– you needn't worry about that.' For all the
clarity of the look, the word *brazen* sounded somewhere in
Wilfred's mind.

Mr Taverner went on: 'You wouldn't mind the place being
what many people would call haunted? You remember – I told
you. (I'm using that word because I can't think of another that
would cover the odd goings-on, though it doesn't fit, in my book,
what seems to go on in the Yellow House.) Would you mind?'

Wilfred hesitated. He felt strongly that he must speak the
truth.

'A bit,' he muttered at last. He wished that the question had
not been asked; yet it would have seemed worse, somehow, if
Mr Taverner had kept silent.

'I give you my word . . . I'd say my solemn word, only I'm
never solemn . . . that there's nothing to worry about. You'll
get used to it; we all have.'

Mr Taverner stirred his tea, into which he had put, as usual,
large quantities of sugar.

Yes, but none of you are ordinary people.

The words remained unspoken, and Wilfred made his decision in the manner of peace-lovers the world over: suddenly, without thinking out the matter any further.

'All right, then. Yes, and I can't thank you all enough.'

On a fine morning in the middle of January, Derek got into the 1938 car, now in order after a fortnight's absorbed work on it by himself, and, with Mr Taverner beside him working the map, began to drive straight across England towards the mountains of Wales.

He had made a faultless first excursion at the wheel, with Mr Taverner, nearly a week ago.

'I've nothing to teach you; your mate was right,' the latter had said on their return to the Yellow House after the car had been backed into its shed.

'Wot say?' Derek asked dreamily.

'You do have a genius for cars.'

'A natural, eh?' Derek, who seldom smiled, did so now, and his face became a younger boy's, good-natured and sweet.

'Like to drive her down to Wales on Wednesday?'

The smile broadened. 'Bit risky.'

'So is everything,' Mr Taverner pronounced.

'Well — no licence, I meant.'

'Oh, that. We'll take a chance.' Mr Taverner shook his head. 'Naughty Lafcadio . . . all the same, we will. You'll have to have some lessons, for form's sake, and take your test, of course.'

'Think I'll pass?' Derek grinned.

'I know you will, *and* first time.'

'T'isn't many blokes do that, not nowadays.'

'You will.'

Now they were on their way.

Strengthened by kindness and good food and praise and sleep and new clothes and a job ahead, Derek looked, not only a different boy, but the same boy made happy; his body seemed

more solid inside the sheepskin jacket that was a present from
Miss Dollette, his very hair blew thicker in the wind, and his
skin was clearing.

The merciless motorways, the shaped and levelled roads
running between fields under frost, the leafless woods, fell
behind them until, as the brief yellow evening was closing in,
they spun steadily across the delicate, space-age majesty of the
Severn Bridge; and half an hour later saw their first roadside
notice in Welsh.

Down, down they went, as the dusk deepened, between
seemingly endless rows of small, pale brick houses all looking
alike in the cold glare of the street lamps, past little café after
little café glowing cosily, until they saw it – violet-grey to the
pale horizon, with the occasional lonely red star of light from
a ship shining far out: the sea.

'*That* is not my idea of Proper Sea,' Mr Taverner said
severely. 'Proper Sea is Cornwall. This is only the boring old
Bristol Channel.'

'Looks all right to me – what I can see of it. Smells all right
too . . . oh, there's waves . . .'

They were rolling in, white in the last faint light, beyond
a long dark stone causeway spreading half around the bay.
Mr Taverner, who had insisted on taking over the driving to
give Derek the rest he said was necessary, turned to the left
along a pleasant road running between old-fashioned houses
and a little park facing the sea; leafless now, but it would look
pretty in the spring. He put the brake on gently, and drew in
to the pavement.

'Here we are.'

It was a small garage and petrol station, standing on a corner
next to a little house with lights shining in every window. It was
painted yellow; the same clear yellow as the house in Torford.

A nondescript kind of man came forward leisurely, wiping
his hands on a rag.

'Hullo, Guv'nor,' he said. 'Hullo, Derek,' and soon they were
in the house, and being made welcome by a dumpy little wife

and an equally dumpy half-baby, half-toddler ('a boddler – cross between the two,' Mr Taverner explained). And then they were sitting down to supper in a bright little room with the television on, and appetizing smells in the air.

Derek was not silent or shy; he boasted a little about the prowess with the car, glancing at Mr Taverner for confirmation; and Mrs Stanton filled his plate again while she listened admiringly, and with just enough incredulity to add spice to her listening; and the boddler in its high-chair splashed a spoon in the bowl of mush, and then put a wet hand on Derek's, making him laugh. *It's like it was at home before Dad died,* he thought, confusedly, for he was tired with the unaccustomed driving.

They sent him up to bed early, Mr Taverner saying that he himself would be staying there for a few days 'to settle you in, dear boy', and would see him in the morning. 'We'll have a walk along that causeway after breakfast.'

Derek looked out between the flowery curtains, before getting into bed; the sea was invisible, but that great darkness beyond the lamps shining in the little park – you could tell it was there. And listen; between the perpetual Saturday evening drone of passing cars, there it was: the sound of the waves, the waves breaking on the shore. He drew in his head, and shut the window, then looked round his little room.

Christ, he thought, *but Christ – why are they all so bloody kind to me?*

He hesitated a moment. Then, as if making up his mind, he strode across the room and ran down the stairs to the room on the next floor that was Mr Taverner's, where he had just said goodnight to him.

This little house, like the one where he had stayed in Torford, seemed larger inside than it had looked from the road.

He tapped. At once the door opened and there stood his friend, smiling.

Derek stammered at once, not giving himself a chance to draw back: 'Just . . . came to say . . . thanks for everything,

Laf. *Thanks.* I'll . . . I'll be all right now, and I'll send a card
to Mum. I'll be all right.'

Funny he never said anything, he thought, as he climbed the
stairs again. *But he was pleased; you could see that. All the lights
on — very bright it was in there, and that scent. Remember? I thought
it was a bird, first time . . . must be one of those aftershaves . . .
might get one of them. He always uses it. Get the same.*

And, being nineteen, and for the first time happy since that
afternoon six years ago when his father had taken him to see
Arsenal play the Villa, he began a soft clear whistle. Under his
breath; a soft, clear, happy young man's whistle.

'Does he understand?' asked Mr Stanton. The three were sitting round the fire in the living room, Mrs Stanton with some
knitting in hand for the boddler, who was (temporarily — you
never knew) asleep upstairs.

Mr Taverner shook his head. 'No. But I feel he might, one
day. One or two things he's said.'

The other nodded. 'I thought so. Well, he'll do, I'm sure of
that. Good old Guv'nor . . . you never made a bloomer yet.'

'Thank you,' said Mr Taverner modestly, 'so far. No, it's in
our lot, at Torford, that I'm afraid one's blowing up.'

Mr Stanton stared at him in quiet dismay, and he nodded.
'Oh yes. Very dangerous indeed. She wasn't ready. I know that
risks have to be taken, but sometimes I feel it's damned hard on
me. But never mind that now. Jess,' he turned to Mrs Stanton,
'you can find him a girl, can't you?'

'That was just what I was thinking about,' she said, after
a moment's pause, listening, her needles poised. 'Jean Evans,
working at the Marina Café just round the corner. Seventeen.
Very nice. She's got a regular, but I think that's on the turn . . .'

'Like milk.' Mr Taverner nodded. 'Well, I know you'll do
what you can.'

She looked across at him and smiled.

'He's a sweet boy . . . he'll be safe here, with George and
Timmy and me and the cars.'

Mr Taverner did not smile. 'Safe . . . the big word. Not yet, but all right, Jess,' and he told them what Derek had said to him upstairs.

'Nineteen years on the receiving end,' he concluded, 'and a legacy of goodness-only-knows how many generations of resentment and underdoggery. But he got it out – he got out the word *Thanks.* I could have hugged the child.'

He stood up, and stretched his long arms above his head.

'Splendour of God, but my body's tired . . . shall we all go to bed?'

'Remember how tired we were at Verdun, Guv'nor, just before the end?' asked Mr Stanton, with his hand on the light-switch. Mrs Stanton was putting away her knitting.

'That,' Mr Taverner answered, 'is one of the things I have not been allowed to forget.'

17

A death

Mrs Wheeby steamrollered ahead with her preparations for departure to Cousin Fred's, keeping steadily to Dicky's hours throughout the cancelling of the *Daily Telegraph*, the renouncing of her daily half-pint of milk and, finally, the witnessing of her small armchair, few books, and some ornaments and photographs being carried into a van with *Removals* upon it.

'For I couldn't trust any of the smaller objects to the Post, Mr Davis. These are treasures.'

Then it was Wednesday, and she had gone.

Dicky's silvery roulades and the whales (ah, that vast, gliding shadow!) and their other-worldly singing had gone with her. During the long, mooning days – days existing as it were in a pause – Wilfred often thought about the world whence came those long, lifting and descending cries. It was . . . *there*. If his body could have survived the weight of a mile's depth of water; if his human sight could have penetrated the clear, black-green darkness; he could have seen the vast bodies moving through their kingdom, tasted its salt, felt its currents sweeping him along.

He was standing at the gate of Lamorna, actually waving to Mrs Wheeby as Cousin Fred's car bore her away, while these inappropriate reflections drifted upon him; and they were followed by a too-clear knowledge of what Pat and Shirley and

Sheila and Joan would have said had they then been able, God forbid, to see into his mind.

Suddenly, such a longing for Pat swept over him, as he turned away from the gate towards her dusty, desolate, noisy home, that he almost staggered beneath it.

'Morning', said the postman's voice behind him. 'Raw today.'

Wilfred turned blindly. A letter was being held out.

'Oh . . . thank you . . .'

'Bet you won't be sorry when that lot's gone.'

The postman, an elderly man, nodded upwards at the ruddy-faced, Edwardian-moustached, flowing-haired pair of builders lounging in the wreck of the front bedroom window and chatting, unintelligibly – except to each other – as they sucked down tea.

Wilfred went into the house with Mary's letter.

Dear Dad,

Mr T. wrote to me saying we're going to live at your Yellow House. Suits me.

Love in haste
M.

Well! Suits her, indeed. The young were everlastingly rushing into matters with no examination of the probabilities involved, because they would not give a moment of their time to *thinking things over. And when things go wrong, who gets the blame?* thought Mary's father. *Us: Mum and Dad; the adults . . . Oh well . . . so long as she doesn't mind.*

And what of the hauntings? But perhaps Mr Taverner had cleared the way by mentioning the subject.

He began collecting the few things he wanted to take with him. Oxfam and Help the Aged and the rest of them obligingly sent collectors (usually after school and college hours, and disarmingly young and round-faced) to take away many of the smaller objects. The dustmen would have to be bribed to take away what was left.

And then, the night before he left Lamorna for ever, his father died.

Most of Derby Row was indoors, watching *Till Death Us Do Part.*

Kelly had dodged away from Mr Davis's open front door. One or two passing matrons had asked her where was her mum? – adding that she would catch her death, in her nightie like that. So she had retreated into the warm little room she knew as well as her own home, where Samantha crouched in front of the television in the darkness, and Mr Davis was a dim bulk in the ancient armchair.

Kelly continued to wander uneasily between living room and street. The fire glowed dimly, settling into ashes. She glanced quickly now and then at the armchair, settled to stare at the figures on the screen, then scrambled up and went to the door again; backwards and forwards.

'Wanna biscuit,' whined Samantha.

'Well yer – yer –' her sister swallowed one of the bad words Mr Davis had forbidden her to say – 'can't 'ave one. 'E's asleep,' she ended in a whisper, glancing sideways again at the chair.

'Wanna biscuit . . . Kelly, is 'e a stiff?'

Both stared towards the figure in the armchair, just visible in the bluish glare from the machine.

''Course not. Stiffs 'as blood.'

'Wanna biscuit, wanna biscuit, wanna biscuit.'

'Shut *up!*' shrilled Kelly. 'Shut up or – or I'll *do* yer. Stiffs 'as *blood*, I tell yer.'

She ran to the door, tripping over her ragged nightgown, and out into the street, and peered up and down its quiet length. Frost glittered on the pavement and a freezing mist hung in the air. A car was slowly approaching.

She recognized the blue light on the roof, and, child of her generation, reared on *Z Cars* and *Dixon of Dock Green*, ran out into the middle of the road and stood in the glare of the headlights, waving both arms.

The car stopped, and a man got out.

'Here, what's all this?' said a comfortable voice, as she was gently lifted six feet into the air and confronted by a pair of fatherly eyes.

Her thumb went into her mouth, and she ceased to be the efficient woman seven years' worldly experience had made of her, and became all baby, staring and silent.

'Come on, love. What's up? Lost your mum?'

'It's Kelly,' said the younger policeman from the car. 'One of old Davis's, sir.'

The old man's habits were known to the men at the local station, which was not far from Derby Row, and so was his influence on the local children.

'He's over eighty,' the boy added significantly.

'Go in and have a look,' his superior ordered quietly, with a glance towards the bluish cavern with its open door.

Samantha staggered up out of sleep, and blundered across the room and into the younger policeman.

'Now, now. It's all right,' he said soothingly.

She stared up at him, fair hair falling over her shoulders and torn, grubby nightgown, her feet dirty and bare.

'I bet *you'd* like a biscuit,' he blurted out.

'Said a mustn't,' she gabbled, thumb in mouth.

'He won't mind . . . he's asleep. Now, you show me where they are,' he coaxed.

In a moment he had her riding in his arms. He carried her to the door.

The sergeant said resignedly, 'Two of 'em.'

'That's my Sammy,' cried Kelly.

'All right, all right. Here, you have a nice sit-down in the car,' and he arranged Kelly carefully on the seat. Samantha was fitted in beside her.

Then the two men went into the cottage.

'Still warm.' The sergeant stood up, taking away his hand from the broad, white-haired breast. 'Must have been – oh, couple of hours ago. In his sleep, I'd say.'

'"What a lovely way to go",' muttered the young man, frivolity masking other feelings.

'That'll do . . . you seem to know all about it . . . p'raps you know who those two belong to?' He jerked his head towards the door.

'A Mrs Singer, sir. Lives just down the street.'

'Yes, I know her. Go down and tell her, will you? If she isn't in' – *and that's likely enough*, he thought – 'you can take them down to the station. I'll stay here till the doctor comes.'

But Mrs Singer was in, sketchily finishing some long-postponed housework, and half thinking she might just run down to Davis's and see if the kids was there – it was after eleven and freezing cold. When she opened the door to the policeman, she screamed.

'Oh God – the kids – they bin run—'

'It's all right, Mrs Singer. Nothing wrong with them. But they're up at old Mr Davis's, and he's deceased – passed over,' he amended, at her bemused stare. 'You come with me, will you?'

'I was just goin' up to fetch them . . . gone, 'as he? Wasn't a bad old chap,' she added.

'In his sleep,' the young policeman said shortly. He regarded her tolerantly, handed her daughters over to her, recommended a hot drink and bed for both, and began to set in motion the apparatus for disposing of an eighty-seven-year-old body – *male, retired railway worker* – decently, and in order.

'It's almost the first time in her whole life I've been angry with her,' Wilfred said wearily.

It was five days later, and he was sitting at the kitchen table in the Yellow House, red-eyed and exhausted after the bustle of the last week: the paying out, the telephoning and letter-writing and disposing of his father's few possessions. In the middle of it all he had opened his front door to Sheila – or was it Shirley or Joan? – ablaze with interest (or sympathy, or ravenous curiosity) and offering hospitality and help.

'She sends me two lines, a couple of lines, that's all, about us coming to live here,' he now said bitterly to his three silent listeners, knowing too well that he was whining but unable to stop. 'And then a wire – a wire, mind you – she can't come to her grandfather's funeral. And he would have minded, Mrs Cornforth, he would have. That's what upsets me. Two of my wife's friends came with great wreaths – must have cost a fortune. I never asked them – they didn't even like him. And why they showed up I don't know. Well, I suppose I do, really . . . But he wouldn't have wanted their wreaths. He never forgot one Christmas when one of them and her husband came to our place. Called her a cow. And then I had all of them, dozens it seemed like, meaning it kindly, but phoning, and coming round, and saying what would Pat say if she could see how Dad's place looked. Oh, it was well meant, of course, I know that –'

'Always makes one feel worse, when it's well meant,' Mr Taverner said languidly.

'I *know* they thought Father was *low*. Pat did, too; it was the only thing we ever had words about; and all her friends agreed with her. – I *know* they meant it kindly, but . . .'

For the first time in perhaps sixty years, he put his face into his hands. No one spoke. Then he heard the soft rush of champagne being poured into a glass.

'Another sip,' came Mrs Cornforth's warm voice. 'Won't hurt you. Drink up. You're here now, and we all love you, and *we'll* see to it that . . .'

BOOK THREE

BOOK THREE

18

'I'm done for'

Yasuhiro came slowly down the steps of St Paul's Cathedral, relieved to be out in the bitter spring air again.

He did not admire the vast walls the colour of honey, nor the statues, nor even, he told himself, the height of the roof. But he had had to recall the size and height of the figure of the Buddha at Beppu in order to remind himself that Japan, too, possessed mighty monuments.

The exercise had not sweetened his mood.

His mood was one of criticism; he had been critical since he got into the taxi at the airport, and he was also – though he did not like to admit it – disappointed.

Last night, after that very peculiar meal in the ugly eating-room of the hotel in Bloomsbury where he was staying, he had remained in his room reading Auden. Yasuhiro had not 'embraced the West'. His adoration of his own country, and his secret intention to die for it, would remain: a stone torii, unchanged.

But English poetry! Reading it had been like breathing the scent of unfamiliar flowers.

Tokyo was as ugly as London, but its ugliness was familiar; and the miniature beauty of the small town some twelve miles from the capital, where his family had lived in the same house for three hundred years, had changed little in essentials, since 1905, when Great-grandfather and his comrades had flung themselves on the Russian gun emplacements at Port Arthur. The American bombers had done the town little damage, surrounded, as it was, by woods.

Great-grandfather:

A smile of tenderness moved Yasuhiro's proud lips. Following the account of the snow, the cold, the corpses, the dirt and danger, there would always come the climax: 'And nothing to eat but hard biscuit and pickled plums!'

His brain had been imprinted with those plums.

He had passed the morning in writing a letter to Great-grandfather. In the afternoon, he had called on his father's friend at the Japanese Embassy, and had heard roguish jokes about young men and London night life which he had received with the correct, polite laughter due to jesting from an older person in a high position, and with a haughty gleam in his eyes.

So Yasuhiro's first day in England had been dutiful rather than palatable to his natural love of pleasure; and everywhere he went he encountered this cruel English ugliness. He came slowly down the steps of St Paul's, ivory-faced and appearing, if possible, even calmer than usual because he was feeling cross. His camera was slung across the shoulder of his long pale grey overcoat. He would have liked to look at some flowers; he was hungry.

He walked slowly onwards, past shops and eating-places, in the thin spring light. The only beautiful things to be seen were the great clouds, coloured like pearls, drifting quickly through the blue sky above the tall white offices and old houses of dark brick, while the traffic thundered in his ears; and the English hurried past, with their alien faces all looking alike.

What was the name of this street? he wondered, after twenty minutes. There it was, high up on that brown wall.

'Liverpool Street,' he muttered, pausing on a corner and staring about him – and there, immediately opposite, were some flowers: bunches of them, yellow and white and crimson and pale purple, and an old man with a red face selling them.

Yasuhiro crossed the street leisurely, through a small herd of panting cars. This traffic was nothing to one accustomed to Tokyo. He paused in front of the flower seller.

'Lovely daffs,' instantly said the old man.'Fresh narciss.'

'I will have those.' A long finger in a pale glove pointed.

'Forty pence a bunch.' The seller shook out a cluster of half a dozen irises and presented them, clasped in a hand also gloved, in dirty black wool.

'More,' commanded Yasuhiro, and it was a command. 'All.' The pallor and purity of the irises and their shape were ravishing his senses.

The old man, however, had been through the 1914 war, the depression of the '30s, and the Blitz, and commanding tones (now that he was no longer in anybody's bleeding Army) made no impression upon him. Also, he disliked foreigners.

'Wot, the ruddy lot?' he demanded, incredulous and far from overwhelmed with gratitude. "Ow about my girlfriends? Comes out of the offices lunchtime, they do, and buys a button'ole or a bunch for their mams.'

'*All, all,*' Yasuhiro repeated imperiously, thinking that this impoverished old peasant did not understand.

'Oh, all right. Cost yer four quid, though,' and he began to take out the irises from their place among the glowing mass.

'Kwid?'

'Pahnds – pahnds,' said the vendor impatiently. "Ere, I better wrap 'em for yer – this 'ere wind's enough ter – well, ne'er mind – let alone flars.'

He bustled the flowers into a cone of white paper, whence their strange and lovely heads looked out remotely at Liverpool Street. 'Bit free with it, ain't yer?' he added, as Yasuhiro took four notes from his wallet and held them out. 'None o' my business, come to that . . .' – *tourists; plenty of it* – 'Thenks.'

He was not going to add 'guv'nor' to a kid, and he did not feel like saying 'son' to this little bastard. However, he did say 'Larst a week, they will. Keep the stems cut every day and a drop o' fresh water.'

Yasuhiro, who was not little, and who seemed taller than he was in the grey overcoat, strode on, and more than one alien eye glanced at him with interest.

'Sights', of all kinds, have become so commonplace in London's streets in the last few years that no one stares at anybody; but a beautiful oriental youth, dressed in the height of Western elegance and clasping an armful of flowers carefully protected from the wind, at which he gazed down immovably, caused heads to turn. His serenity was irritating. He made no attempt to avoid bumping into people, leaving others to get out of the way of him and his flowers.

When he looked up at last, he was on the corner of a narrow little street. Nearby were steep steps leading up into a vast, arched cavernous building. Some of the other buildings were large and new, others small and old, a mixture of ages and styles with which he was familiar in Tokyo. He glanced vaguely around, suddenly very hungry, and saw that the shop nearest to him sold cigarettes and sweets. No: sweets were a self-indulgence, and followers of Mishima did not smoke.

His gaze wandered across the road, caught by some coloured dresses, unusually ugly even for England, blowing in the wind outside a small corner shop. The March sunlight shone full into it.

He saw a glint of moving silver in a sunray, glittering out of the dimness, and then, looking closer across the crowded street, saw that the tiny light was hanging on a chain about someone's neck. His stare moved onwards, and at last he saw, above silver chain and medallion, a girl's face.

Dark and quiet, in the flow thrown up from the sunray: a Japanese face?

He crossed the street and, inclining his head to avoid the fluttering dresses, went out of the brilliant day into the dimness of the shop.

Mary looked up from a paperback recommended by Mrs Cadman and saw him silhouetted against the bright square of the door.

She saw his face, first, because it glimmered like ivory in
the dusk, and her thought was, *beautiful.* Then she thought –
but it was emotion rather than thought – that this was a man.

Young, very young, but the . . . the *mannest* man she had
seen in all her seventeen years, and the shape of his head,
capped with soot-black hair, and the cool stare, and the set of
his long pale grey overcoat on his slender but strong-looking
body, drew her eyes into a silent, bemused gaze.

Yasuhiro had seen at once that this was not a Japanese girl,
and was annoyed with himself for the mistake. He was also
annoyed with her.

He parted his lips – but she spoke first.

She said: 'Good morning. Can I help you?'

In Japanese.

He was so surprised that he started. Then, angered by this
betrayal of his feelings, his face darkened, and he quickly said
something incomprehensible – more Japanese, Mary supposed.

'That's all I know,' she managed to say sedately. 'Do you
speak English?'

Sweet voice, not loud, thought Yasuhiro. *But I believe she's
laughing at me. You're not going to laugh at me, modern girl.*

'Of course,' he answered coolly. 'I do not want to buy anything.' (This came out so quickly and smoothly that Mary
supposed it to be a phrase from a tourist handbook.) 'Do you
know – can you tell me, about a clean place near to here where
I can eat?' His face had become calm again.

Mary considered. With the usual kind of young man who
came in to finger Mrs Levy's tourist-baits, cheapness would
have been her first consideration in suggesting a café; even the
American boys, unless accompanied by Mom and Dad, never
seemed to have any money. But her eyes had taken in the quality of the overcoat by now, and those flowers, and she decided
that this one did have some money.

At last, after a pause in which they stared unwinkingly at
one another (Mary dreamily, and Yasuhiro with haughty reluctance) she said: 'The only place' – and the words came in a

rush, because she felt they implied a judgement of him – 'that you . . . could stand – would like – is the hotel in the station. In Liverpool Street station. But it's expensive,' she ended, remembering the solemn reference to Prices which Mrs Levy had uttered when concluding her detailed recommendation of the Great Eastern as a hotel in which a successful career-woman (such as Mary might one day become) could with safety dine alone at the age of, say, fifty-six.

'Ah,' said Yasuhiro. 'No good. I spent all my pounds.' He held up the flowers and smiled. 'Hotels, if good, are expensive.'

That was the instant when Mary's heart went through the motion known as *turning over*. Oh, proud eyes and shining young teeth, and delicate face all laughter-creases and small-boy sweetness! *Good grief, I'm done for*, she thought, staring helplessly.

'Oh . . . well, there's the Canton, that's Chinese, a little way down the street,' she muttered; 'that's quite clean.'

'I don't like places to be "quite",' said Yasuhiro. 'I like clean, clean.' He sounded disdainful and moved the flowers again, to the other side of his chest. 'And *not* Chinese.'

'I meant, clean enough.' Mary was beginning to recover her composure. 'I don't know . . . how clean you like places to be.'

'Perfect clean.'

'Well, the Canton certainly isn't *perfectly* clean. But it's . . . clean enough for me. I've been there.' She smiled politely; with an effort, for she felt too peculiar to want to smile.

His eyes seemed to be searching – her face, her hair, the blue overall she wore over her dress . . . *Looking to see if I'm clean?* she wondered, and colour came into her face. She looked down suddenly.

'Thank you. I go there.' He smiled again, socially this time, not so sweetly; turned, and, with his armload of flowers, was gone.

The heavy way that Mary sat down on Mrs Levy's chair could fairly be called collapsing.

She sat, staring out into the busy sunlit street where he had disappeared; and though, for the remainder of a dream-like afternoon, habit kept her working mechanically, she never ceased going over, again and again, every word that they had exchanged. Their remarks had been ordinary, but had sounded peculiar, as if both had been thinking about other things while uttering them (but then, of course, he had been using a foreign language).

She turned her head restlessly; she could see his eyes as clearly as she could see that scarf on the counter; and she continued to dream, in a kind of sweet unhappiness mingled with her usual common sense: *I ought to have got straight up and followed him. Offered to show him the way to the Canton. Don't be crazy. What's the matter with you? A boy you've seen once, for five minutes?*

Four days later, she was 'no better', as she described her state to herself. She was haunted all day and most of the night by his face.

She was beginning to wonder if she ought to see a . . . a psychiatrist or a doctor or something . . . only fancy *telling* anyone! . . . when Mr Grant, encountering her one morning in the hall, beckoned her along the passage that led into his little conservatory.

'Just wanted you to see these,' he began modestly, indicating a dozen white hyacinths, each more than a foot tall and shining in the warm earth-scented air like strangely shaped moons native to some remote planet. 'Nice, eh?'

'Beautiful, Mr Grant,' Mary said dreamily. Her thoughts, straying and uncontrollable since four days ago, wandered on to Sylvie's observation that Mr Grant was *arter her*. It seemed twenty years since Sylvie had said that, or that she had thought of Sylvie.

'And I thought I'd have a word with you,' Mr Grant went on, 'about the new lodger. Came last night. Rather unusual, he is. Some kind of a foreigner. Japanese, I'd say.'

Mary felt faint.

'Now there's no need to be upset,' Mr Grant soothed. 'You're thinking about the war . . .'

Mary was not thinking about the war.

'Is . . . he . . . nice?' she asked, just audibly.

'I wouldn't say "nice" – not that I mean he seems unpleasant in any way, Mary – but . . . proud, I'd say, if you was to ask me. (Stuck-up, Mrs Cadman will have it.) Knows his own value – or thinks he does. Not one of your slap on the back all friends together sort – and *very* well dressed.'

'Not . . . not in . . . in native costume, of course?' *That was utterly crazy, of course.*

'Oh no, a long grey overcoat. Quite Western-style. Cost a packet, I bet,' said Mr Grant. 'Came here Monday evening – just after you got in, it was. Had we got a clean room to let? Well, Mrs Cadman wasn't too pleased about "clean". But there was young Sylvia's, just decorated, and going begging. Mrs Cadman *did* ask for references; he came out with it at once. "You can write to the Japanese Embassy," he says, and writes out the address (I checked *that* in the phone book and it was all fair and above board). Mrs C. wrote off straight away; and yesterday morning, second post, *express*, if you please, comes a letter from some bloke with a name a yard long. Oh yes, Mr Tasu belonged to a family well known to the Embassy and they could swear for him – *vouch*, it said – funny word. I have heard it, but never seen it written before. So he moved in last night. Paid a month in advance. Insisted on it. Very polite, too, only not *friendly*. Quite young. Early twenties, I'd say. Here to learn English.' Mr Grant shook his head. 'But we'll have to see how it goes. Pearl Harbor. You just never know.'

'Thank you for telling me, Mr Grant.' Mary spoke steadily. 'The hyacinths are lovely.'

And she ran upstairs and locked her door and sat down on her bed and began to laugh. She shook her hair over her eyes and rocked with delicious laughter.

Last night, she thought, *while I was lying awake seeing his face, he was downstairs in Sylvie's room. He followed me.*

He had followed *her*.

*

That afternoon, Mrs Levy had to rebuke her assistant for dreaminess and customer-ignoring. And when two Korean tourists came in, Mary deeply blushed.

'Your face went red, Mary,' said Mrs Levy severely, when the girls had wandered out without buying. 'Vy? I know, I know. You remember the atomic bomb and you feel it all your fault. All students and young people the same. Such nonsense. And this is bad for tourism. They don't like it.'

'It wasn't the atomic bomb. I never think about it,' Mary stammered, coming out of her dream.

'The Japanese a very go-ahead people – "going places", as ve say. And vy you didn't say "Good afternoon, can I help you?" in Japanese? I vos vaiting.'

'I'm sorry, Mrs Levy – I forgot. But they weren't –' Mary actually swallowed '– Japanese – I don't think so, anyway.'

'Of course Japanese. Mary! Your face gone red *again*! Vot the *matter* with you this afternoon?'

Mary went back into her dream world, pursued by Hamburg in the '20s and all the other scenes and characters of Mrs Levy's set pieces, including the unfortunate Gretl Tuber.

So numerous and varied had been Gretl's misfortunes that Mary had once followed the account of a peculiarly distressing event by asking: 'Did she die?'

'Die!' Mrs Levy had exclaimed indignantly. 'Of course not. She is dead *now*, because if she still alive she ninety-seven. But die! Of course she did not die. She do very well. Marry a rich man. This very morning I haf a letter from her granddaughter. Has a lofely home in Brighton.'

Mary travelled back to Parliament Hill Fields longing, yet fearing, to see him. As she approached number 20 through the dusk, her eyes seemed to be running ahead of her to see if a light shone in Sylvie's room.

Oh! She nearly stopped, but compelled herself to walk slowly on to the gate.

The curtains were not drawn. The room was lit through a large, pearl-coloured shade; there was an unfamiliar glow everywhere from what seemed hundreds of flowers, and at the table he sat, in white shirt and jeans, chin supported in his palms, reading.

It took the strongest effort of will Mary had ever made in her life not to linger.

She made herself walk briskly up the steps and feel for her key. An instinct – deep, and very strong, and not easy to name – directed her *not to hang round mooning.*

19

Coffee

'Good evening.'

He stood still, not pushing the gate open, just standing, and looking down at her. He was some six inches higher than she was. His expression was impassive – without the intent, dreaming stare of that first time.

'We . . . meet . . . before. In that shop where the dresses are,' he went on.

'Yes.'

Mary's voice was calm but it was almost a whisper. She noticed the alien accent, the strange faint indrawn breath on certain words. She swallowed.

'You had – a lot of flowers.'

'Oh yes. I like flowers.' She saw the faintest nervous movement in his neck as he too swallowed . . . and suddenly she wanted to catch at his arm and give it a little friendly swing. After all, he wouldn't have come to live here unless . . .

'Come, go,' he said quickly. 'Must not stand in the snow,' and he opened the gate and ran up the steps ahead of her. 'Bad, rain, snow . . .' he called without turning round.

Mary went up after him, thinking *manners*, and so dazed that she did not look where she was going. She slipped. But before she could fall, an arm, feeling more like a steel band than an arm, shot out and gripped her and steadied her.

'You don't fall,' said Yasuhiro, smiling. 'I – save you.' The arm shot away again.

'Thanks . . . I'll just . . . get my key.'

She was trying to keep her common sense. *But I don't know a thing about him* was her distracted thought as she felt in her purse. The dream-prince of jet and ivory had faded; and her strongest wish was to run away and hide. *I bet the Embassy doesn't know what he's like at home,* she thought.

Her hand was shaking, and she had difficulty in inserting the key. In a moment he said: 'You would like I help you? Take my key!'

'I'll manage,' Mary said, rather surlily as the door opened.

They went in side by side, though she had a distinct impression of his starting to push ahead of her and then falling back. She turned to go upstairs – and he was looking at her.

'Cheerio,' she said firmly.

'Sayonara,' he said, all smiling mockery, then turned and strode down to the basement.

Mary went upstairs to her attic on shaking legs, saying to herself *don't be so dotty, don't be so dotty.*

She sat on the bed, frowning, as she unlaced her boots. *I liked it better when I could just look at him,* she decided. *He was smashing then.*

What was he now?

Suddenly, she hurled a boot across the room. The thud was followed by a sharper, smaller sound: a knock on her door. She sat still – but her eyes slid round.

'Yes – what do you want? Who is it?' she called at last.

'I am here. Yasuhiro Tasu,' answered the alien voice.

She got up slowly and went across the room and opened the door.

He was standing there, straight and slim, with a quite different expression from the mocking one of ten minutes ago.

'Will you,' he began at once, 'will you come to have – a-coffee-with-me? In my room?'

Mary experienced a fortifying sense of being in command of the situation, this time.

'Thanks. When I've had my supper,' she said, and she did not smile because she did not feel like smiling. Nevertheless, smile or no smile, her acceptance came out before she could stop it. 'In half an hour. OK?'

'OK I have all ready,' and he did smile, causing Mary's fortifications to crumble.

He ran downstairs, and she tried not to think that his smile indicated triumph.

Usually, she enjoyed cooking her supper and took her time over it. This evening, she felt compelled to hurry, and had to decide what she should wear – not that she had much choice; *but what's the use anyway?* she thought sulkily . . . *whatever I turn up in, I bet he's seen hundreds of girls who look smashing.*

But she did give her hair an extra brushing, so that when she presented herself, rather late, at his door, it was raying out around her face like a black silk cloud charged with electricity. She had also renewed the pink paint on her mouth. Her top was patterned with bright psychedelic colours that would have dimmed a personality far stronger than hers; her skirt was neither long nor short, and black.

'You come. Good,' exclaimed her host, flinging open the door in a manner suggesting that he had been standing just behind it. 'Come. Go in.'

Mary looked curiously round. 'I say, it does look different!' she said, anxious that no silences should fall. 'I . . . I had a friend used to live here.'

'Boyfriend?' he snapped.

Mary did not answer. 'I say, it looks smashing . . . all the flowers. And you've got a new lampshade – *three* new lampshades,' glancing up at the newly whitened ceiling. 'Of course, it's just been decorated. Doesn't it make a difference!'

'Boyfriend was sleep here?' he repeated, still standing by the open door and scowling.

Mary liked this.

'No, a girl,' she replied demurely.

'Coffee.' He pointed to the most beautiful cups, saucers and coffee pot she had ever seen, arranged on Mrs Cadman's dreary little table. 'Sit.'

Mary giggled as she took one of the two armchairs.

'Why do you laugh?' he demanded, without looking up, as he began to fill the kettle behind a bamboo screen (*and that's new*, Mary thought).

She looked round – at the tulips and daffodils and irises, and the transformed room; and the black head that she could see behind the tracery of the screen. And suddenly she was full of enjoyment and mischief.

'Because that's what we say to dogs: *sit*, when we want them to be quiet.'

He came out from behind the screen with a jar of instant coffee, and sank into a kneeling pose in front of the coffee cups – looking strikingly graceful as he poured the extract into the pot – then added boiling water, and lifted his eyes and looked at her. Extraordinary sensations went down her back.

'You help me, please?' He was standing with the coffee pot held before him.

'To make the coffee, you mean? But –'

'No. No.' An impatient shake of the head. 'To speak English. Will you help me.' It was a statement rather than a request.

'All right.'

Mary's tone was neither pleasant nor forthcoming. *If that was all he wanted her for, to help him with his English . . .* the enjoyment, the mischief, wavered, sank.

'Thank you. I have no friend in England,' he announced. 'So thank you. You tell me when I make wrong.'

'Speak wrongly,' she muttered.

He set down the coffee pot carefully and knelt beside Mary, leaning back on his heels.

'I speak – no – act – behave too quick,' he said, softening his voice into a kind of liquid, caressing coo. 'I talk – speak you like a dog. I ask you help me. Too quick. Rude. Not Japanese. I am sorry.' And he looked fully at her, and smiled.

Spoken pleadingly, with the weight of a thousand years of tradition behind them, and by a speaker with such eyes and smile, Mary found the halting sentences irresistible. She also felt, because of his ignorance of English and his funny mistakes, as she would have felt towards a little boy whom she could pity and instruct.

She was wrong. Yasuhiro was no little boy. But her illusion helped the moment to pass smoothly.

'That's all right,' she said quickly, crimsoning. 'My name's Mary Davis.'

'Mahry.' He pronounced it with a curious little lift, like an H in the word. 'You like black, Mahry?'

'No, white, please. Just a drop of cold'll do.'

He seemed to gather the meaning of the colloquial sentence, and in a moment a stout bottle of Gold Top was sharing the board with the exquisite cups and saucers; and having discovered that neither took sugar, Mary and Tasu were sitting before the little heater (drunk on North Sea gas) and Mary was wondering what to say next.

'Mahry,' he said at last, meditatively. 'Hard to say, so hard for Japanese. So I don't try to say Mahry. I do not want to be angry with your name. So I say "Mairly". More easy for me. You like?'

It's funny, she thought, I'd almost sooner be upstairs thinking about him than be here with him.

'Good,' with the manner of one who has settled something. 'Now I tell you . . . You know Mishima? Great Japanese *samurai* – hero.'

'Never heard of him,' she said cheerfully. And neither did she hear much of Tasu's impassioned account, being occupied with listening to the sound of his voice and dreamily thinking, over and over again, *I do not want to be angry with your name.*

20

At the Anstruthers'

In a clear sloping hand, Mrs Wheeby wrote to Wilfred: She was very sorry to hear of the elder Mr Davis's passing away, but Wilfred must remember that he had had a good long life and had been, so she had heard, quite a grandad to the children in his road. She and Cousin Fred would be pleased if Wilfred would come and spend the day with them when the weather was more settled. 'Though I must confess,' concluded Mrs Wheeby – in writing slightly shaky after covering nearly four pages – '*well-warmed* as I am in my new home, I do not mind the *wind*. In fact I like to picture it blowing across the sea.'

And she was his affectionate friend, Edith M. Wheeby.

Affectionate, eh? Good old Wheeby, thought Wilfred.

Affectionate? Well, I suppose you might say I feel the same about her, and he put the letter into a folder.

The folder had been a Christmas present last year from the ill-used Joan – or perhaps from Sheila or Shirley – brought back from a visit to Italy. Or it may have come from France or Spain.

All the Shirleys were voracious travellers – abroad was 'so much more beautiful and interesting'. (They scorned to say that tobacco and alcohol were cheaper.)

The east wind did not penetrate the Yellow House. Wilfred had started what he thought of as *pampering himself* in small ways. When Pat had been alive, decorating and endless small jobs in the house and garden had taken up all his spare time, and he had felt that a few minutes spent in pampering would have been selfish. A luxuriously long shave, ten minutes passed in choosing a new tie, and other harmless indulgences left over from a normal male adolescence, had been sacrificed to the demands of family life.

Pat had been understanding. She had not liked, and had said as much, the sight of the aproned man at the sink, and she had not asked him to wash up – ever. But in return for her concession, he had silently made his own sacrifices. Old and Sweet, his tobacco, had been the most cherished of these minor Isaacs.

But now he gradually began to resume his 'pamperings': polishing his shoes to Army standard; venturing on a Swiss breakfast food made of raw grains, brown sugar, dried fruit and other delicious things, instead of flakes in a glaring packet offering him a miniature tank or tin trumpet in return for coupons. The Swiss breakfast food only had a picture of the Matterhorn against blue skies.

It's there, you know, he would think, sitting at his solitary breakfast. *I'll never see the Matterhorn in the flesh, so to speak, not now. But I can think of it being there. Sets you up for the day, as they say. Real and beautiful.*

Not that he needed setting up. He was happy in the Yellow House.

He had always felt fond of Kichijoten – if one could use the word 'fond' about so remote and beautiful a being – and now he felt fond of the toasting-fork, important at those cosy teas in the kitchen to which he was often invited. He loved his cane armchair, and felt affection for his books.

Once he had wandered up to the spacious attics, one furnished only with comfortable chairs and a colour television set; and one even barer, and whitewashed, with a ping-pong table in the middle and a dartboard on the wall.

'Felicity had . . . has – a whole world-full of nephews and nieces,' Mr Taverner had explained.

He had seen no more shadows or – or – whatever he had seen – and surely there were none between his friends; though

Mr Taverner's face might sometimes look as if caught up in a deep sadness, or Wilfred might surprise an expression of fear on the small countenance of Miss Dollette.

Mrs Cornforth was the one with whom he felt least comfortable, because her brilliance and warmth reminded him of Pat's brightness and cheerfulness, and called to his manhood. She would swirl into the kitchen from shopping, fling her parcels down on the table, and pour out a story of some encountered excitement so ringingly and dramatically that it was as good as a play on TV; and such occasions would always leave Wilfred feeling uneasy.

Mary had not written for over a fortnight. It was the beginning of April. The buds were out and the birds nesting, and still she did not write.

Wilfred was so worried that he confided in Mr Taverner, one evening when they were washing up. Wilfred had enjoyed a supper to which he had been invited. Mrs Cornforth was out and Miss Dollette watching a television programme about hamsters.

'Telephone,' said Mr Taverner.

'She won't like that,' Wilfred said unhappily.

'Of course not,' said Mr Taverner. 'Who can forget the furious impatience in a youthful voice when someone over thirty rings them up? Let her, bless her, get on with it. Got the number?'

'Yes, I have, as a matter of fact, though I don't think she wanted—'

'*Natürlich*. Blow all that. Off you pip. I'll finish these,' and he waved a saucepan.

The telephone was in one of the two niches in the hall, facing Kichijoten, and it was possible to talk in some privacy.

'Oh, hullo, Dad,' said Mary's voice. 'Anything wrong?'

'Nothing's wrong *this* end, Mary. But I haven't heard from you for nearly three weeks and—'

'Oh yes, sorry and all that, love, but we've been awfully busy and – and –' her voice changed. 'Dad.'

'Yes, love?' (Oh, what was coming? Pregnant?)

There was a pause.

Then he heard another voice – young, high, yet unmistakably male.

'Hullo, Mr Davis. I am a new friend of Mairly's. Name Yasuhiro Tasu. I am living in Mairly's house. I want to present myself. Good evening.' The last words had the inflection of a greeting.

'Good evening,' Wilfred gulped. *What was this? Mustn't take it too seriously, mustn't be nosey, mustn't* . . .

'Oh, pleased to meet you, even over the phone,' he said, in the manner known as *jokey*. (At least the boy had some manners.) 'Well, it's very cold up here . . .'

'Not very cold in London,' said the oh-so-alien voice.

'And . . . and how are you two young people spending this cold evening?' lilted the father, knowing he sounded idiotic and unlike himself.

But there seemed to be advantages for over-anxious parents in talking to Japanese boyfriends.

'We talk,' announced the voice firmly. 'We sit in my room and talk. About a great Japanese hero, Mishima . . . Spent most of my money this week on flowers,' it added, with a laugh that Wilfred was surprised to find attractive, 'so can't go to cinema. You heard about Mishima?'

'Er . . . no . . . I'm afraid not . . .'

Pip. Pip. Pip.

'Must go. Mairly says "goodbye".' The line went dead.

Looking dazedly around as he replaced the receiver, Wilfred encountered the stare of Kichijoten. It struck him as distinctly sly this evening, and suddenly he shook his fist at her.

Mrs Anstruther, in her over-full life, had made time to 'tackle' Slutty Singer – in her study, where the fact that Slutty was accustomed to going over the rugs with the Hoover every morning did not prevent an unfamiliar sensation coming upon her as she sat opposite her employer, listening to the unemotional yet curiously reproving voice flowing on and on.

Slutty *almost* listened.

Recipient of genuine if incoherent thanks from the men she entertained, she felt little need of kindness from anyone. She slopped along, exercising her gift of strong sexual response, and being feted by those she benefited.

But she was fond-ish of her five children, especially the two youngest, and spent quite a lot of the men's presents on their clothes. The children's meals, though unwholesome and irregular, were abundant; and although they slept in an indescribable bed, and their hair was touched only when some acquaintance of Slutty's snatched up a brush, the cottage just down the street from old Mr Davis's was always warm.

Julia began in as mother, woman-to-woman a tone as she could summon, as if taking it for granted that Slutty would want to get Samantha into a primary school as soon as possible. She talked, uninterrupted, for nearly ten minutes.

Slutty's eyes were taking in Julia's necklace and her (this morning) firmly fastened, smooth hair.

'And now about Kelly.' Julia pushed herself into the new subject, ignoring a slight hoarseness at the back of her throat. 'She ought to go to a nursery school—'

'Costs money, that does,' said Slutty, also hoarse, but from gin and cigarette smoke.

'I was just coming to that. The council is opening Torford's first nursery school this year, in Caversham Road—'

'I 'aven't 'eard nothing about no nursery school.' Slutty's expression was now suspicious; she associated the word 'council' with nosiness and interference. They were her kids, weren't they?

'It's free,' said Mrs Anstruther, 'except for their dinner money.'

"Ow much'll that be?'

'I don't know to a penny, Mrs Singer, but about fifty pence a week, I should think.'

'Might manage that,' mused Slutty, twiddling a strand of hair.

'I'm sure you can . . . You aren't likely to move, are you?
Move house?'

'Er . . .' Slutty stared at the curtains.

'I'm thinking of some years ahead. They do so much better
at school if they've a settled background. Have you a long lease
on your . . . place?'

'Dunno. I'm all right, I s'pose.'

'Yes, well . . . Mr Anstruther and I would always keep an eye
on the little girls, you know. Now –' she turned to her desk.
'Now you're going along to the Town Hall tomorrow to put
their names down for the school.'

She did not add any coaxing 'aren't you?' but handed Slutty
a sheet of scarlet paper, boldly printed in white Roman capitals.
'Here's the address of the Town Hall.' (She'll remember the
colour; not so likely to lose it.)

'Soon got onto old Davis's place,' confided Slutty suddenly.
'Paintin' it up pink already, they are. There's another, up the
other end, wot they've done too. Change the 'ole street, we
reckon.'

'Indeed? Yes, well, of course they're the kind of little places
people like . . . You'll go along to the Town Hall tomorrow,
won't you, Mrs Singer?'

'Might as well,' said Slutty, clasping the scarlet paper and
responding to the briskness in Julia's tone. Then she heaved
herself up, half nodding at her employer, and slouched to the
door.

'Good,' and she smiled. 'Such pretty children, both of them.'

'Ain't bad,' Slutty admitted, pausing at the door, the faintest
sparkle in her eyes. 'Might see 'em on the telly one o' these days.'

Over my dead body, thought Julia, dismissing the mother of
her protégeés with a smile.

Her husband was waiting for her outside the school in the late
afternoon light, beside their shabby car. It struck her that his
appearance matched it.

'Hullo, darling,' she said. 'Anything wrong?'

'Everything, but I'm used to that. No, couldn't stand the office another minute, so I thought I'd come and meet you. You're late. It's nearly six.'

She told him about Slutty and the little girls, to which his comment was 'Christ'. Julia glanced at him.

'Have you been home?' she asked.

'I have. Babette was there. Been in since three. Apparently she cut some game or other . . .'

'Basketball,' Julia put in mechanically.

'. . . wanted to try out some eyelashes she'd bought.'

'Well, Jeremy, I know it's irritating, but she *is* nearly twelve. They see the older girls . . . It's only a phase . . .'

'Look here, Ju. We may as well get this over while we've five minutes to ourselves. I've decided. She's going to the Comprehensive.'

Julia was utterly unprepared. She had taken it for granted that Babette would stay at Redpaths, take her A levels there, and try for a university place. Julia had set her heart upon Oxford or Cambridge.

But something kept her silent. She had turned quickly to look at her husband; had seen the reflected glare from the traffic lights shining on his sullen, ageing face. But it was the lingering March afterglow that was doing the real damage – revealing, with its delicate light, just what had happened to the laughing, loving man she had married.

It isn't life that's done this to him, she thought, in an instant of guilt and repentance. *It's the life I've made him live.*

He did not look towards her, and for a few minutes she did not feel able to speak. Her day had been an unusually hard one; the upper school was in the middle of examinations; that morning her secretary had announced with a stony face that she was four months pregnant. Julia had divined that, beneath the stoniness, there squirmed and howled a longing for the Head to take things over and arrange . . . something. And then the interview with Slutty Singer.

Oh well, she thought, with an uncharacteristic frivolity more like that of her mother (young in the '20s), *there are always house plants.*

Babette was crouching in the living room, by the dying fire. The room was almost in darkness.

'Hullo – what have you been up to?' Julia said, switching on the lights. Babette did not move. She kept her head still and blinked once. 'Yes,' said her mother sharply. 'I see them. They look ridiculous. The eyeshadow's the right colour and you've put it on quite well, but—'

'I know. "If you were sixteen, it would look more suitable,"' Babette interrupted drearily. 'I don't know what's the matter, Mummy. I feel rather depressed. And I was looking forward awfully to these –' fluttering the eyelashes.

'Well, if you cut games – which you know means a row – *and* do that to your eyes – which you know I don't approve of, *yet – and* sit by a fire that's nearly out in a room that's nearly dark – how do you expect to feel?'

Babette gave a reluctant giggle, as her father came in from putting away the car.

'Heavens! Raquel Welch in person!' he exclaimed, striking an attitude.

'No, but honestly, Daddy, how do you think they look?'

'Like something from the souks of Algiers,' he pronounced, after a survey. 'I prefer you straight.'

'I know. *I* think it looks wrong, somehow.' She scrambled up and surveyed herself discontentedly in a looking-glass on the wall. 'They cost nearly a pound, too.'

'Then you've wasted it, haven't you?' her mother said coldly. 'You know perfectly well – I told you – what profits the manufacturers make on those things. For heaven's sake get them off . . . Jeremy, break it to her, will you? I'll get tea.' She hurried out.

'Break what?' Babette was now sitting on the low, old brass fender. 'Something ghastly, I bet . . . I say, what did you mean about Algiers?'

'We'll leave it at that . . . I don't know whether you'll think it's ghastly, but I think it's necessary. You aren't being what the sociological boys call *stretched*, my love, and so you're off to the Comprehensive in September – *if* they'll have you.'

She sprang up, mouth open, eyes widened. A piece of eyelash fluttered to the floor.

'The Comp? Truly? Do you *mean* it? But I say – how's Mummy taking it? Isn't she simply *rampaging*?'

'She seems to think it may work out. Now, as a personal favour to me, Babs,' said Jeremy, on the note he would have used to a beloved woman, 'will you try not to make a fuss?'

Babette's face was crimson. She pulled off the eyelashes from her right eyelid and tried to put them on the mantelpiece but she was staring at her father and missed, and they floated down into the fire.

'*FUSS!* Make a fuss? Do you know they let you wear what you like there? No more beastly mini skirts and jerseys . . . Jane Jones has got a maxi-skirt, all over wigwams, and she's going to have a Tibetan coat for her birthday . . . there'll be *boys! Alan Hannigan goes there!* Jane says you have a man to teach you filthy physics. He's smashing. He plays the guitar in his leisure time to lay a spot more bread on himself . . . fuss? I'm only afraid there won't be a place for me – no such luck.'

'Well . . . I'm glad that . . .' her father said, settling into his usual armchair and taking out his cigarette case, with smiling eyes fixed on her face. 'I didn't know you . . . I thought you quite liked it at Redpaths.'

'Pretended to, to please Mums,' she answered at once.

When Julia came back with the tea tray, what was left of the eyelashes lay on the table, beside a crumpled paper handkerchief stained blue and green. Babette was sitting on the arm of her father's chair and saying earnestly:

'Make-up's dishonest. Jane says it's absolutely OUT, for her . . .'

Jeremy caught Julia's eye, and winked. But Julia lowered her own quite presentable eyelashes as she primly poured out the tea, and would not let herself return the wink.

I've got Giles, she thought, *priggy though he is. And I'll buy some house plants, I actually will. It would amuse me. And I'll hang on, like — a leech, to Samantha and Kelly.*

21

Old Mishima

Mary was sitting in Yasuhiro's room, wondering whether she should ask him, right out: '*Why* do you go on so about this old Mishima?'

She was finishing her second cup of coffee, on a cold, light evening at the end of March, surrounded by the gazing presences of dozens of daffodil buds arranged with intimidating perfection, and feeling strongly that it was time old Mishima bowed out and Mary Davis had a look in.

A delicious shiver caused her suddenly to smile.

'Why do you laugh, Mairly?' demanded Yasuhiro disconcertingly, pausing in an account of his hero's introduction to *Hagakure*, the eighteenth-century manual of *bushido*, which Mishima wrote in 1967.

'I wasn't laughing, just smiling.'

'Did I made a joke?' His thunderstorm look was coming down.

'(*Make* a joke.) No. Can't smile if I want to?' she demanded, feeling impatient.

'Of course, of course. I wish you to do anything you wish (no, *want* sound better) under my roof,' he said grandly. 'But also – *why* did you smile? In that way? You look down in your face. Your hairs on your eyes look like the moon when she is very young, but black . . . (I see in the newspaper the Americans up there again.)'

Oh, go on about my eyelashes, Mary longed to say. *But now, damn, it was the Americans.*

'Well,' she began, 'I expect you'll be furious – you know – very angry –'

Yasuhiro raised his eyebrows, so black and delicate they looked at first glance as if painted, and waited in silence.

'I only wondered why you talk about Mishima all the time,' Mary said at last, 'and – and I was wishing –'

'Continue to speak, Mairly. Please.' The thunderstorm had lifted, and the diamond-sword sparkle had returned.

'I – I –' she could not go on, and also felt it more prudent not to.

He nodded. 'I know. I know it, Mairly.'

'What?' she muttered.

'Wishing to talk about you and about me. I also – too—' he broke off. 'Many, many thoughts.' Then he went calmly on: 'Talking about Mishima because he is a great, great hero. It is my strong wish to follow him. Be like him. Save Japanese old customs, old poetry, old – traditions? – Yes, traditions. And maybe perhaps –' his voice became quieter, reverent – 'to die for the Emperor and for Japan. In honourable war.'

Mary naturally found this incomprehensible.

Born in the early '50s and brought up in an atmosphere of prudent and woolly Liberalism, well laced with Labour theories, war, to her, was both unimaginable and inexcusable. She stared at him, unwilling to start an argument, but wondering, made cowardly by the feelings: *what on earth could she say that would be acceptable*. She said at last:

'Well, I'm sure they're worth saving – your traditions, I mean. (That word's quite right, Yasu.) And the old poetry and the old customs. Only some of them weren't all that good, were they? I mean, the peasants were awfully poor . . .'

Yasuhiro's brows came down, his eyes flashed as all his features seemed to change, while Mary gaped, fascinated. Something sprang up in her memory – a picture – a drawing?

She knew! It was the picture called simply *A Demon*, in the old Japanese Room at Lorrimer House.

'*Bushido* would come back to Japan, then, perhaps,' Yasuhiro said. 'If enough people willing to die.'

'You said that word before – I've often heard you say it. What does it mean?'

She would have liked to add *when it's at home*, an expression of her paternal grandmother's when confronted by a long word, but she refrained.

'Ancient way of the *samurai*, the warriors. I *told* you, Mairly. This very evening about fifteen moments past eight, I told you. Mishima write an introduction to *Hagakure*, a book about *bushido*.' He paused, looking severe.

'Oh . . . yes . . . I'm sorry. Go on.'

'At this time, Mairly, Japan in dirty hands of politicians – and peasants like only refrigerators and coloured televisions. My own uncle now makes – manufactures them in a large factory –'

'"Big" is better,' Mary put in mechanically. 'Sorry – go on.' At last, she was hearing something about his life at home!

'– a – *big* factory in Tokyo. Family business. Thousands of pounds a year. We always have money by land. Now have money by business. My uncle arrange – manage – it all. My father *inkyo* – live in the shade.'

She looked at him enquiringly.

'In the West you say *retire*. Go away from active life.'

'Oh. Oh, I see. Does he – mind? I mean, does he like it?'

'Yes. But likes *pachinko* (ball game for peasants like your bingo) too much.' Yasuhiro laughed suddenly, and looked at her. 'All day, all day. But sometimes play at chess. So now we are all business men. No honour. No *bushido*. Great-grandfather fought at second battle of Port Arthur. And my father fight. Oh yes. Marched down to Singapore. And after he march – commanded? – yes, commanded in the jungle. I wish – I want –' his voice sank, 'to be a warrior. Like Mishima. Also write books, like he.'

'Write books!' exclaimed Mary, almost more dismayed at this ambition than by his military one. 'But you won't make any money, Yasu, unless you get the story on television. Writing's a very hard life.'

'Don't need money,' was the superb answer. 'Shall have plenty. Also, *samurai* despise. (Yes, despise.) Starve, have no home, only take money for fighting sometimes. More usually, fight because like fighting . . . Honourable.'

Mary felt a strong impulse to shake her head over all this. It opened a wide, misty, dangerous landscape, mountainous and frowning, of which she could not help feeling the lure, because it was Yasuhiro talking. But she also felt it was not a *real* landscape.

'Have plenty funds, too,' Yasu added.

'Nice for you,' she said dryly.

Memories of economies in her own home returned – and a sensation of being cut off from Yasuhiro's life came to her as she saw her mother going cheerfully off to work at the Town Hall on biting January mornings. And there he sat, looking smashing, even in snowy shirt and blue jeans: youth's casual international uniform.

'"Soldiers", Yasu,' she corrected sharply, needing to humiliate him. 'You really must learn to use modern words – "warriors" sounds downright daft.'

'"Warriors,"' he repeated softly, his voice ductile as the movement of a snake.

'Now look here –' Mary was beginning. She paused, but only for a few seconds, before going on sedately: 'Why don't you join the Army – *your* Army – then.'

'Army!' He reared up, this time like the snake poised to strike. 'Japan *have* – has no Army!'

His voice changed, and he recited quickly and with an angry smile: 'Article nine – aspiring-sincerely-to-an-international-peace-based-on-justice-and-order-the-Japanese-people-forever-renounce-war-as-a-sovereign-right-of-the-nation-and-the-threat-or-use-of-force-as-a-means-of-settling-international-disputes.'

He paused. 'So – no more Army, Mairly. No more Pearl Harbor.'

'What?'

'I say, no more Pearl Harbor.'

'And a good thing too. So I should hope,' she said firmly. 'It was . . . simply awful.'

'Brave. Heroes. *Seppuku*. Suicide flyers.'

They stared at each other as if they were strangers. *This is awful*, thought Mary.

Afterwards, lying on her bed and thinking about the evening's talk, she understood that this had been a turning point.

She had wanted to say, 'I don't want to hear about that. Let's talk about you and me.' But Yasuhiro's expression, that of the little boy who wants to describe the dogfight, simply would not let her. She behaved like the ordinary good mother and, smiling, murmured: 'Of course I want you to tell me – go on.'

Yasuhiro then disconcerted her by saying approvingly: 'You show nice manners, Mairly. I know you don't *wish* to listen about Shield Society but you say "yes" because polite –' and he then caused her heart to do its familiar over-turn by adding 'I show you my human feelings, you understand. If I were with English young men, students, or old peasant Mr Grant upstairs, I agree, and say "Yes, yes, Pearl Harbor a disgrace." But here down with you I say I think glorious brave flyers. *You* don't think it. But to you I can *say* it, because—'

He stopped, and apparently went off into a meditation; his face became as impassive as a carved Buddha's in any of the temples on his home of islands. In a moment, he looked up.

'"Every geisha is always nineteen years old" – Japanese proverb,' he quoted gaily. 'Sweet, you know, and polite manners. How old you are, Mairly?'

'Seventeen.' She revived at the personal question, though she wondered a little if she were being compared to a geisha? The travel books were always so careful to explain that they were *not* . . . but somehow one was left wondering.

'And I have twenty.'

He spoke thoughtfully, and did not begin his account of the
Shield Society (founded by Mishima with the aim of 'fostering
the military virtues and defending the Emperor') for nearly
a minute, during which he again looked like a Buddha and
mused in silence.

Mary revived still more on receiving this small treasure of
information, and was enabled to support half an hour – nearly
three quarters, as a surreptitious glance at her watch told her –
of secret meetings and sham fights, uniforms, and a great deal
more of what seemed to her dangerous nonsense.

Yasuhiro always broke up their evenings punctually at ten.
As she went up the stairs, leaving him bowing and smiling
ceremoniously at the door, she was thinking *I do know a bit
more about him. And he does show me his human feelings. He said
so. That's something. But the worrying thing is that he MEANS all
that codswallop about Mishima . . . And he really likes it.*

Mrs Levy had had so much cause to reprove Mary lately for
absent-mindedness, forgetfulness and daydreaming that she
was becoming worried.

She realized, now, when her assistant seemed to be
deteriorating, what a treasure she had found: punctual, biddable,
clever at sewing and – thrown in as a bonus – a good listener.
I didn't know when I was lucky, Mrs Levy thought bitterly. *But
I should have known.* Mary seemed different, but modern girls
are all the same. She braced herself, should she be faced with
a sudden giving of notice, to offer a small rise in salary.

But one morning, about five minutes to one, when she
had already peered out through the door and seen, across
the road, Mary sedately descending the flight of steps leading from Broad Street station, and had turned to take down
from its hook her new astrakhan coat (bought through the
good offices of Cousin Maurice, who was in the fur trade) a
customer stalked in.

As if he owned my shop was Mrs Levy's phrase for this customer's gait. However, he was Japanese, and they usually had

plenty to spend and that overcoat (she thought, staring) can't have cost a penny less than sixty pounds.

'Good mornink. Can I help you?'she asked.

'No thank you. I will look around,' said the customer and did so, into what nooks and places of concealment for human beings the shop possessed.

'Of course, please yourself,' said Mrs Levy, proceeding with the donning of Cousin Maurice's astrakhan.

Suddenly suspicion struck her. She glanced sharply at the Japanese man, who was staring haughtily at a display of plastic dolls dressed in tartan kilts. And here was Mary coming across the road, and she was seventeen, and Mrs Levy would shortly be off for the rest of the day.

Maybe they get up to something, thought Mrs Levy. Her suspicions were given startling confirmation by Mary's stopping dead at the shop door and almost gasping 'H-hello!' at sight of their customer, while he, turning, said calmly, 'Hullo, Mairly. I come to see where you work.'

He turned a smiling face on Mrs Levy, and she had to admit that the smile made him look less stuck-up.

'Ach! You know each other!' she exclaimed, eyes popping, eyebrows rising, every feature expressing surprise and interest.

'Yes, he came in about a month ago.' Mary's voice was muffled, as she retired into her nook to take off her coat.

'Twenty-fifth of February,' put in the Japanese man, still politely smiling. 'My name is Yasuhiro Tasu. I am here to learn English.'

'Und I suppose you coming here every afternoon since the twenty-fifth of February learning it off of my assistant.'

'This *is* only the second time. Isn't it, Yasu?' Mary turned to him.

'Yes, vell, all right.' Mrs Levy, seeing by her watch that it was ten past one, decided suddenly to leave the situation to Providence. 'If you don't see anythink you fancy, perhaps you better be goink on you way,' she ended playfully.

'Yes . . . goodbye, Mairly. Good afternoon,' to Mrs Levy,
with a small bow, and he sauntered out.

Mrs Levy turned to Mary.

'Your face go red,' she announced. 'Vy? Und how does he
know your name?' she added. '"Mairly", indeed! He's your
boyfriend?'

This was what Mary had been dreading. Mrs Levy's grand-
motherly interest.

'He lives in my house,' she said quietly, beginning to fix
cards of earrings onto a velvet-covered board. 'I've had coffee
with him, once or twice. I'm helping him with his English.'

Tell the truth or nearly the truth — it's easier and it works better.

Mrs Levy, however, responded in a surprising way. 'No, no,
Mary. You must be pulling my legs! A Japanese in an overcoat
costing sixty pounds to live in Gospel Oak! If you tell me he
stays at the Dorchester, yes, I believe you. But Gospel Oak —
no, no.'

'It isn't a *poor* neighbourhood, Mrs Levy, there are some
nice houses there. You recommended it,' she reminded her, and
began to steer the conversation into less dangerous waters,
'though not so nice as the ones in the Garden Suburb, of
course.' (She knew that Helenslea Gardens in Golders Green,
where Mrs Levy's daughter lived, was her employer's idea of
all that was most desirable in house property.)

'Ach! Golders Green, yes. Really nice homes there. Und
Bishopsvood Avenue! Between Hampstead and Highgate. *Vot*
houses! Princely. — You go on having coffee with that overcoat,
Mary, maybe you end up in Bishopsvood Avenue, who knows?
You help him with his English, my dee-ar,' ended Mrs Levy
with a disconcerting cackle.

As Mary went up the steps to Broad Street that evening, one
of the packed climbing crowd of homebound workers under
the darkening sky, she was thinking that the next time she
saw him, she would ask firmly: *Why did you come into the shop
on Wednesday? Please don't do it again. I don't like it.*

But she had liked it. Too much, in fact.

'Hullo, Mairly,' and there he was, materializing from behind one of the advertisement hoardings ranged down the middle of the platform.

'Oh h-hullo . . . you again . . . you,' she stammered. And then, unbelievably, his hand stole out and – among all those people – into her own.

'Oh Mairly,' he muttered, his English accent gone utterly into chaos. 'Don't be crohs. I want *so much* to see your face. Could not work or read. Come, come go, Mairly. We go away by ourselves somewhere, perhaps look at the River Thames. Come, go.'

He led her off, and she saw only his serious eyes, looking down into her own. The cherishing manner in which he led her through the throng increased her sense of their being alone together as they made their way down the steps against the mounting crowd.

'Did you go home?' she asked presently.

'No. Sat in Saint Paul's. During three hours. Sleep. But perhaps they think I meditate, like a Hindu holyman,' and he gave a mischievous laugh. 'Then went, and drank tea. An awful place, Mairly and the tea made by withering English leaves, I think. A disgrace. Why you ask me?' softly, and bending his head down to her.

'Oh – I was only thinking you must be hungry,' she said shyly.

'So I am, so I am,' in a voice of pleased surprise. 'Both of we hungry, perhaps. Near Saint Paul's is nice place. Smell of fry, but quiet. No cars. We go there. Look!' He paused, and gazed upwards. 'Saint Paul's.'

She followed his gaze. Carving and column glowed pale gold in the afterglow, against the deep blue of the sky. The dome, above them, struck the eye with its darkness as a note from one of the place's own mighty bells could strike the ear.

'I like him now,' said Yasuhiro. 'This afternoon he was my bedroom.'

Mary gave a delighted little laugh.

'You laugh, Mairly,' said Yasuhiro, smiling. 'I made a joke? In English I made a joke?'

'It's the sort of joke Dad – my father – and I think is funny. You know – a bit sort of silly.'

'What is your father working at?' He looked ahead at the darkening street crowded with hurrying people. 'Is he a peasant?'

'No. A civil servant,' she explained, dismissing an extraordinary picture of her father bending over rice fields in a huge straw hat. 'He's retired now.' She swallowed. 'He – what your people call – "sits in the shade" – *inkyo*,' she ended, calmly, but proud of herself.

'You know Japanese word! Oh Mairly, you learn that word!'

'Yes . . . well, I thought if you want to learn some English, it would be handy for me to know some Japanese.'

She was careful to keep her tone light.

'Handy. What does it mean?'

'Oh – convenient – useful. It's slang, really.'

'Works for your government – did work. How great he was?'

'Not great at all. We live in a town in . . . in the eastern part of England, and my father worked for our – local council. It was a small job – work – but responsible. He was head of the department that collects the rates.'

'Rates?'

'Every citizen must pay part of the money they earn to the Government and that pays for the things everybody has: street lighting and free schools and public libraries,' she said quickly and rather desperately. (Oh why must she dish out all this boring stuff when he was beginning to ask her the questions a young man asks a girl when . . .?)

'I understand. Your family is not peasants.'

'I wouldn't say so – no.' Mary was relieved that the question had not been put to her mother. 'Middle-class, I suppose,' she ended vaguely. 'I never really thought about it.'

Yasuhiro appeared to dismiss the subject. 'Here is the place,' he said gaily, as they approached a low flight of steps leading to a calm expanse of stone, set with shrubs in great jars, 'up this. I find him this afternoon.'

'Found it, Yasu.'

'Found it. Now up this steps, Mairly. Over here. See! As I said you. No cars, quiet.'

'It's super,' she said, looking around.

The grey stone spaces, wide and silent, stretched before them in the fading afterglow, shut in by featureless modern blocks of offices made inoffensive by the dusk, mere background for the rich gold light pouring out from shops and cafés.

'Super,' she said again, after a silence.

Across the precinct, against the background of distant traffic noise, came the sound of footsteps.

'Old sound,' said Yasuhiro. 'One of oldest sounds in the world. Hear that sound in Baby-lon.'

She murmured something.

'What you are saying, Mairly?'

'Oh . . . I only said . . . I like the – the kind of things you say, Yasu.'

He was silent for a moment. Then, looking up at the great dome, he spoke a few words in Japanese. In the quiet, she heard his voice as if she were listening to the notes of some tropical bird.

'What? Oh tell me what you said . . .' she almost whispered.

'The beauty we have lost is floating
In the air like dust of gold,' he said slowly.

'That's beautiful,' said Mary, in a moment. 'Did you just . . . make it up? This minute, I mean?'

'No,' with his flashing smile. 'I had many, many thoughts. When I first saw Saint Paul's the thoughts began. I was jealous – envious? – of him. Because he is so big. I wished for Japan to have the glory of the biggest. I . . .' – his voice fell – 'had human feelings that my nation had lost face. Then other thoughts began – came. So few? (Yes, few.) Few beautiful buildings in England. – So I thought . . . and I had feelings . . . and then the poem. A haiku.'

'Is that its name in Japanese?'

'Yes, *Haiku*. Eighteen syll-ables (oh what a word!) Not quite correct in my translation. Has only sixteen. Must work on it. Difficult to translate. Correct in Japanese.' He repeated it, then his face came alight. He turned to her.

'It is for you, Mairly. A present.'

'Oh! Oh thank you, Yasu. I've never had—'

What would any boy in Torford think of this present? And a poem not even about herself! Yet so beautiful. 'I like it very much, truly,' she said, almost inarticulate with embarrassment.

Then he said, gazing not at her but up at the great dome fading into the dark blue of the sky –

'The beauty we have lost is floating
In the air like dust of gold, darling.'

He turned to her, smiling.

'Darling. English word meaning sweet one. Consoles the heart for loss of beautiful old buildings. And now has eighteen English syllables. Come, Mairly, go, coffee.'

But when they were seated in the café, with full cups of coffee and food (over which Yasuhiro raised his eyebrows) in front of them, he broke what was for Mary an entranced silence by saying thoughtfully, 'Doesn't sound correct, the "darling". Feeling correct, shape correct, sound not quite correct in English. W. H. Auden would say not correct. I will work on that. Not proper.'

'It's "right", Yasu. Not "proper",' Mary said resignedly.

She would have preferred the haiku to remain uncorrected.

22

Shock!

It never occurred to Mary that Mrs Cadman had been noticing the evening visits to the basement.

But one evening, as she was making her way downstairs about half past eight to the usual coffee-drinking, she saw Mrs Cadman poised in the hall. (Poised, not loitering; all her movements were quick.) Mrs Cadman glanced up, and a smile came over her pretty-mouse's face.

'There you are, dear,' she said softly. 'I want a word with you. Come in here a minute.'

She opened the door of the large front room, a place of gloomy furniture and dark wallpaper, lit by a feeble bulb because it was never used except when some casual visitor, recommended by a lodger in the house, passed a night on the Kumfi-Slepe.

Mary followed, thinking *blow*, and resenting every second that kept her from Yasuhiro.

She looked at Mrs Cadman enquiringly.

'I shan't keep you a minute, dear . . . you know, your dad told me, over the phone that evening, that your mother had passed over. There's just the two of you now . . .'

Mary nodded, looking calm. Dad had been enlisting Mrs Cadman's interest in case of Trouble. Well, there wasn't going to be any.

'It's just this –' Mrs Cadman went on quickly. 'That boy downstairs comes from a rich family. Mr Grant saw something in one of those business supplements (I can't be bothered with them but you know what men are with their newspapers). It mentioned the names of the ten largest firms in Japan, and that boy belongs to one of them. I remembered the name from the Embassy's letter. Now, just you remember that *money's always useful.* You young people all do so well nowadays. But it wasn't always like that, you know. I was on the stage in the '30s, and we used to be scared stiff of being sacked. Everyone was.'

Oh Lord, thought Mary. *Here we go. Hamburg, only in England this time.*

'. . . but it did teach us the value of money . . . Now I've nearly said my say,' detecting slight signs of impatience, and dropping a cold little paw for a second on Mary's wrist. '*You play your cards right, dear, and MARRY him.* It's a wonderful chance, and he seems a nice boy, too, so far as I can see. Good luck. That's all I wanted to say.'

She nodded, her small face all kindness and conspiracy, in the dim light from the economical bulb.

'Thank you, Mrs Cadman.' The blush seemed to rise from Mary's very heart, scarlet as her blood, but her tone was calm. 'It's – nice of you to be so interested . . . I'll remember.' She was not going to say any more. Not one single word.

'And remember too – nothing . . . much . . . before you're married,' Mrs Cadman nodded and whispered rapidly as Mary made for the door. 'Oh, I know all about the permissive society, but boys don't change that much and they all try it on.'

Mary nodded, and smiled, and fairly scampered down the stairs.

Yasuhiro had left the door ajar. He was kneeling before the coffee tray, and as she entered he looked up.

'Oh,' said Mary, and paused.

'Yes, yes. I put this on. I wear it,' he said. His expression was solemn and melancholy; she could read changes in his face now. He bent again over the cups, sifting coffee into the pot.

'It's super,' she said, coming closer to look at the dark blue robe embroidered with silvery storks and large-petalled flowers.

'My great-grandfather gave me. Is a ceremonial robe. Traditional,' and he sighed. 'Sit down, Mairly, sit down please.'

Mary sat down. She decided against asking him why he was wearing the robe; it would probably be Mishima's birthday or something – if Mishima had ever done anything so cheerful and ordinary as celebrate his birthday.

Yasuhiro, however, explained at once.

'I have a letter this morning.' He slowly raised his lids, and looked at her. 'From Great-grandfather. That is why I wear his present. When the coffee is made, I shall show it to you. I mean the letter.'

'Oh . . . thanks . . . you know, your English really *is* improving, Yasu. It's heaps better.'

'Heaps? It doesn't matter that my English is improving.'

'Of course it matters . . .' (What could be up?) 'Er . . . does he write in Japanese?'

'Of course of course he writes in Japanese,' Yasuhiro said drearily. 'Is very great at using the brush. Very fine letters. Mairly, please put the kettle on the gas fire. My heart is sad.'

'(Gas-ring. The fire is what we sit by.) All right.'

She did so, while reciting in a cheerful tone the old rhyme about Polly doing the same thing, feeling that an effort must be made to lighten the atmosphere.

An evening spent in glooming about Great-grandfather or prosing about Mishima would be an evening wasted – and they had been getting along so nicely! Though it was true that the golden evening by St Paul's had ended, tamely enough, in a taxi ride back to Rowena Road, with Yasuhiro and Mary seated decorously opposite one another practising Yasuhiro's vowel sounds.

'Polly,' he repeated, sitting back on his heels. 'Polly. What is that little song? Is a haiku for English children?'

'Sort of. Yes, I suppose so. We call it a nursery rhyme.'

'A song for British peasants,' he said contemptuously. 'In Japan, the tea ceremony important yet. Takes the pride of the heart away, then calms the heart.'

Mary poured milk into her cup in silence.

'Why is your heart sad, Yasu?' she asked quietly at last, looking at him over the rim of her cup.

'Because . . .' he did not look up, 'Great-grandfather writes to me in his letter that I must think to marry.'

He took particular care with his accent; she noticed, even through the stunning shock, and her only thought was that she must keep quiet, and show no more than friendly interest.

'I know why it be.'

'Is,' she corrected steadily. 'Yes?'

'He is very ancient – old. (I know why it *is*.) Seen the blossom come ninety-three times. Imagine, Mairly.'

'Born in 1876,' she said faintly.

'Yes.' He got up, in one graceful movement. 'I show you his letter.'

He took a folded sheet of dark paper from his sash. 'Excellently fine writing. Study.' He held the paper out to her.

She studied. The ink was very black; the marks so sharp, and so significant-seeming, even to a foreigner, that they suggested tiny drawings rather than letters.

'They're . . . like queer-shaped animals,' she said at last. It was not precisely what she meant, but she was finding it difficult to think clearly.

'Ancient tradition tells that certain letters are – were – so beautiful they came up from paper and talked to scholars . . . why are you amuse, Mairly? It is not a joke,' as she broke into a little laugh.

'Because I like it . . . Come on, Yasu! Your coffee's getting cold . . . you were going to tell me why –' she steadied her voice, 'why your great-grandfather wants you to marry.'

He nodded.

'He is so ancient,' he said at last, 'he feels that he could die and go to the ancestors, without – yes, without – to see my wife and my son, my first son. That is why he writes.'

She drank some coffee, thinking that she must be very, very careful what she said.

Which Yasu was this? The alien young god (Mary did not use those words to herself), the boy laughing with his eyes who made her heart turn over, her pupil whose mistakes seemed to her childish and endearing? . . . None of them. She had not met this pensive, subdued young man before.

'Understand, Mairly —' he lifted his head and looked at her sadly. 'In Japan the parents choosing the wife. Keep a —' he paused, uttered a Japanese word, then shook his head, and thought — 'ah yes, a *list.* They have a *list.* Of suitable girls. Not all parents do this. But still in honourable families. Not like in "the West of wonder".' He gave a mocking smile. 'Here, you choose your own girl.' He knelt again before the coffee tray.

Mary swallowed. 'And have your parents got a list for you?' Her heart felt as if it were dying. (*And what an idea! Of course, over here some people's mums might say a boy would do nicely for someone, but a list!*)

Yasuhiro nodded. 'Oh yes. Some sweet girls, make a good wife. Have sons. Healthy.' He ended on a note of indescribable — could it be boredom? Mary felt the merest shadow of comfort. 'Pretty as first flowers.' He glanced round the room. 'Since I come here, my — taste? Yes, taste, go to live with those dogs.'

'What on earth do you mean?'

'You must know those dogs, Mairly. English idiom. They live in a disgraceful place, I suppose . . . In Japan we have one vase and arrange flowers very, very careful and correct. Visitors bow to that vase before the host when they come to the house. I know how to put a few — little flowers, at home. But *here . . .*' He suddenly seemed to cast his body sideways, as if forced by a storm working in his breast. 'I am so angry, and London is so ugly — and I am so — so — I do not know — human feelings going over me like that wave in the Old Man's picture . . .'

His voice was so low, now, and the English sounds so mangled, that she could hardly distinguish what he was saying. 'And *giri* fight all the time with human feelings and I buy

more flowers than is wanted to look correct. Yes, that's right.'
He broke off, and she could see his chest heaving under the
embroidered robe. 'Must have flowers. Comfort,' he ended.

'What Old Man?' Mary picked upon two of the words in
his rush of speech that she could distinguish.

'Hokusai. It is a picture of a tremendous wave. And boat.
Wave will fall on the boat, perhaps. Is only called "The Wave".
Yes! Is enough that name. So is here with me, Mairly.' He
stopped. She could see the beating of his heart shaking the
embroidery on the breast of his robe.

'I'm sorry you feel so bad . . .' she ventured at last.

Up came his head, his eyes gleaming.

'I'm not bad, Mairly,' with an angry stare. 'These are human
feelings. They go against *giri*, national honour.'

'I'm sorry . . . I didn't mean . . . I meant, I'm . . . I'm sorry
your heart is so sad.'

'It is the only work of a woman, to calm the heart of the
warrior,' he pronounced, and then quenched Mary's instant
indignation, adding, 'Darling. Sweet one. Good real name for
you, Mairly.'

She looked down. There was a silence. Now, if he were
English . . . she was thinking. But he did not move. And the
next thing that she heard, sounding calmly on the quiet air,
was a familiar name.

'But Mishima . . .' (*I cannot stand any more about Mishima*,
thought Mary, grinding her teeth together) 'prefer not to marry.
He . . .' here something seemed to occur to Yasuhiro, and he
paused, glanced at her oddly, then hurried on, 'only have his
man friends, and the *Tate No Kai*. (You call it Shield Society.)
And why should I marry if Mishima never marry?'

'Can't you please yourself, Yasu? You don't *have* to do everything Mishima did, do you?'

'Prefer to give his life for Japan,' said Yasuhiro gloomily.

'Yes, well . . .' Mary, seeking rather desperately for a more
calming subject than enforced marriage or patriotic death,
blundered on – 'that's . . . just it, you know, I'm afraid I didn't

really take in what you were saying the other evening about him and that Society . . . I was rather sleepy . . .'

'Asleep, Mairly? You are asleep when I tell you about Mishima make *seppuku*? Is like a woman, to go to sleep in such a moment.'

'Well, what else do you expect?' she said tartly, stung by this second contemptuous reference in a few minutes. 'And I said sleepy, not asleep. It's different.'

'No,' said Yasuhiro. 'Not. Almost the same.'

'Oh well . . . I'm sorry, anyway. You tell me. It'll cheer you up,' she ended quite wildly – tossed between the shock of hearing about the list, and seeing his alarming agitation, and wanting to comfort him, and trying to keep calm herself.

But, at the end of nearly twenty minutes, she was sitting with her mouth open, gaping at Yasuhiro standing in the middle of the room with his skin almost green and his eyes flashing fixed on some appalling vision in his own mind. She heard with rising horror how his hero had four times made the attempt to disembowel himself in front of a thousand soldiers of the Defence Corps, and four times failed – *tried; failed; tried; failed; tried; failed; tried; failed* – Mary's hands flew to her ears, but dropped again. Then – then – something stood up slowly within herself, from somewhere very deep, and it said: *This must stop.*

Those were its words. It was a voice, speaking within her. She heard its words, and she felt strong and calm and she broke in loudly across the other's unfaltering, sleepwalking voice.

'Yes, and then what happened?'

'His friend cut off his head,' Yasuhiro said.

Then, suddenly, up shot his own head, and from somewhere that was terribly not his lungs, there issued a sound, not loud, not a shout, but a fearful cry. It was the most frightening sound she had ever heard, because it was as if something apart from Yasuhiro, yet living, had cried out from inside him. She sat as if mesmerized, staring at the stranger in the ceremonial robes of Japan, a group of islands at the other side of the world.

'What? What did you say, Mairly?' he asked dazedly, in a
moment, standing with the sweat bright on his forehead and
slowly turning to look at her.

'I said, "then what happened?" And you told me,' she said
hoarsely. 'What – what an awful thing to do. Did Mishima –
ask him to?'

'Yes. Oh yes. He also was member of the Shield Society.'

'What an awful thing to *ask* anyone,' she babbled.

'It was his duty. His duty. And also *giri*.' He came across
to the coffee table and knelt beside it, coiling his body as if it
were a steel spring, without tremor or sway. 'You heard that
sound, Mairly?'

'I heard you – make an awful noise, Yasu.' She shuddered
suddenly, as if overwhelmed by a vision of all the mangled and
bloodied dead, in all the wars of her century, sweeping into
her small cosy world.

'Awful, yes it is awful. I see you shake, Mairly,' with a glance
of approval. 'That is what is the sound to do, make to shake.
Said that the sound, in the war, could call back spirit into the
body of Japanese soldiers. I learn that sound . . .' He stopped
and swallowed some cold coffee.

'*So*,' he lifted his arm and let it fall downwards in one sweep,
like a dark blue wave falling, to his side. 'End of Mishima. Gone
to his ancestors. Finish.'

Yasu went to the middle of the room under the light where
he had uttered the dreadful cry, and took out the letter again
from his sash.

He had forgotten to pull the curtains, and now Mary was
conscious that every passer-by could see down into the brightly
lit room. She was certain that Yasuhiro would not give a
thought to passing peasants, but she did; and she got up, and
drew the curtains.

'Sit quiet, Mairly,' he commanded.

'Sorry.' She flew back to her seat with a suppressed hysteri-
cal giggle, and he looked up.

'Oh yes. I remember – "Sit!" I am sorry. It was rude. Please sit, Mairly. Great-grandfather must be – must have – honour, even in his letter.'

'*Dearest One, Today I have spoken with – the – the –*' he hesitated. 'I don't know the English word – *the nakodo*. (That is the one who arrange the marriage, Mairly.) *And I have instructed him to let me have the – the details* (yes, details) *about –*' and Yasuhiro paused, and uttered a Japanese sound. 'That is – the – name,' he said in a low tone, with lowered eyes.

'Whose name?' Mary said, automatically, because the sound of the utterly foreign syllables had struck her with yet another shock. That girl belonged to Yasu's Japanese life.

'The one taken from the list that Great-grandfather has – keeps.'

'Don't your parents have anything to do with it?'

'In our family, no. Great-grandfather is almost all. So ancient, and a *samurai* – I have told you how he fight – influence?'

'That's right, yes. Go on, Yasu.'

'Then he says, this is the year of the Tiger, so this year I must not marry. Bad fortune. But soon is the year of the Dragon. So . . . he . . . has . . . told the – the *nakodo* . . . to begin . . . the negotiations.'

He was silent, looking down at the sheet of dark blue paper.

'Is that all?' Mary asked at last.

'Not all. No. He says of course of course I should have my work before I marry. Is the custom. But I have no work. But then he says (it is not *giri* for us in Japan to express love so strongly, but he is so ancient, you know) he loves me so much, so very much, he forgive I have not yet chosen my work, and his wish is to see me marry next year.'

There was another silence. Mary sat still, staring at the floor.

The next thing she knew was that he had crossed the room and was standing beside her. She felt, rather than saw, his hand steal out from the great blue sleeve of his robe, and then she felt a tress of her hair lifted.

'So beautiful,' she heard, and the note in his voice was deep and singing. 'Black like that stuff on ancient cooking sauce-pan.'

'Oh Yasu . . .' Mary choked, almost laughing, almost crying. 'Soot, we call that.'

'Sooot,' he murmured, while his hand crept to the back of her neck and she felt the whole mass part, and fall like a veil on either side of her down-bent face. 'Now I see most beautiful part of you. Behind of neck.'

But this was too much for Torford and seventeen years of the culture of the West of Wonder. Mary began to shake hysterically.

'You laugh, Mairly? You laugh when I tell you behind of your neck is so beautiful?'

'No – no – of course it isn't that – I'm glad, Yasu love . . . that is, I mean, it's not the way to say it – the word's wrong . . .' She wiped her streaming eyes. 'It's *back* of neck . . . or *nape*, if you want to be really correct.'

'Ah. Language difficulties once again.' He looked at her consideringly. 'You laugh but you cry also, Mairly. And I, too. You call me "love".'

'Yes, I did,' she said steadily. 'We often use it in England. It's just friendly. I say it to people in the shop sometimes.'

'Yes of course, of course.' Yasuhiro's eyes had their diamond sparkle. 'Now we will go for a walk on that Heef, Mairly. It's a good evening. Come, go.'

'(Heath, Yasu. And *nice* evening.) All right – I'll just get my coat – it's cold.'

'And I put on my jack-ette. Surprise for people to see cere-monial robe walking on Heef.'

'Yes, wouldn't it be.'

She did not think, while flinging on her coat. She did not cover with a scarf the hair he had called 'So beautiful'. She did not want to waste one second of the time that might be spent with him. That Japanese girl was thousands and thousands of miles away, at the other side of the world. But Mary Davis was going for a walk with him this minute, and by all the tribal traditions of Torford that gave Mary Davis the advantage.

He was waiting for her in the hall, wearing a white shirt, jeans, and his expensive coat.

'You know, Mairly,' he said meditatively, as they went down the steps, 'in Japan we don't often say that word "love".'

No, thought Mary, *I bet you don't.* She made a vague responsive sound. Then she said, feeling a desire to turn the conversation: 'You know, Yasu, your English is *good.* I mean you do still have trouble with some sounds, but – your – you can *express yourself.*'

'Ah. Can say what is in my heart.'

'Well, yes. I suppose so.'

'Not all,' he answered, with a return to gloom. 'But I shall tell you, Mairly. In Tokyo are still some old houses. Beautiful. Poor places but beautiful. Little, small. In one of these houses lives Mr Richard Cumber-ledge, and he is a lush.'

'A *what?*'

'Drink too much saki. Also too much whiskey. American whiskey. Used to be a novel-ist in England, sixty, nearly seventy years gone, now, and was much admire. Says he was friend of many famous writers. Thomas Hardy. He is now old, old, almost ancient as Great-grandfather, but used to teach English at Tokyo University where I studied for my degree, but now has small little pupils to teach in one room – few? – yes, few.'

'Oh, that's where you were . . . I was wondering.'

'Why you were wondering, Mairly? It is quite natural ordinary circumstance me being at Tokyo University.'

'No. Oh *dear.* I meant: I thought "Where was Yasu at – which university was Yasu at?"'

'Ah. Understand. Yes, I was there three years. But sent away.' He smiled wickedly. 'They did not like what the acts I do. With the *Tate No Kai.*'

'That . . . Shield Society. Did you belong to it?'

'Yes. Yes, Mairly. With all my human feelings and *giri. And* have my degree. Myself and three friends. The student-riots, and authorities consider Shield Society upset – disturb – angrify –'

'Make them angry?'

'Yes, yes, the Americans. So myself and friends sent away from university. But I have degree, so if I want to work in unworthy office, any firm in Japan please to have me. From Tokyo University, you see.'

'You're lucky, then,' Mary said firmly, not approving of this smugness. 'Lots of the girls at my school had brothers and boyfriends who got good degrees but can't get jobs.'

They were walking under trees already showing a shadowy fullness of buds. The air smelt of dead leaves and of spring.

'I think perhaps Mr Cumber-ledge was not a friend of Thomas Hardy,' Yasu said meditatively in a minute, 'because once he said to me he was also friend of Oscar Wilde and sit with him in coffee bar called Royal. But Mr Cumber-ledge would have been small small boy when Oscar Wilde sitting in that bar. I learn from Mr Cumber-ledge many English idioms. "Those disgraceful dogs." He often said about them . . . here is the Heef. Run, Mairly!'

Side by side they raced off, across the grass towards the dark hill rising against the afterglow.

Mary soon fell behind, panting, for Yasuhiro ran like a deer. She could just distinguish his smiling face through the twilight as she climbed breathlessly to the summit. He was holding out his hands to her.

'I like to hear you say that word love to me, Mairly,' he said, as her hands came up to meet his and he pulled her to his side. 'I hope – yes, hope – that you will say it many times often.'

23

Ride in a hired car

'You don't quite understand, Mrs Cornforth, if you don't mind me saying so. The fact is –'

'Yes?' Katherine said encouragingly. (*Her voice kind of, well, woos you is the only way I can put it,* thought Wilfred.) After a pause in which he did not reply she hurried on: 'Oh I *do* understand, Mr Davis. I am *good* about people. I do know what makes them tick. Please let me have that – God knows it's about all I have got, and even that I'm not allowed to use,' she ended, sounding almost bitter.

'I didn't mean anything offensive or – or unkind, you know that. I only meant, well, I suppose most fathers aren't downright afraid of their daughters, and I am afraid of Mary. Not that she's ever done anything really wrong, you understand me, except that running away – that did shake me, I don't mind telling you. Sometimes I think I'll never get over it. With her mother not gone six months. But –'

'That's love,' pronounced Katherine, '– being afraid.'

She lent forward and lifted the heavy brass tongs and carefully fitted a fragment of coal into a red cave. 'When one loves, one is afraid.'

'Well, perhaps that's so, Mrs Cornforth. But I can't help feeling it oughtn't to be.'

'Oh!' Katherine laughed. 'If we get onto "oughts" we'll be in deep water . . . not that I'd mind for once.' She turned to him quickly, and he noticed how her eyes shone. 'Does it ever strike you that life here is – well – just a bit dull?' and she laughed again. 'Shallow water, in fact?'

Wilfred did not quite like her laughter.

'Dull?' he repeated, shocked into vehemence. 'No it does not, Mrs Cornforth. Peace, perfect peace is what I'd call it, speaking frankly.'

'And isn't that a wee bit dull?' she teased, leaning back in her chair. 'I'd like . . .' she paused, and her eyes slid round at him while her lovely head remained motionless, her red-brown hair flowing in the sunlight like a nimbus, 'a . . . challenge, now and then. Something to get my teeth into, in fact. But don't mind me. I'm only being naughty. I was a tigress in one of my incarnations, I expect, and I miss the taste of blood.'

He was silent. A blast of Torford's east wind, coming across twenty miles from the icy sea, sprang at the drawing-room windows and rattled them.

'I've often wondered about your fires, you know,' he said next. 'Aren't we in a smokeless zone?'

'Oh, Felicity and I leave all that kind of thing to Laf. So boring.'

'But how does he – I mean, if we *are* in a smokeless zone?'

'Laf's all right, dear Mr Davis. Never worry about Laf. With his wit and his detachment and his charity and his cool, nothing's likely to upset *him* – you keep your anxiety for that daughter of yours . . . trendy little girl, taking up with a Japanese!'

He became aware that he was bathing in a gentle warmth that did not come from the fire, and that it was troubling, because with it went a sensation as if someone or something were murmuring within him: *Beware! Don't! Look out!* He lifted his eyes and met the full gaze of Mrs Cornforth's fixed upon his own. A slight smile curved her mouth.

There had been silence for some time after her last mocking sentence, and now Wilfred felt how long that silence had been and how – the word sprang into his mind and bloomed

there, like some brilliant flower – *sweet.* But always there was
that voice murmuring *No! Don't! Beware!*

Katherine did not speak. *It's as if her eyes were kissing me,*
he thought, and the warning voice deepened and turned to
an iron command: *Look up, look beyond!* He made his eyes
leave hers, and let them be drawn to the windows whence
poured down a brilliant, unmoving light. There, in the deep
blue, towered one dazzling golden-white cloud – sculptured,
impregnable.

'Well,' Katherine said, getting up gracefully, 'I'm going to
play the piano,' and she made an indolent movement of her
long arms. 'Do try not to *fuss,* dear Mr Davis. Why the hell
don't you telephone your Mary?'

A little later he heard the distant notes of the piano. *Katherine
playing Vivaldi rather badly on the whole,* Mr Taverner called
these sessions.

Wilfred looked vaguely at the window. The great cloud had
dissolved, the sky was full of flying shreds of grey, and the hard
light and the east wind poured against the panes. The voice
in his head or heart or spirit was silent now, but he thought:
*That was funny. Narrow escape. Don't want to spoil things here . . .
besides, at my age! And . . . I don't really like her. Kindness itself,
of course, but I don't.*

It was a discovery.

This was a Saturday afternoon. Silence, sweetened by the distant
notes of the piano, was in the Yellow House. But Wilfred could
almost feel the vigour of the awakening spring rushing through
the streets beyond the clear panes and their faded curtains: the
Torford Wanderers, splashed and scarlet-faced, were racing
through the biting air across the churned mud of their home
ground; the first tennis players of the season were gradually
turning from bluish-white to a healthier pink in their scanty
skirts or shorts; even a few bathers were wading out through
the icy foam of the high tide whence that wind was coming.
And lovers at every table, he thought, in all the coffee shops.

I'll go for a walk. See if the primroses are out in Fredaswood, he decided.

Visitors to Torford interested in local history assumed, wrongly, that the wood on the hill had been a grove sacred to the goddess Freya. But the truth, though less interesting, was not unromantic. A merchant successful in groceries, who had bought the land in 1778, had given it to his daughter, who had died young in childbed.

An hour later, Wilfred was walking, as briskly as the marshy ground would allow, along a grassy ride in this wood, between swaying saplings of birch and maple.

He paused, and stooped. There were the primroses, pale greenish-yellow in their nest of crinkled leaves, sheltered from the wind by a low, mossy bank. He picked a small bunch and carefully wrapped their stems in a polythene bag brought for this purpose, to protect them from the warmth of his hand.

With this, his enthusiasm for the walk declined; he began to feel chilly, and was relieved to see coming towards him, as he emerged onto the road, the bus that would have him in the town in twenty minutes. Good to feel the seat under him and the padded back supporting his shoulders.

If I'd been alive two hundred years ago, I'd have been plodding through that wind on Shanks's mare, he thought, watching the dazzling new green of the thorn hedges stream by; *funny how when you think about the past you always assume you'd have been comfortable . . . most people were damned uncomfortable. But used to it, I suppose . . .*

He enjoyed his walk, in spite of the wind, arriving home in a double glow of warmed blood and approving conscience, and able to report to his friends on the state of the buds in Fredaswood, over the high tea to which he was invited in the kitchen.

'The dripping toast is dead, long live Gentleman's Relish,' observed Mr Taverner, whose turn it was to deal with the bread. 'Shall I mention cucumber? I shall not. The year goes on quite fast enough as it is. Katherine dear! That jar. Can't we have the little grey one?'

'Oh you are an old – I don't know what you are, Laf. I like it. It's the last thing poor Olivia made before she killed herself.'

Katherine paused, with the primroses suspended above a black pottery jar of a shape deliberately irregular and aggressive; its handles were formed of the clay pinched out into two shapeless protuberances, and the base was adorned with a purplish-red blotch low down on one side.

'Exactly. It looks like just that. Do put it away, love.'

'Laf,' Miss Dollette murmured.

'The grey *is* better,' Katherine muttered in her turn, opening the cupboard where the vases were kept. 'You're right – as usual. But she *was* my friend . . .'

'Ha! The front door. Wilfred, will you go?'

Wilfred had hardly heard the conversation, warmth and food after copious inhalation of icy air having produced drowsiness, and he went across the hall, past Kichijoten glowing in the late light, thinking of nothing at all.

It was a shock to open the door to Mary.

'Hullo, Dad.' (How pale – and she looked older! And no suitcase!)

'Hullo, love! Well, this is a pleasant surprise, on a cold Saturday evening. Come in, out of that awful old wind . . . everything all right?' he could not keep himself from adding, as she followed him into the house.

'Perfectly, thanks,' she answered steadily, then put her arm round his neck and drew his face close and kissed him. Unhurriedly – as she had not kissed him for a long time – as if she were renewing something long-loved and familiar.

'I just thought I'd like to see you,' she said.

'Well, you know it's a treat for me, dear.' *Why had she glanced at the statue of Kichijoten, then looked away, with that sudden hardening of expression?* 'Had your tea?'

'No. I left the shop at half past, as usual, and I was just crossing the road when I thought – "There's that five-forty, I

could be with Dad in just over the hour." So I went straight
over to the station, and here I am.'

Her determined smile accompanying the words served as
a greeting to the three sitting at the tea table. A place was
unfussily made for her, with pleased words of welcome, and
Wilfred reflected upon the advantages of living with people
he thought of as *belonging to a higher walk of life*.

The fact was particularly advantageous on occasions when
there was concealed anxiety, or, as he now suspected, some kind
of a crisis in a beloved life. The pleasant social tide swept over
all secrets. It could not heal, but at least it made the moments
easier. Even Mrs Wheeby would have thoroughly investigated
Mary's unexpected arrival and her reasons, while as for Sheila
and Joan – the very air seemed picked bare as he imagined *their*
cries and questions and comments.

Only Mrs Cornforth's shining eyes slid round mischievously
from time to time to Mary's face, and he liked her none the
better for it. He was proud of Mary. She kept up a quiet but
unfailing flow of the smallest of talk – the weather, London, her
journey, her job; even a mildly amusing picture of Mrs Levy
was presented, with a background of Hamburg. He had not
suspected that his child could entertain an audience. But he
did not know that both love and fancy had been aroused from
their sleep by a Prince who was also a Poet.

After tea, the others tactfully went about their own affairs,
and he suggested to Mary that they should go up to his room.

They settled themselves beside the fire, somewhat dimmed
by the light of the setting sun, which streamed into the room.
The peace rose softly about Wilfred, but could not surround
him completely because of the expression in Mary's eyes.

'How's business going, love?' he asked at last, using a euphe-
mism; his father had always said 'work'.

Mary roused herself from a silent staring into the fire. 'Oh
all right, I suppose.' Pause. 'I ought really to get something
better paid, but I don't know – *she* suits me and I like the work
and –' She broke off, looked down, and was silent again.

How difficult it is to love – wisely and unselfishly to love! The thought passed vaguely through the father's mind as he too gazed downwards. *How difficult.*

'I can't think how you manage at all, love – in London, on about seven pounds a week.'

'Nearly eleven, Dad, with what you give me and what's in my account. I don't eat all I'd like to, that's all.'

'But that's – awful, love!' he exclaimed. 'What your mother would have said I don't know. Not eat enough! I thought you looked thinner.'

'It's always good to lose weight,' she said austerely.

'I could easily manage a bit more, you know.'

'Oh, that's all right, Dad, thanks all the same. It's easy managing if you just stay at home evenings.'

The tone was quiet, but it was bitter, and it disturbed him.

Mr Grant, sitting peacefully over the gas fire and reading an account of that day's bomb explosions, while mutters of *murdering bastards* and *I'd give them four minutes' warning* escaped his pursed lips, was interrupted by a loud and haughty knock on his door.

That's milord or I'm a Dutchman, he thought, and did not hurry himself in laying aside the newspaper, getting up, and crossing the room. His shoulders squared themselves, and his head went back. He gripped the door handle, swung the door wide, and stood there, staring into the insolent eyes of his Japanese tenant.

'Well, my lad, and what can I do for you?'

'Where is Miss Mary Davis?' Yasuhiro demanded.

'How should I know? Me and Mrs Cadman don't go spying. Pay your rent, keep yourself respectable, and go your own way, is our rule.'

As the other inhabitants of 20 Rowena Road were all over sixty, and terrified of everything in the contemporary world with the exception of Tide and paper handkerchiefs, Mr Grant could feel confident that this liberal attitude would not be abused.

'She is not in her room. I have knocked at the door.'

'Well, if you nearly bust through it, like you just done this one, p'raps she didn't feel like answering.'

'Then I turn handle. But it is locked,' Yasuhiro went on, as if nothing had been said.

'That's all right. *Her* room, isn't it? – No, I *don't* know where she is. Out, I expect. Saturday night – only natural. So you be off, please.'

He paused. Then, his feelings needing expression, he went on severely: 'And you'd better mend your manners. I was sergeant in the Rifle Brigade for fifteen years, and we had a few like you. *Fire-eatin'*. 'Eroes on the bloody field o' battle, and walking on people's faces in between fights to keep yer 'and in . . . I know.'

Glare met glare – then Yasuhiro's expression changed: smoothed, polite.

'I am sorry. I am rude.' A dazzling smile, which was not returned.

'And we don't want any soap today, thank you.'

'You were a warr— a soldier?' Yasuhiro asked suddenly. 'In last war?'

'That's right. Rifle Brigade 1923 to '47. Finest regiment in the Army. 'Course, they have to bugger it about, they always do, and it isn't what it was (come to that, what is?). But the tradition's there, and we done our duty.'

'Ah. My great-grandfather was a sailor. Become Admiral. Fight at Port Arthur. Still happily alive in our house.'

'Port Arthur? Crikey, he must be getting on a bit . . . Russki-Japanese war, wasn't it? Keeps healthy, does he?'

'He has yet some strength, thank you for him. That Rifle Brigade – I have heard its name.'

'Yes, you might have . . . your lot come up against us in Burma. Ah well, let the best man win, is what I always say.'

Mr Grant, having, so to speak, inflicted loss of face on the enemy, was preparing to execute a tactical retreat when he recollected that Mrs Cadman was all for encouraging friendly relations between Mary and this blighter.

'You and Mary had a row?' he demanded.

'No oh no. Friends. But . . .'

Mr Grant took what he called a dekko at the young face, which now appeared troubled. *Bit of a boy*, thought Mr Grant. *Can't be above twenty.*

'S'pose we ask Mrs Cadman?' he suggested. 'I know she's got a phone number.'

'You don't get out much in the evenings then, love?' said Wilfred.

A shake of the head.

'That boy,' he said, resolutely but making himself use a casual tone, 'the Japanese boy – is he still living in your house?'

Nod. Mary's expression became expressionless.

'Doesn't he take you out in the evenings? It's what most boys and girls do, if they're friends.'

'We've been out once. To St Paul's. At least, we went to a café near St Paul's.'

'Doesn't sound exactly lively,' her father said dryly.

'Oh, he's lively enough, most of the time. Tales about cutting off people's heads, and Great-grandpop fighting in some battle about ninety years ago. Never a dull moment, really.'

'Doesn't sound quite your cup of tea, love.'

'A lot of it isn't. But . . .' she was silent again, and he was pondering what his next remark should be when there was a sharp rap on the door and the cheerful voice of Mr Taverner. 'Mary! Wanted on the telephone.'

She got up reluctantly, saying 'It'll be old Levy or Mrs Cadman. No one else has the number. I suppose she wants me to go in tomorrow. Shan't be a minute, love,' and she went out.

Wilfred shook his head, and began to pack a pipe with Old and Sweet.

'Hullo?' said Mary in the silent hall, under the benign eyes of Kichijoten. The world seemed shut out and miles away: and the next instant everything had faded and there was only one voice.

'Mairly? Why did you go away from me? In that way?' it demanded angrily.

Mary's impulse was to say, slowly and distinctly, 'Well – I – am – damned.' She resisted it, and said, on a desolate note she did not know was in her voice: 'I just wanted to see my dad.'

'Oh. So you did not go away in a rage of temper?'

'Of course I didn't go away in a rage. Why should I?'

Now he'll have to explain why he's said nothing to me but 'Good morning' and 'Good evening' for the last week.

'Well, I think you are perhaps in a rage because I have not ask you drink coffee. For seven nights, I have not ask.'

'Seven? Is it really that long?'

'You are sarcasm at me, Mairly.'

'No I'm not. Why should I be?'

'Because – I tell you previously – I have not invite you to drink coffee.'

'So what?' she said hardly, after a pause.

'My heart is sad, and I have many, many thoughts.'

She just prevented herself retorting: 'And what about my heart?' and stood listening, in silence.

'You come home and I tell you those thoughts.'

'I'll come home tomorrow.'

'Come now. At once, Mairly.'

'What, tonight? It's after nine, and I'm tired.'

'I come to fetch you away in a Godfrey Davis.'

'Who – what Davis?'

'Godfrey. Car hire firm. Very reliable. I have used, when not wanting to walk along ugly disgraceful streets to our Embassy. You say, and I come. Near eleven o'clock I shall be at where you are. Perhaps half hour after eleven.'

'No – thanks,' she said, after a pause for consideration, in which she imagined a two-hour ride alone with him in a fabulous car. 'I'd like to be with Dad for a bit. But if you like . . .'

'What if I like? You tell me, Mairly.'

'I'll get the 11.11 to Liverpool Street tomorrow morning. It gets in at 12.25.'

'We go back together to Rowena Road by the train from enormous Broad Street, and I show you my heart.'

Her step was quicker and her expression different as she came into her father's room.

'That was Yasu,' she said, sitting down by the fire. 'The Japanese boy. You . . . you'd better learn his name, Dad. It's Yasuhiro Tasu.'

Wilfred obediently repeated the exotic sounds.

'We've had a spot of bother,' she added offhandedly. 'But it's all right now. Well, what's your news?'

Her father had no news, and was famishing for her confidence. They went to bed early.

Wilfred always looked forward to the few moments before he fell asleep in the Yellow House. After his door was shut for the night, he was accustomed to hearing various quiet sounds which seemed to indicate that the house was still wakeful and, in some manner which he could not analyse, *busy*. This activity, whatever it might be, was wholly agreeable to him; soothing him before he drifted off into those dreams of an unearthly clarity and beauty which had begun to visit him. The continuous subdued sounds suggested the working of something mysterious, fruitful and happy; and even if he should awaken in the small hours, he would lie restfully, listening to the living silence.

On Sunday morning, Mary was cheerful over the breakfast he insisted on cooking for her.

'Is this what you usually have, love?' he enquired, sliding a fried egg onto its couch of bacon.

'Gosh, no. I can't rise to that. Often bacon and egg is my supper.'

'Mum would say it was your duty to yourself to eat properly.'

'I know, Dad. But it costs money – *money*,' was the absent answer, as she sat down at the table. *Raw egg and bean paste. Sounds simply disgusting. But I suppose one would get used to it.*

'I eat *enough*, you know. I don't use up all that energy. I'm not charging about in the fresh air all day,' she added, noting his expression.

Wilfred shook some of his Matterhorn cereal into a bowl. He longed to ask questions about that boy. But 'it' might not even be serious. He himself had so little experience! Rose Carter when he was twenty-two, and then a peaceful blank until Pat, when he was forty-seven.

'Dad.'

'What, love?'

'You may as well know . . .'

God, what was coming?

'Yasu's rich.'

'Rich, is he? Well . . .' Wilfred just stopped himself saying, *Why doesn't he take you out somewhere nice, then?*

'Yes. His family make colour TVs.'

'Then what's he doing living in your house? From what you've told me, it's clean and respectable enough but not what you might call luxury, is it?'

'No it is not,' Mary said, with decision. 'But it's all right, I suppose, though everybody in it but me and him is about ninety.'

'Seems funny –' Wilfred spooned up the last of his chopped nuts and grains: '– you wouldn't think . . .'

'Well –' she was not looking at him, '*I* never met anyone like him. Honestly, sometimes I think he's a bit off his trolley – but clever, too. He writes poetry. And he says things . . .'

'What sort of things?' suspiciously.

'Oh, funny nice things – you'd like them.'

'And you – you like him, do you, love?'

The tone was dry, carefully drained of a teasing note.

Mary's head was turned towards the window. There followed a longish pause.

'I don't know if I do or not,' she said calmly, at last. 'And I don't know if he likes me. All I know is – when I don't see him – and he seems to feel the same – here, don't you move, I'll do that.'

She got up and began clearing the table. 'On here? Right? Quite the little housewife now, aren't you? – All I mean is – *don't worry*. I know what I want. Have, since I was twelve.'

This affair, thought Wilfred watching the apparently calm young woman stacking cups . . . *this affair is a very different affair from love under the indifferent shadow of the Town Hall. Mary's a bit too sensible, perhaps*, he thought. *And this being bowled over by a Japanese boy who writes poetry is a sort of – letting the other side out, as it were.*

'It's just that I don't know if he's *all right* yet, so I'm not doing anything in a hurry – even if I have the chance to,' she ended wryly. 'Here – what's the time? Gosh, if I'm going to catch that train I must get my skates on.'

The delicious interlude was over. She was off on her own path again, moving towards her own future with absent, though always affectionate, answers to his carefully casual questions.

'Dad. Mr Taverner says he'll drive me to the station.'

A last-minute kiss and embrace.

'You're sure you're really all right here, Dad? Really fitting in and all that?' she whispered unexpectedly as they went down the stairs. 'We don't seem to have had a minute for a real natter, the time's gone so fast.'

Yes. You hadn't been here two hours before that young blighter was on the phone and off you went into Disneyland, thought her father dourly, while chirping aloud that it had been a nice little flying visit and take care of yourself and goodbye. He squeezed her firm young arm.

'Oh, I forgot to ask you last night –' said Mary, as the 1938 car rattled through the streets of Sunday Torford, past the combustion-engine worshippers cleaning their idols, 'can you

let me have a copy of that photo you took of that goddess you
made up, in the snow. You know, at Christmas, Mr Taverner?'

'Willingly.' Mr Taverner slightly turned towards her.
'But . . .'

'You'll let me pay you for it, won't you, please? I know how
expensive colour films are.'

'I'd be delighted to give you one, Mary, if I had one. But I
haven't. The thing's a blank.'

'How funny,' said Mary, wondering if Yasu would be there
when her train got in. 'It was a perfect morning for taking
photos, wasn't it, and so bright with the snow. Quite blank,
was it?'

'Absoballylutely blank,' he said solemnly. 'Now, if you're
going to catch that train, I had better step on it.' He accelerated.

'It is funny,' Mary said dreamily again.

'Isn't it? Remarkable, really.'

He was waiting for her at the barrier, and, having greeted her
with a silent, brilliant smile, led her in his usual style through
the crowds as if they had not existed, and up to a large handsome car complete with grey-uniformed chauffeur, parked like
a peacock among London sparrows, in the side road that led
down to the station.

'Godfrey Davis, Mairly. Please go in.'

Mary went in. She looked furtively at the immaculate grey
back of the chauffeur in the front seat and hoped that the coming conversation would not be too personal.

When the car was gliding away, Yasu did not at once begin
to talk. He had seated himself beside her, but at the far end of
the long seat. Presently he said:

'Better only you and me. You think so, Mairly, love?'

'Yes. Thank you, Yasu. It was kind of you.'

She was not going to exclaim: 'You call me love!' though it
was the first time, and her heart danced. He had the behaviour
of last week to explain.

'This is same kind car my father has in Japan. Will not let me drive it, though,' and he laughed.

She laughed dutifully also.

'Peasant is a nuisance but necessary,' Yasuhiro went on, indicating the driver. 'Now, if you want, I tell you some of my many many thoughts.' Mary's eyes were fixed on the necessary peasant. 'All of last week I think and think.' Yasuhiro's eyes turned towards her, and a little smile tilted the corners of his mouth. 'What I think concerning, Mairly?'

'Yasu, hadn't you better not – I mean, let's wait until we get home, shall we?' she interrupted, and moved her head forward in the direction of the chauffeur.

'Of course of course. Sensible. Always peasants listen, sometimes even dare repeat what heard, though not in our house. Beautiful weather now. Trees budding. Sun shining. How was in Tor-ford? Making geisha conversation, I think,' and Yasuhiro began giggling and she joined in.

But even as the childish, rather silly sound bubbled out of him, his eyes, dark and glittering, remained fixed on hers, making her heart beat faster, bringing the feeling that every moment spent away from this stranger from the other side of the world was not real. Only when they were together was her life actual.

She stood by the gate while he tipped the chauffeur, staring dreamily down the length of Rowena Road, which was lined with cars.

'Now you go eat lunch, I go eat lunch. Disgraceful place, no servants to cook and bring to us,' said Yasuhiro, whose feudal instincts appeared to have been aroused by the presence of the peasant and the use of Godfrey Davis. 'All the same, we eat. Then go for walk on that Heath and I tell you what I have do.'

'Done, love.' It slipped out.

'Again, again, you call me "love"!'

'Yes. And you behave once more like you did last week, and I'll never call you "love" again for the rest of our lives. So you remember.'

She was trembling, though she spoke firmly, staring up at him.

He turned from the front door, for as usual he had darted up ahead, and smiled down at her.

'Oh Mairly. How much I like to hear you say "the rest of our lives"! Yes, in our lives we will rest beside together. But not always rest, have much doing together. Perhaps I even take you travelling with me. See E-gypt.'

'Thanks.'

But it was a murmur. Her thunder had been stolen by this agreeable prospect.

She tapped on Mrs Cadman's door before going up to her room.

'Hullo, Mrs Cadman, just wanted to let you know I'm back.'

'That's right, dear – have a nice time?'

'Short and sweet, thanks. Dad asked to be remembered to you.'

Dad had done no such thing. But Mary knew that he would approve the graceful little lie.

'Thank you, dear. Keeping well, is he? Settling in nicely?'

'Oh yes, thank you.' She was poised to be off.

'Such a carry-on you never heard, last night.' Mrs Cadman lowered her voice, and the plastic rollers confining her hair under a net seemed charged with importance and mystery. 'A phone call booked to Japan, if you please, and him asking me would I please wake him up when the phone went at three in the morning. (Different time over there, of course.) Well, I said, seeing you're the age you are and I'm the age I am, No. You have this alarm clock, I said, and that'll wake you up all right. "Unless he passes over in the night from blood pressure," Mr Grant said. (Not meaning it nastily, but really!) And there was I, fast asleep, and never heard a thing. But Mr Grant was awake. That wound he got at that Kidney Ridge always aches a bit in the spring. And he heard him jabbering away in Japanese for nearly an hour. What it must have cost! Well, I said to Mr Grant, there's the money to pay for it, and at least he's honest, and he'll be responsible, and Mr Grant heard him reverse the charge, thank goodness, or I would not feel comfortable; you know what muddles that post office makes. Got everything you want for your lunch, dear?'

Tinned pilchards and bread and margarine.

'Yes, thank you, Mrs Cadman.'

Mary went upstairs thinking about the telephone call to Japan. An hour! It wouldn't take an hour to ask how Great-grandfather was and get the rest of the family news. Could he have been *explaining* something to *them*? Listening at midday, all those thousands and thousands of miles away on the other side of the world? After nine o'clock, when he had talked to her, and knew that he was forgiven?

'Mary –' Mrs Cadman's voice came softly up the stairs. 'It was me gave him your number, dear. Mr Grant told me he was asking where you were – seemed a bit upset. (Well, *that* never does any harm.) Mr G. thought it was a nerve. But *I* thought, oh well, a little oil on the wheels, you know.'

'That was all right, Mrs Cadman.' Mary paused, then added: 'Thanks very much, as a matter of fact,' and smiled.

Mrs Cadman was smiling too, as she almost tiptoed down the stairs, the sunlight making a contemporary version of the halo around her plastic rollers. And Mary, opening the tin of pilchards, was thinking how sickening it was to have two old women poking into her beautiful love story. Kindly meant, of course, and simply sickening ... And oh, what had the telephone call to Japan been about?

24

The photograph

They were climbing a broad hill, crowned by a beech in brilliant green leaf with a seat beneath it.

'There we will sit,' announced Yasuhiro suddenly, pointing. But an elderly lady exercising two dogs was also making for it. 'Now we run,' he added, and leapt away, Mary following, enjoying the race but ashamed of this frank grabbing.

'Ha! We win!' he announced, flinging himself onto the seat. 'Go away, go away, dogs, back to the shameful place where you live,' to the two young boxers who had finished the race with them and wanted to make friends.

'Carlo! Benita! Come here at once,' called the elderly lady, and they bounded away.

'I like this Heef,' Yasuhiro announced in what Mary now recognized as his social voice (*doesn't want to start talking seriously*), surveying the bright, green-gold prospect. 'But too many beastly peasants.'

The landscape was dotted with strolling figures, many elderly like the lady of the boxers, but others young: bearded and Chinese-moustached, or with flowing hair and ample skirts billowing in the wind.

'People must get a breath at the weekend, Yasu.'

'Of course, of course. Fair enough, as you say here. But does not mean I must like. Appearance *affronts* me. (I learnt that word yesterday – *affronts*.)'

'Good for you . . . you'll find it useful.'

He slowly turned his eyes on her.

'What you are meaning, Mairly? Sarcasm, perhaps? Ah yes. You mean I am too often affront?'

'(Affronted.) Well, you do rather go on about peasants. Other people have a right to exist, you know.'

'I do not say they haven't . . . But also I have a right to be affronted. (*Western democracy!*) Dirty, looking poor, no shape to outline of them. Important to Japan. Shape and outline – same thing? I must think about meaning during next week.'

'You do that, love,' Mary said smoothly, wishing to steer the conversation into less impersonal waters.

'You see, Mairly,' he swept on, 'these peasants are not beautiful. Spoil landscape. Yes, spoil.' His tone was hard, his eyes flashing. The artist was awake and exasperated.

'Everybody can't be beautiful,' she snapped. 'How about me?'

'Different.' His hand shot out and gently took her own. 'You are beautiful *to me*. Do not care one solitary damn (also learnt this yesterday) what other people think.'

Mary was silenced again. She made no coy protestations. They sat for a moment in silence while his gaze rested arrogantly upon her white, downcast eyelids, then she tried again.

'Well, tell me what you've been doing this weekend?'

He looked out over the bright landscape, then began slowly:

'Last night, Mairly, it is Saturday night, I made a telephone call to Great-grandfather in Japan (it was daylight there, you know when night here – "small hours" is the name). And why do you think I do this, Mairly?'

'How on earth should I know? Did you want to know how he was?'

'Was what?'

'(Oh dear.) His health, I mean.'

'Not truly. Will die soon, and we all know this; he too. No. I telephone to him to break news. Break, like you break an ugly stone because is perhaps bad news – bad news for them my family. Wait.' He put up a hand. 'Confused thoughts in heart – human feelings fighting with *giri* – and I forget my English.' He drew in a slow, deep breath and expelled it. Mary sat with lowered head, looking at her linked fingers. Her heart was heaving.

'No. I telephone to him to tell him not to make any more arrangements for me to marry.'

Now Mary did look up, startled, and met the triumphant sparkle of his eyes. He nodded.

'Yes, that is what I say to him, Mairly. And I do this because, I tell him, I marry you.' As he said the last word, he put out his hand again and took hers as if he were about to lead her out onto a path that they would follow together. *Into the misty, mountainous land of danger, where he lived?*

She looked down at the long, ivory fingers, and tried to catch at her feelings. Here was what she wanted. But she was drowned in love. She could not think clearly. Did she want it now? There was a pause.

She made what was, so far, the strongest effort of her life.

'That's . . . I mean . . . thank you, Yasu, love,' she said faintly. 'But . . . I'm not . . . absolutely certain that I . . . want to marry you.'

'Not marry me, Mairly,' he exclaimed loudly, withdrawing his hand. 'But I see you in the shop. I love your face, like a Japanese girl in an old fairy story. I follow you to unworthy Rowena Road. And now you are not wish to marry me?' His English had become almost unintelligible, and she found this unbearably moving.

'Oh Yasu, love, don't be hurt. Don't be angry. Aren't you just a bit – afraid – to marry someone not Japanese?'

'You learn husband's country customs. Woman's duty.'

'Well, yes. If I married you, of course I should. It isn't that. It's just that I – I don't like some of the customs.'

'What customs? You explain me,' and he put his arm around her shoulders and parted the veil of her hair; and then she felt his fingers begin, gently and with feather-like delicacy, to stroke the nape of her neck. It was lulling; she seemed to be moving towards sleep. But she roused herself.

'That old – I mean Mishima, Yasu. I don't like you being so – so devoted to him. All that stuff about dying for Japan. And I thought that business about the head-chopping-off was simply awful. And as for that other carry-on – simply disgusting . . .'

She faltered, for he was nodding in a satisfied manner.

'Of course, of course. Sweet gentle woman.'

'You see, I think it's bad for *you*, Yasu.'

'How can it be bad for young man to admire virtues of *samurai*?' The fingers stopped their stroking abruptly, and he stared.

'Well –' Mary gulped and struggled on. 'Suppose – we were married, and you were still mixed up with that Shield Society, and they tried to hijack a plane or assassinate the American ambassador or something, and you got killed –'

'Ah. Yes. Understand. Fear for husband. This is right for a woman. But for me, glory of death – for Emperor and Japan.'

'I don't *care* about glory or the Emperor or Japan!' She drew away from the warmth of his body and the faint spice-like scent that always clung to his clothes. 'I care about *you* and – and any children we might have. Your great-grandfather's always talking about you having a son. Be nice for him, the son I mean, having his father killed by the police, wouldn't it?'

'Glory of Japan,' repeated Yasuhiro. But he said it mechanically, and his fingers resumed their stroking while he stared away over Hampstead Heath.

'What did he say on the phone? When you told him,' she said in a moment, more quietly.

'Said must see a photo of you.'

'Oh well. I've only got snaps.'

'Snaps no use,' decidedly. 'Must have good, large photo.'

'Is that *all* he said, Yasu? Just about the photo?'

'Said also was not surprised I want to marry Western girl. Said he did . . . expect this. I tell him, you see.' He bent towards her and she felt his breath on her cheek. 'I tell him my human feelings, Mairly. In my heart is much, much loving for you, and I tell him that. Also that you are sweet, gentle, not mobogirl.'

'What's that?'

She spoke languidly, leaning against him.

'Modern girl.'

'I love you too, Yasu,' she said softly.

There followed a mutual inclining of the two dark young heads, and a kiss.

'There's Dad,' she said in a moment. 'I'd have to leave him . . . and he's . . . he'd be so lonely. So surprised, too, he'll be when I tell him about – everything.'

'Of course of course. Understand. And I ask his agreement. And then, if he like, he come with us, live in Japan.'

'Oh Yasu! Would you? He's only got me now. It would make all the difference. You see, some of your customs are so . . . strange.'

She just managed to substitute *strange* for *dotty*.

'The family of husband and wife are important, both. But husband's family most important of course of course. Is Honourable Dad all the family you have?'

'There's Aunt Beatty. That's Dad's sister. But we only keep up with her at Christmas and Easter.'

'Ah. Then we think of her no more. Is old and will soon die.'

'She isn't old. She's five years younger than Dad and he's only sixty-seven. You really *must* stop saying that kind of thing, Yasu. Right out, like that. People don't *like* it, in England.'

'But is true. Sixty-two ancient, love –'

He inclined his head towards her again.

'All the same,' said Mary, when the kiss was over.

'Kissing a Western custom, not Japanese. But good,' said Yasuhiro, all sparkle. 'I tell you what we shall do, Mairly. Two acts. It is the moon of May. Now she is young. After our work, each evening, we walk together on this Heath and talk. You tell me about your human feelings. I tell you my own. Right?

(A young man in the Free Library told me this use of word today. Colloquial.)'

'Right,' said Mary. 'What's the other "act"? ("Thing" is better. "Act" sounds a bit funny.)'

'(Thing.) Oh – send large good photograph of yourself to Great-grandfather.'

Yasuhiro studied eight hours at his English in the languages school and at the local Public Library. (On the latter, his comments were a mixture of contempt and wonder.) He also stalked the streets of Soho looking for a theatrical costumier's where he could hire a Japanese dress for Mary to be photographed in. Mary had suggested that she might save trouble by wearing his dark blue robe with the silver storks and chrysanthemums.

'Make trouble,' Yasuhiro cut in sharply. 'Insult to Honourable Great-grandfather for woman to wear man's dress. His present to me.'

'Thank you.'

'You are sarcasm at me, Mairly. Please shoot down the bird of anger that is flying in your heart. Because you are woman, gentle and sweet, I love you.'

'Oh well. So long as you do.'

'I do, Mairly. Oh so very.' The little skirmish ended in an embrace so strong that her senses were shaken.

The next evening he showed her, with an expression of distaste, a white cotton kimono almost covered in green, orange, purple and blue storks, bridges, pagodas and little men in wide hats, accompanied by an *obi* of shocking pink.

'Is worn by dancing peasants in some play called *The Mikado* (insult, I think). The man tells me, in the shop. I tell him it is a horrible horrible robe, and he is surprised. I shall take it back to the shop. Very disgraceful taste. And affront Great-grandfather.'

Fortunately, at another, smaller theatrical hire shop, recommended by Mrs Cadman, all kindness and curiosity, he found a plain light blue kimono with a white *obi*; and when Mary had gone upstairs with it and come down transformed, he nodded.

'Good. Very well, Mairly. Now he see only your face and beautiful hair. No silly men in hats or horrible colours.'

'Aren't I going to have some of those gorgeous hairpins? I was looking forward to that.'

'Of course not. Of course not. *Going too far*, as you say here. Un-necessary. Now tomorrow, we find respectable shop and have the photograph taken.'

The result, when collected by him some days later, looked startlingly Japanese. Mary hardly recognized herself, so strongly did the dress seem to emphasize the length of her eyes and the calm of her expression (Yasuhiro had been present at the sitting, and would not allow her to smile). As she looked at this grave young woman, who might have been quite twenty-five, she felt a bewildered sensation, as if she had taken some paces forward into Yasuhiro's own country.

25

Deadlock

On this morning in early winter, the flower arrangement in the niche consisted of one white iris, a purple-flushed bud, and a spray of grey-green eucalyptus leaves flown in from Australia. The charcoal smouldered in the brazier adding its humble, familiar warmth and faint smell to the blaze of the central heating and that of the sunlight, chill and wintrily-bright at this season, beating against the closed screens.

Admiral Kouei-fei Tasu's daughter-in-law had brought in the letter and the parcel a few minutes ago on her morning visit, putting them down on the sleeping dais before him and then making her obeisance with what his eyes, though dim even with the assistance of the miraculous new glasses, could detect as an unseemly haste. She was wearing Western dress, and her hair in a Western style, and she knew that he disapproved of both. She was anxious to get out of the room.

Such signs of the decline of his authority in the family were increasing daily. Strong and helpless anger swept across his spirit, then a deep sadness. He killed both feelings as if they were mutinous sailors, and turned to the letter and parcel.

'Now –' he murmured. 'Now I shall see.'

He opened the letter first.

Ha, the boy had not made the mistake of repeating what he had said, ten days ago, over the telephone. That would have been a waste both of time and precious space in the letter. He knows that it would have annoyed me, thought the old man, *and that I wish for news of him. He does not know that I famish for news. It is imprudent and cramping to the growth of their spirit, to allow the young to know how much we love them.*

Honoured and most beloved Great-grandfather,

Now that your heart-child has talked with you, his spirit is calmer, though large raindrops hang from the petals of the azalea, showing that a storm has passed. The struggle between my duty to the family and my human feelings has been fearful, as if demons fought. This dutiful one has begun to talk with the chosen girl about the differences in our customs and beliefs. Yes, *her beliefs.* Condescend, dear and most honoured one, to bend your warrior spirit to an understanding of this fact, hard as a stone: it is necessary as the downward flow of water that I *explain to,* and – pray do not avert your noble head – *even argue with* this girl of the West. Their women, as you know, expect such condescension; and perhaps this particular humble stepper-out upon the path of life may so condescend, because he is the stronger. Also I know – again, bend your honourable spirit to understanding! – that she would *actually refuse to marry me* if I did not so argue and explain. That would crack my weak and unworthy heart.

Dear and venerated one, you have sometimes turned your ears from the contemplation of wisdom, where you sit in the cool and scented shade, to hear from this beginner, of the Shield Society. He knows that in your wisdom, hanging like a fruit of perfect ripeness from the tree of your years, you believe that the future way for Nippon lies along the paths of trade and commerce rather than that of the *samurai.* But he knows, for love gives insight when it is true love, that this belief is bitter to you, eaten as a sour herb is, for medicine, rather than

as a sweet fruit for delight. O noblest of warriors, guide
of my days and pillar around which my heart's affections
twine, you suffer – you! – and eat this herb for the good
of Nippon.

How will your venerated spirit respond to the fact that
Mary Davis shares your own opinions about the Shield
Society, but more strongly?

'Ha – good, good,' the old man muttered. 'In age the heart
grows cowardly. Love rules in the place of honour. (Alas.)
Hi-jacking, assassination, civilian bombings, all are desirable in
a conflict, but my deadly fear is that *he* will die or be maimed.'
He read on, eagerly.

Her reasons are admirable: a woman's. She fears for my
life, and sees in the mirror of her mind the fate of our
future sons, growing up in the storm of life without the
ruling hand of a father. Will your stainlessly upright
warrior soul contrive to believe that, reason as I may, *I
cannot bring her to share my views?* Stranger yet, strange as
the mist shapes that arise from the lake at evening, I find
this difference, and even her *stone-hearted will*

– the expression used was the strangest in the very wide
choice offered by the writer's native tongue –

attractive. Her obstinacy draws me, as the fisherman
in the moon pulls the tides of the sea. It is as if I had
discovered a new star in a familiar constellation, finding
will and thought in a gentle, loving woman. I confess this
only to your beloved self, and humbly wonder whether in
the course of your varied path through life you yourself
have come upon another such case?

Here the Admiral uttered a short sound, remote yet warm,
as if the spirit of affection itself were amused.

Condescend, O most honoured Great-grandfather, to inform me at your leisure whether there is dismay in the family, considerable or overwhelming, at my *choice*. I will not venture to insult the goodness of your heart by asking you to speak for me.

The letter concluded with those sentences which in Japanese express the deepest veneration.

'He knows well that I shall speak for him. *I* also know that, for all his dutifulness, he will have his way,' the Admiral muttered. 'Now, for the photograph.'

But it was sealed with that detestable Western invention, a transparent ribbon smeared on one side with some sort of glue, which ancient fingers find so difficult to unfasten. The Admiral clapped his hands sharply, and at once a screen at the far end of the room slid aside, and there entered a thickset man in a dark robe, who approached with bent head. He bowed almost double with hands crossed over his breast, then looked up enquiringly. The Admiral held out the parcel.

'Remove the outer paper.'

The body-servant had the Sellotape off in an instant, and unwrapped the parcel, revealing a second wrapping of white paper pattered with gold stars, which he also removed. He did not glance at the contents.

The Admiral held out his hand and the man approached and handed him a coloured photograph on a grey mount, then resumed his submissive position.

The Admiral studied the picture. His gaze, through the pebble-lenses enlarging his eyes so that a semblance of youth was restored to his marvellous face, moved steadily and slowly over the photograph, taking in the hint of dimples at the mouth corners, the rounded chin, and the strong throat rising from the soft line of the blue robe.

'It is there in the eyes,' he muttered at length. '*Mind*. Not the demon-curse of learning, no. Will and obstinacy, perhaps, rather than pure Mind. But it is there. Victory will be *his*.

No easy victory. But victory, because the woman-qualities are strongest. See!' – suddenly holding out the photograph to the servant. 'The Western one whom the pride and flower of our House wishes to marry.'

Jizo drew in a hissing breath as he took the photograph and subjected it to a stare, ravenous with a curiosity of which no trace appeared on his broad, battered face.

'What does my faithful one think of the lady's honourable face?' demanded the Admiral at length. 'Speak from human feelings.'

'Western lady in dress of Nippon. Pleasing. A great honour for the lady,' was the stolid answer.

As no sound or movement came from the figure seated on the dais, he ventured in a moment to put the photograph down at his master's feet, then said, in as soft and coaxing a tone as his hoarse voice could manage, 'Will the very honourable one be pleased to eat now? The hour grows late, and perhaps the very honourable one is a little wearied by the consideration of these important matters, and in need of strength.'

'Yes. Yes, I will eat now. Cause these –' he held out the packet and photograph – 'to be taken to the honourable mistress-san.'

For he had noticed the thirsty glance that his daughter-in-law had cast at parcel and letter.

On Hampstead Heath the evening walks and the three-hour-long arguments went on.

Mary felt that deadlock, stony and immovable, had been reached.

Yasuhiro's English had improved during these weeks spent in forcing out, in a foreign tongue, his strongest feelings. The mispronunciations and errors that had touched her, because of their childishness, had ceased. This hurt her, but she would not let herself tell him so. *The tougher he thinks I am, the better,* she thought.

'You want sons, I suppose?' he demanded one evening. 'Yes of course you do. Then you make a bargain with me. I give you sons, you agree that I support Mishima and Shield Society.'

'I'm not making any bargains, Yasu,' she said tiredly, 'and you can't promise to give me – or anyone – sons. It hasn't been found out how to.'

'Ancient methods in Japan often successful.'

'They may be. They aren't being tried on me. Does your family believe in them?'

'Oh I never discuss such. Servants' talk. But old nurses say they know. Honourable Great-grandfather's old servant say you have a pleasing face – I forgot to tell you.'

'Big deal,' snapped Mary, and was punished for her pertness by having to give an explanation.

'All in my family please with your face. They say typical woman-face,' he said next.

'Yes, well, I suppose that's a bit of good news. (We could do with some, at least I could.) Have you written to Dad?'

'Have here.' He touched the pocket of his jacket.

'Can I see it? Not now, silly. When we get home. I'm not a cat – I can't see in the dark.'

'Is all sealed up and stamped. Also, I don't wish you to see. Important subject between men.'

'Considering I'm half the "important subject". . . .' Mary broke off, turning away to stare angrily over the dim, sparkling valley full of London. In a moment, her control regained, she turned to him. 'And there's another thing, Yasu. I haven't mentioned it before because I thought we'd better get the other thing settled first . . . What about your work, job I mean? What are you going to do?'

He did not answer at once. Then he said slowly, 'My family, you know, Mairly,' he said slowly, 'have much much money. Factory, machines (what is called 'plant', love.) Land, too. True money, this. Unaffected by stock market.'

'That's useful,' she said dryly. At the moment this confirmation of Mrs Cadman's hopes did not excite her at all. 'But we'll have to have some of our own, won't we? – If we ever do get married, that is.'

'We marry, love. Great argument, great battle. But in the end at last, we marry.'

'. . . and I don't suppose you'll want *me* to work,' she plodded on.

'Of course, of course. You will work. Become *shokaba no hana* (*office flower* – which we call girl working in office). Make tea for directors, never rise above humble position, sometimes made to clean out office loo.'

'*Thank* you!'

'Mairly, *Mairly!*' He caught her to him in a hug. 'Where is English joke-sense? I am *joking* with you. You think my wife *work*? Never never no never. Arrange house, manage servants, look after old parents sitting in shade. And Great-grandfather leave me all his money. Arranged,' he ended calmly. 'Much, he said to me.'

'Oh. Then you'll have a . . . private income?'

'Very private and secret. Not even tell you.'

'I don't want to know, thanks, so long as you give me enough to manage on decently. That *does* make a difference. But I should think you'd *want* to work at *something*. What will you do with yourself all day, while I'm putting that charming *moxa* powder on the children when they play up?'

Nothing had driven home to her more sharply the utter alienness of his country's customs than what he had told her of small children, adored throughout Japan, who were sometimes punished for extra naughtiness by placing on the skin a pinch of a powdered, burning herb called *moxa*.

'I have told you, Mairly, only certain old-fashion families do this, uninfluenced at all at all by the West . . . What should I do with myself? Study, read, go for walk, see lovely interesting world, eat delicious food arranged by good wife. And write, of course, of course.' He turned, and smiled at her.

'But that wouldn't be *work*, love.'

'Why should I work? I am not a peasant.'

'You can say that again,' she muttered, and a silence fell.

They walked on side by side, over the young grass, under the starlit sky, through the air scented with spring. She did not know what he was thinking; she was wishing she was peacefully engaged to an English boy, with a steady job in an office or a bank, or even studying medicine; and a dear little single-diamond ring; and Dad pleased; and the wedding presents, and perhaps even a house . . .

No, a house would be out of their range. (It was, nowadays.) *And she loved Yasu. She loved Yasu.*

He's raving dotty about some things, she thought resignedly, as they swung together down the hill, *but I'm not. And I'm getting to know him better every day, in spite of all the arguing. And in a way — though it's a bit much, I must say he's what they call a challenge.*

'Why do you laugh, Mairly?'

'I was just thinking of you as a challenge, love.'

'Explain, please. The word is unfamiliar.'

'Well — you're very different from me, and — and it's as if I had to kind of face up to something, and defeat-conquer it — sort of.'

'A fight.' He nodded, after a pause. 'Like two *samurai.* Respect each their courage but fight until one is killed. Yes, I understand.'

'No one's getting killed. You do . . . exaggerate, love.'

'It was a met-a-phor-ical saying. You are a challenge to me, as well, yes. Will you call me *Shirjin,* when we are wife and husband, love?' and he caught her hand and swung it as they walked.

'Depends what it means,' cautiously.

'Means "master". Japanese wife have the custom to say this.'

'I should laugh, Yasu.'

'Laugh? Why laugh? Not a joke.'

'No, it isn't a joke . . . but we're *friends,* Yasu. You don't call a friend "master".'

Mary was silent as they turned their steps towards home.

She was weary of the unending argument. She had assembled all her reasons, backed by some of her strongest feelings; and they had seemed to her unanswerable in their truth and strength, and he had ignored them, merely saying, over and over again, that glory and honour were necessary.

26

Invited visitor

The ink was the blackest Wilfred had ever seen. And his name on the large blue envelope seemed formed, rather than written. *Formed,* he thought. *More like a drawing. Even makes 'Davis' look important. Now who is it, I wonder? Mary's Yasu. I bet. What's he on about? Hope it isn't* . . .

'Good God,' he observed in a moment, and lifted his eyes from the page, and looked helplessly around his peaceful room.

Most honoured Mr Dad-Davis,

I want very truly and sincerely to marry (become the husband) to your only daughter Mary Patricia Davis. I am twenty years, only son of formerly noble Japanese family now ashamed to confess to you manufacturing those coloured televisions. My great-grandfather, Admiral Kouei-fei Tasu, has more than ninety years and has leave me all his stocks and shares, much of them. Mary wishes truly and sincerely to marry me but is *making her mind* (like old-fashion English bed. Colloquial.) Some differences in opinion. If this happen, I shall be true honoured if you kindly agree to come away with us, Mary and myself, to Japan. Live in our house. A large place, and the garden much spoken of for peacefulness and beauty, even disgraceful tourists knocking on the door with cameras. Anxiously I await for your honourable answer.

I send you respectful greetings.

Yasuhiro Tasu

Well, thought Wilfred dazedly, *well . . . couldn't be put better, could it? And asking me to go, too. All those miles and miles away. Never heard anything like it. I shouldn't lose her. But Japan! Last place I ever . . . really, it's quite bowled me over, that it has.*

He hastily drank some tea, then sat staring uneasily at the letter while his thoughts whirled on.

'Course, nothing's what you might call settled yet. Might all blow over. Young people. Change their minds.

There was a tap on his door, and he went across the room and opened it.

Mr Taverner was there, holding out a telegram.

Its allright dad love I want to
marry him so please say yes
Love Mary.

Her and her telegrams!

Wilfred was still in his Marks and Spencer dressing-gown, and it was nearly eleven o'clock; but he pulled the girdle tighter and, holding the telegram and the handsome, important-looking letter in front of him as if they were about to explode, he hurried through the sunlight and the silence, across the hall under the gaze of Kichijoten (slightly quizzical – was that the word? – this morning), and rapped at the kitchen door. Mr Taverner's voice called 'Hullo!' and he went in.

Mr Taverner was alone, finishing breakfast with *The Times* and a large old pewter coffee pot.

'Hullo – I'm idling – come and idle too. Telegram not bad news?' he added, his tone changing, as he leant forward to pull up the chair onto which Wilfred almost sank. 'You look rather shaken.'

'Nothing really wrong, thanks – only a bit of a shock, as you might say. Just you read these,' and he held out the telegram and the letter.

'From Mary's Japanese friend? I wondered, when I saw it this morning . . . I know you'll forgive me; elderly bachelors tend to become inquisitive.'

His eyes travelled down the letter, then turned to the telegram.

'Well,' he pronounced, 'all very dignified and filial, isn't it? Couldn't be handsomer . . . but apart from the tone, which is Japanese traditional, the important bits are "some differences in opinion" and "kindly agree to come away with us" – don't you feel that?'

'Exactly. Exactly so, Mr Taverner,' Wilfred said, using a little phrase that had often served its turn in his Town Hall days. He felt grateful. 'I knew you'd understand. I'm not really worried about Mary, she's so sensible . . . only sometimes I feel she's a bit *too* sensible, if you know what I mean. If there's anything in her that *isn't* sensible, p'raps it's got to come out, and falling for this Japanese boy is how it shows – if you take my meaning . . . I've never got over that running away to London. Fairly stunned me, that did.'

'What an unusually good father you are,' Mr Taverner observed unemphatically, and Wilfred looked down.

'Don't know about that,' he said rather surlily. 'I've tried to be . . . That I can say. I'll have to see him, of course. Won't I?'

'Of course. You'll ask him up here?'

'You don't think – go down there myself?'

'Well, in your position I wouldn't. Let him come to you. He'll expect to, anyway. You'll "lose face", as his people say, if you go to London. His sense of family duty and respect will be satisfied if he comes here. Very important, to them. They are the most extraordinary race, I do believe, on the face of this planet. They have some glorious qualities – courage, devotion, passion. No cosiness: beauty and honour before everything. Hence their ruddy uncomfortable houses and customs.'

'Well, it's a bit of a staggerer – going off to live in Japan at my time of life. All that bowing and kneeling, and never a decent cup of tea again. It's all very well for you to laugh, Mr Taverner. I'm not tea-mad, but don't they put scent in it or something?'

'I'm sure they don't, though there is a naturally scented kind. You could get your Mrs Wheeby to send you out a supply of Tetley's every three months or so.'

'I suppose . . . Yes, I'll have to see him. I wish I knew a bit more about the Japanese.'

'The important thing is whether he can love. The power of loving isn't confined to any one nation, fortunately.'

There was a pause. Wilfred was looking down at the letter.

'Above all,' Mr Taverner repeated, 'the power to love.'

He sat quite still. The sunlight reflected back from the whitish-yellow walls seemed to hover about him in concentrated radiance. His hands were motionless. A mysterious picture, delicate and small and clear, appeared suddenly in Wilfred's inward eye: a pale, remote, seated Buddha, the corners of his lips lifted in the faintest of smiles.

'Mr Taverner –' Wilfred hesitated '– do you think that power – the power to love, I mean – can be learnt? Like you would a language, so to speak?'

'Yes, I believe it can, thank God. But one has also to realize that some people haven't the capacity to learn, and that *is* a mystery.'

'And of course we can't tell about this boy,' said Wilfred, tapping the letter.

Mr Taverner shrugged. If he can love, it'll be like a volcano.'

'That'll suit Mary. (Don't know how I know that, Mr Taverner, I just do.) She's a deep one.'

'The volcano and the lake . . . it sounds like a poem. I notice you haven't said anything about Great-grandfather's stocks and shares.'

'They'll be useful. I'm not denying it. And if he was a student living on a grant, I would feel different, I admit. But I know, and I'm sure you know, money's no use without two people – getting on.'

His sentiments, so difficult to express, collapsed primly into the final words, and Mr Taverner laughed.

'I feel they do "get on" – that's what's drawing them. I also feel they'll hold – in spite of these differences of opinion.'

'Then you think I should – give my consent, Mr Taverner?'

A shrug. 'Oh my dear man, you must know I can't say anything of that sort. It's up to you.'

'Yes, I suppose it is.' Wilfred sighed. 'What Pat would have said to my ending my days in Japan, I don't know . . . Besides, the fact is I'm quite contented here with all of you, specially now I know Mary's probably going to be settled. All right for her, she's young.'

'I'm glad you're happy with us.'

The tone was gently dismissive and Wilfred went away at once with a murmur of 'Well, thank you, Mr Taverner, that's cleared my mind a bit.' He had a faint sensation as if the interview had been closed and a door had been quietly shut.

There had been a shadow growing in the Yellow House for some time, and Wilfred had refused to look at it or think about it.

Gradually Mrs Cornforth's moods had come to be linked with this unease – those moods of excitement which were the cause of the occasional flash from Mr Taverner's eyes. Lately the moods had been quieter: fewer stories about the raffish group in the town whose company she frequented; more evenings on which she was to be found in the long drawing room, doing nothing, sitting by the window staring at the pale, boarded-up, empty house opposite, or looking listlessly into the fire. She wore almost every day a favourite dress: full-skirted, of yellow cotton printed with flame-coloured flowers, announcing that she adored it and would wear it until it fell to shreds. And as the air grew warmer and the birds more frenzied in their singing, and the leaves opened into their myriad shapes, her personality seemed to grow. Silent, or relating some tale, how her eyes shone!

Wilfred did not truly enjoy her tales. Other people's business, Pat would have called them; and his own verdict was that Mrs C. made them seem like some TV play and *sort of took the seriousness out of them.* Because that incident, that she made so funny, meant the break-up of a marriage . . . But she was enjoying it. You could see she was. Not that she ever said a word that was really downright offensive.

And although Mr Taverner and Miss Dollette only looked mild over the stories, saying little, Wilfred knew that they disliked the display.

For it *was* display, and a relishing, and (he suspected) a distortion.

P'raps she'll take herself off. Can't say I'd be sorry. Kind, and pulls you in a funny kind of way. But I wouldn't break my heart. More peaceful without her.

Well, I've had a bit of a think and a bit of a chat and you'd best get down to it, my lad. – Now, have I got a really posh bit of notepaper? No I haven't. Trust me. I'll get dressed and pop round to Cole's.

There was a light tap at his door. 'Mr Davis?' said the voice of Miss Dollette.

He went across and opened it, thinking: *She's the sort for me, really. Not dangerous.* And before he could feel surprise at the last word appearing in his thoughts, Miss Dollette was saying: 'Oh Mr Davis, I thought you might perhaps be able to make use of this?' She was holding out some writing paper of a deep cream tint, and some matching envelopes.

'Why Miss Dollette, are you a thought-reader or a good fairy? I was just this minute going to pop out to Cole's, I've got a rather important letter to write.'

'Oh, then I'm glad I . . . happened to come across this . . . no thought-reading . . . that's – that would be rather a burden, to tell you the . . . but as for *the other* . . .' She spoke almost in a whisper as she was turning away. 'That's *exactly* what I've wanted to be since I was three years old. A good fairy.'

Dressed, he sat at the table staring at the writing paper. *Get on with it, man. You've only got to ask the boy to come and see you.* He bent over the table.

Dear Yasu,

I call you this, as my Mary always does and it seems more friendly. Thank you for your letter. I appreciate you asking my permission. But I am sure you will realize that I must see you and talk matters over. So will you come and spend the night of the sixteenth and then we can have a good long chat? Give my love to our Mary.

Yours sincerely

Wilfred G. Davis

PS I particularly appreciate your thoughtfulness asking me to go with you both to Japan.

There, that'll have to do.

He did not read it through but stamped the envelope, and went out to the pillar box on the corner of Moultie Avenue (known inevitably to the local young as Mouldy Avenue), and posted it.

No sooner had he heard the faint sound signalling that it was irrevocably on its way than he wished he had written differently. He began to dread the boy's arrival (a Japanese), and decided he must have had one of those blackouts people seemed to have so conveniently nowadays, even to think of going to live in Japan. While as for handing his Mary over to a foreigner . . .

Wilfred G. Davis you must have been mad, and he wiped his forehead. *Oh well, I can always phone and say I've changed my mind.*

But that won't change theirs, he thought despondently, strolling home through the May breeze. *The next thing'll be keeping the engagement party dark from Sheila and Co.*

*

Mrs Cornforth was coming towards him down the sunlit passage, in her red and yellow dress, singing softly an air he knew came from some opera: sunny, Italian music.

'Gorgeous warm day,' she called, and he explained about Tasu.

'Oh that'll be marvellous – what fun! I'm dying to see him – I'm sure he's simply gorgeous to look at. It'll be perfectly all right about a room –'

'I'll pay, of course,' Wilfred said stolidly.

She shrugged. 'Just as you like. It only goes into the Do Gooders Box.' At that moment Miss Dollette came out of her room, and Katherine swooped round with a swirl of coloured skirts. 'Darling, here's Mary's boy asking to come here for a night on the sixteenth. It'll be all right, won't it?'

'We shall be very glad to see him,' was all Miss Dollette said, smiling, and went on her way with Katherine following.

Wilfred, having said 'Thank you', was brought up short at the door of his room by the ringing sound of Katherine's voice from the head of the stairs.

'Oh *why* not, Felicity? I'd adore to – and they adore flowers.'

A pause; he stood with his fingers on the handle. Miss Dollette must be saying something.

'Of course it wouldn't. He'd expect it. Oh well, even if he didn't, it would be such a lovely surprise.' Another pause, and then the resonant voice in real anger – 'Oh what a coward and a *prig* you are! Don't you *ever* want to do anything different?'

After that, he heard no more. The two went down the stairs, and he realized with a little shock of shame that he had been *eavesdropping*, and went into his room and shut the door.

Wanted to put a great bunch of flowers in his room, I suppose, he mused. *Kind of her but I wish she'd – keep out of things. Now let's see, when's the sixteenth? Cripes, day after tomorrow. Better get in some sherry, I suppose.*

27

Samurai combat

When he opened the front door, Wilfred's first impression was one of beauty and hauteur, two things not often encountered on the doorsteps of Torford. The young man wore a long grey overcoat fitted to a slender waist. He stood very still, against the background of pale, deserted houses and evening light; his hair just touched his wide shoulders.

'Good evening,' he said, and his beautiful face broke into a dazzling smile. 'Here I am, Yasuhiro Tasu, as we arrange. I had a good journey, thank you for your kind enquiry. It is a very nice evening. Mairly is quite well. I send – bring – you her dutiful love.'

'Thanks,' said the prospective father-in-law dryly.

In a few seconds the visitor had used up every sentence his host had prepared, to fill those first awkward moments of arrival. 'Come along in. Have you had tea?'

Wilfred felt conscious about the last word. He and Pat had always used it in the sense of a large meal, with meat or cheese, bread-and-butter and cake, eaten about six. *Dinner or supper* could be the terms used by this young hero for his last meal of the day, for, in addition to the race difference, Wilfred felt one of class.

'Oh yes, oh yes, thank you.' Yasuhiro, carrying a small suit-case, was following him into the house, 'on the train . . .' The flute-like, yet unmistakably male, voice died away, then resumed in a different tone: 'Most beautiful house I have seen in England. It is *very* beautiful. Congratulate you on your taste, Mr Dad.'

Wilfred, amused and pleased, turned a smiling face over his shoulder. 'I mustn't take the credit, you know. It isn't my house. Some friends let me have a room here.'

'Peaceful harmony, like ancient music or calmness of the forest,' continued the oh-so-alien voice.

'I'm glad you like it.'

Yasuhiro kept up an easy babble about the houses in the road and their derelict state ('oh yes, the bombing. Must let the by-gones be the by-gones, necessary'), their age and their architectural style.

While relieved at not having to bring out his own limited store of small talk, Wilfred did wonder if his guest always talked so much?

It would send me round the bend, he thought. *But it's better than shyness. Perhaps he's nervous.*

But his first impression convinced him that Yasuhiro could never be nervous, in any conceivable situation.

Mary had certainly picked up something – except that it was *he* who had picked up *her*. Yes. That was what he must remember. He, Wilfred Davis, was the father of the chosen one, and this boy had come here expressly to get his consent to their marriage.

'Want a wash?' Wilfred blurted, at the door of Yasu's room.

'Thank you, thank you, I am quite clean. But loo on the train wasn't. I am astonished that the British people can endure – bear, *stick* such dirtiness.'

'Too many people and not enough staff nowadays . . .' Wilfred answered vaguely. 'My old dad worked on the railways,' and he waved the guest into his room, where the evening sunlight sparkled on the sherry decanter that had been one of Pat's prides.

'Most beautiful again,' Yasuhiro murmured, gazing around. 'And Solomon-seal and tradescantia flowers arrangement very un-us-u-al. (Daring mixture – has no meaning, I suppose? Of course of course no.) Excuse that I stare. I know it is not the

custom in England. I should say "nice-place-you've-got-here",'
with a sidelong glance and a smile that Wilfred thought of as
more natural.

'Sit down, Yasu, and take your coat off.'

'But . . . perhaps I show you my heart,' gracefully and rapidly stripping off the coat to reveal a suit of palest grey which
caused his prospective father-in-law to think *Cripes, that must
have cost a packet.*

'You'll have some sherry, won't you?' Wilfred thought that
his Pat would have been pleased with him; he was doing the
honours well. And he was pleased when the boy stood, attentive, inclining slightly, until the glasses were filled and he
himself was seated.

'Yes, I show you my heart-thoughts – if you are kind to
listen,' Yasuhiro went on.

'Fire away.'

'Ah – like a gun. British colloqui-al-ism.'

'Yes – well – it means – you know – get started, tell me.'
(*Heart-thoughts. I like that. Expressive. But Mary said he writes
poetry.*)

'It doesn't sound polite, perhaps. What I will say.'

'I can take it,' Wilfred said playfully.

'Mairly has told me you are the kindest of fathers. Different
in Japan. Fathers often what West call *severe.* It is our custom.
But here, easy to hurt a kind heart.'

'That was nice of you, Yasu, to worry.'

'And when I arrive here, all is har-mo-ni-ous,' he went on,
looking around at the golden-white walls and shining furniture,
'and – I am surprised.'

'I like it myself,' Wilfred confessed. 'But when Mary's mother
was alive, we had things different in our house. She liked a bit
of colour.'

For an instant an older man seemed to look out of Yasuhiro's
eyes.

'Understand,' he said gently. 'Happiness with wife covers all
shapes and colours with beauty.'

'That's just it,' Wilfred exclaimed. Then, suddenly becoming embarrassed, 'Here, I'm forgetting my manners,' and he held out a packet of cigarettes. 'Do you smoke?'

'No oh no!' Yasuhiro exclaimed, so vehemently as to startle Wilfred. 'I am a follower of Mishima. Fitness of body, iron of soul. We do not smoke. Bad, bad habit.'

'All right, son – glad to hear it – you don't mind if I do?' drawing out his baccy pouch and reaching for his pipe.

'Of course of course, all habits permitted in house of the honourable host,' Yasuhiro answered, with his social smile. 'You arrange charming flowers yourself?'

'Lord, no, I can't arrange flowers.'

'Family Tradescant breed these flowers. Unusual name. I look for name in dictionary in disgraceful Public Library. Names interest me.'

'Mary said you were working very hard at your English. But Yasu –' Wilfred looked down at the fingers pressing the tobacco into his pipe. 'Why do you call the Public Library disgraceful? I've found them pretty good, especially in the last ten years, much better than when I was a boy, fifty years ago.'

'Allow me to say honourable face does not look so ancient.'

This was the kind of remark that Japanese made in books, and Wilfred, while suspecting mere politeness, felt more at ease. After all, one had read the *Mr Moto* stories.

'Oh, young in heart, you know, young in heart.' But he was not going to be deflected. 'Why is it disgraceful, Yasu?'

Yasuhiro's lashes went down for an instant, then swept up. 'Favourite word. Mairly say that I use it too much and in wrong sense. For me means – it means bad, ugly, wrong. Most of all, ugly. Those libraries us-u-ally ugly places.'

Wilfred contemplated giving some information about spending the ratepayers' money, then decided against it. He changed the subject.

'All right if you come down to . . . supper with my friends, Yasu? It's nearly time. They'd like to meet you. But if you'd prefer a bite up here alone with me, just say so.' His heart sank at the prospect.

'I am pleased to meet your friends, thank you. But to have meal alone with you would be enjoyable. Honourable host decide,' with a quick little bow.

'Then downstairs, I think. Livelier for you.'

'What honourable host decides pleases me.'

Wilfred, glancing at the clock, wondered if such politeness went on all the time in the boy's home in Japan. *A bit of a strain,* he decided. *And those ambassadors or whatever they were – talking about some peace treaty or other in Washington while their chaps were actually bombing Pearl Harbor. Can't trust 'em. But there must be some decent ones, I suppose.* He rose. 'Let's go down, shall we?'

Yasuhiro got up in one movement, suggesting a spring, and Wilfred almost grinned – *pretty dull for the boy and he must be hungry – no wonder he sprang.*

But then Yasuhiro stood aside while he went through the door, and the impulse to grin was replaced by embarrassment, for no one had ever deferred to him like this in his whole life. The people who had come to see him at the Town Hall, in his position as Rates Supervisor, had invariably been intent upon their own rights or wrongs, and determined to show him that they were not afraid of him. *It's only manners,* he thought, *but I like it – from Mary's boy.*

The three in the kitchen were all occupied, Mr Taverner uncorking wine, Miss Dollette putting out napkins, and Katherine Cornforth setting in the middle of the table a white porcelain bowl filled with crimson nasturtiums and their leaves. As Wilfred and Yasuhiro came in, she looked up and smiled brilliantly, then swept forward with hands outstretched.

'Well! At last,' she exclaimed. 'Yasu himself. Mary's told us *so* much about you, and we're all *terribly* glad to have you here.'

Yasuhiro's answering smile was as brilliant, but without warmth; his bow, though low, was stiff.

'Pleased and most honoured to be here,' he said.

Introductions followed, and two more ceremonious bows, but no more outflung hands, to Wilfred's relief.

The meal, one suitable to a summer evening, began in easy silence; Wilfred realized, for perhaps the first time in his life, how much of talk is due to a nervous fear of quiet, and also how composed Yasuhiro was now, eating shrimps and salad.

After supper, Katherine said that of course Yasuhiro would like to go round the garden, because the Japanese were so marvellous at gardens.

Dammit, that's – that's cheek, Wilfred thought.

'Come on, Yasu.' She slipped her arm through his and began to draw him through the little scullery to the back door.

'I see that garden is beautiful as house,' he said, allowing himself to be led away. *The place where the plates are washed,* he thought, as they passed through the little room opening off the kitchen. *No machine for that washing. Do they make the peasant-father wash them with his hands in exchange for his room and food?*

'Now – own up! You expected to see some ghastly thing like a photograph in a gardening catalogue, didn't you?' Katherine lightly shook his arm.

'I have seen the house. *So* I did not,' was the smiling answer.

'Felicity,' turning her head, 'what's the name of our tree?'

'Elder,' Miss Dollette softly supplied, from where she was lingering at the door in the afterglow.

The ripple of the Tor was audible, the last light fading from the sky above the black houses beyond the meadows and the railway line; a few lights, and here and there the bluish glow from a television, shone from the windows.

The tree leans above the stream to give protection and shade, even as Great-grandfather leans over me where I dash and sparkle in the sunlight of my youth, Yasuhiro was thinking. *Oh, my heart weeps silently for home!*

'Most pleasing,' he repeated, 'and that flower, the Seal of Solomon, is that its name?'

'Yes – it loves the shade,' Miss Dollette put in, raising her voice slightly, for Katherine had taken them into a stroll round the oval lawn, and they were at the far end of the little expanse. 'There are some white violet buds gone to seed, but it's too dark to see them. Funny little round black things. You wouldn't expect white violet buds to—'

'Felicity darling!' Katherine interrupted imperiously. 'Can't you go and entertain Wilf or something? I've got something simply frightfully important to say to Yasu.'

Miss Dollette turned at once, silently, and went indoors, where Wilfred was in the middle of a low-voiced appeal to Mr Taverner.

'I can see she only means to be kind, of course, but I've *got* to talk to him and it's so difficult, him not being English and all that, we'll need all the time we've got. I can't understand it, Mr Taverner – Mrs Cornforth isn't like those friends of Pat's, nosey or anything. I don't mean to be unkind . . . her heart's in the right place of course, but—'

'Of course. It's very tiresome, dear man. But calm down. He'll get away in a minute. And *les défauts de ses qualités*, you know.'

'No, I *don't* know, Mr Taverner. I got a place at what was then Torford Grammar School, but I never could study French.'

'I'm sorry, Wilfred. I only meant that if Katherine weren't so warm and eager to help people, she wouldn't be capable of buttonholing a complete stranger like that.'

'*I'm sorry I spoke out,* Mr Taverner, but it's Mary's *whole future.*'

'Well, give them another five minutes. Then we'll break it up.'

Wilfred went to the window and stared gloomily out.

'I'm old enough to be your mother,' Katherine was saying in a lulling murmur as they paced slowly along in the twilight, 'and I do so want to help you . . . and Mary, too, of course . . . such a sensible girl . . . that was the first thing I thought about her when I met her: *how sensible.* I simply *must* ask you something, Yasu.'

Her voice sank mysteriously. The arm she held remained stiff, and although Yasuhiro's head was courteously inclined towards her, he was silent.

'*Do* tell me what you saw in her. I know one *never* understands what attracts people to other people, but really – Mary – to most people – the only word I can use sounds rather unkind – she'd actually seem *dull*.'

'I know the word, Mrs Cornforth,' he said. 'It means not bright, not shining.' His tone was expressionless.

'I only meant until one gets to know her, of course,' Katherine added hastily. 'But you do agree, don't you? To most people . . .' No answer. She tried again. 'You see, Yasu, it *intrigues* me, because you're simply the very last kind of person one would *expect* to be attracted to her. Aren't you?' She shook his arm gently. 'Oh come on, Yasu! "Give", as the Americans say.'

'You are very kind to offer such interest, Mrs Cornforth,' he answered slowly, and Katherine stopped dead, and stood staring as he spoke, 'but I don't want to do anything suggested by Americans. Want only, oh so much, to grind them into powder like the beans *we* eat for our break-fast. Now if you excuse, I return to your honourable house. I have important affairs to talk about with Mary's father.'

He was gently pulling his arm away.

The first part of his sentence had come out on an extraordinary note indescribable in words; it was almost a growl, and it conveyed an impression of alarming, and naked, force.

There was silence in the summer dusk.

'I'm – sorry,' Katherine said at last, breathlessly, in a shaken voice. 'I didn't think I'd ever hear *that sound here*.'

'*Samurai* fighting cry,' he said lightly, as they strolled back to the house. 'It brings spirit back to dead bodies . . .'

Katherine said nothing. Her head was turned away.

28

Epic

Wilfred was accustomed to interviewing strangers.

It had been part of his work at the Town Hall during the thirty years he had passed there; his reponsibilities increasing as time went on and his reliability and conscientiousness establishing themselves in the opinion of his superiors. He knew how to look people in the eye without giving offence, and how to receive glances, charged with helpless annoyance, without showing any in return.

But the dark, bright eyes now looking into his own had no expression but courtesy.

Wilfred almost sighed.

'About your job, Yasu –' he began. 'Got any ideas yet?'

'None. Not at all. No. You see, not necessary to toil in shabby business because Great-grandfather will die soon, and he has leave to me all his stocks and shares. This I tell you in my letter. Also, my family has large large house – much room for Mary and perhaps for many children. Sons. I hope for you, also, Honourable Mr Dad. (Please do come.) Therefore good situation. Don't you think. So?'

This appeared to dispose of the situation, and more than satisfactorily. But not for a lower-middle-class, old-fashioned Englishman.

'Well, that sounds very nice, of course . . . But won't you want to do some kind of work?'

Yasuhiro shrugged.

'Why to toil if you have money? Go around, look at beautiful world, play at games with my children, be with sweet wife. Plenty to do, plenty.'

What has been called the *Protestant work ethic* was shocked in Wilfred.

'But – but –' he hunted about for reasons that should not seem idealistic or moral '– you'll be so bored, Yasu.'

'Only bored when toiling in office of disgraceful factory. How could I be bored while swim, climb, do *kendo*, read, look at beautiful white moon, go to Apurimac, marvellous marvellous place?'

'Where's that?' Wilfred asked after a pause. He had to say something, because he felt he was getting nowhere in the argument.

'Is in Peru. I have seen coloured photograph. Waterfall going down hundreds of feet into pool so clear cannot know if it *is* water. Trees stand all around watching. Oh wonderful.'

'Yes, well, you could always see that on holiday – and wouldn't you—'

'Not "always". Forests everywhere rapidly destroying by pol-lution. Hurry, hurry to see in time. Also before disgraceful tourist come.'

'– want a house – home – of your own?' Wilfred retreated helplessly from Apurimac. 'I'm sure Mary will.'

'Wife want what her husband want,' proclaimed Yasuhiro.

'Don't you believe it. Sometimes, perhaps. Not always.'

'Then she learn. Duty to do this. But I am rude. I interrupt you, Mr Dad.'

'They only learn up to a point. In England wives have minds of their own, you know.'

'Men have more strong minds,' and Yasuhiro smiled, a man-to-man sort of smile, which Wilfred found endearing.

'Some of us have, and some of us haven't . . . When it comes to Mary having her own home, I think you'll find she's got a very strong mind of her own. She's been brought up to believe that's the – er – natural way to live. A lot of trouble's caused by young people living with their parents – I've seen it.'

'Custom, in Japan. Or, if trouble, then parents speak strong to young people, and trouble all gone.'

Wilfred wished, feelingly, that this could be the case nearer home. He shifted his ground of attack.

'Besides, how about your own parents? Won't they want a bit of peace? You're – what? – twenty-one? They must be getting on.'

'Oh yes, Father old now. Sit in shade, as we say. My mother more young, wear Western dress.'

Wilfred shifted ground again.

'Wouldn't you feel – well – I mean, living on inherited money—'

'What is in-herit-ed, please? Expression not familiar.'

'Money someone left you when they died.'

'Answer number one question first. Then give reasons. My father does not like peace. Enjoys play at tennis, play at *pachinko* (Japanese game). Cheerful person. My mother cheerful also. Get around.' Yasuhiro paused for a long time. 'Pleased to have only son and daughter-in-law living in their house. Daughter's father also.' He paused for a long time. 'I tell you my heart-thoughts, Mr Dad. Parents *not* pleased I want to marry girl from the West.'

Ah, now we're coming to it. Just what I thought.

'But I go straight to Honourable Great-grandfather, talk to him on the telephone . . . Great influence with parents. So now good situation.'

'Glad to hear it,' Wilfred said weakly.

'And about stocks and shares. They are not *stolen* money. Honourable Great-grandfather earn this money being great sailor. Put money in Stock Exchange. Now much much more. Good situation also.' He smiled triumphantly.

'But – I don't feel it's *right*, Yasu,' Wilfred said at last, experiencing that sense of confusion that is almost sorrow, which overcomes certain people when arguments which they feel strongly to be right are swept aside by other, more forceful minds.

'But is not *wrong*, Honourable Mr Dad. How is wrong?'

'Well, er, how about all the millions of people in the world who haven't enough to eat?'

'Oh, die soon. Relieve pop-u-lation ex-plosion. Good situation.' Yasuhiro waved a hand.

'Or – or who don't have a nice home?'

'Cannot help,' and he smiled.

'It's – it's so damned *selfish*,' Wilfred burst out.

'Why selfish? I am ready to die for glory of Emperor and Japan.'

'Let's hope you won't have to.'

'Strongest wish,' Yasuhiro said, and the muscles of his jaw tightened.

At this point, Wilfred almost gave up, and thought of suggesting that they should go down to join the others, or that he should teach Yasuhiro to play Old Maid or something . . . Militarism, on top of everything else. He was more than anxious about Mary's future now: he was seriously troubled.

'But Yasu, that would mean war, wouldn't it? You can't want a Third World War?' Yasuhiro continued to smile in haughty silence. 'We'd none of us last more than a few minutes – use your head!' Wilfred went on vigorously. 'How about your beautiful world – all blown to pieces, or made' – he hunted for the word – 'infertile?'

'Japan have the Bomb by then,' was the steely answer.

'And a lot of good that'd do, wouldn't it?'

'Honourable host's opinion correct of course of course,' and Yasuhiro retired into the social manner.

Wilfred then made an effort. For him it was a strong effort, because he was accustomed, in arguments outside office hours, to retreat into good-humoured but obstinate silence, into pipe-fiddling, into changing the subject; even occasionally, when his antagonist was very pig-headed, into hypocritical agreement.

But this argument was different; this time he had to stand firm, because it was for Mary.

'I never see the point of arguing about war,' he began at last. 'One never gets anywhere. And you, at your age, aren't likely to understand how I feel at mine. I've been through two of 'em. You haven't.'

'Not my fault! Not born at right time! (Excuse, I am rude.)'

'You can thank your lucky stars you weren't – It's all right. You weren't rude . . . It wouldn't be like the last one, you know, any more than that was like 1914.'

'Glorious death for Japan,' Yasuhiro repeated.

'For you, perhaps, if that's what you want. But how about all the millions and millions of other people? You aren't using your imagination, Yasu. How about Mary – and the children, perhaps.'

'This is how Mairly says. I see that your honourable mind is like her mind.'

'Natural, isn't it, seeing I'm her father.' He leant forward. 'Look here, Yasu. I want to give my, er, consent. But I, er, more than that of course I want Mary to be happy—'

'If she marry me she will be happy.'

'Yes, well, perhaps . . . But look here. All this stuff about dying for Japan, it worries me. Who'd take care of her and the children if you went off and got killed?'

'Family take care of honoured widow. Duty in Japan. Western ideas, throw widow away like plastic container. Not in Japan.'

'Yes, I expect they would. But she'd be very unhappy and lonely if you got killed.'

Yasuhiro shrugged. His mouth was set sulkily.

Wilfred breathed a heavy sigh, half of exasperation, half in preparation for what he was about to say. He spoke steadily, when he did speak.

'And suppose I said you've got to give up these ideas or *I won't* give my consent? How'd you feel then?'

Colour came into Yasuhiro's face. He sat very still. He did not raise his eyes; only said, in a low voice:

'That would hurt my heart so much so much that I would crack. Like por-ce-lain plate. Heart of Mairly too, I think. But of course word of Honourable Mr Dad is final.'

Wilfred was so surprised that he could only sit and stare. So much for his ideas of rebellious, uncontrollable youth! He was shocked out of his astonishment when Yasuhiro added pensively: 'We both commit suicide, I think. (National tradition, you know.) I have expected this – in my heart-thoughts. Mishima is right when he says love not possible for modern boy and girl in Japan or anywhere.'

'Whoever he was, Mishima was talking rubbish!' Wilfred almost shouted. 'All we need is a bit of give-and-take between you and me. As for suicide – that's all nonsense. I never heard . . .'

Yasuhiro slowly shook his head, still staring at the floor.

'Painful and sad to live with cracked heart. Suicide better.'

Wilfred sat looking at him in despairing silence. He, the girl's father, had the power to stop the whole thing, just by saying 'No'. *Like some old chap in Victoria's reign.* He couldn't believe it. Yet he was certain the boy meant what he said.

The room was quiet. A summer stillness held the air, and faint light, from a moon made gold by the earliest hint of autumn mists, showed in at the window between the curtains. Under the occasional bellow of a passing train and the remote drone of traffic, the singing of the stream was audible. Wilfred found his tired thoughts wandering off into nowhere.

'Yasu,' he said slowly at last, with a feeling of coming back into the real world. 'How about writing all this?'

Yasuhiro looked at him attentively.

'Mary tells me you write poetry. Why don't you write something for – for the glory of Japan? Something really splendid. Make you famous and all that. It's just an idea . . .' His voice trailed off as Yasuhiro did not answer.

'Mishima was writing,' he said at last. 'Stories.' He hesitated, then leant towards Wilfred, lowering his voice almost to a whisper. His eyes had the ingenuous light of a very young boy's. He was transformed, and Wilfred could only stare.

'Mr Dad, you are Mairly's father. Tell you now my very secret heart-thoughts, as only to my Honourable Great-grandfather. I do not wish to die for glory, or commit suicide. I wish to live with Mary and enjoy beautiful world.'

'That's all right,' Wilfred said after a pause. 'I understand. It's all right, Yasu.'

He was moved, and therefore he was embarrassed. The sight of Yasuhiro's changed and softened face, and the half-whispered confidence, brought the thought that this boy from the other side of the world might one day be a son to him, supported and supporting, loved and loving. Wilfred did not use these words in his thoughts. *Get on together all right* was how he translated them. He had to turn his head away until he 'felt better'.

Yasuhiro appeared to have gone off into a reverie. He got up silently and moved across to the window and stood with his back to the room, staring out into the dusk.

He did not say anything, and gradually the voice of the stream below the window began to be heard. Wilfred heard a soft crackle of words.

'"He sings swiftly and low to himself in the dark, the clear Stream Spirit." Is a poem. What we call a *haiku*. I make English translation. Good one. Correct, too, in syll-ables.'

'Very nice.'

But Wilfred had had enough. He said firmly, 'It's past nine. How about us going up to the TV room and watching *Ironside*?'

Wilfred slept late, and awoke through one of the exquisite, confused dreams which had blessed his sleep since he came to live at the Yellow House, to be aware of a by no means subdued knocking on his bedroom door.

'Hullo – what's up – come in,' he called drowsily, less than half awake.

The door opened with some energy.

'I am here, Honourable Mr Dad. Forgive the rudeness that I wake you from desirable sleep. But car hired this morning waiting at the front door. To drive me back to London. So I wish to speak to you before departure.'

'Oh – well – you're a sharp mover, aren't you? Nothing's wrong, I hope? Mary didn't phone or anything?' Wilfred sat up in bed, gazing dimly at the elegant grey-clad shape in the doorway.

Strange – strange that this little peasant, this minor official of the British Government, is my father-in-law to be, mused Yasuhiro, *behind his sweet-smiling mask. His thin hair is disordered on his scalp, his sleeping-robe is in tasteless colours. But he is not without intelligence. He even has some imagination. And his poor peasant-heart has what has been called the American and British virtue – kindness. I shall honour him, as it is my duty. I, even I, actually feel some softness towards him.*

'Nothing is wrong. I have spoken with Mairly on the telephone. Already.' Yasuhiro giggled. 'She is angry that I awake her so early. (Wake her up.) But when I tell her I am going back to disgr— to Rowena Road, she is angry once more. But I *wish* to tell you . . .'

'Oh . . . well . . .' Wilfred, sitting up in bed, was trying to refrain from smoothing his hair and rubbing his eyes. 'Fire away.'

'And I wish to tell Mairly, at once very quickly. *I have got first lines.* Poem concerning heroic suicide of Mishima. Write this for glory of Japan.'

'Oh – well – that's fine, Yasu. Congratulations. Very glad to hear it . . . Had your breakfast?'

'No. Hunger increases strength of senses – to see, hear, and feel heart-thoughts. Eat when I get back to London. Irri-ta-ting detail at this moment.'

'Sorry.'

'– Will be demon-poem. Very terrible. Stir up the heart-feelings. Peasants all over the world will "swallow" and know tra-gic story of Mishima who died for ancient Japanese traditions.'

'Er – will it be a long poem?'

'Ep-ic,' was the prompt reply. 'Long poem concerned with great tragic happenings. Much made in Ancient World. Often sung to musical instruments. (This I learn at Tokyo University, second year English course.) Now, Honourable Mr Dad, you give your much-wished consent I marry with Mairly?'

There was a pause. Wilfred, sitting up in bed with his hair on end, did not feel at his most capable, and when at last he spoke, it was slowly.

'You know I'd like to, Yasu. But – does it mean that if you write this poem you, er, won't want to die for Japan?'

Yasuhiro nodded slowly, standing very straight with his arms at his sides.

'Yes, Mr Dad. (Of course, if war came, I would have to fight.) But – I have told you – in my heart-thoughts I wish to live, not die for glory of Japan or commit suicide. So this poem, which I make *very* long, *very* glorious, great work, shall be a – kind of dying. *Such* work, you understand, *so* difficult to make great, tragic, true.'

I suppose, Wilfred thought, *this is the best I shall get . . . at least he doesn't want to cut his stomach open any more. Really –!*

I'd better settle for it.

'Right you are, then, Yasu. I give my consent. And I hope you'll both be very happy together – as happy as Mary's mother and I were.'

The next instant he was looking down at the top of a black, bowed head, as Yasuhiro knelt before him with hidden face.

'Here – I say – get up – this won't do, son!'

But Yasuhiro was up before the embarrassed sentence had finished, colour in his own face.

'Heart-thoughts go over me like Hokusai wave. Now I go, Mr Dad. Bye-bye. I shall now tell Mary.'

A smile like the rising sun itself, and he was gone.

*

I lose face, Yasuhiro was thinking as, his telephone call made, he leant back in the car rushing towards London. *I, a member, the last male member, of the family descended from a second cousin of the Divine Emperor in the reign of the first English Elizabeth (holy cow, what a name) knelt to a slightly-less-than-peasant minor official. It is fortunate that no one saw me or knows of the loss of face except the man himself.*

He stopped the car outside the gates of the Prince Charles Hospital, where flowers were being displayed to tempt visitors, and suggested to the vendors that they should sell him their entire stock and deliver it to Mr Davis in Hardy Crescent in return for fifteen pounds. The offer was refused with incredulity and demands to know who he thought he was. The chauffeur was smiling, and Yasuhiro resumed his journey, with the loss of face unrepaired.

And yet, he thought, *my heart sings like a bird set free.*

29

Sylvie again

Mary's views on weddings chimed in perfect tune with those of the less advanced women's magazines: the importance of The Dress, the temporary unimportance of the bridegroom (all he had to do was to *be there*, and on time); the details of the reception; a white wedding, of course – every minute point and custom which the sociologists and psychiatrists and feminists are knowledgeable or contemptuous about.

Only at the threshold of the bedroom did her imagination become vague, and her thoughts begin to march in the clinical order directed by the educationalists of her generation. She was informed, but incurious. Love had neatly stepped in over the heads of the technical experts and, in his ancient way, bound his bandage over her thoughts and her young senses. What no one had prepared her for, when the time came, was the mutual, laughing sweetness.

They ought to tell you, she was to think to the end of her life. *Really they ought.*

When Mrs Cadman, happening to encounter Yasuhiro in the hall at Rowena Road, excitedly suggested that the large front room would be plenty big enough if Yasuhiro and Mr Grant just shifted the couch into the hall, he was silent for a moment.

'I had thought,' he began at last, 'to hire a room at some hotel.'

'Oh you don't want to do that, wasting your money – it'll be no trouble. I shall enjoy it. Miss Wayne was only saying to me this morning, it'll liven us up.'

Yasuhiro's impulse was to demand what-the-hell business it was of Miss Wayne's? – a figure encountered by himself occasionally on the stairs, and of which he retained only the dim impression that it was female and advanced in years. Now, apparently, this vague entity was arranging the celebrations for his betrothal. However, he said courteously: 'I hope that Honourable Miss Wayne will come to drink champagne with other welcome guests. But, Mrs Cadman—'

'Now, I don't want to hear another word about it! That's settled!' cried Mrs Cadman, showing symptoms of that apparent mental unbalance which overtakes women when weddings, christenings or funerals are being arranged, and sweeping him aside as if he were a spider. 'We'll have the big room and I'll make one of my cakes – it's for Mothering Sunday, really, but it won't matter for once – I've got the recipe somewhere, and there's that cut-price place in Dartmouth Street, you can get your champers there, that'll save you a bit, you don't want to bankrupt yourself before you start – who's coming?'

'Flowers,' was the gloomy answer.

'Flowers? Who's he?'

'Flowers from a flower merchant. Hundreds and hundreds of flowers. I shall order. At this time dahlias most beautiful. Also early chry-san-the-mums. Can be so arranged to mean rejoicing.'

'Well, that'll look lovely, I'm sure . . .'

Yasuhiro was about to add that rejoicing could be as well expressed by a single spray of almond blossom, but refrained.

Hundreds of flowers were what would be necessary to impress upon the coarse minds of the guests the honour and the position – even now, in Japan's Age of Degradation – of the Tasu family. If he suggested a spray of almond blossom – even though it was flown across the world from a land over which spring was now trailing her green cloak – they would only think that his family had not the money to buy more. *It's a mournful situation*, he thought in English, *to have no taste*; and he looked even more courteously at Mrs Cadman.

It was Monday morning, just after lunch, and Mary now came down the stairs, dressed for work in blue trousers and sweater under her dark green coat. The trousers were a gesture of defiance. Yasuhiro said that Japanese women of good family averted their eyes from them, and Mrs Levy said Mary had not the figure for them.

Mary thought it prudent to lay in reserves of self-will against the future and continued to wear them.

'Ah, here's Mary, she'll decide everything,' exclaimed Mrs Cadman.

Mary and Yasuhiro had hardly stopped talking to one another since the previous morning, but they had not yet reached the engagement party.

'What've I got to decide?' she said. 'Want to walk me to the bus, love?' to Yasuhiro, who unsmilingly inclined his head.

'Your engagement party, girl, wake up!' Mrs Cadman was enjoying being carried away.

'Oh well . . . I thought we'd get the wedding settled first.' Mary glanced at Yasuhiro, smiling, and he flashed back a polite smile and her heart sank. *He's going to have his way*, she thought.

'We have Japanese cere-mony,' Yasuhiro was announcing as he and Mary set off down the road.

'Yasu! Every girl in England chooses what kind of a wedding she'll have – and the dress and everything! It's the custom . . .'

'The custom in Japan is wedding held at the family house of the man. And only low, un-traditional girl wears Western dress. Of course of course all will be Japanese.'

'Well, it isn't the custom over here.'

'You look so pretty – nice in Japanese wedding dress, Mairly, ornaments in the hair that you like; and you have *white* dress same as English girl, only better shape. Japanese girls also wear white on wedding day.' He paused. 'But *all* white, *only* white . . .'

'I haven't said a word to Mrs Levy yet, blast it. She'll never stop going on about it.'

'. . . in Japan, white is death-colour.'

'What!' Mary stopped and stood staring. 'Well, that's cheerful, I must say.'

'Death colour, yes. White robe and sash means death of the bride to the family of her father.'

Mrs Levy's reception of Mary when she came on duty at one o'clock had never been warm, and since her assistant's fall into dreaminess and absent-mindedness, it had become fretful. The idea that Mary might one day leave only occurred to Mrs Levy to the accompaniment of scoffing inward laughter.

'Ach, Mary – there you are. I think you are not coming. It's five minutes past one.'

'Is it?' Mary glanced at the clock on a shelf. 'Sorry.'

'Sorry, sorry, it's better to be on time than sorry. But modern girls all the same.'

'But I bet not many of them are going to marry a rich Japanese boy.'

Mary spoke unhurriedly, with her back to Mrs Levy, while she was hanging up her coat. Silence followed, and she did not look round.

She slipped on her working overall and turned, deliberately. Disappointingly, Mrs Levy was not sitting staring with her mouth open, but had returned to the account book in which she was entering figures.

'You vish you vere,' she said at last in a dry tone. She did not look up.

'Well, I am.'

'A joke I can enjoy, but lies are different. When I finish this column, I go off to lunch with my daughter. She has a new au pair, German girl, very good housewife.' She bent over the book again.

'But it's true, Mrs Levy. I am going to marry him.'

Mrs Levy compressed her lips and shook her head and continued to add up new pence.

'All right, then. He's coming here to fetch me this evening—'
Mrs Levy put down the pencil.

'I shall be with my daughter at the cinema, as you know, Mary, because I haf told you ve go to see *Fiddler on the Roof,* seventh time. Today you are vorse than usual.'

'– and I hope you'll come to our engagement party.' Mary felt a sudden pity for the shreds of rusty hair and the scored sallow old face. 'I don't know the date yet—'

'Ha!'

'– but we'll be sending out the invitations.'

'Thank you. That I will wait for, an invitation. On a card printed with your name, I suppose? Ha!'

After this exchange, Mary settled to work on innumerable details involving the arrangement and display of small plastic and base metal souvenirs, outrageously overpriced, and valueless but for the harmless associations they awoke in the minds of those who brought them home. Mrs Levy shut the book with a snap, locked it away, and put on her smart black coat and hat and went off to meet her daughter.

Mary stood by the counter, idly watching her employer cross the street. Why should she go on working? Dear old Dad would manage to pay for the engagement party, and even squeeze out something for clothes. He had some money now he'd sold the house.

She sat down: to have a serious think, with the cigarette whose occasional smoking had caused raised eyebrows and a reference to his hero ('Mishima was very against this habit. Weakens the body'). Mary had retorted 'So what', and continued to smoke. She stared absently out past the bright, blowing dresses, at the strolling crowds touched, even in the City, by the golden languor of this unusually beautiful autumn.

The first thing was to fix the wedding date.

Here or – or in Japan?

Terror suddenly seized her. Ten thousand miles away, on the other side of the world, and strange; stranger than anything seen on television *because it was real.* Because real people lived there and worked, and ate, and had babies, and died. But in another way – a foreign, strange, utterly alien way. And she was going to live there.

But I'll have Dad. The thought was like sudden warmth in the air of deadly cold. *If he wasn't coming* . . . Never had she banished a thought because it was too frightening to face. She did so now.

They walked through the damp, leaf-scented darkness. London growled quietly to itself and glowed and sparkled in its vast valley.

'You understand, Mary,' Yasu said, presently. 'I decide. I must stay in England to finish my studies. You notice how I have improve in my words?'

'Yes, love, you've improved all right.'

'I was – suppose – to come for one year. It would please Honoured Great-grandfather if I did this, seeming to him firm in my intentions like the unbending rock. And you, Mary, are the flowing water that winds around it, changing shape because of the rock shape.'

'Thanks.'

He glanced at her sideways, and smiled. He was developing a taste for English humour.

Mary was thinking about the simile. He was going to use all his formidable will to turn her into water or a bowing willow or something, and she intended to remain Mary – either Davis or Tasu, honourable *san* or not. She was going to stay Mary. *And he knows it*, she thought.

'Yes – if you stay on for the year that'll mean February,' she said. 'When did you think of us getting married?'

Her tone was casual but she did not feel casual. This was the moment.

'Soon soon, quickly,' was the flattering answer. 'After February perhaps when the cherry blossom comes.'

'April,' she said thoughtfully. 'And – and here or in Japan?'

'In Japan, Mary, of course of course. Dark iris, twilight flowing water –' and his arm swept round her body and drew her to him as they walked. 'This will please my family *so much*. Truly, is absolutely im-possible to have a disgraceful English marriage ceremony. So ugly. It would un-doubtedly offend the ancestors,' he added in a lower tone.

'April, then,' Mary said firmly, thinking it prudent to ignore the last part of his sentence. 'Early or late?'

'Depends upon two circum-stances. When is the cherry blossom here? And what are prog-nos-tica-tions. (I learnt this word yesterday, in thinking and planning for our ceremony.) Prognostications, yes – of the astrologers.'

'Cripes! Astrologers, now. What on earth have they got to do with it?'

'We must have a fortunate date, love. Otherwise bad situation.'

'Oh well, that's all right. I can see that.'

Mary, growing up in an age which denies faith yet thirstily needs its morning-paper ration of magic as it needs tranquil-lizers, swallowed the astrologers with hardly a gulp. 'Early April, then?'

'Yes. The tenth day of April, if the astrologers say this is fortunate.'

'April the tenth,' she repeated.

Then Yasuhiro paused. They were under a great maple tree, whose pale, dying leaves faintly reflected the glare in the sky over London. His arms drew her close.

'British kiss,' murmured Yasuhiro. 'Date of our marriage.'

The kiss was given and taken.

'You like that, Mairly?' he asked, drawing away from her a little.

'Oh yes – sweet – little celebration –' she gasped. 'Oh Yasu, I do love you. I do, I do.' She stopped, ashamed.

'So I do love you, Mairly. For life-long. As the Pine of Takasago. And here's another present for you. You shall choose the date of this British engagement party.'

*

Mary decided to invite Mrs Wheeby, Mrs Levy, her father's three friends at the Yellow House, and – if she could find her – Sylvie.

When she showed the list –which included all the other tenants – to Yasuhiro, his only remark was: 'I shall send an es-pecial invitation to your father.'

'But *of course* he's coming, Yasu! Not ask Dad! What an idea!'

'But if I send to him *person-ally*, from me myself, and say the party will be without him a waterless desert, it will please him. Also it is my duty as future son. *Giri* demands.'

Whether the old peasant comes or not, it will be a waterless desert, he was thinking – in English now. *But I'll order six bottles of their whisky. And we'll have saki – 'a foreign custom'. Peasants and tourists like that. How beautiful I could make this party if I were at home! But I must bow my head, like the young pine to the storm. May I not break!* For he was beginning to feel swellingly cross.

'Whisky!' said Mary, on hearing of this intention. 'You'll have everybody drunk – not but what old Grant won't like it, and Dad won't mind.'

'Mr Grant won't like the whisky?'

'No, I meant he *will* like it (your English is lots better, love, but still not quite how we talk) – and cripes, we don't want six bottles, two'll be plenty.'

'Then I supply a long table, food from a shop, and flowers, flowers, cover in flowers,' he snapped. 'Hide and conceal that room.'

'Oh all right – but Mrs Cadman was going to make her special cake—'

'We'll put it away behind a flower vase,' almost shouted Yasuhiro, and Mary decided to change the subject.

Asked if she happened to know Sylvie's address, Mrs Cadman put a considering finger on her chin.

'I know you said she lived somewhere near,' Mary suggested.

'Now, where was it? She did tell me, when she took the room. Unless it was all lies, of course. Bel something. Belfast?

(No, that's Ireland.) Belsize? Can't be. That's over Hampstead Way. Belmont! That's it. Fourteen Belmont Street. It's round Queen's Crescent way, off Kentish Town Road, and the house is next to a fried fish shop.'

Mr Grant, who could be relied upon to come up with useful information, only needed half a minute's thought to produce the name and address of a local printer who, struggling with advancing bankruptcy, was prepared to undertake small jobs; and before she set out to find Belmont Street, Mary handed in at his shop the invitation, beautifully scripted on a sheet of his blue writing paper by Yasuhiro.

Mr Wilfred Davis
requests the pleasure of
your company at an
Engagement Party
to be held at 20 Rowena Road, Parliament Hill
Fields, NW5 on December 1st from 2.30 and onwards
to celebrate the engagement of his only daughter Mary
Patricia Davis to Mr Yasuhiro Tasu, only son of Mr and
Mrs C. H. Tasu of Tokyo, Japan.

Round Queen's Crescent was what Mary thought of as *an awful part.* The small streets of early Victorian villas were in all the squalor of demolition: the inhabitants would not in any case have thought of putting their rubbish anywhere but in their front gardens, where the few dying bushes of laurel occasionally gave shelter to a powerful, immaculately groomed motorcycle.

However, there was a more cheerful sight, a group of small shops with fine cabbages glowing in the window of one, and (striking sign of progress) fluttering outside another a rackful of pornographic magazines which, ten years earlier, would have been cowering under the counter. Was this Belmont Street, looking little changed from forty years ago? And there was the fried fish shop. But next to it, number 14 was only a white gap strewn with crumbling plaster and the miscellaneous rubbish of years. *Blow,* thought Mary. *As though there wasn't enough to do, and I've only got half an hour. I'll try the fried fish shop.* A stoutish young woman was banging about behind the counter, in a smell of stale fat, fish and synthetic scent. Mary was opening her mouth to say 'Sorry to trouble you but do you happen—' when she stopped, staring. The greenish hair, though worn now in the shortest of spiky cuts; the eyes that matched it; the long nose . . .

'Sylvie!'

The familiar sulky look vanished, replaced by the equally familiar one of malicious excitement.

'Look 'oo's 'ere!' Sylvie exclaimed. 'Never thought I'd see *you* again . . . How'd yer find me? Ma Cadman, I bet. Guess what?' she ended, on a burst of triumph.

What of her could be seen behind the counter assured Mary that she was some eight months pregnant. Her purple, orange and green dress ended just below a great bulge. Mary decided to play fair, and shook her head.

'I'm married,' announced Sylvie. 'Been married about five months. Mind yer, *I* wasn't all that crazy about it, neither, but –' patting the bulge, *"e* kep' on at me, saying it wasn't fair to the kid, and Mum moaned – so we done it. ('Course, I'd've 'ad another abortion, if they 'adn't kep' on about it.) Had a smashing wedding, though. Down at St Peter's. Show you the photos some time . . . You still in the same job?' she ended, on a patronizing note.

Mary nodded, but with a smile, and Sylvie looked at her sharply.

'Cor, you are an old dozy! I'd a bin out of that, by this time. You look just the same – I dunno, though. You do look a bit different, somehow.' She giggled. 'Haven't been up to anything, have yer? I bet not – you aren't the sort.'

'No . . . but I am engaged,' Mary said at last, and heard her own voice, deep and soft in contrast to Sylvie's shrill one. She never used to notice Sylvie's voice.

'Go on!' screamed Sylvie. ''oo to?'

'He's Japanese,' was the calm reply.

'Go on! I don't believe it! 'Ooever gets engaged to Japs? Where'd yer meet him? In the shop, I bet.'

'Yes.' Mary knew there would be no chance to explain anything.

'Where's yer ring? Lessee it,' and out shot a hand, fat now, but the nails painted with the familiar green varnish.

'They don't have them in Japan, it isn't the custom.' Mary wished, not for the first time, that it was.

'Saved 'im a bit, that did,' Sylvie grinned. 'When you getting married, then? Got yer dress yet?'

Mary shook her head.

'They don't have our kind of wedding dress, either,' she said quickly. 'Mine'll be white and scarlet. I'll probably be married over there, anyway.'

'Goin' all that way? Catch me!' Sylvie screamed. 'I said to Chris, you're stayin' right here where I know a few folks, I said. He was all for sellin' up and goin' out Barnet way. I soon stopped that, I can tell yer . . . Japan! Sooner you than me . . . Can't believe it, and you always the quiet sort. I bet you don't want to go to no Japan, do yer?' she added, surprisingly. But at that moment, a fat young man came in from a side door, slid an arm round her, and gave her bottom a prolonged pinch, at the same time winking at Mary.

Imagine kissing him. However, he seemed amiable enough.

'What yer come round fer, then?' demanded Sylvie, having asked one or two more casual questions. 'Thought yer'd 'ave me on, I bet.'

Plainly, she did not believe what Mary had said.

'Just to ask you and er – Chris – to the engagement party. You'll get a card, of course—'

'"Of course" – get her! Better get a move on, then. They'll be pulling this place down any day now. Given us another shop in the new block o' flats. Wot do we live on meantime? Air?' and she shrieked with laughter. 'Engagement party – yes, I bet.'

'It's on December the first, at Rowena Road. In the big front room – you remember,' said Mary.

'Should have thought you could find somewhere better than that tatty old—'

Here Chris surprised Mary by saying in a hearty voice, 'Thanks a lot. We'll be there – if the Battle of the Bulge don't come off,' and he jerked a thumb at his wife.

30

The party

Dear Mr Davis,

You must forgive me for not acknowledging your very kind letter sooner, but I have had a tiresome toe. After the unavoidable delay I will make haste to reply with all speed.

I have thought the matter over thoroughly, after receiving the invitation to the engagement party from Mary, and also discussed it with Fred, who has been *most* kind and helpful, and I hope that you will not take it amiss if I tell you that I must decline. I have already written a brief note to Mary. In the third person.

There is no point in beating about the bush with an old friend. (I hope I may say friend.) And to you I will admit that my reason for declining is that I never can get over Mary running away like that and taking up with that poor creature. Treating her father so casually. No, I cannot overlook it. I hope she will be happy in her new life, though she will find it strange at first. (No doubt you will remember I always did have a liking, from early childhood, for 'Things Japanese'). Do as you think best about telling her my reason for declining. I merely said

I had a previous engagement. I shall not send a wedding
present.

Concluding in thanking you for your kindness in
saying you would like me to be there. I hope we shall
meet soon. Perhaps, later in the year, you will come to
spend a day here.

Always yours very sincerely,

Edith Wheeby

Wilfred was reading this letter, in the afterglow, as the train
thundered its way across the quiet Essex landscape towards
London. It was of no use to gaze out at the fields of stubble,
and trees already pale in the dying foliage of autumn because
the rain snatched him past them. He didn't want to look at his
fellow passengers, and he had forgotten to buy the *East Essex
Herald* at Torford station. He had nothing to do, and so he had
taken out Mrs Wheeby's letter.

His friends at the Yellow House had also been asked.
Mrs Cornforth had showed obvious disappointment when
Mr Taverner had said, without explanation, that he was sorry
their attendance was not possible.

Wilfred had felt relieved by this decision; he foresaw that
the occasion could be *what you might call sticky*, though he was
pleased that Mary had invited his friends.

He glanced out of the window. Rows of dark brown brick
houses, pierced by threatening whitish towers that caught the
last yellow light of day, had replaced the fields of aftermath.
The train was running into Ilford; in a few more minutes they
would be at Liverpool Street. He stood up, and began to take
his case down from the rack.

Broad Street was a high, dim, echoing cavern, refreshing
to nerves battered by the bellowing of the train; and Wilfred
settled down in the second, local train to enjoy the twilight
going past, with house lights shining through the dusk.

The party had been going on since half past two. What
state would it be in?

Rowena Road looked forbidding, its grey-and-white houses orange-lit and bordered by a double line of parked cars. *But respectable*, thought Wilfred as he rang the doorbell of number 20. *Respectable.*

The door flew open and there was Mary. (Nice big hall, and no smells.)

She took his case from him. 'Found your way here all right, then? Come in, I'll show you your room. Like a wash? It's on the landing.' She was leading the way upstairs, laughing and rubbing her eyes. 'Don't mind me, I've been asleep.'

'Asleep?'

'Yes. We did start at half past two, but things sort of fizzled out, somehow. Miss Wayne and the other old things always rest in the afternoon, and Sylvie and her Chris can't make it until their shop shuts at eight, and Mrs Levy may not come at all, she thinks it's a come-on.' Mary giggled. 'So Mr Grant and Mr Cadman and Yasu and me got started by ourselves. We sat around chatting –' She was leading him across the landing. 'Yasu started on that old Mishima – need you ask – and I fell asleep . . . Here we are.' She opened a door, and put his case onto the bed. 'And you should have heard Mr Grant!' She was lingering at the door. 'I shouldn't think Mishima ever heard anything like *that* while he was with us – might have done him a bit of good if he had! And Yasu took it. I thought he'd go for Mr Grant with a bit of *kendo*, but he was just awfully polite. Only he went kind of greenish (he does, when he's worked up) –'

'Where is he now, then? I hope he hasn't gone off somewhere, if he's worked up?'

'Oh no. It's only rage. I'm used to it. He's downstairs, making us some Japanese snacks.'

Mary had learnt never to say *Jap*. It implied contempt.

'Well, love, come on down when you're ready. Right down, into the basement. Gosh, you ought to see the big front – it looks smashing. But not till the others come . . . Hurry up. I don't want to miss a minute of you.'

She was gone. He stared at the shut door, glowing with happiness at her last words.

She looked unfamiliarly older, in a silky dark green dress with a square neckline that showed off a necklace of stones glowing with fire. *This was how Yasuhiro's wife would look, perhaps, the mother of his children (Max, Hugh and Cilla, in that order). The young Tokyo matron. And would the Japanese snacks be raw fish?* He sighed, and went across the landing to wash.

She was waiting for him at the bottom of the basement stairs. From behind a door, pluckings and twanglings and nasal chantings came out into the stuffy air: sounds incongruous and foreign.

'That's Yasu's favourite group, the Dwarf Trees. I can say it in Japanese but it nearly breaks my jaw.'

'Are you learning Japanese, dear?'

She shrugged. 'Picking it up – I'll have to tackle it a bit harder when I get out there, of course . . . You'll have to dig into a lot of titchy little pots, I'm afraid, love. He's set on giving us real Japanese starters.'

She opened a door, and there was Yasuhiro, managing to look dignified in a striped butcher's apron over his dark blue ceremonial robe. Open packets, glittering polythene wrappings and bright pink shrimps were scattered on a table in a corner. His wand of office was a wooden spoon.

He came forward. 'Welcome, Honourable Mr Davis.'

Wilfred observed with dismay that his host's face was faintly greenish.

'Oh . . . hullo, Yasu. Nice to see you again. Are you cook this evening?' Wilfred said.

Yasuhiro looked at his spoon with dislike.

'Such is my high position – my job. It was the idea of Miss Wayne. She lodges in the house. She told her idea to Mrs Cadman. I wanted to hire a cook for the evening, you know, but Mrs Cadman and Miss Wayne and old Mr Grant said it would *save money* if I did the preparations.' He sighed heavily. 'It isn't necessary to save money. But good manners to agree with guests. So I buy a cook-book about Japanese cooking and read it, and now I am making these starters.' He smiled. 'Don't be afraid to eat, Mr Davis. I follow the instructions carefully.'

While talking, he was gently pushing forward a big armchair, into which he settled Wilfred with light touches of his long fingers, while the spoon waved gracefully.

Mary was busy at the side table. A faint delicious smell came to Wilfred as the boy moved.

'Understand, Mr Davis, this work is not pleasing to me,' Yasuhiro murmured. 'I do it to please Mrs Cadman and Miss Wayne.'

'It's all right – son.' The last word was muttered. 'I never could stand that kind of thing myself – not a man's job – though I can make a cup of tea now *and* wash up as well as anyone.'

'My words are spoken in the shadow of the pine trees, Mr Davis.'

'Eh?'

'In secret, it means.'

'Oh yes – yes of course . . .'

Yasuhiro smiled, and shot up from his kneeling position, and went over to Mary at the table.

What it is to be twenty, Wilfred thought, watching the two as they moved about the room. *I'm as tired as a dog after that journey, those diesels are enough to kill you – 'shake you about like a pea on a shovel,' as Pat used to say . . . Those flowers must have cost a packet.*

There were seventy large dahlias, arranged in those corners where their purple, crimson and white would light up the shadows; the effect of the colours was extraordinary; and after a little while it became impossible for Wilfred to look at anything else. What with the flowers' still watchfulness, and the sweet scents from Yasuhiro's robes – and surely Mary had been putting stuff on herself, as well? – and the pungency of some powder smouldering in a little brass pot, he dozed off.

He was aroused by a triumphant cry of 'Corn in Egypt!' and awoke with a start and the confused impression that a female form was about to collapse upon him.

'It's all right – she's found her glove. She must have dropped it when she came in from church this morning,' said Mary's voice, laughing. 'Dad! Wake up. Here's Mrs Cadman.'

'It's a shame to disturb you,' said Mrs Cadman, straightening up from almost beneath his chair. Her appearance struck him as agreeable: a mouse in pink and orange. 'Yes, here I am, Mr Davis, and pleased to see you in the flesh after our chats on the phone.'

'And on such a happy occasion,' boomed a voice behind her, where Mr Grant stood slightly at attention. 'Found your way here all right, then?'

There followed some discussion as to whether Rowena Road was easy to discover 'amidst the intricacies of Lower Highgate'. (The phrase was Mr Grant's, Mrs Cadman vowing that she had never heard it used by anyone, before or since.)

Wilfred became aware that someone was being steered up to him by Yasuhiro: a small, thin, commonplace, elderly person, wearing, despite the fact that it was December, a bright summer dress. An older man hovered in the background.

'Here is Miss Wayne,' said the host in his most mellifluous voice. 'Is Mr Davis, Mairly's father, Miss Wayne. Honoured guest,' he added, to Wilfred, 'has said to me it seems a wicked waste of money to have so many flowers when millions of Indians are starving. Perhaps I leave you to dis-cuss this inter-esting question,' and he swept away with a swirl of his robe. (Wilfred saw, with dismay, that the greenish tint had deepened.) The hovering male form remained unintroduced, and drifted into a corner.

'Well so it does,' repeated Miss Wayne, almost in a whisper, but firmly, 'doesn't it, Mr Davis? (It is Davis, isn't it?) I'm afraid my hearing isn't quite what it was, and foreigners never can pronounce names properly, can they? Aren't there a terrible lot about? I declare, sometimes I don't know if I'm in Highgate or South America. And the price of everything! Is it as bad up your way, Mr Davis?'

A conversation followed about half-newpence, and biscuits, upon which Miss Wayne appeared to subsist. Wilfred was wishing he were alone with Mary and Yasuhiro, watching them and enjoying the scents and the brilliant flowers.

The table had been cleared, and there appeared a number of little bowls of white and grey-green porcelain, into which Yasuhiro began rapidly spooning exotic-looking liquids and solids, while Mary, unaided, lugged up four heavy old chairs and shepherded everybody into them, including the elderly male who was now presented as Mr Bailey who-used-to-work for-Camden-Council.

Miss Wayne whispered to the company at large that she had read that one sat on the floor to eat in Japan, and she was glad they hadn't got to.

Mary, rapidly distributing white paper napkins printed with black storks, cast one glance at her betrothed as if daring him to overhear and comment; but he maintained his host's smile while serving Miss Wayne with cold rice garnished with pieces of lobster.

'Should be oc-to-pus, Miss Wayne, to be truly Japanese,' he beamed, as he filled her bowl. 'But not possible.'

'I'm thankful it isn't,' she retorted, still in her near-whisper, and valiantly began to pick over the *sushi* with her fork.

The interest of identifying pieces of chicken and scrambled egg – ('This dish is called *tamago-dombui*') – amidst a background of rice quickly promoted discussion; while the warm, bland-tasting liquid with which Yasuhiro filled and refilled the tiny cups led to laughter, and then loud laughter. When Yasuhiro's thirst for revenge on these peasants was a little slaked, and when he had caught his prospective father-in-law's eye, the bottles were whisked away and seen no more until later that evening.

Nevertheless, they were all unusually cheerful as the little party moved upstairs to the big front room, Mary and Yasuhiro having gone ahead, with Wilfred wondering who would do the washing-up? Certainly not the host. The guests were agreeing that all those little bites of things they had nibbled were tasty enough.

'More like canopies,' whispered Miss Wayne. 'What they have at those cocktail receptions. I've read about them. Well I never!'

The door of the big room had opened. There stood Mary and Yasuhiro side by side in the doorway, hand in hand and smiling.

I feel a right Charlie, Mary was thinking.

As the five elderly guests approached, the two hosts inclined in a deep bow. Yasuhiro's ceremonial robe gleamed in its solid splendour, Mary's necklace glinted soft fire. Behind them could be seen a glow of flowers, and the white cloth of a long buffet table. Blue incense coiled slowly in the soft glow from many large orange-coloured lanterns.

'Well!' cried Mrs Cadman. 'You've been busy! I wouldn't know my first-floor front. I did see some men carrying things in, but I kept my promise and I never said a word. The *flowers!* You naughty boy, you must have ruined yourself!'

Yasuhiro smiled.

'Quite a fairyland,' Miss Wayne whispered.

'You like all this, Mrs Cadman?' enquired Yasuhiro graciously, advancing. 'British food this time – salmon, tur-key. Mary choose it. Also whisky. And champagne. Correct for engagement party. We eat and drink later, when other honourable guests arrive.'

At that moment the other guests had arrived, and were standing on the doorstep in what might have been an awkward silence had not Mrs Levy broken it by observing that *it was quite a place to find, and no taxis about, and, her daughter's car being in use that evening to take her to a very smart party, she had not been able to offer it to her mother here. Und so there is a party after all? She had had her suspicions*, nodding and smiling meaningly.

Sylvie, in a yellow and purple dress down to her ankles and scraped-up hair, giggled and said they were chancing their arm, too. Mrs Levy, eyeing the bulge approvingly, said that if there was a party, she hoped it would not go on too late; sleep was zo necessary just now, for Mrs—?

'Pollitt,' put in the young man. 'Mr and Mrs Pollitt,' and Mrs Levy was just saying had they been married long and was there any other family, when the door was opened by an elderly man.

Mrs Levy's eye rushed past him and swept over the hall. Wilfred had opened the door because no one, in the uproar over the buffet and the flowers, had heard the refined ding-dong of the bell.

'Good evening. Do come in. Mrs Levy, is it? I'm Mary's father.'

'I am glad to meet you, yes glad.' Mrs Levy extended a black-gloved hand from the sleeve of a mink jacket (Nephew Maurice was in the fur trade). 'I haf heard much about you from Mary.'

'Nice things, I hope . . . Hullo there!' to Sylvie. 'Nice to see you again . . . Hullo,' shaking hands with the young man.

'I gotta go upstairs,' Sylvie announced, dragging at her green kiss-curl.

'It's her condition,' confided Chris to Wilfred.

'I go vith you,' and Mrs Levy put a hand on Sylvie's arm. 'Another woman is good at such times.' It would also give Mrs Levy a chance to inspect the upper storey.

'Here – she ain't goin' to have it now,' protested young Pollitt. 'Leastways, I hope not . . . You can manage, can't you, Sylvie?'

'Ach! This is *Sylvie?*' The hand darted back as Mrs Levy stared.

'Bet you've heard about me from Mary, too,' Sylvie grinned.

'It's different now. You are wife and mother-to-be,' said Mrs Levy recovering. 'Ve must all be young once. I myself, in Hamburg—'

Here Sylvie broke away to hurry upstairs, waved on by the flustered Wilfred; and he led Mrs Levy to the big front room, leaving Chris to await his wife. An attempt to help Mrs Levy take off the jacket was resisted.

'I keep this on. Chilly these autumn evenings,' said Mrs Levy firmly.

Mary stood chatting to Mr Bailey, wishing that it was an ordinary engagement party, with just a few bunches of flowers, and food prepared by an understanding mum, and an ordinary, nice, shy young man for a fiancé. It was too much: too many flowers, too much food and drink and – and too much *foreignness*. It embarrassed her, and she still had, at the back of her mind, the memory of that conversation with Yasuhiro two days ago, when he had given her the necklace. It haunted her uncomfortably.

'Oh Yasu – it's – it's beautiful. Thank you a million times, love. And – I haven't a thing, really, to give you. Not like this . . .'

'What thing do you like best in all the world, Mairly love? (Presently, later on, it will be our son.) But tell me now – what you like most?'

She lifted her eyes, and looked at him. But he shook his head impatiently.

'Not me – not me. Of course I know *that*. I mean, what do you like *for yourself*?' There followed a pause while she thought. Then she gave a conscious little laugh.

'Oh. My own way, I s'pose.'

'*Then, one day, you give me your own way, Mary*. That will be my present from you.'

And, in spite of the necklace, and his face close to her own, her instant thought had been: *not if I know it.*

But then she saw between the flowers the face of Yasuhiro, grave and courteous, as he listened to Mrs Cadman, and all other feelings were swept away in the glow and glory of the fact: *we're going to be married.*

'Mary love –'

She turned, at once the competent young hostess.

'– here's Mrs Levy.'

'Hullo, Mrs Levy. I'm glad you could come.'

Mrs Levy responded by starting back six inches with her eyes fixed on Mary's neck.

'*Gott im Himmel*, Mary, those are fire opals!'

'Yes, pretty, aren't they –?'

'My cousin Harry works in Hatton Garden, taught me how to distinguish—'

'– they're my engagement present from Yasu. Like my ring?' She held out a hand, where a great stone glowed. 'They don't have them in Japan, really, but he knew I'd like one . . . to . . . show to people. It matches.'

'So I see,' said Mrs Levy dryly. 'Vell, Mary, I make a mistake. You are engaged, and you *zeem* to be a very lucky girl. I say *zeem* because it's only sensible to look ahead like a sophisticated woman . . . yes, sophisticated . . . What a show of flowers! While you were about it, you should haf take a *really* nice room at the Westchester Hotel. It's in Holborn; new hotel. You can get—'

'Mrs Cadman very kindly said we could have this one, and I didn't want a lot of fuss with waiters and things. Mrs Cadman! Here's Mrs Levy – you know, you've talked to her on the phone.'

'Und vere is the boyfriend?' Mrs Levy acknowledged the introduction with a brief smile, as her eye sped unerringly to where Yasuhiro stood, now solitary, beside the salmon on its silver dish.

'I'll take you over,' said Mary, more than willing to hand Mrs Levy to one capable of dealing with her.

'We have met before,' announced Mrs Levy, fixing Yasuhiro with her eye. 'You come in to see the place vere Mary works.'

'Yes, it was so,' said he, sweetly. 'Good evening, Mrs Levy. I am honoured that you come to our party.'

'I nearly didn't come – what's your name – didn't catch it –'

'Yasuhiro Tasu,' with a smiling bow.

'I was invited at last moment to another party, very smart, Golders Green, friends of my daughter. I almost don't come. She has a beautiful home, standing one and a half acres of ground, worth thousands.'

Yasuhiro's eyes were expressionless as a lizard's. His mouth curved in the gentlest of attentive smiles.

'I have not visited Golders Green. But seen the name on
Underground stations. It is in the open country?'

'Oh no, not isolated at all, very good communications and
every amenity you could vish for. I don't suppose you and Mary
haf any chance of getting home of your own, not for years und
years? Terrible price places are –'

'We shall live in the house of my family. Near Tokyo.'

Mrs Levy's eyes glittered with pleasure. 'Oh vot a mistake!
Oh I am so sorry! Such a bad start, living with relations! Vy
not save your money? Get a mortgage.'

Yasuhiro looked down for a moment; he saw in his mind's eye
the ancient wooden walls and the roof of grey-blue tiles, tilted
like a smile on the lips of some wise old man; the harmonious
tint of the golden reed curtains, and the pale straw-paper of
sliding shutters; the long, low, modest yet regal place that had
held his family for three hundred years.

'It's the custom in Japan,' he said gently.

'Terrible overcrowding everywhere. Of course, I own my
home. My daughter, too. I haf six bedrooms.'

Here Mary brought up Sylvie to be introduced, and Mrs Levy
was spared the anguish of hearing that Mary's new home had
forty rooms, and stood in the Japanese equivalent of seventy
acres. Yasuhiro would never have shown such execrable taste
as to proclaim these facts, but Mrs Levy would have drawn
them out of him.

Sylvie could only stare and mutter, but Chris surprised his
hostess by saying loudly 'Congratulations –' and then, to everybody's mounting embarrassment, plunging into a humorous
account of the horrors of the married state, delivered with what
used to be called guffaws, while his merry little eyes darted
sideways glances at Mary.

'She'll do yer, boy. She'll have yer down for the count before
yer know whether it's August or Saturday night. I'm warning
yer. I bin through it. Look at me. Lost a stone the first six
weeks –'

'Oh you liar!' Sylvie screamed.

'You take my advice and scarper while you got the chance –'

'You joke,' said Yasuhiro, while his smile became stony.

'Joke! It's no joke, I can tell you, mate –'

'It's . . . kind . . . of you. But believe that I can protect myself from these dangers. There will be difficults, of course of course. But expect these when Japanese marries Western girl.'

Here Mrs Cadman, sharing the general conviction that Chris had been fortifying himself before arrival, bustled up and started firmly to chat to Sylvie.

The glassy-eyed hush was broken, people were steered into groups of two, and Wilfred, seeing that the greenish tint had become permanent, joined Mrs Levy in her critical survey of the turkey.

'What a beautiful jacket. Is – is it mink?'

Mrs Levy turned graciously to inform the semi-whisperer that it was, indeed, mink.

'Mink. I have read about it, of course, but I've never seen any. Would you mind if I just felt it?'

Admiration of her possessions was almost Mrs Levy's favourite form of conversation. She allowed the gesture, then suggested that they should sit down. She speedily turned the discourse to an uninterrupted description of the comforts and devices in her daughter's house, with hints about the enormous sums they had cost, and the continual fears of her daughter and herself that they might 'have bugglars'. As Miss Wayne's own life was darkened by a fear of burglars and what they might be plotting to do to the top-back at 20 Rowena Road, she soon wished that the monologue might have stayed with the glories of electric percolators and blankets.

No one was completely at ease. The hot, rich breath of money was too insistent, and Yasuhiro, as host, lacked the desirable mateyness. ('Looking at them as if they were beetles,' thought his future wife resignedly.) Nevertheless, by degrees, the atmosphere thawed – even became lively.

There was a great deal of alcohol, though party manners, and fear of their women, prevented Mr Grant and Chris from drinking as much as they would have liked. One glass of champagne transported Wilfred, though Mary's expression of quiet happiness would have been enough for him.

Mrs Levy and Mrs Cadman exchanged glances when Sylvie screamed and slapped people, and the former also derived some entertainment from pricing everybody's clothes. When this was done, she fixed her eyes upon Yasuhiro moving gracefully from guest to guest, and, so far as her nature would permit, marvelled.

Miss Wayne had a technique for dealing with social occasions: she did what she considered her duty first, then made the very most of even the smallest chance of any enjoyment. She seldom came away from places that most people would have called hopelessly dull without some grain of pleasure to chew on.

She now crept from group to group, sipping a glass of champagne, and paused beside talkers to listen, occasionally putting in a murmured contribution. The lovely light from the lanterns, the hundreds of flowers, and Mary's necklace and ring – what a sight it all was! Her eyes moved shyly from face to face, and came to rest on that of her host.

He had returned to the salmon and taken his former place beside it. He stood looking out across the softly lit, flowery room.

Homesick, poor boy, thought Miss Wayne. *I'd like to just say a word . . . show him someone understands . . . but they always say in those books you mustn't pry with young people . . . well, I could just say how pretty everything looks*; and she made her way towards him.

He felt her creeping advance almost before he saw it. It was the last straw. Chris had just been commenting on the salmon: it wasn't too bad, he handsomely conceded, but if he, Chris, had known beforehand, he could have got it for them wholesale. Yasuhiro had thanked him, smiling over clamped teeth.

And now here was Miss Wayne.

He whirled round on her like a blue and silver dragon.

'Miss-Wayne – you *still* think wrong spend money on flowers when Indians starve?' His English was fragmented.

'Yes . . . Mr – I'm afraid I didn't catch your name . . . I do think so.'

With what was plainly, to him, a heroic effort, she looked straight at him. *Here it was,* she thought: *the face of triumphing Youth, heartless and strong, as it smiled from other people's televisions, or was witnessed while one crept past it in the street.*

Yasuhiro experienced an emotion unfamiliar to him: shame.

He smiled, his real smile, and then he made her a bow from the waist, so low that she saw the silky black top of his head for a long instant before he came slowly up again. The gesture was unmistakably one of admiration, and she could only stare. But slowly her heart warmed with happiness. She said nothing.

'Miss-Wayne, Mairly tells me you go very much to a church. Would it please you take all these flowers tomorrow to your church?'

'Oh yes. You are so kind. But *all* of them?'

'You won't feel these flowers wicked – un-worthy – to be offered in your church because they are bought with money which might have gone to starving Indians?'

'Oh no . . . of course not. So beautiful . . . nothing so beautiful could be wicked, I'm sure.'

'That, about the flowers, you said, was a poet's thought.'

'Well!' murmured Miss Wayne. 'However shall I get all that lot round to Holy Trinity?'

'Mary shall help. And her father,' ordained Yasuhiro, disposing of their Sunday morning lie-in. 'I will arrange it.'

They exchanged smiles, and she moved away to the shelter of Mrs Cadman's company. *How sweet he looked when he really smiled! A nice boy underneath, I expect,* thought Miss Wayne.

At half past ten the salmon and turkey were served, with various exotic salads from different countries discovered by Yasuhiro at the end of his Japanese cookery book and included for the fact that they looked pretty.

'It's Arab,' Mary confided on a warning note to Mrs Cadman, holding out one of the salads on the thinnest plate Miss Wayne had ever imagined, with a pattern of Japanese ladies in pink and grey robes walking beside grey waterfalls.

'Arab?' Mrs Cadman studied the small, highly coloured mound. 'Well, I only hope it isn't encouraging them.'

Towards half past eleven, Chris started making facetious, and Mrs Levy solicitous, remarks about the necessity of Sylvie's getting her beauty sleep. Yasuhiro stood, ready to make courteous farewells and accompany each guest to the front door.

The final surprise was sprung when two large, luxurious hired cars were discovered waiting to take the visitors home.

In they got, Chris loudly announcing that he and Sylvie would have one of their own next year, while Mrs Levy excused herself for accepting the lift by saying that of course her daughter's car would have been there to fetch her if it had not been fetching her daughter from the very smart party in Golders Green.

The door shut on the tenants at number 20.

Something blue and silver shot past them as they stood chatting for a moment in the hall. It disappeared into the basement.

'What on earth's the matter with *him*?' exclaimed Mrs Cadman.

Mary shrugged.

In so short a time as instantly to fill their minds with pictures of robes being hurled all over the room, back flashed Yasuhiro: face greenish, hair disordered, dressed again in the uniform of world youth.

'Well,' Mrs Cadman was beginning, 'I'm sure—'

'I go for long walk,' he said, in that very low, almost growling voice which had once dismayed Mary, and, sweeping round to face the little group as he stood at the front door, he added: 'I hope the party successful. Hope all honoured guests enjoy flowers, lights, British food. Miss-Wayne,' a short bow towards her, 'you are very brave. *Samurai*-woman. Goodnight.'

The door slammed. They heard feet tearing along the pavement, then the sound died away.

Miss Wayne blinked. *Samurai?* Oh yes . . . she had read . . .

Mr Grant shook his head. 'It was that young Pollitt. Not a bad chap, but low. Not an idea about anything. Needs eighteen months in the Guards – only they'd never take him. A stone off him in weight wouldn't hurt, neither.'

'Over the Heath, I expect,' muttered Mrs Cadman. 'Sooner him than me, this time of night.' She shivered, then turned to Mary. 'Aren't you a bit afraid of him getting mugged, dear?'

There was a pause.

'I'd be really sorry,' said Mary, 'for anyone who tried mugging *him.*'

31

Katherine

It was late afternoon on the following day, and Mary and Wilfred were sitting in the dining room at the Great Eastern Hotel, which is apparently built into Liverpool Street station, and finishing a rather sumptuous tea, Wilfred standing the treat. The trains were blaring and bellowing below, but their noise was muted by thick walls and distance. Wilfred's train left in about twenty minutes.

'A bit selfish, isn't he, love? Don't think I'm knocking him, but these things do make all the difference, once you're married.'

'Selfish! You can say that again. *And* a racist, *and* a militarist – a sort of poor man's Hitler, I suppose. Oh, a nice old picnic it's going to be, being married to him.'

She smiled, looking absently out across the long room where the Danish businessmen were getting their first taste of English tea. Her father studied, a little wistfully, the young face.

'You know I don't mean to butt in, love, but – are you *quite* sure it's going to be all right? Isn't it – well, more than a bit risky?'

'Getting married's always risky,' pronounced Mary, biting into the last cress sandwich, 'and, mind you, he is other things as well.'

'How do you mean, other things?'

'It's a bit difficult to explain. I'd have to use corny words like *honourable* and *patriotic*. And then I'm always thinking about him,' she ended suddenly, in a mutter, and the blood ran up under her skin.

Her father looked away. No, it had never been like this for him.

'We'll be all right, Dad,' she said in a moment. 'It'll be interesting, in a way.'

Interesting! Really, the young nowadays. What would Pat have said if he had called the prospective joining together of their two lives 'interesting'?

He glanced at his watch.

'I must be moving . . . Where is he, this evening?'

'Off to his *kendo* class – funny occupation for a Sunday evening, whacking at each other with great sticks, but he likes it. I think he's getting the party off his chest.'

Wilfred and Mary had already pleasurably dissected the party. It was plain what the host's feelings had been. But when Wilfred had seen him briefly that afternoon, Yasuhiro had seemed restored to serenity, even cheerfulness. Yes, he had walked on that Heath for four hours, getting back (he had not said 'home') at half past three, with more lines of his poem firmly in his head. 'And they are true,' he had said, fixing Wilfred with his clear dark eyes. 'Good situation, Mr Davis. Now I *work*.'

'What I can't get over is him staying in bed till twelve this morning,' Mary said, as they went down in the hotel lift to the station.

'He was out till after three, love. And everybody likes a lie-in of a Sunday if they can get it.'

'I know – I didn't mean that. But taking it for granted that Mrs Cadman and I would clear everything up properly. Not even bothering to get up. You can see he's been used to servants all his life.'

'Well, I expect his family has, love.'

Mary made a small face, and they made their way, under the vast ribbed roof amid echoing thunders, to where Wilfred's train waited.

It was making direful preliminary noises, and he hurried into it.

He hung out of the window, and she stood beside it for a moment.

'Bye, love. I'll phone you,' she said, smiling, as the monster began to move.

She's beautiful, her father thought in surprise, as he drew in his head. *She always was, to me, of course. But now – why, several people stared at her this afternoon. I don't mean startlingly beautiful, of course, more like . . . like a healthy young tree or fresh grass, really. That kind of beautiful.*

Settling himself in a corner seat, he glanced casually round at his fellow travellers, and his eye stopped at a slight, pale woman whose clothes contrived to give an impression of elegance, and whose fair hair straggled from under a fur cap. She had a briefcase on her lap and was about to open it, when she looked up and met his eyes. A smile slowly appeared, and she leant forward.

'Isn't it Mr Davis? . . . that wasn't *Mary?* Was it?'

'Yes,' he said proudly. 'That was Mary, Mrs Anstruther. I've just been down for her engagement party, as a matter of fact . . .'

'There! What did I tell you? Congratulations.' She touched the seat at her side. 'Come and sit here and tell me all your news.'

'I'd like to, Mrs Anstruther – I'm a bit full of it all, to tell you the truth.' He moved across to the indicated place.

The faintest flowery scent came from Mrs Anstruther's coat. Her earrings were of carved white coral. Following an experienced guiding murmur, he opened his mouth to begin.

For nearly fifteen minutes, he related Mary's history for the past year, answering his hearer's skilful questions. When he finally announced the proposal that he should accompany the engaged pair to Japan, Julia actually stared.

'Oh, one never knows!' she breathed.

'What did you say?'

'I was thinking aloud. It's just that the most unexpected things happen to the most ord— to the nicest, but really the most . . . everyday . . . people. Do you think you'll like living there?'

'I'll be with Mary, so nothing else matters much,' Wilfred said, and Julia nodded. 'But there is that raw fish and sitting on the floor and all that,' he wound up by saying. 'I've got the fare home for us both, and I'm hanging on to it, Mrs Anstruther . . . That old chap running it all, over ninety. There's almost bound to be differences. But we could do with a bit of that sort of authority over here, in my opinion.'

'Oh, I don't think we must encourage the idea of the old managing affairs for the middle-aged and the young.' Julia's slight smile was cold. 'It's unhealthy.'

'Ah, there I don't agree with you. Things have gone too far the other way, to my mind.'

Wilfred glanced at her nervously. Her expression had become haughty and sad.

'I hope all's going well at Redpaths?' he said, nervously. 'Her mother would have been so – so upset at Mary's leaving – like that. We both had such a high opinion of Redpaths, and I'm sure it's done a lot for Mary – nice manners, and that.'

'Thank you, yes. We flourish.' *He saw I was rattled and he's trying to comfort me. Dammit, I will not be comforted. I wish I were a reincarnation of Mrs Pankhurst.*

Silence fell. The four other passengers read and dozed. Lights came on in the carriage; London began to seem remote, and last night's party to have the air of a dream. Wilfred was thinking with quiet enjoyment of the people in the Yellow House. Then something stirred in his memory.

'Mrs Anstruther –'

The face she turned to him was gentle and friendly.

'Those two little girls, Samantha and Kelly, Mrs Singer's two . . . My old Dad always kept an eye on them. Well, the whole street did, for that matter, but he was sort of special with them. He passed over several months ago.'

'I'm sorry to hear that. Peacefully, I hope.'

'Yes, in his sleep . . . Well, you know how things get about. I heard you were going to keep an eye on them. I just wondered how they're getting along. Carrying on his interest, you might call it, I suppose . . . Pretty little things, both of them – nearly always round there whenever I looked in. I just wondered—'

'Too pretty.' Her tone made him stare. 'They think of little else but becoming pop singers. But I hope to see them come through *that* ambition. They're all right. They're both in care, for the present, at that very good foster home, Bryant House, in Macclesfield Road. It's run on the family system, there are about twelve children and an unusually satisfactory house-mother and father. Of course, with children of that background, semi-literate and precocious and encouraged in every undesirable attitude by their own families, it's not easy to tell whether they're really well-adjusted. But they ought to be capable of adapting. They've been experiencing the extended family in *practice* ever since they were born. That may have helped them to settle down.'

'But are they happy?'

The question seemed to irritate Julia. She almost snatched her suitcase off the rack as the train drew in to Torford, ignoring his movement to help.

'Happy? Who's happy, Mr Davis? We have to make do as best we can, with what we've got, and what we can get . . . No, no taxi, thanks, my husband's meeting me. I've enjoyed hearing about Mary. Let me know how she gets on – and you, too. Don't forget I mean it. Goodbye.'

She was gone, hurrying away with her hair tumbling down, into the Sunday evening crowd dispersing into the chill, slightly misty air. But as he was lifting his own case down from the rack, he heard her voice again.

'Mr Davis –'

He turned. She was back at the carriage door, giving an impression of hovering before taking flight again.

'Sammy and Kelly come to us to play, every Saturday afternoon. I truly am keeping an eye on them. You mustn't worry.'

As soon as Wilfred opened the door of the Yellow House, he felt a new atmosphere.

Something had gone.

The calm and gentle gaiety of the hall had vanished. His glance moved across to the staircase, as he stood hesitating, with the open door behind him letting in the chill air of evening, and then he saw, with an astonishing disturbance along his nerves, that Kichijoten's niche was empty.

The drawing-room door opened, and Mr Taverner looked out.

'Hullo. Nice to see you back. How did it go?'

'Where's Kichijoten?' Wilfred demanded.

Mr Taverner shrugged.

'She's had to go.'

'But why? What's the matter? Not – burglars, or vandals?'

'Oh, nothing like that.'

'I was only thinking – an isolated place like this – at least it's isolated since demolition started.' Mr Taverner was now going slowly upstairs, and Wilfred was following. 'We're in a dangerous district. I've heard people – dropouts, thugs, I don't know – go past at night, singing. (If you can call it singing.)'

'All districts are dangerous, my dear man.'

'Will she – will Kichijoten be back soon?'

'I don't know. She's been – the hem of her robe has been slightly damaged, and it takes time and patience to put such things right.'

'*Patience?*'

' Especially, as we all know, in dangerous centuries. (I expect they had the deuce of a job getting a stone quern repaired, in the twelfth. That was one of the dangerous ones. Great changes. Always dangerous – *and* painful.) Come in and have some sherry – I want to hear about the party.' He paused at the door of his room, and looked at Wilfred enquiringly.

Wilfred had never seen Mr Taverner's room, but as soon as he was invited to see it, all the slight peculiarities and small mysteries surrounding his mysterious friend seemed to coalesce, and to present themselves before him as one large question mark. *I'll get to know a bit more about him* was the thought that crept into his mind.

The walls were light green, the bed narrow, the shelves crammed with detective stories and thrillers. The well-waxed floor was covered by two or three mats of shining yellow reed.

Mr Taverner indicated an armchair: large, shabby, and so charged with persuasion and age that it suggested a person rather than a piece of furniture.

Wilfred hesitated. 'Isn't that yours?'

'When I start feeling no one else ought to sit in that, the end will be near . . . You try it.'

Wilfred settled himself in the comfortable old thing. *It's as if it was some friend of his,* he thought, staring out between the half-drawn curtains at an almost dark sky with one streak of light. 'A sorrowful red eye,' he remembered reading in some book.

Then he glanced round the room. There was only one object in it that suggested personal life: the photograph of a beautiful, dark man in his early forties on the wall above the desk.

'Cheers.' Mr Taverner handed him a glass and lifted his own. 'To Mary and Yasuhiro —' and Wilfred muttered the names as he drank the toast. Mr Taverner had got hold of the boy's name all right — but that was like him: *always interested in other people's affairs, but in a — a — civilized way, not nosily, like Sheila and Shirley and Joan . . . and if I don't tell them soon, they'll find out and then God help me.*

'How did the party go?'

For an instant, Wilfred had a strange flash of memory. He was home from his first day at school, and his young mother was eagerly questioning him. With the flash there came such a feeling of safety! Then he returned to the present, and went into a description of the party, lingering on the quantity of flowers and the prettiness of it all.

'I'm relieved to hear that appalling little girl Sylvie has got herself tied down,' said Mr Taverner, when the tale was ended, 'though I never cease to marvel how the most shrink-inducing

people manage to find *someone* willing to shoulder them for
life . . . Did I tell you about young Derek?'

'That boy who was here at Christmas? No . . . You know,
Mr Taverner, I was glancing through some book of poems,
the new kind, at the Library soon after he left here, and I saw
one – it was about a boy with *Born to Lose* branded on his
shoulder. Not really, of course. Just how the writer imagined
him. It made me think of young Derek.'

'Yes . . . but that brand can mean less than it seems to, you
know. A bit of our old friend Drama, there; Byron, and the
legion of the Damned, and so forth. *Look at me, I'm going to
Hell.* Easier – and more noticeable, don't forget – than trying
not to go there. And so few are admitted, anyway! Oh, it's an
exclusive club, Hell . . . Derek's going to be all right now. A
pretty, motherly little girl's found him, and he's found her, and
they're going to start life in a caravan, Derek's saving up for
it. They won't marry at first. Those friends of mine he's living
with are helping him. They've put him on to a local farmer
who'll rent him a scrap of land, not too outrageously. The girl
isn't greedy, either. Amazing!'

Wilfred remembered, with a small, guilty pain Pat's plan for
redecorating the house every three years, the re-carpeting and
re-upholstering, the right glasses for drinks, the good-natured
unflagging driving of himself until he had reached the highest
position at the Town Hall that he could hope for.

He switched himself back to the present.

'Miss Dollette and Mrs Cornforth well, I hope?'

'Mrs Cornforth . . . will be,' Mr Taverner said. 'Miss Dollette
is not quite as happy as usual.'

'Oh? Nothing serious, I hope . . . *I'd* better get used to the
idea of change,' he went on. 'This time next year, it all seems
to point to me being in Japan.' Mr Taverner looked at him in
silence, above his interlaced fingers. 'I must say I'd sooner stay
here. Born here, grew up and worked here, married here, lost
my Pat here – yes, it'll be a wrench all right. But Mary wants
me to go, and she'll be there wherever I land up. She'd go, of

course, even if I didn't – but I think she's just a bit nervous. East is East, and all that. 'Course, I shan't interfere – unless I see her put upon. That would be different.'

'Wouldn't it be rather difficult to "interfere" with that particular son-in-law?'

'I'm not so sure, Mr Taverner. I wouldn't be surprised if he wasn't as tough as he makes out.'

'That's a shrewd remark. What do you base it on?'

'Oh – one or two little things, I suppose. And he's a poet. You think of a poet as, well, not tough.'

'Quite wrong, dear man, they're as tough as the proverbial old boot. They have to be, to get the poetry written.'

'Did you ever know a poet, Mr Taverner? Really well, I mean?'

'Once.' He held up the bottle, questioningly.

'No – thank you all the same. I must go and unpack, and then I've got to work out a route to Mrs Wheeby's. I'm going over there for the day on Tuesday, and it's a bit dicey with transport.'

Wilfred was standing at the open door. The atmosphere pervading the silent, softly lit golden-white walls of the passage flowed out and touched him, persistent as the faint, disturbing scent of hawthorn.

'Mr Taverner?'

His host had sunk back into the big armchair. He looked across attentively, but the mask was in place.

'Everything is all right, isn't it?'

'Not just now,' Mr Taverner said after a pause. 'And I won't say "Don't worry". For a little while, we must worry, all of us in the Yellow House.'

Wilfred stared. Then, suddenly irritable, he said shortly: 'Oh well, I'll be getting along. I'm a bit tired, carting all those flowers round to Miss Wayne's church this morning in a force six gale. No picnic, I can tell you. Thanks for the drink.'

'See you at supper,' Mr Taverner smiled.

Wilfred shut the door.

*

No peace, Wilfred was thinking, as he went along to his own room. *You find a place where the people are so decent they seem more like – like – good spirits – than anybody in this world. Things straighten out fine for Mary. And then, damn me if we don't all have to worry about something . . . I'm not told what. Not even here, there's no peace.*

He went down to supper feeling aggressive and disliking the feeling.

'In the dining room, tonight!' Mrs Cornforth's voice, bell-like and excited, startled him as she whirled past with a sheaf of gladioli, dahlias and copper leaves in her arms. He followed her into the room.

The table was set; it glittered with silver and gleamed with glass. She stood over it, her red hair glittering, too, in the light, and began to arrange the flowers and leaves. The fern scent breathed strongly from her dress.

'It looks grand,' he said uneasily. 'I didn't know we were having company.'

'We aren't,' she carolled, moving the heavy silver forks about. 'It's to welcome home "the father of the bride".'

'Well, that's very kind of you –'

'And I bought up every flower in Parkinson's. Felicity may enjoy creeping round the suburbs for bits of weeds – I don't,' and she thrust some red leaves before Mr Taverner's place. 'I'll be in the doghouse, of course, for making those little so-and-so's do the silver – but it's good for them, they're getting too big for their new boots as it is . . .'

She laughed. 'Now I have done it, haven't I? Naughty Katherine.' She was not looking at him. Her voice died into an angry mutter as she thrust red chrysanthemums into a silver bowl.

'Seems a lot, all that, just for – us,' he said feebly at last; he would have liked to go away – to the kitchen, upstairs again, anywhere. But her beauty, and something else that was frightening yet imperative, kept him lingering – fascination, curiosity.

She glanced across at him, and laughed.

'Well, we're the only ones who'll enjoy it. Fat chance there is of getting the kind of company *I* like invited *here*. Give me the goats, every time, Wilfred. They're more fun and more of a challenge too – if you *must* moralize –'

'I don't think I moralize, Mrs Cornforth,' he said, after a pause in which irritation and fear rose in him like a tide. 'I'm fairly broad-minded, I like to think, for a man of my upbringing . . . and education.'

'You're a dead, nice bore,' she said, rearranging some leaves, not troubling to look at him. 'There!' Now she did look up. 'It's out. And do I feel better? No! I don't.'

She sat down at the table and put her face in her hands.

Wilfred was feeling actual, physical pain in his heart. He did not love her; the word had never come near his thoughts of her. He slightly feared and disliked her in comparison with his feelings for the other two. But she was a beautiful woman . . . and . . . and . . . *I know I'm well over sixty and I've had a perfectly ordinary life . . . I'm not tall, or clever,* he thought. *But my life's been interesting to me,* he thought passionately . . . *That was the cruellest thing anyone's ever said to me. I've always done my best.*

She lifted her head, and looked across at him and laughed. 'You're a sweetie, too.'

'Thank you. But it was a rotten thing to say, Mrs Cornforth, and you know it. And . . . I don't feel all that grateful for being called a sweetie.'

She shrugged. 'Oh God. I'm sorry, I'm sorry. I'd hoped we were friends enough for you to take the truth.'

Wilfred pressed his lips to keep back a furious, confused sentence, and at that moment Miss Dollette came in, carrying two pale green candles.

'Here you are, darling – are they the right colour?'

'I said *jade*, not that washed-out . . . I've been needling Wilfred.'

'Well, you like needling, don't you?' Miss Dollette said faintly, fitting the candles into silver sockets. 'Did you enjoy it?'

'For about three seconds.' Katherine laughed again. 'Is the stuff ready? I'll get it.' She hurried away.

Wilfred stood, undecided, still feeling resentment and pain. For an instant, he wished he were sitting at the table in Shirley's bright, cheerful home, or Joan's, playing one of those card games which he used to dislike so much, with Sheila's husband's red, tamed face opposite. Then the picture faded. Miss Dollette was his friend – and there was no need, with her, to hide troubled feelings.

'What's up with Mrs Cornforth?' he asked bluntly.

Miss Dollette looked up slowly.

'She's bored, Mr Davis, and when Katherine is bored it – it can be dangerous.'

'*Dangerous?*' He stared.

She nodded, rearranging the place settings that Katherine's fidgetings had disturbed.

'You – you don't mean she's mental or anything like that?'

'Oh no. Nothing like that. But boredom makes some people dangerous – and cruel.'

'But that's like some teenage delinquent!' Wilfred burst out. 'Mrs Cornforth must be over forty.'

She shook her head.

'Mr Davis – no – dear Wilfred – I'm a coward, and always have been, though I'm trying very hard not to be. My heart is still beating too fast because of what I said to Katherine just now, and I'm wondering if I was right to say it, and I'm so afraid that if – if anything happens, it'll be *my fault.* You see, I love Katherine. She's all I've always wanted to be and never could: warm and brave, and loving towards people. (Oh! I'm so *afraid* of people.) She's like a golden dragoness – but a *good* one. And, you see, it was I who asked that she might come with us.'

There was a pause. Her soft voice seemed to linger on the air.

He shook his head. 'I'm sorry, it's all beyond me.'

'Oh, I know. It must be. It's such a *big* story, you see, the story of the Yellow Houses. But will you be patient, especially with her? Will you, if I ask you? Just be patient? Don't try to understand, just accept and wait for what – what is going to happen?'

Before he could answer, there was a cry from the hall. 'Laf! Laf! Supper!'

The voice rang through the house like a beautifully toned bell; the colour of her hair, and her fiery dress, and the copper leaves she had strewn on the table, were all in the sound. 'Blazing hot!'

She swept in, carrying a tray, and set the covered casserole on the table, and in a moment Mr Taverner entered and took his place.

'Glory and splendour tonight,' he remarked, as he began to serve the food.

'That was me,' Katherine said instantly. 'I'm tired of cosiness in the kitchen.'

'So. Well, it *looks* very civilized. Congratulations.'

'Oh you know I can do it when I want to.'

He glanced at her, but said nothing, and they began to eat. Wilfred, steadily packing into himself what seemed the first real food he had eaten for a week, could feel an extraordinary warmth – atmosphere? – pulse? – stealing towards him from where Katherine sat.

It was a cloudy night. The curtains were not quite drawn, and between them the sky showed a pale, sinister red from the reflected glare of the town's lamps and those in the road itself – temporarily erected following complaints to the council of orgies in the dimness of the newly created wasteland. And Wilfred could make out a leaping, golden-red glare, low down. The dropouts must have lit a bonfire on the space directly opposite the Yellow House.

32

Three journeys: three destinations

'Why do you just sit there staring? Why don't you go out and *do* something for them?' Katherine's voice seemed to strike him like a blow.

'Oh, Mrs Cornforth – yes, I was thinking about those kids. As for going out – I don't really feel I could do anything useful if I did,' Wilfred said. He had actually started at her words.

'Young bodies! – souls in agony and deadly peril!'

'I don't believe it's as bad as all that, really. I run into my old colleagues at the Town Hall from time to time, you know, and I hear things—'

'You don't really *care*.'

'I care all right, Mrs Cornforth, but I'm – I'm getting on, you know, and – as I was saying, I've heard about that bunch out there. They're just teenagers, out for a lark.' His hand went to a pocket for his handkerchief. His forehead was sweating.

'You shut your eyes. You shut them tight. You might be blind, for all you see. And you choose to be like that. You *choose* to be blind.'

'I think you're trying to quarrel with me,' he said desperately.

He did not dare to glance at the other two. From far off, from very far away, he felt a breath of coolness and comfort, and remembered, crushing his handkerchief in his damp hand, the fern-scented linen of that *other* handkerchief – the one that had led to his sitting where he sat now – trembling and full of strange fears.

'Anything for a bit of life!' she said, and he had not believed that her voice could sound so coarse. He could see, out of the corner of his eye, the slight movements made by Mr Taverner and Miss Dollette in the act of eating, and again he felt comforted. But he was sweating in the uncanny heat pulsing from her. He now felt her to be his enemy.

There was silence – but no lessening of danger. *Danger?* He tried to make his tone reasonable.

'It was always a quiet, decent little place, Torford –'

'Yes,' she said bitterly. 'That was why Laf chose it.'

Mr Taverner put down his knife and fork, and said 'Katherine'. She whirled on him. 'Yes, "Katherine" – the outsider, the one who shouldn't be here – the one who's sick of this half-dead, half-alive set-up, and the whole boring idea.'

'You knew the plan,' Mr Taverner said, 'and the rules. I told you myself.'

'As far as you *are* a self, I suppose.'

He shrugged. 'Oh Katherine. And will you, can you, I ask you for the last time, *be careful?* Felicity and I have done what we set out to do—'

'One retired clerk patted off to sleep, and a half-baked boy sent down to Wales to a boring job. Big deal!'

'We don't want the work ended here by . . . I need not tell you, need I?'

'Oh yes you need – I'd like you to. One of my troubles is that I've never known enough.'

'You've been told all that you were ready to know.'

'But I'm a bit "unreadier" than you throught, aren't I? Your nice, comfortable Yellow Houses seem milk-and-water *to me.*'

'Not milk, Katherine. But certainly water. Cold water, in a cup. That's the motto of the Yellow Houses and on that they work. They always have.'

All had risen, and were standing.

'Always!'

'For nearly two thousand years,' Mr Taverner said, without raising his voice. 'Since the Wanderings ended. Since the cities began rising, all over Europe. Since the first Yellow House, in half-ruined Rome in the year 350 AD. That was the best, that's our model, because they had more to struggle with. The idea of small comfortings, small advances, small foundations on which larger things could be built, was so new. People were more like you, Katherine, in those days, fiery and unchastened. Our work seemed – so small in those days.'

'I didn't know they were as old as that,' she muttered, and was silent.

Wilfred, too, was silent; keeping so because he felt that, at last, veils were being lifted. So it was an Order, a Brotherhood, of some kind, as he had suspected.

'Well,' Katherine said at last, 'the Yellow Houses aren't enough for me.'

'I know, dear one.'

'So what's to happen to me? I'm not going to stay here, in this one. I'll go mad.'

'Don't be silly.'

'It's *all right* for you and Felicity,' she shouted, snatching up a glass and dashing it to the floor. 'Can't you *see*? You're *all right*. You've got things to do – well, one thing, made up of a lot of little fiddling things – and you do it. But I' – she drew in breath as if it hurt – 'I want *more* to do. I want to reach out, and haul in, until my arms ache and my hands are bruised and I'm *used. I want to feel used. Can't you understand?*'

'Of course I understand, Katherine, I'm not a half-wit. You put it very clearly indeed. And I do you the justice to be certain that if you *were* bruised and hauling and stretching and aching, you would feel fulfilled, whereas I should merely be uncomfortable and wanting a bit of peace, and – useless. You're a natural fisher of men; women included, of course. Now where do you want to go? Tell me.'

Wilfred was watching Katherine's beautiful, troubled face. For an instant, terror flashed into it.

'Katherine!' Mr Taverner called sharply. 'No! That's a temptation – away with it!' and Wilfred saw her expression of agonized fear change, and fade, and pass.

'However full your dotty little mind is of drama,' Mr Taverner was saying, 'don't indulge in *that* sort of nightmare-dreaming. Felicity and I and the rest of us can't imagine what it's like there. You really must stop being – so ambitious, Katherine. Our Master Himself didn't go there. He did once refer to it, but He never went there, and you know why.'

'Because,' she said slowly, 'there's no hope there.'

'Exactly.'

'And,' Mr Taverner went on, his tone becoming dry, 'it's an exclusive place, as I said the other day to Wilfred; you'll never qualify. In fact, dear Katherine, *you're* going to end up somewhere, and as something, very different.'

She looked at him, questioningly, almost as a child would, and he nodded. Then he said something that Wilfred did not catch, and this surprised him, because, until now, every word that Mr Taverner spoke had been distinct. And Katherine – the fiery, passionate, trouble-making Katherine – drooped her head like an ashamed little girl, and was silent.

In a moment, Mr Taverner laughed, and up came her head.

'Well, I shan't – like it.'

'"You will "when you get there", as they say.'

'I'm not sure if I believe it.'

'It's true, darling – or will be.'

'Oh . . . well . . . then I can go to the other place, the second one?'

'If you truly want to, Katherine. You may not like that, either, you know, when you're there.'

'Oh I will – I will. There's hope, there, and I can help and love –' She whirled round on Wilfred, and, before he realized what was going to happen, put her arms round him and pressed him to her soft full breast and kissed his lips. 'Sorry I was a bitch, love.'

'It's – it's all right,' he stammered. 'It's – quite all right, Mrs Cornforth.'

'Goodbye,' she said, smiling at him while tears started from her eyes, and, gathering her skirts in both hands, she ran from the room.

'Trust Katherine for the perfect exit,' murmured Mr Taverner. 'Now I suggest that we sit down again. I would like to see a truly dramatic situation in which everybody was lying back in armchairs. The food is lukewarm by now, and I certainly don't want mine . . . How about you?' to Wilfred, who shook his head.

'I'll just sweep up that glass,' Miss Dollette said, but Mr Taverner held up a hand.

'Leave it, dear.'

'For them to do?'

'Yes. I've a reason.'

'I was only wondering if they would – now. You must have noticed, ever since things changed for them, their manner is different. They may feel, well, that it's below their dignity.'

'They'll do it.'

'I'm so glad for them,' she murmured.

'It's Katherine . . . I didn't tell her. I want her to find out for herself. She's exactly their idea of a goddess, of course. I wonder if she'll say "Big Deal" about the change in them?'

The conversation was carried on in low tones while the two rapidly cleared the table. Wilfred, suddenly, silently joined in the task. *Blow all this mystery,* he thought, stepping round the fragments of glass on the floor. *When you think you've got everything clear, it starts all over again. I'm fed up with it.*

'I think I'll go to bed,' said Miss Dollette when the laden trolley had been wheeled into the kitchen. 'There's going to be so much to do, and I'm tired.'

'You and I will sit awhile?' Mr Taverner suggested to Wilfred. 'Katherine has gone out – did you hear the front door slam?'

'They have lit the fire,' Miss Dollette called to them as she went upstairs.

'Good,' Mr Taverner called back. 'Next year they'll have the stubble fires lit for them.'

*

In the drawing room the newly kindled flames danced their light over pink walls and apricot satins. They settled themselves, and Mr Taverner opened a box on a table beside his chair and held it out to Wilfred.

'Cigars, eh? Well, thank you – quite a treat.'

Slowly the rich smell of the smoke filled the room. Wilfred leant back and watched it curling upwards, and wished he felt as peaceful as it looked, and that Pat might be sitting opposite, instead of that long, lanky, mysterious man.

'A vicious circle,' observed Mr Taverner. 'That's why we have to, we must, go on.'

'What for? Why?' Wilfred demanded bitterly.

'To learn. But we can choose. We can learn, and go on, or we can stay in the circle.'

'I didn't know you were religious,' said Wilfred, insolently. He stared at Mr Taverner. And Mr Taverner looked back at him, with his faint smile, and was silent. Wilfred suddenly looked down at the floor, penitent and ashamed, and saw in his mind's eye a clear picture of a statue: one of those Indian statues of a god sitting cross-legged, broken into fragments. But the piece of warm-hued stone holding the lips still offered its slight, infinitely comforting, smiling message.

'Sorry,' he said at last.

'My dear man, it's all right.'

'The fact is, I'm . . . flustered. You know I've been happy here, with you and Miss Dollette, as happy as I could be anywhere without my Pat. But you must admit it's a funny house . . .'

'I hope so. I shouldn't like to live in a place that wasn't funny. Katherine wants to, and the place where she's going to work is never funny. Ironic, yes; funny, no. By God (who gave us funniness) no.'

'You know very well what I mean. And this time I'm not going to be put off with yarns about haunting. I don't believe you, and that's flat.'

'I hoped you wouldn't.'

'*Hoped* I wouldn't? – Do you think I *like* all this mystery, and talk about "helpers" and – and all that? What did all that mean about Mrs Cornforth wanting to go to some place where there's *"no hope"*?'

'I told you. Hell is an exclusive club,' Mr Taverner answered lightly. Yet Wilfred received a disturbing impression of controlled desperation under the lightness.

'*Hell?* But no one believes in that nowadays! Even the Church doesn't.'

There was a pause. Then Mr Taverner went on: 'Katherine spoke without imagination. She doesn't truly want, of course, to go to that – it isn't a place – where there's no hope.' Even the slight colour that usually gave an appearance of health to his face had faded. 'Talk of something else – now – at once. Please.'

'She must be mental,' Wilfred said, after a pause. He was scared. Vague thoughts skimmed through his mind of phoning Sheila or Joan, packing a bag that night and going over to Mrs Wheeby. *She'd understand. She and Cousin Fred are my own sort.*

'Oh no. Far from it. And don't mistake, dear man. Katherine is going much, much further than you or I or Felicity will.'

'I'm glad to hear that, somehow. You know, I never could really like her, not as I do you and Miss Dollette. But there's something about her . . . You want her to be all right, somehow. I don't know . . .'

'She will be,' nodded Mr Taverner. 'She will be all right. I'm sure.'

'But you keep on sort-of-*dodging*, Mr Taverner! What *are* you and Miss Dollette doing here? Is it a kind of, well, a community for helping people?'

'Certain people, yes.'

'Certain people . . . I've wondered sometimes what you would do, you and Miss Dollette, if someone really vile turned up here wanting help – a sadist, for instance? Someone who enjoys hurting and being cruel, someone *really bad*?'

'They wouldn't. Not our pigeon.' Mr Taverner got up and stood by the mantelshelf, and carefully rested his cigar on an ashtray.

'But . . . aren't those the people who really need the help?'

'They're the kind Katherine wants to help. And will.'

Wilfred gave it up, for the moment. He felt, and he knew, that he was 'getting nowhere'. Every new fact that he seemed to discover only opened out onto more unanswerable questions. He suddenly felt excessively tired and his thoughts turned, with refreshment and relief, to the happy fate of Mary. Plenty to deal with there! And it was all straightforward! Difficult, perhaps, and unfamiliar, but straightforward. *Earthly* . . . funny word to think of. He made a last attempt.

'Mr Taverner . . .'

Mr Taverner looked at him attentively.

'You said something when we were having supper about there having "always" been Yellow Houses. In foreign cities . . . In Rome. *Yellow* Houses, you said. Why yellow? Were they always yellow?'

'Always.' Mr Taverner nodded, leaning an elbow on the mantelshelf. He looked very tired.

'Why was that? Not that it isn't a beautiful colour. I remember the first time I saw it, looking out of our kitchen window at home. Not quite like sunlight. Softer, somehow. – Why were they yellow, Mr Taverner? Is that the – the Brotherhood's colour? Kind of a badge, I mean?'

'It's said to be the colour of the light in the highest region. The spiritualists could tell you about that.'

'Oh – Spiritualism. When we were engaged Pat and I went into that a bit – and going to different churches and that sort of thing . . . And we decided at last that it was enough if you respected the Church and tried to lead a decent life . . . I don't fancy Spiritualism, never did . . . What's the joke?'

'You make it sound like sardines on toast.' A clock in a corner chimed quickly and silverily. 'Midnight. Shall we turn in?'

The old-fashioned phrase came to Wilfred comfortingly, helping to restore his feet to the earth. He got up.

'As late as that? I'd no idea.' He paused, surveying the long, gaunt form standing beside the fire. 'Don't think you've got away with taking me in, Mr Taverner. I know the garden path when I see it, even if I don't know what's at the end of it. You've hardly told me a thing. But if your Brotherhood's like the Masons – secret, you know, except to members – that's all right with me. It's been – you've been – very kind to me. Don't know how I'd have managed without you and the Yellow House, in fact—'

'That's the point, dear man. That's the whole point.'

'Say goodnight to Mrs Cornforth for me, will you? And say of course I don't bear her any malice. Give her my – well, just say I wish her well. I do, too. Goodnight.'

'Goodnight. Sleep well.'

Wilfred shut the door. He crossed the hall, yawning as he went. The hall looked, for all its peacefulness, a little sad without Kichijoten. But no doubt she would be back soon. It would be all right. Things usually seemed to work out all right in the Yellow House.

He went to bed and slept for eight hours without a dream.

He overslept, and had to hurry over washing and shaving and his breakfast. His train left at half past nine, and the station was twenty minutes' walk away, and he dared not wait for a bus.

He hastened down the stairs and across the hall. The walls looked peculiarly bright this morning, and as he went he tried to remember exactly what Mr Taverner had said about their colour on the previous evening, but it was useless; he retained only an impression of mystery and – yes, there was that vague feeling of size, bigness somewhere. *The highest region.* The words returned suddenly. Well, if you believed in heaven at all, it might well be that colour. Only better, of course. Better.

He gently opened the kitchen door.

They were lingering over breakfast, Mr Taverner and
Miss Dollette; he rustling through *The Times* and she with
her embroidery, a length of rose linen with a half-finished
pattern of dazzling marguerites. She was carefully drawing a
thread of snowy cotton into place to begin a new petal. Both
looked up and smiled as Wilfred put his head round the door.

'Just to say good morning and I'm off.'

'You'll have a bright evening,' said Miss Dollette, 'though it
looks as if it might darken over this afternoon.'

'Yes . . . well, I'm prepared.' He laughed, touching his raincoat. 'Cheerio, then.'

Mr Taverner lifted his hand for a moment and smiled.

'Goodbye, dear man.'

Miss Dollette echoed softly, 'Goodbye,' and Wilfred shut
the door.

Irritating and exhausting frustrations followed, attaching to
the shortest journey: late buses; no buses; buses that crawled
because of traffic; and trains that went too fast to be enjoyable;
inexplicable ten-minute dead stops outside stations; and the
occasional addition of tremendous thunders from passing jet
liners. But when Wilfred saw Cousin Fred's house, he immediately felt calmer.

Here was a row of the small red-brick Edwardian villas
that he liked best; here were the small front gardens, the net
curtains – no, they'd be nylon nowadays – and . . . and the
respectability that he had longed for since he was fifteen and
beginning to find his parents' cottage, cosy and loved though
it was, rather rough.

The unchanged '30s atmosphere in Cousin Fred's house
soothed him. Everything, from the light oak furniture to the
jazz-patterned curtains, belonged to the days before the world
began to go mad, the days before the Second War. The pictures
were all of pretty scenery, sunlit or moonlit. Little dogs of
metal or china sat about on shelves looking saucy or pathetic.
The cat was named Tiger, but was of a noticeably un-tigerish

appearance, and the drama in Mrs Wheeby and Cousin Fred's joint life was generated by a theory that 'Tiger would Have Dicky in a Flash if he got a Chance', and acted out daily in many a hasty shutting of doors and windows and loud alarums from garden or kitchen, though Wilfred was soon convinced that if Tiger had really wanted Dicky he would have Had Him, for neither Cousin Fred nor Mrs Wheeby moved as quickly as they supposed they did.

But the familiar peace! The solid enjoyment of a treacle pudding, the bottled beer, the half-hour nap in the afternoon, and the slabs of plum cake with the thin bread-and-butter Pat could never be bothered with at four o'clock.

The sun was setting as he left them, standing in the doorway to wave him goodbye; for he would not let them accompany him down the short path to the gate, saying that the evenings got very chilly.

So he turned to wave to them, as they stood in the lighted doorway with the unfashionable comfort of their hall visible behind them: Mrs Wheeby wrapped and shawled and scarfed and muffled against draughts, yet with eyes wandering from the departing guest to take in the clear sky and its one low star, and Cousin Fred, two feet taller, looming protectively behind her.

Happy, thought Wilfred, turning up his collar against the evening chill as he hurried down the road; *really happy, I'd say. And more like a married pair than cousins. Nice to see that, nowadays.*

After a journey worse than that of the morning, for he had unwisely let himself in for the very middle of the frenetic rush back to their dens of the daily workers, he came out of Torford station to see the last of the husband-meeting wives edging the car bearing her exhausted junior executive out into the ordered chaos of the maelstrom. It was dusk now; the red lights burned with their false romance along the narrow old road jammed with vehicles. Already mist loitered in the leaf-less trees. He was walking homewards, when he heard what he thought of irritably as *someone yelling*. At first he felt only annoyance at anybody increasing the infernal racket all around him. Then he realized that he was hearing his own name.

'Wilf! Wilf! Want a lift?'

Joan – or was it Shirley or Sheila? – a rosy face smiling through the window of a car immediately opposite him, imprisoned in the block. He hesitated.

'Buck up! – the lights'll change any minute. Hop in.'

He hopped, slamming the door, and scrambling. *Damn*, he thought, and braced himself for Joan's – yes, it was Joan – questions.

But Joan kept her eyes on the car just ahead, and said nothing for two or three minutes; and then, in the quick, shy tone she and her friends kept for certain occasions, said:

'Terrible, isn't it?'

She did not look at him. Then, in a moment, she added: 'Haven't you heard?'

'Heard what? I've been with friends in Chelmsford all day. I haven't heard anything. That loony Nixon been pressing buttons again?'

'Oh no, nothing like that. It's your friend – that woman in the pink coat – Mrs Cornforth, did you say? She's dead. Drowned.'

The traffic had stopped again. The air outside the car seemed to beat and shake, and his hands were cold and his mouth dry and his heart leapt, then settled to a steady hammering. He felt sick, staring at Joan.

'But – she can't – what happened?'

'Got caught in the tide – or that's what they *think*. It was in this evening's *Standard* – didn't you see it? This morning, it was, quite early.'

'I tell you I haven't seen or heard *anything* – are you *sure*?'

'Of course I'm sure. Everybody was talking about it at coffee this morning. The police are certain she's drowned, although they're still looking for the body. They'll have to wait to see if it's washed up further down the coast before they can issue a statement – *presumed* drowned, I suppose it'll be, until then . . . The tide's terrible round Vikor, of course – I've heard it comes in as fast as a galloping horse.' Joan broke off, as she turned the car down a less crowded street. 'She's lived here about a year – I used to see her around last Christmas. She *must* have known what the tides are down there – we all do. (All of us with kids, anyway.) Suicide, it *must* have been. She always looked to me like the sort that might take her own life. – What?'

'I said "Take it, and do something with it",' he said hoarsely.

'Sorry?'

He did not answer.

'Didn't you see her this morning before you left, then?'

'No,' he answered faintly. 'No, she wasn't up when I left.'

Joan looked satisfied, as if 'lying in late' were all of a piece with suicide. What she said, however, was: 'Oh well, we mustn't judge, must we? What that poor soul must have gone through, to take an action like that! Did you ever see any signs of *strain?*'

'No, I didn't.'

'But you lived in the same house, I thought you said?'

'She was a bloody nuisance,' he shouted, fumbling with the door of the car, as the traffic lights held them up again, just beyond the road leading to the 'poor' end of the town. 'Cheerio – thanks,' he added over his shoulder, and scrambled out and, darting perilously between the cars, was across and down the road leading into Hardy Crescent before Joan could shut her mouth, or get the shocked look off her face.

Enjoying it, he thought savagely, walking fast between the small, dimly lit shops and the empty ruinous houses and glaring snack bars. *Enjoying every minute of it. Oh God. How could I say a thing like that? How could I?*

He was almost sobbing as he hurried along and his thoughts raced with him. *The worst thing is, the worst thing of all is, I meant it. She was a bloody nuisance. We all got on so nicely together, and were so peaceful and – almost happy – and she upset things. She did. She upset things.*

Clearly, as unmistakably as he heard the noise of the passing lorry through which it came to him, he heard the voice of Mr Taverner saying: *Saints have to upset things.*

Saints? He lowered his head, and shut his eyes for a moment, as if to drive off grief and bewilderment and fear; and when he looked up, he saw Hardy Crescent before him – the graceful houses blanched and still in the false moonlight of the lamps.

It's all got so awful, he was thinking as he drew near to the Yellow House. *For two pins I'd chuck living with them, and ask Joan – or Mrs W . . . it would only be until April. Suit me really down to the ground, that would, a room at Cousin Fred's. ('Course, I'd pay them.) No mysteries or tragedies there.*

Then the horror and grief came back, and as he pushed open the gate of the Yellow House, he groaned. The mist hung thick and icy. The last Japanese sunflowers and chrysanthemums lay in withered swathes at either side of the path. He looked up at the windows . . . and saw, with a sickening shock, that they were curtainless.

He ran up the steps, and, breathing fast, fumbled for his key, and managed to get it into the lock, and swung the door back.

He knew what he would see . . . what he would find.

Nothing. Emptiness. Gone. And the walls glimmering wanly in the reflected glow of the street lamps. The stairs, still seductive to the eye, though carpetless, curved upwards into the darkness.

He switched on the light by the door and instantly the hall was gently glowing with the colour which, if Mr Taverner had spoken truly, was literally heavenly; and on the air there lingered faintly the scent of fern, the woods and moss fragrance that he had first breathed on Mr Taverner's handkerchief just over a year ago. Tears came to his eyes. Slowly he began to climb the stairs, switching on lights as he went. Slowly he entered room after empty room, their bare walls singing in that holy colour, or with the rose of sunset, the green of spring woods.

At least they had left him these ravishing colours.

His footsteps echoed from room to room as he made his wretched pilgrimage, everything forgotten but the loss of his friends. Not a fragment of string or an old cardboard box or a scrap of newspaper was left to prove that anyone had ever lived there, and, in his own room, his few personal possessions were stacked neatly. He gulped at the neatness – that would be Miss Dollette. The few books, the photographs of Pat and Mary, his old television set and armchair, and the wardrobe full of worn clothes.

Where would he go? What would he do, until April?

But it was not that. He would manage. He had Mary, and he had some money. It was the longing to hear, and the expectation that at any minute he *would* hear, Mr Taverner's voice, or see the light glinting softly on Miss Dollette's hair as she came quietly down the long passage towards him, smiling. And ready to explain . . .

Ah, explaining!

But there was nothing. Silence, and his echoing footsteps, and nothing.

He paused at the door of Katherine's room and put his hand on the knob, then stood for a moment listening, staring at the bright, silent landing; seeing her body rolling to and fro in the darkness, in the icy sea out beyond Vikor Sands, with her red coat drifting around her. Katherine, who had made this emptiness and silence.

Saints have to upset things.

Slowly, he opened the door. He did not want to; he was frightened at the thought of what he might see; but he wanted to give her room a last look. He turned on the light.

The walls glowed like a dark red rose, the air was scented by Katherine's scent. He made a little groaning noise, strange and weak, as if grief itself had given tongue, looked slowly around, then turned off the light and shut the door.

Presently, I'll have to think, he thought as he walked – lightly now, for the noise of his own footsteps seemed to intensify the silence. *But not yet. I'll look into the dining room. There might just be something . . . Where shall I go tonight?*

Down the stairs he crept, and across the hall, all the time with that overwhelming sensation of walking away from something; leaving something irrevocably behind him; and up to the dining room. Again, for the last time, he opened a door on a room that he knew would be dark and empty. And it was dark, utterly dark, and utterly silent. His gaze travelled hopelessly, as he stood for a moment by the half-open door, into that silent darkness. And then he noticed the scent. Not fern or moss. Something else.

Straw. The smell, faint and dry and pure, that comes up from stubble-fields when the harvest is over. *That's a very old smell,* he thought dreamily, pain and sorrow drowsing while he breathed it in; *it must be one of the oldest smells in the world, that must.*

What was that glittering on the floor? Oh, the glass. The glass Katherine had broken last night. Miss Dollette had wanted to sweep it up and Mr Taverner had said she was to leave it. It caught the light from the hall; that was why it glittered.

But what was the dim glow – the faint, shining circle – of golden-green that was forming slowly above it? He began to feel warm; very warm, unnaturally warm, in that house now so cold, but he neither minded this nor was he frightened. It was as if he were entranced, as he stood, holding the door half open, with the silent hall behind him, watching the growing of the two golden-green blurs – larger and larger and larger. Suddenly, *they formed.*

Then he saw them: 'the helpers' – the rough, rudimentary sketches for human forms; the maliciously smiling ones, the two who had haunted his memory.

They were not looking towards him; both were stooping, and the male held – of all the unexpected things in the world – a dustpan, while the female slowly, unwillingly, was sweeping the broken glass into it. The expression on each brown, flattish face was identical – dislike of the task.

Even as Wilfred fully realized that they were there, they looked up. The male thing, staring at him from under long black brows, deliberately motioned the female to put down her brush, while he, as deliberately, put down the dustpan. Then, with the implements of their work lying at their sandalled feet, both slowly rose to their full small height, and he saw that they were *clothed*.

Both wore robes that seemed woven of wheat, at that point in its ripening when the green is almost, but not completely, changed to gold; while barley and oats, fully ripened, jutted from bosom and loins in a decorative pattern, as if growing; and the glossy black head of each was crowned with the flowers that grow in the harvest fields: poppies, and cornflowers and marguerites.

He saw that they were changed in another way, too: their malicious smiles had vanished; and, as they stared at him out of their round, black eyes, the sullen look brought by their work also disappeared. They stood motionless, their hands at their sides. Then, slowly, in a way that made him think of children proud of their robes and new honours, each inclined a head towards him in greeting, and both smiled. The smile, almost, of children. (Almost, not quite. Something unknown, something he could not define, lingered.) Their smiles were so warm that his heart moved towards the pair in tenderness and wonder, and he smiled in return.

They had gone. The room was dark again: the glow vanished, as though it had never been. Only the scent of straw lingered in the air.

He was suddenly terrified. He slammed the door on the darkness and its inconceivable vision, and turned desperately to face whatever else might be coming towards him through the silent house. He stood for a second or two, staring wildly at the gold-white walls . . . and then the front door bell rang, loudly and imperiously.

He started towards it. Of course! They had come back. He would open it to Mr Taverner in his white coat and Miss Dollette in the old-fashioned cape-coat she wore to go shopping . . . Katherine! All wet, with streaming red hair darkened by the sea . . . oh, no . . .

He ran to the front door and dragged it open.

'Dad! Love, are you all right? We've been phoning you all day. What's the matter?'

Mary. His Mary, solid and handsome in her old green coat and a black fur hood, looking at him with anxious love. Behind her stood Yasuhiro, and beyond him Wilfred saw a car drawn up to the gate, with a uniformed chauffeur at the wheel.

'I'm all right – had a bit of a shock, that's all,' he said weakly, letting himself be kissed and shaken hands with. 'They, Mr Taverner and Miss Dollette, they've gone . . . and Mrs Cornforth . . . worse, I'm afraid—' he broke off.

'Well! I liked them all right, but I always did think there was something a bit funny about them,' said Mary. 'Only they didn't seem the sort that can't pay the rent, did they—'

'So are we going, Mr Davis?' Yasuhiro struck in authoritatively. 'To Japan? My great-grandfather,' his face and voice lost all expression, 'is dying, and wishes to see me before he joins the ancestors. They telephoned to me this morning at Rowena Road. Much to arrange, you know. Embassy book places for us on the plane. You will come with us of course too, won't you?'

'Now come on, love. No argy-bargy,' said Mary, with precisely her mother's tone. 'You haven't the ghost of an excuse now . . . What's funny?' staring. 'I say, *are* you all right, Dad?'

'Nothing – it's nothing. Just the shock. Mrs Cornforth, too . . . dreadful. But my things . . .'

'Where've you *been*, all day? We started phoning you almost as soon as Yasu got the news – that was about ten this morning. He came into the shop and whipped me off as if I were being hijacked. Here, you come upstairs with me.'

'Must hurry, Mary,' warned Yasuhiro.

She gave him a significant glance over her father's shoulder, and, slipping her arm into Wilfred's, began to lead him across the hall to the stairs.

He let himself be led. Following on that evening's shocks, the comfort of leaning on these two young, strong, confident creatures was inexpressible; and he made no attempt to assert himself beyond muttering that of course he would go with them

to Japan, and he was sorry to hear about the old gentleman's
illness, and . . .

'H'm.' Mary surveyed his stacked possessions. 'Better phone
Help the Aged in the morning. Didn't Mum have some buddy
who worked there? But we'll take your clothes.' She opened
the cupboard and began piling them over her arm.

'Yes, Shirley Bates. – Mary, *don't* phone her – we'll never hear
the end of all this . . . and there's poor Mrs Cornforth, too—'

He broke off. Truly, and if he stopped to think, Katherine
was not poor at all.

'All right, love. Whatever *is* up? But never mind now, you
can tell me in the car. All right, then. Oxfam, not Help the
Aged. You don't want any of this old junk – any of this, do
you? Here, I'll take Mum's photo.'

He shook his head, numbly looking his last on small objects
he had loved for fifty years.

'OK, then. Let's go . . . here, don't fall out! What's so interesting out there?' as he opened the window and leant out into
the still, misty night.

He drew back into the room, seeing in his mind's eye the
Tor moving sluggishly six feet below, white cartons and scraps
of newspaper glimmering unwholesomely in its defiled current.

Even that had gone. Even that.

Down the stairs, following Mary, for the last time. Across
the hall where Kichijoten had presided. Lights switched out
by Yasuhiro. The door shut. Shut on the Yellow House. For
the last time.

He looked back, once, at the serene little columns on either
side of the porch, the calm facade set with the dark eyes of
windows. It was empty, now, the Yellow House, and he was
going to Japan with his daughter and . . . his son. The car moved
off, the chauffeur guiding it carefully over the uneven road.

'We're going to a hotel,' Yasuhiro announced. 'You must eat
a good meal, Mr Davis, with wine. All this is a sudden shock
for a man sitting in the shade.'

He smiled; his social smile, and Wilfred's heart sank.

'Imagine, Dad! Mrs Levy kept me for ten minutes this morning, with Yasu having fits in the car, while she tried to fix up some scheme for me sending over Japanese souvenirs that she could sell at cut price! Can you beat it?'

'The mind of a peasant. They think only of the profits. Unfortunate situation for them, really,' Yasuhiro said tolerantly.

'Mrs Cadman sent you her kindest wishes and so did old Grant. You warm enough, love? Have a bit of blanket,' and she leant forward to arrange a rug, with gentle care, over his knees.

He murmured something, unable for the moment to speak. He had not felt so loved, so taken care of, since his small hand had rested in the big warm one of his father, sixty years ago, on one of their rambles over the low hills visible from the cottage windows. *Never see them again.* A deep sadness swept over him.

Something made him glance up, and he met the gaze of Yasuhiro's dark eyes. Slowly the beautiful haughty face softened, and warmed into a smile.

'Yes,' said Yasuhiro, 'we must take good care of our father,' and in his turn he leant forward and rearranged the rug. More symmetrically, Wilfred noticed. He also noticed that the rearrangement allowed a slight but noticeable draught to play about his knees, and felt a sudden instinct to laugh, and thought *It mayn't be so bad, after all.*

He glanced out at the little streets of Torford going past, seeing them for the last time.

What a day it had been – what an evening – what a year . . . and now, at the end . . . what was the *good* of it all, all the mysterious happenings at the Yellow House? What was it all *for?*

'*Even the grass* –' It was Mr Taverner's voice, coming to him inwardly and clearly above the low, luxurious humming of the car's engine – '*even the grass shall be saved.*'

In the autumn of the following year, the wheatlands in that region of France called La Beauce lay reaping-ripe under the sun. A car could drive for a day without losing sight of their dark gold vastness, with the wind rippling over the miles of heavy, drooping heads — 'the Corn-Rabbit walking', as the mothers of the Old Europe used to say to their children.

Wheat and barley, rye and oats, and the great sky; the great sky, and wheat and oats, barley and rye . . . And the dry silky rustling that is the voice of the corn godlings talking.

On the outskirts of one of the small villages in the heart of this region, workmen were employed on a sunlit morning in covering the walls of an ancient, solidly built house with a wash of whitish-gold, as if the colour of the ripe wheat had been mixed with that of fresh milk.

The new owner leant leisurely on a gate, watching: a tall, lanky man, wearing a white raincoat.

THE HISTORY OF VINTAGE

The famous American publisher Alfred A. Knopf (1892–1984) founded Vintage Books in the United States in 1954 as a paperback home for the authors published by his company. Vintage was launched in the United Kingdom in 1990 and works independently from the American imprint although both are part of the international publishing group, Random House.

Vintage in the United Kingdom was initially created to publish paperback editions of books bought by the prestigious literary hardback imprints in the Random House Group such as Jonathan Cape, Chatto & Windus, Hutchinson and later William Heinemann, Secker & Warburg and The Harvill Press. There are many Booker and Nobel Prize-winning authors on the Vintage list and the imprint publishes a huge variety of fiction and non-fiction. Over the years Vintage has expanded and the list now includes great authors of the past – who are published under the Vintage Classics imprint – as well as many of the most influential authors of the present. In 2012 Vintage Children's Classics was launched to include the much-loved authors of our youth.